The wooden weapon keened,
a low hungry sound.

Get up, I told myself. *Get up, you stupid bitch. That thing is threatening Japhrimel.*

It worked. Fury poured through me, a rage red and deep like hot blood from a ragged hole. My legs straightened. I gained my feet in a stumbling rush and threw myself forward, the Knife held in the way my *sensei* taught me, flat against my forearm for slashing, the pommel reversed with its claws digging into my wrist.

Burn, a half-familiar voice whispered inside my head. **Burn them. Make them pay.**

Shapeless yells rose, Lucas yelling my name, Leander screaming, McKinley letting out a cry that shivered the air. Everything vanished but the enemy in front of me and the need to make him—whoever he was—*pay.*

In blood.

BOOKS BY LILITH SAINTCROW

JILL KISMET NOVELS
Night Shift

DANTE VALENTINE NOVELS
Working for the Devil

Dead Man Rising

The Devil's Right Hand

Saint City Sinners

To Hell and Back

Dark Watcher

Storm Watcher

Fire Watcher

Cloud Watcher

The Society

Hunter, Healer

TO HELL
AND BACK

LILITH SAINTCROW

www.orbitbooks.net

New York   London

Copyright © 2008 by Lilith Saintcrow
Excerpt from *Night Shift* copyright © 2008 by Lilith Saintcrow
All rights reserved. Except as permitted under the U.S. Copyright Act of 1976, no part of this publication may be reproduced, distributed, or transmitted in any form or by any means, or stored in a database or retrieval system, without the prior written permission of the publisher.

Orbit is an imprint of Hachette Book Group USA

The Orbit name and logo is a trademark of Little, Brown Book Group Ltd.

Orbit
Hachette Book Group USA
237 Park Avenue
New York, NY 10017
Visit our Web site at www.orbitbooks.net

Printed in the United States of America

First edition: January 2008

10 9 8 7 6 5 4 3 2 1

ATTENTION CORPORATIONS AND ORGANIZATIONS:
Most HACHETTE BOOK GROUP USA books are available at quantity discounts with bulk purchase for educational, business, or sales promotional use. For information, please call or write:

Special Markets Department, Hachette Book Group USA
237 Park Avenue, New York, NY 10017
Telephone: 1-800-222-6747 Fax: 1-800-477-5925

For Nicholas Deangelo.
Peace. Another charm's wound up.

Tempt not a desperate man.
—Shakespeare, *Romeo & Juliet*

I was a-trembling because I'd got to decide forever betwixt two things, and I knowed it. I studied for a minute, sort of holding my breath, and then says to myself, "All right, then, I'll go to hell."
—Mark Twain, *Huckleberry Finn*

TO HELL
AND BACK

Prologue

There is more than one way to break a human," he said, softly. "Especially a human woman."

I hung between sky and ground, the constellations of Hell overhead and sterile rock underneath, the icy inhuman heat of a place far removed from my own world lapping at my skin. I had come looking for my own clean death in battle, and found this instead. This indignity.

The Devil doesn't believe in killing you, if you can be made to serve.

I will not scream. The world narrowed, became a single point of light as the writhing claws slipped below my flesh and the wet sounds of the thing that would break me to his will echoed against stone walls. I will not scream. I will not give in.

I did scream. I screamed until my voice broke itself again as the scar on my shoulder woke with frigid hot pain, my body healing even as he tore at me. I fought as hard as I could. I am no stranger to fighting, I have fought all my life.

None of it mattered.
Nothing mattered.
I died there. In Hell.
It was the only way to escape something worse.

1

Darkness closed velvet over me, broken only by the flame of a scar burning, burning, against my shoulder. I do not know how I wrenched myself free, I only know that I *did*, before the last and worst could be done to me.

But not soon enough.

I heard myself scream, one last cry that shattered into pieces before I escaped to the only place left to me, welcome unconsciousness.

As I *fell*.

Cold. Wherever I was, it was *cold*. Hardness underneath me. I heard a low buzzing sound and passed out again, sliding away from consciousness like a marble on a reactive-greased slope. The buzzing followed, became a horde of angry bees inside my head, a deep and awful rattling whirr shaking my teeth loose, splitting my bones with hot lead.

I moaned.

The buzzing faded, receding bit by bit like waves sliding away from a rocky shore. I moaned again, rolled over.

My cheek pressed chill hardness. Tears trickled hot out of my eyes. My shields shivered, rent and useless, a flooding tide of sensation and thought from the outside world roaring through my brain as I convulsed, instinct pulling my tissue-thin defenses together, drowning in the current. Where was I?

I had no prayers left.

Even if I'd had one, there would be no answer. The ultimate lesson of a life spent on the edge of Power and violence—*when the chips are down, sunshine, you're on your own.*

Slowly, so slowly, I regained my balance. A flood of human thought smashed rank and foul against my broken shields, roaring through my head, and I pushed it away with a supreme effort, trying to *think.* I made my eyes open. Dark shapes swirled, coalesced. I heard more, a low noise of crowds and hovertraffic, formless, splashing like the sea. Felt a tingle and trickle of Power against my skin.

Oh, gods. Remind me not to do that again. Whatever it was. The thought sounded like me, the tough, rational, practical me, over a deep screaming well of panic. *What happened to me?*

Am I hungover?

That made me laugh. It was unsteady, hitching, tired hilarity edged with broken glass, but I welcomed it. If I was laughing, I was okay.

Not really. I would never be *okay* again. My mind shuddered, flinching away from . . . something. Something terrible. Something I could not think about if I wanted to keep the fragile barrier between myself and a screaming tide of insanity.

I pushed it away. Wrestled it into a dark corner and closed the door.

That made it possible to think a little more clearly.

I blinked. Shapes became recognizable, the stink of dying human cells filling my nose again. Wet warmth trickled down my cheeks, painted my upper lip. I tasted spoiled fruit and sweetness when I licked my lips.

Blood. I had a face covered in blood, and my clothes were no better than rags, if I retained them at all. My bag clinked as I shifted, its broken strap reknotted and rasping between my breasts. I blinked more blood out of my eyes, stared up at a brick wall. It was night, and the wall loomed at a crazy angle because I lay twisted like a rag doll, pretty-much-naked against the floor of an alley.

Alley. I'm in an alley. From the way it smells, it's not a nice one either. Trust me to end up like this.

It was a sane thought, one I clung to even as I shivered and jolted, my entire body rebelling against the psychic assault of so many minds shoving against me, a surfroar of screaming voices. Not just my body but my *mind* mutinied, bucking like a runaway horse as the *something* returned, huge and foul, boiling up through layers of shock. Beating at the door I had locked against it.

Oh gods, please. Someone please. Anyone. Help me.

I moaned, the sound bouncing off bricks, and the mark on my shoulder suddenly blazed with soft heat, welling out through my aching body. I hurt everywhere, as if I'd been torn apart and put back together wrong. The worst hurt was a deep drilling ache low in the bowl of my pelvis, like the world's worst menstrual cramp.

I could not think about that. My entire soul rose in rebellion. I could not *remember* what had been done to me.

The rips in my shields bound themselves together, tissue-thin, but still able to keep me sane. The scar pulsed, crying out like a beacon, a flaming black-diamond fountain tearing into the ambient Power of the cityscape. The first flare knocked me flat against the ground again, stunned and dazed. Successive pulses arrived, each working in a little deeper than the last, but not so jolting.

Breathe. Just breathe. I clung to the thought, shutting my eyes as the world reeled under me. I made it up to hands and knees, my palms against slick greasy concrete as I retched. I don't usually throw up unless poisoned, but I felt awful close.

Too bad there was nothing in my stomach. I curled over on myself, retched some more, and decided I felt better.

The mark kept pulsing, like a slow heartbeat. Japhrimel's pulse is slower than mine, one beat to every three my own heart performs, like a strong silt-laden river through a broad channel. It felt uncomfortably like his heartbeat had settled in the scar on my shoulder, as if I was resting my head on his chest and hearing his old, slow, strong heart against my cheek and fingertips.

Japhrimel. I remembered him, at least. Even if I couldn't remember myself.

I cursed, in my head and aloud as I found the other brick wall confining this alley. Drove my claws into the wall, my arm quivering under the strain as I hauled myself to my feet. I couldn't afford to call on him. He was an enemy.

They were all my enemies. Everyone. Every single fucking thing that breathed, or walked, or even touched me. Even the air.

Even my own mind.

Safe place. Got to find a safe place. I could have laughed at the thought. I didn't even know where I was.

Not only that, but where on earth was safe for me now? I could barely even remember *who* I was.

Valentine.

A name returned to me. My name. My fingers crept up and touched a familiar wire of heat at my collarbone—the necklace, silver-dipped raccoon baculum and blood-marked bloodstones, its potent force spent and at low ebb. I knew who wore this jewelry.

I am Valentine. Danny Valentine. I'm me. I am Dante Valentine.

Relief scalded me all over, gushed in hot streams from my eyes. I knew who I was now: I could remember my name.

Everything else would follow.

I hauled myself up to my feet. My legs shook and I stumbled, and I was for once in no condition to fight. I hoped I wasn't in a bad part of town.

Whatever town this is. What happened? I staggered, ripped my claws free of the brick wall, and leaned against its cold rough surface, for once blessing the stink of humanity. It meant I was safe.

Safe from what? I had no answer for that question, either. A hideous thing beat like a diseased heart behind the door I'd slammed to keep it *away*. I didn't want to know right now.

Safe place, Danny girl. I flinched, but the words were familiar, whispered into my right ear. A man's voice, pitched low and tender with an undertone of urgency. Just the way he used to wake me up, back in the old days.

Back when I was human and Jace Monroe was alive,

and Hell was only a place I read about in classic literature and required History of Magi classes.

That thought sent a scree of panic through me. I almost buckled under the lash of fear, my knees softening.

Get up, clear your head, and move. There's a temple down the street, and nobody's around to see you. You've got to move now. Jace's voice whispered, cajoled.

I did not stop to question it. Whether my dead lover or my own small precognitive talent was speaking didn't matter.

The only thing that mattered was if it was right. I was naked and covered in blood, with only my bag. I had to find somewhere to hide.

I stumbled to the mouth of the alley, peering out on a dim-lit city street, the undersides of hovers glittering like fireflies above. The ambient Power tasted of synth-hash smoke, wet mold, and old silty spilled blood, with a spiked dash of Chill-laced bile over the top.

Smells like Jersey. I shook my head, blood dripping from my nose in a fresh trickle of heat, and staggered out into the night.

2

The street was indeed deserted, mostly warehouses and hoverfreight transport stations that don't see a lot of human traffic at night. There *was* a temple, and its doors creaked as I made it up the shallow steps. It could have been any temple in any city in the world, but I was rapidly becoming convinced it *was* North New York Jersey. It smelled like it.

Not that it mattered right at the moment.

The doors, heavy black-painted iron worked with the Hegemony sundisc, groaned as I leaned on one of them, shoving it open. My right leg dragged as I hauled myself inside, the shielding on the temple's walls snapping closed behind me like an airlock, pushing away the noise of the city outside. The damage to my leg was an old injury from the hunt for Kellerman Lourdes; I wondered if all the old scars were going to open up—the whip scars on my back and the brand along the crease of my lower left buttock.

If they did open up, would I bleed? Would the bleeding ever stop?

Take out all the old wounds, see which one's deepest.

The voice of panic inside my head let out a terrified giggle; my chattering teeth chopped into bits. The door in my head stayed strong, stayed closed. It took most of my failing energy to keep that memory—whatever it was— wrestled down.

Every Hegemony temple is built on a node of intersecting ley lines, the shields humming, fed by the bulge of Power underneath. This temple, like most Hegemony places of worship, had two wings leading from the narrow central chamber—one for the gods of Old Graecia, and one for Egyptianica. There were other gods, but these were the two most common pantheons, and it was a stroke of luck.

If I still believed in luck.

Jace's voice in my ear had gone silent. I still could not remember what had been done to me.

Whatever it was, it was bad. I'm in bad shape.

I almost laughed at the absurdity of thinking so. As if it wasn't self-evident.

The main chamber was dedicated to a standard Hegemony sundisc, rocking a little on the altar. It was as tall as two of me, and I breathed out through my mouth because my nose was full of blood. I worried vaguely about that—usually the black blood rose and sealed away any wound, healing my perfect poreless golden skin without a trace. But here I was, bleeding. I could barely tell if the rest of me was bleeding too, especially the deep well of pain at the juncture of my legs, hot blood slicking the insides of my thighs.

I tried not to think about it. My right hand kept making little grasping motions, searching for a swordhilt.

Where's my sword? More panic drifted through me. I

set my jaw and lowered my head, stubbornly. It didn't matter. I'd figure it out soon enough.

When I held my blade again, it would be time to kill.

I just couldn't think of who to kill first.

My bag shifted and clinked as I wove up the middle of the great hall, aiming for the left-hand wing, where the arch was decorated with dancing hieroglyphs carved into old wood. This entire place was dark, candles lit before the sundisc reflecting in its mellow depths. The flickering light made it even harder to walk.

My shoulder pulsed. Every throb was met with a fresh flood of Power along my battered shields, sealing me away but also causing a hot new trickle of blood from my nose. My cheeks were wet and slick too, because my eyes were bleeding—either that, or I had some kind of scalp wound. Thin hot little fingers of blood patted the inside of my knees, tickled down to my ankles.

I'm dripping like a public faucet. Gods. I made it to the door and clung to one side, blinking away salt wetness.

There they sat in the dusk, the air alive with whispers and mutters. Power sparked, swirling in dust-laden air. The gods regarded me, each in their own way.

Isis stood behind Her throned son, Horus's hawk-head and cruel curved beak shifting under Her spread hand of blessing. Thoth stood to one side, His long ibis head held still but His hands—holding scroll and pen—looking startled, as if He had been writing and now froze, staring down at me. The statues were of polished basalt, carved in post-Awakening neoclassic; Nuit stretched above on the vault of the roof, painted instead of sculpted.

There, next to Ptah the Worker, was Anubis. The strength threatened to leave my legs again. I let out a sob that fractured against the temple's surfaces, its echoes coming back to eat me.

The god of Death regarded me, candles on the altar before Him blazing with sudden light. My eyes met His, and more flames bloomed on dark spent wicks, our gazes flint and steel sparking to light them.

I let out another painful sob, agony twisting fresh inside my heart. Blood spattered, steaming against chill stone. This might be a new building, but they had scoured the floor down to rock, and it showed. My ribs ached as if I'd just taken a hard shot with a *jo* staff. Everywhere on me ached, especially—

I shut that thought away. Let go of the edge of the doorway and tacked out like a ship, zigzagging because my right leg wouldn't work quite properly. I veered away into the gloom, bypassing Anubis though every cell in my body cried out for me to sink to the floor before His altar and let Him take me, if He would.

I had given my life to Him, and been glad to do it—but He had betrayed me twice, once in taking Jason Monroe from me and again in asking me to spare the killer of my best and only friend.

I could not lay down before Him now. Not like this.

There was something I had to do first.

I kept going, each step a scream. Past Ptah, and Thoth, and Isis and Horus, to where no candles danced on the altars. The dark pressed close, still whispering. It took forever, but I finally reached them, and looked up. My right hand had clamped itself against my other arm, just under the scar on my left shoulder, each beat of Power thudding against my palm as my arm dangled.

Nepthys's eyes were sad, arms crossed over Her midriff. Beside Her Set glowered, the jackal head twitching in quick little jerks as candlelight failed to reach it completely. The powers of Destruction, at the left hand of Creation. Propitiated, because there is no creation without the clearing-away of the old. Propitiated as well in the hope that they will avoid your life, pass you by.

What had been done to me? I barely even remembered my own name. *Something* had happened.

Some*one* had done this to me.

Someone I had to kill.

Burn it all down, a new voice whispered in my head. **Come to Me, and let it burn away. Make something new, if you like—but first, there is the burning.**

There is vengeance.

Between Isis and Nepthys, the other goddess lingered. Her altar was swept bare, which meant it was probably the end of the month wherever I'd landed. Offerings to Her and to Set were cleared away at the dark of the moon.

Unless they were *taken.* Which happens more often than you'd think.

I folded down to my knees, each fresh jab of agony in my belly echoed by my dragging right leg and a thousand other weals of smoking pain. My fingers were slippery with blood, and I kept swiping at my face. I tipped my chin up.

My eyes rested on Her carved breasts, the stone knot between them. The shadows whispered and chuckled again, soft little feathery touches against my skin and ruined, flapping blood-crusted clothes.

Her face was a male lion's, serene in its awfulness, the disc above Her head most likely bronze but still lit with a random reflection of candlelight, turning to gold. My eyes met Hers.

"Sekhmet." My aching lips shaped the word.

The prayer rose out of my Magi-trained memory, from a page of text read long ago in a Comparative Religions class at the Academy. Psions are trained to almost-perfect memory, a blessing when you want to remember an incantation or a rune; deadly misery when you want to forget the sheer maddening injustice of being among the living.

Or when you *have* to forget, to stay sane. When you must push away something so monstrous your mind shivers like a slicboard over water as violation strains to replay itself in the corridors of your brain, the place that should be the most private of all.

I did not whisper. My ruined voice crept along the walls, flooding the air with husky seduction. "*Sekhmet sa'es.* Sekhmet, lady of the sun, destructive eye of Ra. Sekhmet, Power of Battle, You who the gods made drunk; o my Lady, *n't be'at.* I evoke You. I *invoke* You. I *summon* You, and I will not be denied."

No answer. Silence ate the end of the prayer. The ultimate silence.

I tipped my head back.

A scream welled out of me, out of some deep numb place that was still fully human. However wrecked and shattered that place was, it was still mine, the only territory I had left. Everything had been taken from me—but by every god that ever lived, I would take it *back.*

Just as soon as I could figure out who to kill first.

The prayer beat inside my head, an invocation as old

as rage itself. *I invoke You. I summon You, I demand You, I call You forth and into me.*

Sound careened and bounced against stone, echoes like brass guns tearing the air itself, the walls of the temple creaking and groaning as I howled. My lips were numb and my body finally failed me. I slumped over to the side, my head striking the floor with a dim note of pain, my fingers clutching empty air. Blood smeared between my cheek and the stone, and as my vision wavered Her lips pulled back, teeth gleaming ivory-white as the rushing of flame surrounded me. I spiraled again into oblivion. This time it wasn't dark, and there was no blue glow of Death's far country.

No. This time I descended into blood-red, the sound of an old slow heartbeat and the running liquid crackle of flame. I fell, again, and this time I felt no pain.

I don't know how long I was out. It seemed a very long time. I would surface, hazily, and something would push me back down. Two things never varied—the feel of softness under me, and a low rasping voice, even and quiet. And the third thing: fever, sinking through my flesh like venom. Each time it rose, the cool cloth on my forehead and the voice would drive it back.

The voice was familiar and unfamiliar at the same time. Male, a low whispering tone, produced by a human throat. Or was it only that the ragged pleading in it sounded so human?

"Don't you dare give up on me, Valentine." Hoarse and harsh, a throat-cut voice, suffering through the syllables. "Don't you *dare.*"

My eyelids fluttered, shutterclicks of light pouring into my head, scouring. The light was from a candle on a bare, sticky wooden table, glimmering in a ceramic holder. The candleflame cast a perfect golden sphere of light, and my naked skin shrank under the weight of a sheet. The room was warm.

"Hey." Lucas Villalobos's lank hair was mussed and dirty; flecks of dried blood marked his sallow face. The river of scarring down his left cheek twitched as an odd expression filled his yellow eyes and exposed his strong, square white teeth.

He was grinning. With *relief.*

Now I've officially seen everything.

I let out a sharp breath, my right hand feeling around slick sheets. The thin mattress was getting harder by the second. I felt every individual slat of the low cot.

I flinched and blinked. Stared up at Lucas. Managed a single, pertinent question.

"What the *fuck?*"

"That's more like it. You're one slippery bitch, Valentine."

Another question surfaced. "How . . ." I coughed. My throat was a dust-slick river of stone. I hurt all over, heavy and slow. But everything on me was working. My belly ached, way down low, as if I carried a hot stone.

Another hot rill of bile worked up my throat.

"I got ways of trailin' my clients." He shrugged, picking something up from the nightstand. He slid one wiry-strong arm under my shoulders and tipped tepid chlorinated water down my throat.

It was the sweetest taste I'd had in ages. He took the cup away despite my sound of protest, stopping me from getting sick on it. I didn't think I'd retch, but I wouldn't put it past me.

"You disappeared six months ago." He shook his lank hair back, rolling his shoulders in their sockets as if they hurt. He wore a threadbare Trade Bargains microfiber shirt, but his bandoliers were freshly oiled, resting on re-inforced patches. "I been knockin' around tryin' to find you, keep one step ahead o' everyone else. Two nights ago I found you in Jersey, of all fuckin' places." He paused, as if he wanted to say more. "Care to tell me how the fuck you managed to vanish like that?"

I sank back onto the thin mattress. Shut my eyes. Darkness returned, wrapped me in a blanket. "Six months?" My voice was just as ruined as his, but where Lucas's harsh croak was a raven's, mine was cracked velvet honey, strained and soft. "I . . . I don't know."

"You was in pretty bad shape. I didn't think you'd make it."

Relief rose up, fighting with pure terror as I strained to remember what I could, tiptoeing around the huge black hole in my head . . .

My sword chimed as I dropped it, my boots ground in shattered dishes and broken glass, and I had her by the throat, lifted up so her feet dangled, my fingers iron in her soft, fragile human flesh. The cuff pulsed coldly; green light painted the inside of the kitchen in a flash of aque-ous light. She choked, a large dark stain spreading at the crotch of her jeans. Pissed herself with fear.

My lips pulled back. Rage, boiling in every single blood vessel. Heat poured from me, the air groaning and steaming, glass fogging, the wood cabinet-facings popping and pinging as they expanded with the sudden temperature shift, the floor shaking and juddering. The entire house trembled on its foundations, more tinkling crashes as whatever Pontside and Mercy and their merry crew of dirty fucking Saint City cops hadn't broken as they searched the house shattered.

It is your choice. It is always your choice. *Death's voice was kind, the infinite kindness of the god I had sworn my life to. If I denied Him, He would still accept me, still love me.*

But He should not have asked this of me.

She was helpless and unarmed, incapable of fighting back. But she was guilty, and she had lied and murdered as surely as any bounty I'd ever chased.

Anubis et'her ka . . . Kill. Kill her kill her KILL HER!

I could not tell if the reply was Anubis, or some deep voice from the heart of me. But she can't fight back. This is murder, Dante.

I didn't care. And yet . . .

"I didn't kill her," I whispered. "The healer. I didn't . . . I walked away. I went to a phone booth, and I called Polyamour."

"She told me so. She was the last person to talk to you, near as I could figure. Nobody else knows. I had a hard enough time gettin' her to give *me* anything."

I could see why. Lucas Villalobos was every psion's worst nightmare. We knew what he charged for his help. Only the desperate bargained with him, and I hadn't had time to tell Poly he was on my side.

"Valentine?" Lucas restrained himself from shaking me, thank the gods. "Care to tell me where you was?"

I thought about it. Where *had* I gone?

My heart thudded, a sharp strike of pain inside my chest. Clawed fingers, digging in—

Lucas grabbed my wrist, locked it, and half-tore me out of the bed as he backpedaled to avoid my punch. We went down in a tangle of arms and legs, my claws springing free and slashing at empty air as he evaded the strike. *"Stop it!"* he yelled, producing an amazing amount of noise through the gravel in his throat. *"Calm the fuck down!"*

The sheet tangled around my hips. One of Lucas's skinny, strong arms locked across my throat, his knee in my back. "Calm down," he repeated, in my ear. "I ain't your enemy, Valentine! Quit it!"

I froze. My heart thundered in my ears. I felt my pulse in my wrists, my ankles, my throat, in the back of my head. Even my hair throbbed frantically.

It was true. He wasn't my enemy.

Who was? What had *happened?* "I don't know," I whispered. "I don't know what happened. The last thing I remember is being in that phone booth."

It wasn't strictly true. I knew I'd left the phone booth and gone . . . somewhere.

Pretty damn far, a sneering little voice spoke up inside my head. *You went right over the moon. Right over the goddamn moon and into the black, sunshine.*

Lucas was out of breath. "You calm?"

I'm not anywhere near calm, Lucas. But it'll have to do. I stared at the floor—filthy boards, dirt squirming in cracks, my narrow golden hand spread in front of my face to keep me from being mashed into the ground. I still had my rings, but each stone was dull and empty, no spells sunk into their depths. I had used them all.

When?

I coughed, racking. Wanted to spit. Didn't. "Let me up."

He complied. I made it up to sitting, my back braced against the cot, the sheet wrapped around me. Lucas squatted, easily, his yellow eyes on my face. Just like a cat will stare at a mousehole, patient and silent.

I shut my eyes. Breathed in. My shields were in bad shape, ragged patches bleeding energy into the air, heat simmering over my skin as my demon metabolism ran high. The surfroar of human minds outside this small room was just as loud as ever, but it wasn't crashing through my head. The discipline of almost forty years as a psion stood me in good stead, trained reflex patching together holes in the shimmering cloak of energy over me, little threads spinning out to protect me from the psychic whirlpool of a city.

Almost forty years, last time I checked. I didn't even know what year it was.

The absurdity of the situation walloped me right between the eyes. Danny Valentine, part-demon bounty hunter and tough-ass Necromance, and I didn't even know what goddamn decade I was in.

I bent over, wheezing. Lucas rose to his feet and shuffled away. I laughed until black spots crowded my vision from lack of oxygen, fit to choke as the candleflame trembled and the bare white-painted walls ran with shadows.

Lucas came back. He settled down cross-legged, and when I could look at him again, swabbing hot salt water from my cheeks, he offered me the bottle. It was rice wine, fuming colorlessly in my mouth. I took a healthy draft and passed the green plasglass bottle back to him. He took a swig, didn't grimace, and tossed it far back. His throat worked as he swallowed.

I wondered who the blood on his face was from. Discovered I didn't want to know. There was only one thing I needed to know from him.

"What the fuck's going on?"

He shrugged, took another hit off the bottle. "You disappeared and all hell broke loose. Your green-eyed boyfriend's tearin' up whole cities looking for you, and he's not too choosy where he looks or how hard. Your blue-eyed girl was scrambling to keep away from him at first, but she pulled a vanishing trick too, about a month ago. Everyone wants a piece of Danny Valentine, and I nearly got my head taken off a few times lookin' for you myself. I never been so happy to see a datband trace go live in my *life*."

So that's how he'd tracked me, with a datband trace. I was glad nobody else had been close enough to me to slip that code in. "Six months." I stared down at my hands. The battered black molecule-drip polish on my fingernails was almost gone, the fingernails themselves translucent gold.

Claw-tips. I could extend them, if I had to, and rip the sheet to shreds.

A year in Hell is not the same as a year in your world. Eve's voice floated through my head.

Why would I think of that now? I'd been out of action for six months, six months I couldn't remember. Six months I would probably, if I was lucky, never get back. I didn't *want* to remember them.

What do you do now, Danny? Japhrimel's looking for me, and Eve . . . Has he done something to her? Where have I been?

It didn't matter.

"What do you think we should do?" I whispered. I was fresh out of ideas.

Lucas took another mouthful, handed the bottle to me. "I think we should contact your boyfriend. There's other shit goin' down too, Valentine. Magi casting circles and invoking, and things coming through."

"Isn't having something come through the *point* of Magi casting circles?" I took a hit of rice wine, let it burn all the way down into my chest. It wouldn't do a damn thing for me—my part-demon metabolism mostly shunted alcohol aside now.

But the idea of getting drunk was so fucking tempting I wondered if I should find a vat of beer or something stronger.

"Not when Magi keep getting torn apart, even when they're just casting regular sorceries. The Hegemony's issued a joint directive with the Putchkin Alliance. No Magi are allowed to practice for the foreseeable future."

I stared at him, my jaw suspiciously loose. *"Sekhmet sa'es,"* I breathed, a thrill of fear running along my skin. "A joint directive?"

No Magi practicing meant the corporate shields of gods-alone-knew how many companies weren't being worked on. The glut of work could be ameliorated by some Shamans, but the finer industrial thieves were probably having the time of their lives. All sorts of other effects would ripple out through the economy—the potential loss in tax revenue was enormous. The setback in research labs would cost a hefty chunk, too.

"I ain't no coward." Lucas gave me a straight yellow-eyed glare. "But I can't see keepin' you alive much past sundown if we break cover. There's just too much fuckin' flak up there. Your green-eyed boy will keep you alive, and I confess I'd like a little backup m'self."

Now I have *officially heard everything.* For the man they called "the Deathless" to admit to wanting backup was thought-provoking, to say the least.

Thought-provoking isn't *the word you want here, Danny. The word you want is* terrifying. I sighed, swallowed another slug of clear fiery liquor. Even if I couldn't get drunk it was a calming ritual. My stomach rumbled a bit, subsided. I should have felt ravenous.

I only felt slightly unsteady. Nauseous. And *heavy,* my limbs filled with sand. "I need clothes. And weapons." *Where is my sword?* I badly wanted to close my hand on a hilt, hear the deadly whistle as a keen blade clove air. I wanted *my* sword, the sword my teacher had gifted to me.

I came back to myself as the bottle groaned sharply in my clenched hand, thick green plasilica singing with stress. Lucas eyed me.

I had to force my fingers to relax. I breathed deeply, in through the nose, out through the mouth. Just like the first and last meditation instruction every psion has hammered into her head—*breathe, and the mind grows still.*

I wish that was true. My datband gleamed on my wrist, which looked suddenly naked without the thick cuff of silvery metal.

The Gauntlet, the demon artifact that marked me as Lucifer's little errand girl. Where was it?

That was another thought I didn't want. I pushed it away.

"You got it." Lucas levered himself to his feet. "You got any idea how we're gonna find your boyfriend?"

My fingers tingled, and the scar on my shoulder burned, shifting. I could *feel* the ropes of scarring writhing against the surface of my skin. "We won't have to." My voice sounded very far away. "Sooner or later he always finds me. One way or another."

When he did, I would at least be safe for a little while. Everything else was just noise.

"Good thing, too. You get in *more* fuckin' trouble." He shuffled away, past the table with the dancing candle-flame. Halted, his shoulders coming up and tensing. "Valentine? You okay?"

Do I look okay to you? "Yeah." I set the bottle down and scrubbed my hands together, as if they were dirty. I *felt* dirty. Filthy, in fact. Maybe it was the room. I dearly wanted a shower. "Is there a bathroom around here? Any hot water?"

"There's a bathroom. Knock yourself out." He started moving again, a fast light shuffle barely audible even to my heightened senses. "Spect you might want to get cleaned up." He vanished through the door.

I wanted to scrub myself raw under some hot water. Still, I had more important work to do. I'd left Japhrimel trapped in a circle of Eve's devising, and told him it was war between us. He probably wasn't going to be happy with me in the slightest.

It didn't matter. My fingers crept up to the mark on

my shoulder, its frantic dance against my skin oddly comforting.

Japhrimel. The word stuck in my throat. *Even if you are angry at me. Even if you're furious. I* need *you.*

My fingers hovered, a scant half-inch from touching the moving scar. I pinched my eyes shut, my skin crawling, and curled over, my arm coming down to bar across my midriff. I *squeezed* myself, earning a huff of air from my lungs in the process. I was tired, and however good hot water sounded I suddenly didn't want to visit the bathroom.

There might be a mirror in there, and I didn't want to see myself.

Why not, Danny? The soft, mocking voice of my conscience came back on little cat feet as darkness swirled against the candle's glow. My cheek hit the floor, and I pulled my knees up. Lying down seemed like a good idea. A *really* good idea.

What are you so afraid of, Danny? Huh? Answer me that.

I didn't want to. So I just lay on the dirty floor and nailed my eyes shut, waiting for Lucas to come back.

3

I jolted up out of a deathly doze when I heard the foot-steps. Lay, my eyes closed, every inch of my skin suddenly alive with listening.

I'd scooted back under the rickety cot, seeking blind darkness. It just seemed like a good idea, especially with so many people looking for me. I was too exhausted to fight much, especially with my shields so fragile.

The fact that hiding under the bed wouldn't necessarily keep me safe never occurred to me. If it had, I'm not sure I would have cared.

Under the bed the floor was even filthier, but the wall next to the cot felt cold and solid against my back. I pulled my knees up, twitching the sheet under me and dispelling the urge to sneeze at the dust suddenly filling my nose. With that done, I *listened*, my sensitive ears dilating.

There. Four sets of footsteps. One very light, brushing the earth, one shuffling equally lightly—Lucas—and the third, a tread of heavy boots.

The last set I would have known anywhere. It was a noiseless step, quiet as Death Himself, but the mark on my shoulder woke with renewed soft fire spilling all the way down my arm.

My eyes squeezed shut. Shame woke, hot and rank, pressed against my throat and watering eyes. I didn't want him to see me like this.

Like what, Danny?

I couldn't name it even to myself.

The door opened. The footsteps had gone silent.

I *felt* him come into the room like a storm front over a city, his attention sweeping the walls once and focusing, unerringly, on the small dark space where I huddled on my side, curled up as tightly as I could without breaking my own bones.

The door closed, and he filled up the room like dark wine in a cup. The black-diamond fire of a demon's aura almost blinded me, with my shields so fragile and torn. OtherSight blurred through the veil of the physical world, showing me the thick cable of my link to him, a bond cemented by blood. His blood, and mine.

He'd *changed* me, given up Hell for me, and bargained to regain a full demon's Power as well. Lied to me. *Hurt* me, held me up against a wall and shaken me, left me sleeping alone while he hunted Doreen's daughter as I'd begged him not to.

Every time the water got deeper, I found out he'd known the game from the beginning, and was playing against me.

And yet, he always came for me. My heart swelled, sticking in my throat like a clot of stone.

There was a slight sound as he reached the cot. I managed to open my eyes.

A pair of boots, well-worn, placed just so against the

dirty floorboards. I saw the edge of his coat, too, liquid darkness stirring a little. He must have been agitated for his wings to move so much.

I saw something else, too.

The tip of a familiar lacquered indigo scabbard.

He eased himself down to sit cross-legged facing the bed, his coat flaring away along the floor. Set my sword down with a precise little click, just out of reach.

His silence was so absolute the candleflame's hiss became loud. I saw his knees—a pair of worn jeans ragged at the hems, and the scarred leather of his boots tinged with darkness. He'd been wading through something liquid, up to the ankles.

I didn't want to know *what*.

I stared at the sweet curve of my sword, lying quiescent and tempting. Hot water boiled out of my eyes, tracked down to touch the dirty, blood-crusted hair at my temple. My vision blurred.

Japhrimel said nothing.

It took every remaining erg of courage I possessed to make my right hand unclench. I eased forward, bit by bit, silent as an adder under a rock.

The mark on my shoulder flared again, Power spilling from it and coalescing, a cloak of black-diamond fire closing around my battered shields. It was the equivalent of a borrowed coat, the weight of so many psyches shunted aside from my shivering mental walls. Along with the soft caress of Power against my skin came something else— my rings beginning to swirl with deep light again.

Japhrimel's strength. Given without reserve or hesitation, as simply as he might have poured water into a cup. I let out an involuntary sigh, my arm falling limp to the floor. The relief was overwhelming. No more shouting of messy normal minds trying to get *in,* trying to drown me. The blessed silence was almost enough to make me weep with relief.

He *still* said nothing. His silence was sometimes like speaking, a complex patterned thing. But not now. Now his silence was simply the absence of every sound, a breathless feeling of waiting.

I realized, as if I'd known it all along, that he'd wait there for as long as it took for me to gather myself. He would let me make the first move.

He'd wait forever, if that was what it took.

Two sides of a coin, the betrayal and the waiting. I wished he'd just choose one and get it over with, so I could fight for him or against him.

I inhaled sharply, catching the last half of the sigh in my teeth. When I spoke it took me by surprise, my voice rusty and disused for all its velvety half-demon roughness.

"I guess I don't look so good." The words trembled.

Great, Danny. Can you sound any more fucking stupid? The darkness behind my eyelids had knives in it. Every one of them was pointed at me, and quivering with readiness. The black hole in my memory yawned.

Japhrimel didn't stir. When he spoke it was soft, even, and soothing, the most careful of his voices. "I care little for how you *look,* Dante."

More sharp relief, tinged with deep unhealthy shame and a dose of panic, made my heart thud frantically inside my chest. "Something happened to me." *I sound about five years old and scared of the dark.*

I'm really going to have to work on my vidpoker face.

"Indeed." Still very quiet. "I am still your Fallen, you

are still my *hedaira*. Nothing else is of any importance."
He paused. "It is . . . enough that you are still alive."

I flinched. *You don't get it.* Something boiled below
my breastbone, something sharp. Claws, sinking into my
chest, something wriggling and squirming against violated flesh. "Something *happened* to me."

"Your sword was delivered to me two days ago, by the
Prince of Hell's messenger." His shielding didn't quiver,
but I knew enough of the faint shadings in his voice to
read terrible, rigidly controlled fury in him.

Japhrimel was a hairsbreadth away from rage. The
thought, for once, didn't frighten me. Instead, it filled me
with a sick unsteady glee.

I *wanted* him to be angry.

"I left you," I whispered. "In Eve's circle." *Trapped. I
told you it was war between us.*

"That is of no account." He didn't shift his weight, but
I got the idea he would have waved the idea away with
one golden hand. Just gone, *poof,* like so much smoke.

"You're mad at me." *I sound like a stupid girl on a holovid soap.* I opened my eyes, stared at the light of sanity
and the beautiful curve of my sword, its scabbard a mellow indigo glow. "I *left* you there."

"I did not expect you to release me. In fact, I demanded
that you do so in order to make you more valuable in the
escaped Androgyne's eyes, so she would keep you alive
as a bargaining chip and not slaughter you to revenge herself on me." Japhrimel sighed, a slight colorless sound.
"I expected to collect you soon enough. I broke free of
the Androgyne's trap and searched for you, but you had
disappeared. I found no trace of you in the city but your
perfume, and the knowledge that a door had recently been

opened into Hell. Then I knew Lucifer had taken you, and the game had changed."

"Oh." I began to feel slightly ridiculous, hiding under the bed. He sounded so calm, so rational. I didn't feel ridiculous enough to risk leaving this safety, no matter how flimsy it was. "I don't remember." *I'm beginning to get a bad feeling about what I don't remember.* I felt so *heavy*, every particle of flesh weighed down by gravity. Had it always been this hard, this tiring to draw breath?

"I suspect that is a mercy of short duration. Events are afoot, *hedaira*. I think it best we do not linger here." He didn't shift his weight.

"What's going on?" I didn't think for a minute he'd tell me anything. Keeping things from me seemed to be a real hobby with him. I wondered if he got any satisfaction from it.

Then I had to swallow that thought, because he opened his mouth again.

"I have not only declared war on Vardimal's Androgyne, but on the Prince of Hell himself. I intend to kill my Maker, *hedaira*, and to do so I will need your help."

My help? Killing Lucifer? I shut my mouth, opened it to speak, and shut it again. I felt like a fish tossed onto shore, and probably looked just as ridiculous. If anyone could see me under the bed, that is.

Is that who I have to kill to get myself back?

Somehow the idea didn't seem laughable at all.

"Do you hear me, Dante?" The fury was back, circling just under the surface. I had sometimes thought I *knew* him, the demon who had Fallen and bound himself to me. This rage was something new, and the only thing scarier than its icy crackle was how good he was at keeping it tightly reined and controlled. "I have not only Fallen but *rebelled.* Yet I will not yoke myself to Vardimal's Androgyne in the Prince's place. I shall make you a bargain, my curious one. If you wish me to lay aside my claim on the rebel Androgyne, I ask that you help me defeat my Prince."

My heart squeezed itself down to a concrete lump in my chest. Blackness rose from the hole in the floor of my mind, threatening to choke me or tip me into howling insanity. I struggled, my rings popping and snarling with sparks—no spells in them, but pure Power fluxing and trembling through metal and stones. Moonstone, amber, bloodstone, and silver, each ring bought and charged and worn continuously. The rings had seen me through countless bounties, never leaving my skin even while Japhrimel murmured in my ear in a Nuevo Rio bedroom, the taste of his blood in my mouth and the feel of his body imprinted on mine, my bones crackling as he *changed* me into something else. Something more than human, or less, depending on how you looked at it.

"Why?" I whispered.

"Is it not enough that I will?" Tension crackled below the surface of his familiar voice. I should have been terrified.

What's enough, Japh? My right hand crept out. My wrist looked fragile, too thin; my fingers slid out into the flickering candlelight along the dirty floor. My sword was a little too far away, so I edged forward, moving my heavy recalcitrant body like a sled on reactive-greased runners. My hip bumped the cot above me, my head barked itself on a metal support.

The lacquer of the reinforced scabbard was cool and

slick under my fingers. My left hand slid out from under the bed too, and I groped empty air for a terrifying moment, thinking maybe he'd changed his mind or I was hallucinating.

Japhrimel's fingers threaded through mine. I found myself dragged out of my sheet and from under the cot like a stuffed toy, almost limp. He flowed upright, carrying me with him and ignoring my sudden panicked flinch, every inch of my body shivering as terror rose with a blinding snap like the sound of a hammer on a projectile gun.

Air flirted and swirled unsteadily as he pulled me against him, his coat separating in front as his wings spread, wrapping around me and pulling me into the shelter of his body. The musk-cinnamon smell boiling from his skin closed around me, a heavy drenching scent, and my knees buckled.

Damn him. He still smelled like *home*. Like safety. Except something trembling under the surface of my skin told me safety was just a word. I doubted I would ever feel safe again.

He dropped his face to my tangled, filthy, blood-caked hair and inhaled, shuddering, his bare chest feverishly warm with the heat of one of Hell's children. And I surprised myself again by starting to scream—but the screams were muffled by wrenching sobs as I pressed my face into the exposed hollow between his collarbone and his shoulder, his arms and wings around me and the only haven I had left safely reached at last.

That's the problem with being a tough girl. The crying fits never get to last long enough.

The bathroom door yawned like an open mouth. I stared at it like a rabbit stares at a snake. I'd wrapped the sheet around myself again, clutched my sword's slim hard length, and perched guiltily in the one chair. Japhrimel settled himself on the edge of the cot, his eyes burning green and half-shuttered.

I couldn't look at his eyes. I glared at the open door, daring it to come get me, if it wanted me.

Outside the room, I heard a muttered question. Lucas's answer reassured me.

Since when did I find Lucas Villalobos reassuring? The world had indeed gone mad.

Tall, saturnine, gold-skinned demon, sitting motionless on the edge of the rucked bed. Japhrimel's coat fell away from his knees, clasped his throat with a high Chinese collar, and trembled just a little under the gold of the candle's uncertain light. His face was familiar, winged eyebrows and sharp nose, the architecture of his cheekbones unfamiliar to anyone used to human faces, his lips thinned and held in a straight line, betraying nothing. His hair had grown out, a fall of darkness softening the harsh lines of his face. The length was new—he'd always kept it trimmed, before.

I wondered again how I could have ever thought of him as ugly, long ago in the dim time of our first meeting.

He finally stirred slightly. "We should go, Dante. It isn't wise to linger."

My legs trembled, but I hauled myself to my feet. Pulled the sheet up, tucking it under my arm to keep it wrapped around me, and cast around for my bag. "Fine. Where are we going?"

"Don't you want a shower?" He very carefully didn't

look at me, but the edges of his coat ruffled again. Light ran wetly over its surface. "I seem to recall you have a fondness for hot water."

I spotted my bag, lying on the floor. It looked very small and very sad, its knotted strap and stained canvas a reminder of . . . what? Something terrible.

Panic trembled under my skin until I took a deep breath, just like I would calm a rattling slicboard. *One thing at a time, Danny. You've got your sword and Japh's here. Just take it one step at a time.*

"There's a mirror in there." The queer flatness of my tone surprised me. For a completely ridiculous objection to the idea of a shower, it stood up pretty well the more I thought about it.

Japhrimel rose, slow and fluid. He ghosted over the floor, his coat now making no sound as it moved with him.

I searched for some way to ask the question I needed most answered, and failed miserably. "Lucas said you were looking for me."

He shrugged as he pushed the bathroom door open and flicked the switch inside. Electric light stung my eyes, flooding a slice of none-too-clean tile. "I seem to spend a distressing amount of time doing so."

I opened my mouth, but a wall-shattering sound smashed through whatever I would have said. Japhrimel stepped out of the bathroom, his fingers flicking. He stopped, his coat rippling and settling and his eyes not quite meeting mine. "There is no mirror." The words turned sharp and curt. "Be quick, and careful of glass on the floor." His stride lengthened, and my Fallen brushed past me on his way to the door.

My pulse slowed down a bit. I caught my breath, my knuckles white around the scabbard. Lacquered wood groaned as my fingers flexed, battle between my will and my unruly body joined again.

Japhrimel halted, between me and the door. His head dropped, and if I hadn't been shaking so hard myself I might have sworn he was trembling. His hair whispered as it brushed his shoulders, strings of darkness. "I would counsel you also to be careful of me," he said, softly. "I do not think I am quite . . . safe."

You know, of all the things you could have said, that's one of the least comforting. My mouth had turned dry and glassy, a tide of terror rising up against my breastbone. "Are you saying you'll hurt me?" *Because, you know, I wouldn't put it past you. Even if I am really glad to see you.*

Go figure. Ten minutes with him and I was already feeling more like myself. Except I felt so goddamn heavy, my body weighed down with lead.

And I had no real clue who "myself" really was anymore. Details, details.

His shoulders hunched as if I'd screamed at him. "I would not," he said, clearly and softly, "hurt *you*. But I am not quite in control of my temper. You could cause an injury to someone else, by way of me."

Great. That's really reassuring. The familiar bite of irritation under my breastbone spurred and soothed at the same time. "Oh." My fingers relaxed, a millimeter at a time. "Japh?"

He said nothing, and he didn't move. The shaking in him communicated itself to the air.

"Thank you." *I'm going to have to rethink any plan that includes cutting loose of you.*

My Fallen's black-clad shoulders dropped. The sense of breathless fury in the air waned, swirling uneasily, ruffling the candleflame and touching the creaking walls.

"I told you I would always come for you." As calmly as he might have told me what was for lunch. "Be quick, Dante."

I hitched the sheet up on my chest and edged for the bathroom. There was nothing to be scared of in there, now.

4

We were still in North New York Jersey, deep in the festering wasteland of the Core. Japhrimel brought me clothes—a Trade Bargains microfiber shirt, a pair of jeans too new to be comfortable, and a pair of boots in my size that would need hard use before they were anything close to broken-in. With Fudoshin's comforting weight in my left hand, I almost felt like myself again.

I came out of the bathroom rubbing at my hair with a towel that had seen much better days. Once I scrubbed the crusted blood and filth away, I felt scraped-raw and naked, but at least I'd stopped bleeding. The city dozed outside my borrowed mental walls, a pressure I didn't have to directly feel to be wary of.

If a psion's shields broke, the mind inside those shields could fuse together in meltdown, just like any delicate instrument after a power surge. I was lucky my brain hadn't been turned to oatmeal.

Lucky. Yeah. I was lucky all over, lately.

My heart slammed into my throat.

Japhrimel stood by the door, his eyes half-closed and burning green. "How do you feel?"

I took stock. I felt like I'd eaten too much and now had to lie in the sun to digest, like a lizard. A slow heavy cramp wended its way through my belly, and I sighed, testing my arms and legs. I could still make a fist, and my toes wiggled when I told them to. "Fine." *I don't feel quite like myself, but after the week I've had, I don't blame me.* A half-hysterical sound caught me off-guard, and I clapped my right hand over my mouth to trap it.

Stop it. I struggled for control, peeled my hand away from my mouth. I locked my fingers around the hilt instead. A simple motion clicked the blade free and it leapt up, three inches of steel shining, oiled and perfect. My voice turned into something else, cut off savagely midstream.

Blue fire tingled in the steel. Fudoshin hummed, ready for blood to be spilt. "Just fine," I repeated, my eyes locked to the blue shine. "Where are we going?"

"We must leave here." Did he sound uneasy? "There is much to be done."

Does it involve killing someone? If it does, I'm all for it. I slid the blade back home with an effort. *Not now. Soon.* "What's first?"

"First we must have a small discussion." He had gone utterly still. "There are some things we must say to each other, and they are not comfortable."

Great. Why don't we just get a sedayeen *arbitration specialist? I hear they're cheap this year.* "Like what?" *He's going to ask me why I left him trapped in that circle and let Eve get away. He's going to ask me where I was, what happened to me.*

Japhrimel paused. Electric light slid lovingly over the planes of his face, touched the wet blackness of his coat. The edges ruffled, his wings responding to agitation. When he spoke, it was the gentlest of his voices, and he held himself very still. "You were taken to Hell." The question ran under the surface of the words.

I closed my eyes.

How much did Japhrimel know or guess? "It hurt," I heard myself say, in the flat odd voice that only showed up when I was talking about the past. That was a relief—it was over and done, now. The worst had happened.

I winced as soon as I thought it. Thinking the worst has happened is a sure way to invite Fate to serve up another heaping helping of gruesome.

"Did you take anything from the Prince? Accept any gift, eat anything? Even a single mouthful of water, a single bite of food?" Gentle, but tense, the words straining from a dry throat.

Tierce Japhrimel sounded worried.

"No." *I don't think you'd call it a gift.* Black unhealthy humor rose in my throat, I pushed it down and away. *Don't think about that, Danny. You'll go mad.*

"Are you certain?"

I nodded, my jaw set so hard I could feel my teeth groaning. If they hadn't been demon-strong, those teeth, would I have shattered my own jaw?

It was an unpleasant thought.

"You accepted *nothing* from the Prince or his minions?"

There wasn't any accepting involved. "Nothing." My jaw eased up a little. I could speak, now. The darkness behind my lids was more comforting. "He dragged me through a door and into Hell."

"What happened?"

A delicate touch—the brush of his callused fingers against my cheekbone. Gently brushing the line of my jaw, turning and sliding down the hollow of my throat.

Back when I was fully human my neck was bigger, a slope running down to my shoulders, the cord of the sternocleidomastoid muscle well-developed. Now, the cervical curve was better designed, demon bones capable of taking a greater hit and the muscles running just slightly differently to provide more leverage and flexibility.

Japhrimel's palm met my throat. His warm fingers curled, his thumb stroking just where the tension had settled. When I swallowed, harshly, my skin moved against his.

My eyes flew open, his face filling my vision, familiar and oddly, terrifyingly different for a split second before I recognized him.

What could I tell him? How could I possibly put it into words?

"He hurt me," I whispered. "Then I fell out of Hell and Lucas found me."

"He hurt you?" Calm and quiet, as if I couldn't feel the fine explosive quiver running through his bones. His eyes burned green, lightening two awful shades until they looked . . .

Like *his*. Like Lucifer's. Like they could strip me down to bone and burn until not even ash remained. I tensed, muscle by muscle, staring into his eyes. My breath drew itself in, held against the back of my throat. My chin jerked down in a facsimile of a nod.

Very softly, the most human of his voices turned into the brush of cat's fur. "Tell me, beloved. Tell me what was done to you."

The words refused to come. They sat in my chest like a stone egg, like the heaviness in my belly, like the betraying weakness of my treacherous body. I smelled cinnamon, and musk—the darker smell of Japhrimel's pheromones, the lighter overlay of mine, blending together to make a bubble of safety and climate control. The walls creaked and groaned sharply as Japhrimel's aura cycled up into the visible, streaks of blackness painting the air like colored oil on water.

I held his gaze, only capable of doing so because at the back of the green light, at the very center of the hot darkness that was his pupils—not round like a human's or slit like a cat's, but somewhere between the two—a different darkness moved.

Before he'd bargained with Lucifer to regain a demon's Power, his eyes had been humanly dark, and it was that I saw in them now. The darkness hadn't been eaten by the green light spilled over his irises.

It was there, *under* the light. How had I never seen it before?

"He hurt me." The little-girl whisper wasn't me. It *couldn't* be me. "I don't want to talk about it."

His hand fell away from my throat, leaving cold bareness behind. His eyes held mine. "Then you do not have to." Japhrimel's tone was still killing-soft, but its edge was not directed at me. "When you wish to, I will listen. But first, answer me this. Did you accept anything from the Prince or his minions, anything at *all?*"

Of course not. Nobody in their right mind takes a gift from a demon. Except me, of course. I'd taken gifts from Japhrimel too many times to count.

"No," I whispered. "There was no accepting involved,

Japhrimel." *And if you ask me that one more time, I'm going to scream.*

"He merely . . . hurt you?" His voice scraped and burned along the edges of my numbness.

"He hurt me enough. I *said* I don't want to talk about it." I turned on my heel and took two steps away toward the bathroom door again, stopped restlessly. Despite the shower, I suddenly felt *filthy*.

"We are not finished."

I stopped. My hair brushed my shoulders, the mark pulsing with soft velvet heat. My rings swirled with light, my aura settling down under the healing weight of Japhrimel's.

He was holding me together, the cloak of a demon's Power easing around me like a caress. Each successive wave from the scar on my shoulder worked in a little deeper, thin filaments spinning across the ragged gaps in my shielding, patching them. My wrists and knees felt naked and vulnerable, but the slim heavy length of my sword in my left hand more than made up for it.

My skin crawled. I wanted to scrub myself again, with a wire brush if I had to. Shock had kept me numb before, but I wasn't numb now.

Not even close.

"What else?" My brittle tone would have been a warning to anyone else.

His footfalls were silent, but I felt each one against my back, my skin roughening instinctively under its tough golden perfection. Warm hands touched my shoulders, and he turned me to face him, with gentle inexorable pressure.

His skin used to be so hot, before. When I was human, and my flesh was humanly cold.

What am I now?

I didn't know.

He held my shoulders and examined my face, his gaze a physical pressure over my cheekbones, my mouth, my forehead. His eyes didn't frighten me now, despite their green glow.

His mouth was a thin line, his hair falling over and shading his burning eyes. The air in the room jolted once, as if hit by a projectile cannon. I flinched, but Japhrimel held me still and deathly silence fell again, wrapping around both of us.

When he spoke, it was quiet and level, each word evenly spaced. "I will repay the Prince tenfold for any harm done to you." His inhaled breath was a slow hiss as his eyes locked with mine.

I wonder if that's supposed to make me feel better. Shame rose, hot and vicious, and I tasted copper. He held me for a few more moments, and whatever he saw on my face must have satisfied him, because he let go of me. "We have little time, and must leave now."

"Where are we going?" I suppose I sounded normal— if by *normal* you mean *like a ten-credit-per-minute vidphone sex queen.* Something in my throat was permanently broken, thanks to the Prince of Hell's habit of strangling me.

It was a favor I longed to return, and with Japhrimel firmly on my side it might just be possible.

Maybe.

If Japh really was on my side.

Oh, gods above, Danny, don't start doubting him again.

"We have an appointment to keep." His shoulders straightened as he stepped away from me. "Come."

I shivered, a reflexive movement. Any other time, I would have flinched under the plasgun charge of Power and cold fury in Japhrimel's voice. "Japhrimel."

He paused, his coat coming to rest with a slight betraying flutter.

"Where are we going?" *Don't just order me around, dammit. I've had all I can take of being ordered around.*

Five seconds of absolute silence ticked by before he replied. "Konstans-Stamboul."

My shoulders dropped. *Great. Wonderful. Making progress. Why are we going there?*

He strode out of the room as if he expected me to follow.

So I did. What else could I do?

5

Ten hours later, on a hover bristling with demonic shield-ing, we were in Konstans-Stamboul. I spent most of the journey on a narrow shelf of a bed in one of the hover's three cabins, grateful for a chance to simply rest. There were sounds under the well-tuned hum of hover transport—Lucas, other voices. I didn't care; Japh had brought me on through the cargo bay so I didn't have to see anyone.

I was grateful for that. I didn't *want* to be seen. I wanted to be alone.

I'd like to get a good few hours of meditation in. Even praying wouldn't hurt if we're going near a temple. It was a reflexive internal movement, a reaching for the faith that had always sustained me. The space where that faith had been was an ocean of bitterness, and I shivered like a child with a mouthful of sour candy as I buckled the rig on. It was new and custom-made, oiled leather holding two 9 mm projectile guns in low holsters, a 40-watt and a 20-watt plasgun (60-watts have a habit of blowing up in the hand), and a collection of knives, from two main-gauches long as my forearms from wrist to elbow to a thin flexible stiletto on the inside of one strap. The steel had faint dappled marks in the metal, as had all the knives Japhrimel had produced for me.

He understood good gear, the Devil's assassin. At least we always agreed about that.

The rig was going to chafe. The leather hadn't been broken in yet, despite its oiled softness. My other rig was gone.

Don't think about that.

I rolled my shoulders back in their sockets, breathed in, and felt the familiar weight of weaponry settle into shoulders and hips. My hand tightened around the scabbard, and I let the breath out in a soft hiss.

Armed and dangerous again, Danny. I dropped, with a jolt, fully into my skin, and opened my eyes.

Japhrimel stood just inside the door, watching me arm myself. "Are they acceptable?"

"I've never had a problem with any of the gear you get me." My voice was flat and weary, my face frozen into a mask. "You have a good eye for steel."

If I hadn't glanced up at him, I might have missed the faint smile touching his thin lips. "A compliment indeed, coming from you."

I checked the guns. They cleared easily, the projectiles clicking as I spun them, reholstering. The plasguns whined as I drew them, and I finished by testing the knives. The smallest stiletto was a bit sticky in its glove-tight sheath, but that was only to be expected, and if I had to draw it I probably wouldn't need it quickly anyhow. No, it would be a quiet draw, quiet as slipping the blade between ribs, as quiet as a prison cell with a lock that needs picking.

Japhrimel had even remembered the type of projectiles I usually carried ammo for, Smithwesson 9 mms with interchangeable cartridges. I had ammo in my bag, but I wasn't sure if my bag could take much more abuse.

Just as I thought it, Japhrimel raised his arm. I heard faint voices outside—Lucas's painful whisper, mostly; the others were just murmurs.

My bag, its strap no longer knotted, dangled from Japh's hand. He held it like it weighed nothing. "I repaired some small damage to this. I thought you would want it." He paused. "Even though it does still smell of Hell. I could not mend that."

A lump rose in my throat. I crossed the room, the new boots stiff and making each step oddly clumsy. I took the bag, ducked my head, and settled the strap diagonally across my body. When I looked up, Japhrimel was still staring down at me.

We stood like that, my head tilted back, his shoulders no longer ruler-straight but slightly slumped. His eyes were fixed on my mouth, their green glare hooded and alert.

I searched for something to say that would lead me on to the next thing that had to be done. *Roll with it, Danny. Get with the holovid.* "Thank you." I would have licked my dry lips, but the way he was staring at them stopped me. A flush of heat went down my body, followed by a wave of panic nailing me in place. "Don't look at me like that."

His eyes swung up to meet mine. Tension sparked in the air between us, a circuit closed or broken. Either way, it snapped once, then twice, as his hands came up to touch my shoulders. Leather creaked; the rig wasn't anywhere close to broken-in.

Great. If I have to sneak around it's not going to be very quietly. I swallowed several times. The funny coppery taste in my mouth didn't need an introduction.

It was fear. I was afraid of my own Fallen.

How was I going to work around that?

Work all you want, I told myself. *But there's someone who needs killing first. Then you can take your sweet time and figure out everything you've ever wanted to know.*

My voice surprised me. "I have to kill him." I searched Japhrimel's face, looking for the hidden human darkness in his glowing eyes. It was there, if I could just look deep enough. "I *have* to kill him. You have to help me."

He nodded, a short sharp movement. His coat ruffled along its edges, a rustling sound.

He did not ask who I meant.

"No more tricks. No more lies or plans I don't know about. No more hiding."

Another short nod. He looked as if he would say something, stopped.

"Promise me, Tierce Japhrimel." I could not sound any more deadly serious. My belly twitched, the skin flinching as if I expected a suckerpunch. "*Promise* me."

"What could I promise you that I have not already? I am in rebellion for your sake, is that not enough?" His quick motion arrested my protest, he laid one finger against my lips. "Come with me."

I flinched, covered it well enough. "Where now?" As if it mattered.

"We have an appointment. One I never thought I would keep." His mouth twisted bitterly at one corner, a swift snarl. It should have chilled my blood.

It didn't. For some reason, I felt a jagged burst of relief inside my chest. He'd promised.

It would have to be enough.

6

Konstans-Stamboul is an amazingly low-built city. Zoning laws are tight and archaic here, and the traffic is mostly wheel or airbikes, with a generous helping of slicboards. There aren't many hovers, and the freight lanes over the city are full of slow silvery beetles marching against a sky often starving-deep blue, old pollution and new citybreath laying a bowl of refraction over dreaming blocks of stone buildings mixed with concrete and weathered plasteel.

In the midst of this, the white walls and piercing towers of Hajia Sofya rise like a flawless tooth in otherwise-shattered gums. Graceful and pristine, the temple thrums with agonized centuries of worship and belief—Old Christer, Islum, Gilead Evangelical, and finally the multicolored, multilayered hum of Power collected consciously by psions coming to pray to their personal gods and normals coming to propitiate those same gods. Belief like sweat dews the white, white walls, and everywhere in the city you can *feel* the temple looming, a heart pumping slowly but surely.

There are other temples in Konstans-Stamboul, but none of them feel like Sofya. That's how psions refer to her—*Sofya*. And even more familiarly, as *She*. There are only two temples referred to in the feminine singular—Hajia Sofya, and Notra Dama in Paradisse.

Vann crouched easily on the grated plasteel floor of the hover, tossing what looked like brown knucklebones onto a square of dark leather painted with three concentric rings. He didn't *look* like a psion, but I supposed a Hellesvront agent working for Japhrimel might pick up a little divination here and there.

McKinley slumped in a chair, his head tipped back and a pale slice of throat showing. He wore all black, as usual, and his left hand lay cupped on his knee, more metallic than ever, glowing in mellow Stamboul light falling through the portholes. He looked tired, dark bruised circles graven under his closed eyes.

Lucas leaned against the hull, peering out a porthole, his yellow eyes slitted and the river of scarring down his face red and angry-looking. He rested one hand on the butt of a 60-watt plasgun, stroking it meditatively. Leander Beaudry, his cheeks scruffy with stubble over his accreditation tat, very pointedly didn't look at Japhrimel. He sat in another chair bolted to the floor, his knees drawn up and his sword across them. His emerald glowed, a spark popping from it as I stared at his familiar, suddenly-strange face. He looked so . . . human. He even smelled human, the odor of mortality a spice against the scent of *other* everyone else in the hover carried.

Even me. My thumb rested against the katana's guard.

"We're exposed here." Lucas didn't acknowledge my presence with anything else. "How long we staying?"

"We shall be leaving shortly." Japhrimel's heat against my back was comforting. He stood close, shadowing me

in a way he never had before. "As soon as we have collected what we require."

McKinley's eyes showed a faint gleam under the heavy
lids. They rested on me, those little gleams. I didn't like
it. The sandpaper-on-skin distaste I always felt for him
rasped at me. The little clicks as Vann threw the bones
irritated me too.

I wondered if I could kill either or both of them before Japhrimel intervened. I actually even started planning how to do it, a thin unhealthy joy rising behind my
heartbeat when I imagined slipping my katana free of its
sheath and letting the rage take me.

*The first few steps would be forward, gathering mo-
mentum and leaping, committing myself while McKinley
was still in the chair. The sword would clear sheath with
a musical ring, and the strike would be an upward diago-
nal, so that even if he tried to leap to his feet he would
walk into it. He wouldn't take the easiest way out, kicking the chair over backward, because it was bolted to the
floor. The second stroke would be a reverse, wrist twisting and hilt floating as the blade sped back down, and it
would finish him and position me for a crouch to launch
myself at Vann—*

McKinley's dark eyes unlidded themselves halfway,
his lashes rising with agonizing slowness. He looked at
me like he could read my mind.

I'm sure my face reflected what I was thinking. I could
feel it, a chilling little smile pulling the corners of my lips
back, showing strong white demon-altered teeth.

McKinley didn't move. His Adam's-apple bobbed as
he swallowed, but there was no stink of fear from him.
Instead, he examined me from under half-closed eyelids,

wearing the same set expression he might use to watch a poisonous but not terribly bright animal, one to be cautious of despite its inherent stupidity.

The friction on my nerves got worse. Vann said something I didn't quite catch, his stance changing just a fraction as he crouched fluidly over whatever he was doing.

Japhrimel's hand descended on my left shoulder, his fingers curling around and tightening over his mark in the sensitive hollow under the wing of my collarbone. "There is no cause for alarm," he said quietly. I had no trouble hearing *his* voice through the sudden rushing noise in my ears. "It is, after all, natural."

McKinley shrugged, a lazy movement. "Doesn't look like she agrees, m'Lord."

Japhrimel's thumb stroked the wing of my shoulderblade, brushing one of the rig's leather straps. The touch burned through me, clearing away the sick unsteady feeling of violence.

He irritates me, but that's not a reason to kill him. What am I thinking?

I didn't know. And that was dangerous in and of itself.

Silence stretched out until McKinley closed his eyes again. Vann scooped up the bones and the leather square, rolling them into a neat packet he tied off with a leather thong. The resultant little thing disappeared into his clothes and he rose with swift economical grace. "Will we be accompanying you, my Lord?"

The way the two agents spoke to Japh—with careful deference but absolute trust—rubbed me the wrong way too. It wasn't that they were so respectful. I of all people understood the need to be cautious where demons were concerned, especially if you work for them. But the lack of unease told me these two had known Japh longer than I had, and that I didn't like at all.

Sekhmet sa'es, *Danny, are you* jealous? *Of a couple of Hellesvront agents?* I slid away from Japhrimel's hand. He let me, but I didn't miss the sudden tension in the air as I crossed the hover in swift strides, my new boots and rig creaking, to stare out the porthole next to Lucas's.

"You will be accompanying me, but not in the usual manner." Japhrimel said it carefully, giving each word particular weight. "Your task will be to protect what is most precious to me."

Silence spread out in ripples again. I peered out the porthole, seeing the edge of a landing pad, a bare weedy empty lot, and the unmistakable slumped tenements of Konstans-Stamboul's poorer section. This wasn't quite where I would have picked to park—a shiny hover sitting around in this neighborhood would draw attention. Thick, golden late-afternoon sunlight dipped every surface in honey.

My fingers tightened on the sheath as the silence grew more intense. I felt eyes on me, didn't turn around. What was I supposed to do?

"Very well." Japhrimel sounded like something had been decided.

Lucas let out a soft breath, a tuneless hum. I glanced over, meeting his yellow gaze. A thought froze me, seeing the river of scarring running down his face.

They called Lucas the Deathless, and the rumor was that he'd done something so awful even Death had turned His back on the man. I'd always assumed Lucas had been a Necromance.

What if I was wrong?

"Lucas." The word was out of my mouth before I was aware of speaking. "Can I ask you something?"

He shrugged, turning his gaze out his own porthole. "We stick out like a hooker in a Luddite convention, parked here." Under the threadbare yellowing shirt, his wiry shoulders were hunched. Call me sensitive, but I got the idea he didn't want to answer any questions just now.

"I thought the same thing." Thin amusement rode the edge of my voice. I rolled my shoulders back in their sockets, settling the rig. "I just wish I could stop getting my clothes blown off me and bloodied."

"Quit gettin' yourself into trouble with demons." He jerked his chin toward his right shoulder, a movement I belatedly realized took in the silent and visibly unhappy Leander. "Boy's learned his lesson."

"You don't have to call me a coward, Villalobos." Leander's voice was soft, the professional whispering tone of a Necromance. We who enforce our will on the world with our voices learn to speak softly. It's also kind of an affectation—a whisper is better than a shout when it comes to scaring the hell out of someone.

I don't usually feel like scaring the hell out of someone. People—at least, *normal* headblind people—are simply scared of psions as a whole. It's xenophobia and fear of the unknown all wrapped up in one economical package, with lingering hatred left over from the Evangelicals of Gilead and their theocratic North Merican empire making a festive bow. The Seventy Days War and the fall of the Republic were years and years ago, but people have long memories when it comes to hating the different.

"Not callin' you a coward, Beaudry. Think it's your

smartest move." Lucas gave the whistling gurgle that was his laugh.

I turned away from the porthole, looking at Leander directly. A scintilla of light from the emerald embedded in his cheekbone sent a swift bolt of something too hot and nasty to be pain through me. "What's going on?"

The Necromance shrugged, an economical movement. His katana rattled unhappily inside its sheath, and his shielding shivered as the charged atmosphere stroked at it. His eyes were shadowed, and the inked lines of his accreditation tat shifted under scruffy dark stubble. "Your friend doesn't like me, Valentine." He didn't have to point for me to know it was Japhrimel he was talking about. "But if I strike out on my own, I'm looking at trouble. I'm associated with you now. So do I stick around and wait for your pet demon to take more of a dislike to me, or do I find a hole to hide in until this blows over?" A short bitter laugh, and he palmed his face wearily. "Except things like this don't blow over. I'm just unhappy. I'm not a goddamn coward."

"Nobody's saying you are." My eyes fastened on the emerald, alive with green light. He still had his connection with his psychopomp, with whatever face of Death had revealed itself at his Trial.

He was a Necromance. His god hadn't forced him to spare a traitor's life.

Except my god hadn't forced me, had He? No, He had simply *asked*. I could not blame Him. Who did that leave to blame?

Anubis—The prayer started inside my head, I shoved it away. I would not call on Him.

Not now. Not like this. The determination was raw and painful, heavy sunlight on already burned skin.

"So I'm in." Leander's tone said plainly, *That's that. Don't push me.*

I considered him for a long moment. He was right. I'd stepped in over my head this time, worse than usual. The hideous beating secret inside my brain was almost as black as the traitorous tingling on my cheekbone where my own emerald flashed.

After all my worship, all my love, and all my service, my god had let me down just when I needed Him most, by even *asking* the sacrifice of me. How could I reconcile my faith to that? I had been *forced* to spare a killer's life. I had been used by the god I loved.

Would another Necromance understand my pain?

Why don't you ask him over coffee, Danny? Whenever you can take a moment out of your busy schedule of being dragged into Hell and strangled to death by demons.

I scraped together the most tactful thing I could think of to say. "Fine. You're in." *Just stay out of trouble.* I half-turned again, meeting Japhrimel's eyes.

My Fallen stood with his hands loose at his sides. It was the closest to bored I'd ever seen him, but he also had a look I didn't like at all. A look of listening to some sound I would never be able to hear, no matter how hard I strained my better-than-human senses. It was only a millimeter's worth of difference in the set of his mouth, a slight tension in his winged eyebrows, but it was as loud as a shout to me. I'd spent long enough looking at him to know.

He'd worn that look a lot in Toscano, before our life together had gone merrily to Hell.

Icy spider-feet walked up my spine. "You have a problem with that, Japh?"

He considered me, his eyes burning incandescent green. The raggedness of dark hair falling over those eyes helped make his gaze a little less awful, as did the thin oval of human darkness behind the glow.

He ended up saying nothing. It might have seemed like the wisest course, considering the way my right hand itched for my swordhilt. I wasn't used to this kind of simmering rage.

Still, I didn't *dislike* it. It felt clean. Cleaner than the dark thing pulsing in my head, at least.

"See?" I swung back round to face Leander. "You're in." Another thought stopped me, so fast I snapped off the end of the last word. A sudden inspiration. "My very own Necromance to hang around. Just like getting a puppy for my birthday."

The sharp intake of breath, for once, wasn't mine. It was McKinley's. His eyes flew open, and I could swear Vann went white under the copper tone of his skin.

Wow. Maybe I just said something right for a change. Either that or I've just made a huge mistake. Guess which way my luck's running lately.

Japhrimel nodded. "As you like, my curious." No more than that. No color to his voice except simple acceptance.

I wished I could figure out whether he was giving in because it didn't matter in the long run *what* I did. It was pretty damn likely.

There you go, Danny old girl. You're thinking like yourself again.

The trouble was, I wasn't sure I really was thinking

like myself. It's hard to tell when you're not sure who you are anymore.

"My Lord." Vann clasped his arms behind his back, standing poker-straight. It looked ridiculous on him, especially with the fringe hanging off his leather coat. "I would remind you—"

"Not necessary, Vann." Japhrimel said over the top of him. Not dismissively, and not with any real heat. But his face settled and set, a demon's essential oddity closer to the surface than ever before, and my heart turned over inside my chest.

He wasn't human. It should have bothered me. It should have reminded me of the thing beating like a diseased heart inside my skull, the memory sleeping uneasily behind the strongest door I could make to shut it away.

It didn't. Instead, I saw the thin line of his lips, the fineness of his eyelashes, and the raggedness of his hair. I saw the oval of darkness behind his burning eyes.

I saw the man—no matter if he was a demon—who always came for me.

Whatever was on my face might not have been pleasant, but it seemed fine by my Fallen. His mouth relaxed into a half-smile, one corner quirking up in that sardonic expression that meant he was enjoying himself. As if I'd made an unexpected move in a game of battlechess, or done something that pleasantly surprised him.

I liked that look.

But what I liked even more was the thought that I might have some sort of control over my relationship with him. A little bit of control might sound like a small thing, but it was the difference between screaming insanity and some kind of rational shape to the inside of my head.

I actually felt happier than I had in a long time. Maybe I shouldn't have, but there it was. But still, my arms and legs were heavy, and deep in my belly a stone sat, dragging me down.

"So." I actually sounded perky. *Chalk up a winning gravball goal for Danny Valentine. It's about time.* "What's this about an appointment?"

7

I hadn't thought it would affect me like this.

Sofya's outer beauty was nothing compared to the magnificence inside. I'd seen holostills and travelogues, but they . . . nothing could do her justice. The blue, white, yellow mosaics had been carefully restored, domes soaring with mathematical precision above the standard Hegemony sundisc, its burnished glory little match for the piercing shafts of dying russet and gold sunlight falling through space harmonized, sanctified, and made agonizingly sweet by centuries of Power, praise, prayer, and above all, sheer undiluted *belief.*

Belief is what magick works on, after all. And so *much* of it is bound to give anyone who works the highest art humanity's capable of a high cleaner and sweeter than Clormen-13.

The temple was also heavy with demonspice and a tang of mortality's decay—a heady stew when added to the *kyphii* incense swirling hazily through the interior and the sweet blue-black resin they use in temples in this part of the world. The time to find any temple deserted is dusk, when incense grows heavy and shadows skitter with a life of their own. Normal humans instinctively avoid places of Power after dark, and psions are just waking up as the sun goes down. It's like a psychic shift-change for the entire world.

The gods, in this slice of the world, were mostly Old Graecian. Hermes with winged sandals and helmet, Héra in Her place of primacy, Apolo's small statue next to the more massive Artemisa Hekat holding a bow and touching the head of a sleek marble greyhound. Hades was there, shadowed by Persephonica, with Her basket of flowers echoing Demetre's horn of plenty. Âres crouched behind His shield, shortsword thrusting belligerently up. Aphroditas swooned on a long couch, Her naked body glowing triumphantly.

There was another long gallery of gods, mostly Old Perasiano, along with a round shield of calligraphy for the remnants of old Islum, enduring its last death here in a part of the world it once ruled, just like Novo Christianity. The Religions of Submission had a good run, but once the Awakening had happened and people could speak directly and reliably with gods . . . well, they just didn't make sense anymore.

At least, to most reasonable people.

I'm not really up on my Old Perasiano, but I recognized Ahra Mzda, as well as Ah'rman, His destructive shadow-twin. There was a rough carved stone for Allat, who hadn't been Perasiano but who made sense, given the once-popularity of Islum in this part of the world.

It was beautiful in a way only sacred space can be. For just a moment the spell of beauty and belief closed around me like a warm bath, almost dispelling the twitching heaviness in my belly. But the emptiness of my naked face, my emerald still twinkling unnecessarily from its grafted roots on my cheekbone, hit me like a slap.

What was I doing in a house of the gods, now that my own god had asked me for more than I could give? I had always been so certain, so sure of being cradled in Death's hands. Now I couldn't even look at Hades's dour shadowed features under his anachronistic crescent-peaked helm. He was just another of Death's faces, not the slender canine head of my own personal psychopomp, but my eyes skittered away from Him all the same.

I couldn't look Death in the face anymore.

I tore my eyes away and paced into the temple, Japh-rimel's step soundless behind me. He was alert and wary, the cloak of his Power against my skin drawing together more and more tightly, covering me with a mantle of warmth.

I was grateful for that, even as I shamefully averted my eyes from one of Death's faces. Our little group made next to no noise except for the creaking of the blasted new rig, announcing to the world that I was wandering around even more loudly than the light-filled scar of my aura on the ambient landscape of Power.

Kyphii filled my nose. Gabe Spocarelli had always been burning the stuff, its fragrant bite filling her house. Except now her house was empty, everything inside it searched and possibly broken, and Gabe was dead.

Another reason not to look Death in the face. If I went into the blue land where my god resided now, would I meet my oldest friend? Would she ask if I was protecting her daughter, like I'd sworn to? Would she ask me if I had avenged her death?

Would her soul believe me if I told her I'd tried?

The temple spun around me, a spiked wheel of sanctity and belief. I took a deep breath of *kyphii*-laden air, the Power contained in those thrumming walls bleeding out in organ-tones of deep red and deeper violet just at the edge of hearing, rattling my bones. The floor clicked underfoot, permaplas mosaic tiles distressed to look like old chips of silica glass, and in the middle of the vast empty bell of the deserted temple a monstrous cramp gripped the lowest regions of my belly, sinking its rusty teeth right through me.

Japhrimel's arm circled my shoulders. "Dante?"

Vann swore. There were little clicks as he and McKinley moved up to what I recognized as cover positions— and I would have cared about that, really, if the pain hadn't been eating me alive, a blowtorch in my guts. Lucas swore too, but more quietly, and I heard the whine of an unholstered plasgun.

The temple shivered like a parabolic mirror swiveling on jeweled bearings. The Power in the walls turned to streaks of oil on a wet surface as I collapsed, only Japhrimel's sudden clutching hand keeping me from spilling writhing to the ground.

What the hell it hurts oh no now what?

I *felt* it, the thrumming in this building even older than the Republic of Gilead. A darkness lived at its very roots, and as fresh pain gripped me I bent over without even the breath to scream. My emerald sparked once, twice, green glimmers in the gloom.

Pain eased, in dribs and drabs. I hung from Japhrimel's hands, limp and wrung-wet, sweat standing out in great clear drops on my skin. "—ohgods—" I managed, in a

very small voice. "I think I'm going to . . ." *Throw up.
Pass out. Something.*

"Do what you must. I thought we had more time."
Japhrimel's hands were gentle. Too gentle. I would have
preferred him to use the iron-under-velvet strength he was
capable of, because if he was being this exquisitely careful, something was *most definitely wrong.*

"More time for *what?*" I gasped, my legs shaking. The
only other time I'd felt this unsteady was when I had my
worst bout of reaction fever after landing in a slagheap
on a bounty in Hegemony Suisse. I'd thrown up so hard
I'd been weak and shaky for days and almost burst a few
blood vessels.

Back when Doreen was still alive.

I didn't need that thought. I had enough keeping me
occupied. "I think I'm all right." I shook Japh's hands
away—or would have, if I could have stood up on my
own. My legs refused to obey me. They'd turned into wet
noodles.

*Is it me? Am I not allowed in temples anymore? Anubis,
my Lord, my god, why? What have I done? I spared the
traitor You wanted me to spare.*

But I'd cursed Him, hadn't I? I had cursed my god bitterly, down in the very roots of my being. I'd thought it
could not matter. I had been *sure* it would not matter. I
had also lied, broken my sorcerous Word, and betrayed
everything I held dear.

No wonder sacred space did not want me.

The voice came from nowhere, skittering through the
temple's shadows like thousands of pairs of decorative
insectile feet, pricking hard and hurtful against shivering
skin. "Kinslayer." It spoke Merican, but the accent was

pure demon, twisted and wrong. "How dare you enter this place?"

I managed to raise my head. Shadows gathered between the swords of dying sunlight, and the house of the gods rustled with currents of uneasy Power.

Japhrimel's sure steady grip on me didn't change. "Sephrimel. I greet you."

"You greet me. How courteous. How *dare* you enter here?" The insect feet turned to pinpricks of fire, and Sofya's entire interior shuddered. It was a demon's voice, but somehow wrong. It was a voice of casual power, full of a demon's terrible alienness. There was something else in that voice, something that twisted hard against my bones. It was as if a murderous forgotten artifact, old and blind in a corner, had suddenly risen up to demand attention—and blood.

Japhrimel sounded just as he usually did. Calm, quiet as a knife slipped between ribs. "I have come for what you stole. It is time."

The owner of the skittering voice stepped out of shadows that shouldn't have held him as casually as a human might step from one room into another.

He was tall and gaunt, as starved-looking as I've ever seen a demon. Golden skin drew tight over bones as architecturally beautiful as Sofya's own grace. His hair was an amazing shock of clotted ice, twisted into dreadlocks pulled back and looped several times with hanks of red silk. The hair looked like it had drained the life from him, and his baggy black robe, belted with a length of frayed rope, didn't help. Narrow golden feet, callused and battered into claws, rutched against the mosaic floor. His hands were skeletal, the claw structure built into fingertips and wrist musculature clearly visible with no extraneous flesh to disguise it.

His eyes. Dear gods, his eyes.

They were dark, not incandescent with awful power. Black from lid to lid, but not empty. No, his eyes were grieving holes in a face that had drawn itself tight around a sorrow like a burning stone in the throat.

Like the burning stone in my belly.

I met his gaze, and the gripping pain in my belly coalesced around a hot hard fist buried in my flesh. I knew that grief.

I'd lost people too. Their names were a litany of pain, each one a different scar on my still-beating heart. My social worker Lewis, killed by a Chill junkie. Doreen, slaughtered by a demon intent on breaking Lucifer's hold on Hell. Jace, throwing himself past me to take on a Feeder's *ka*. Eddie, dead in his lab, betrayed by his *sedayeen* research partner. And Gabe, my best friend, lying tangled in her garden, dead protecting a traitor my god had asked me to spare.

Each anguish rose up to choke me as I stared into those black, black eyes. Whoever this demon was, he had lost something.

No. Not something. Some*one*.

Another cramp unzipped me. I spilled against Japhrimel, the agony drawing a curtain of redblack over my vision. I lost sight of the white-haired demon. Japh murmured something to me as I inhaled sharply, wondering who was making that soft mewling sound of pain.

It was me.

"You have lost whatever wit you once possessed." The demon's voice was now a bath of terrible icy numbness.

"So it is true. You have Fallen, committed the sin you punished others for."

"What talk is this of sin, between us? You have spent too long with humans." Japhrimel braced me, the scar on my shoulder spilling warmth into my racked body, fighting with the hideous clawing in my belly.

It hurts it hurts oh Anubis—I dragged in another breath. "*Anubis et'her ka;* oh my Lord my god, *please*—"

Again the pain retreated. It left no relief in its wake. How could I call on Him? Why would He answer me? I was a traitor to myself, and this was my punishment.

But it *hurt*.

"I have spent my penance with mortals. *You* still reek of Hell and murder, Kinslayer." His voice was rising, and the entire temple throbbed. I had a sudden uneasy vision, between flashes of pain so immense it was like drowning, of Sofya's white walls weeping blood like an injured tooth.

Breathe, Danny. Breathe.

But I couldn't. Not until the swell retreated and I found myself sweating and shaking, wrung out, hanging in Japhrimel's hands. *Fine time to have an attack of nerves, sunshine. What the hell? I was feeling fine.*

But I hadn't been feeling fine for a long while, had I? Stumbling from one terror to the next, staggering from one suckerpunch in the gut to the next, spilling from horror into agony and ending up at numb grief each time.

My eyes cleared. I didn't look up at the demon's face again. "I think I should wait outside," I whispered. The urge to retch rose and passed through me, so immense it felt like all my insides were trying to crawl out the hard way.

Nobody paid any damn attention. Lucas had gone silent and still as an adder under a rock. Leander's pulse thrummed audibly, the only human heartbeat I'd heard for a while. Vann and McKinley had their laserifles trained on the dreadlocked demon.

That hair's amazing. I wonder if he smokes synth hash and rides a slic in his spare time. He looks like a sk8 in Domenhaiti. All he needs is permaspray stains on his fingers and a few circuit wires in his hair.

The thought sparked a jagged laugh. Why was I always *laughing* at times like this?

"I do not dispute that," Japhrimel said, still calmly. A steady bath of Power flushed from his aura to mine, working in to meet thin wires of flame running through the core of my bones. "I have merely come to claim a certain article from you. It should please you to hear that I am ready to use it for its intended purpose. McKinley."

I snapped a glance at the black-haired Hellesvront agent, who slung his laserifle's strap over his shoulder and stepped forward. Japhrimel, without so much as a glance down, transferred my weight to the agent by the simple expedient of pushing me. I spilled against McKinley like a newborn kitten, my legs useless and the rest of me not far behind.

What the hell? Another cramp was gathering, my belly quivering with anticipated pain, something trying to climb up through the space caged in my ribs, twisting and clawing.

"Japh? *Japhrimel?*" I'll admit it. There was no room for pride. My voice was the thin piping squeak of a child caught in a nightmare.

Maybe he can make it stop. Oh please, please make it stop.

No wonder my god didn't want me. I was praying to a demon, the only intercession I had left.

"It's all right." McKinley closed his right hand over my arm, bracing me so I didn't go straight down to the floor. "Just relax, Valentine. It's okay."

This is not anywhere near okay.

A new quality crept into the stillness. It was the unsettled boiling of air about to erupt with violence, and Japhrimel moved out in front of us as Vann stepped in, laserifle socked to his shoulder. Even Leander had a plasgun out, though he was chalk-white and visibly shaking, his eyes flicking between me and the pair of demons who faced each other on Sofya's pebbled floor.

Seen so close, the difference was startling. The white-haired demon was more than human, true. It screamed from every pore and angle of his frame.

But Japhrimel was more, too. If the other demon was a candle compared to the weak shimmer of a human's aura, Japh was a halogen lasebulb, burning hot enough to scorch plasteel.

He hadn't looked like that compared to Lucifer, had he?

My brain shivered away from the idea. *Eve. What is she doing now? Where is she?*

The thought enraged the tearing thing living in my vitals. Pain swelled, blackness bulged under the surface of my mind, and whatever Japh and the other one said was lost in the fact that I was pretty sure I was dying here in Hajia Sofya.

The blackness swelled, pulsing obscenely as something *alien* fought for control of my brain and agony-wracked

body. Out. I had to get *out* of the temple and away from
whatever divine anger was punishing me.

Unfortunately, McKinley thought otherwise. My
sword dropped to the floor with a clatter as I feebly tried
to fight his hands off me. Then the most amazing cramp-
bolt lanced my belly and I went down to the floor, scrabbling for my sword to cut out whatever monstrous thing
was growing in me.

I convulsed.

Sudden coolness ran from the crown of my head down
through my flesh, a river of balm. I gasped, mouth working like a fish's, and was aware of a slick pattering sound
and Leander's muffled curse. The pain in my belly turned
back into inert heaviness, as if I'd swallowed something
indigestible, lodged in the bowl of my pelvis.

My hands searched fruitlessly for my sword. Warm
bony fingers caught my wrist. *"Avayin, hedaira."* Weary
kindness in each syllable. "Peace, beautiful one. Be at
peace. You will not die of this."

Are you sure? Because I really think I might. I collapsed
against the unforgiving floor, pebbles of mosaic digging
into hip and cheek. They felt cool and good against my fevered skin, as the darkness struggled to birth itself inside
my head and the thing in my belly twisted. I heard my
own breath, a panicked whistling I wasn't sure I liked.

The kind voice wasn't familiar, and it turned unkind
again. "She carries *a'zharak.*" Each word laden with disgust and some other, less definable emotion. "This is how
you treasure your prize?"

"I made no claim to be the best of my kind. I make no
claim to be the best of *yours* either. The Prince seeks to
control my link to her world. She has suffered for it—and

suffers now." Japhrimel sounded just as tired, and just as sharp. "I did not come here for my sake, but for hers."

"Then it is *her* I will help, Kinslayer. Draw your minions away."

The heavy spiked agony in my belly crested again, and the bony hands of a starving demon clamped down with inhuman strength. A hissing breath of effort filled my ears, and I screamed as the weight was suddenly torn from me in a rush of blood and battered viscera.

Leander yelled. Lucas let out a shout of surprise, and the sounds smashed the calm of the temple's interior. I curled around myself, endlessly grateful for the cessation of pain, and passed out for one brief starry moment as chaos erupted around me.

8

The water was full of knives, and as I thrashed it drained away, liquid weightlessness replaced by the agony of cutting.

No. You can't go yet. A familiar voice, the words laid directly inside my consciousness, as I struggled to escape, flesh a prison and my soul the struggling captive, digging her way out with broken fingernails as sharp edges pressed into numb flesh, invading.

Blue flame rose, the entrance to the land of Death, and not even the fact that my god might well deny me the comfort and rational clear light of What Comes Next could deter me. I strained toward that blue glow.

There are times when Death is not an adventure, but an escape from a life descended too far into Hell. Any hell.

Not yet. Maddeningly, the voice barred my way. The knives retreated, my skin still numb. I couldn't tell if I was bleeding or just cold, if I was standing or lying down, if I was alive or something else.

Then the light came, a sharp living light, not the glow of What Comes Next that lifts the soul up and away on a streak of brilliance. This was a human light, and as I *blinked I heard the sound of dragging footsteps on wet stone and felt arms around me, stick-thin but very strong.*

I blinked again. A dizzying moment of vertigo, and the world came into focus, into clear heartstopping detail. The light was coming through the window.

Along the edge of each window ran a thin line of gold. It poured through each pane of glass, a curtain of sunshine dancing with infinite dust-motes.

It should not have surprised me to see sunshine when I dreamed of Jason Monroe.

He sat cross-legged on the floor, looking up with mild interest, blue eyes catching fire under the flood of light. It glowed in his hair, a human furnace of gold, and he was again the young Jace of the first violent flush of our affair. The Bolgari chronograph glittered on his wrist, and he wore a white T-shirt, muscle flickering underneath as he lifted the sword a little, balancing it on his palms.

The room was a surprise. It was Jado's room, the room at the top of the stairs where my sensei *gave out his prized swords, one at a time, to his most trusted students. Only here, the wooden racks along the wall were empty, and the mellow hardwood floor was scratched and scarred, white paint on the walls chipped. The window was bare, and the hall beyond the open doorway stood empty as a soymalt 40 can rolling down the street.*

"Nice." Jace was barefoot, in jeans, and the fine golden hairs on his forearms glistened in the light. "I like this venue, too."

He actually spoke, *instead of the words being laid in my head like a gift. And no wonder the voice that called me away from Death was familiar, for it was his.*

Breath left me in a walloping rush. I sank down to the

floor, finding myself in a tattered blue sweater, ripped jeans showing pale human skin underneath. In these dreams, I was human again. My nails were painted red with molecule-drip, and my hair was tangled, dull with black dye, and full of split ends. "I'm not dead." *Three words, through the lump of misery in my throat, forced out despite myself.*

It dawned on me, through the fog of light and the good smell of dust and paint and fresh air, as if the room breathed summer wind through every crack. "And I don't think I'm really dreaming," *I whispered.*

His grin widened, the smile that had brought no short-age of female attention his way. "Got it in one, sunshine. We have a little time, here. A little space."

"I miss you." *The simple truth of it frightened me, took shape in the air, looming invisibly behind thick syrupy golden light.* "Why are you doing this? Why didn't you let me die?"

"You're being dense. What else would I do for you?" *A shrug, his face turning solemn. The sword eased back down, into his lap, across his knees.*

It was his dotanuki, *the sword broken by the shock of his death. Not precisely broken, just twisted into a cork-screw and leaking agony into the air, the agony of a soul ripped from its moorings by a Feeder's* ka. *My eyes traced the familiar scabbard, and every question I had never asked him rose in my throat and stung my eyes.*

"Gabe," *I whispered.* "Eddie."

"You did the right thing." *His hand twitched, as if he would reach forward to touch me. Then it relaxed, and his fingers trailed over the familiar wrapped hilt.* "It isn't like you to kill a defenseless woman, Danny. You would *have hated yourself for it. Later, that is. When you calmed down."*

I shook my head. "That's not what I meant." And he still hadn't answered me. Why would he call me back, of all people? He was dead too.

I'd failed him just as surely as I'd failed everyone else.

"You wanted to ask if I see them. I can't tell you that, you know that. Go into Death and ask for yourself, that's your question." He sighed. "You're always asking the wrong fucking questions, baby."

"When did you get so goddamn shallow?" I flung back at him. It was easy, the reflex of a fight. Always better to fight him—I have always been more afraid of the damage a soft word could do.

I suppose he might have even understood that he was the only person I had ever fought so hard.

The question was, had he understood it while he was alive?

"You're a lousy Shaman. Loa work better when they're cajoled."

"You're not a loa." I was fairly certain of that, at least. Had he been one of the spirits the vaudun Shamans of the world traffic with, he wouldn't have bothered to wear someone else's face. I've only caught glimpses of them, since they have little use for Necromances. But no loa would appear in another skin here, in whatever dream-space this was.

They do not dress, while they are at home.

"Other people get loa. You get me."

It dawned on me in slow stages. I stared at him, at the bump on his nose, where a break from a bounty he'd run with me as apprentice and backup had gone horribly wrong in Freetown Hongkong. We had just barely made it out of there alive, and he had never bothered to get the break in his nose bonescrubbed. No, I'd set it with a heal-charm, and he'd left the tiny imperfection there, saying it would teach him to be more careful when facing a bounty with a laserifle in close quarters.

"Like a familiar?" I hazarded, prickles spilling down my back. Lucifer had given me Japhrimel as a familiar, long ago. I knew most of the rules where a demon familiar was involved, except for maybe the one about letting the demon fall in love with you.

But what are the rules when your dead boyfriend shows up as a meddling spirit?

"Like, and unlike." He nodded approvingly, his fingers smoothing the hilt. It was a familiar movement. Whenever he rode transport or discussed the finer points of hunting bounties, his fingers would move, slightly. On a swordhilt, on the butt of a gun . . . or on my hip, gently, as we shared a bed late at night.

Long, long ago. Before Japhrimel. Before everything.

I couldn't help myself. I had to. "Japhrimel."

Jace's eyes flicked down to his lap, rested on the sword. "I can't see a lot about demons from here, Danny."

"That's not what I asked."

"It's the only answer I'm giving. I'm not going to stop watching your back because of him, Danny girl. You're heading into deep waters, and you'll need all the help you can get."

Sekhmet sa'es, can the water get any deeper? The thought must have shown on my face, because he laughed. It was the short, bitter bark he used while hunting, a *sound that brought back memory upon memory until they crowded in the sunlight, shadows passing the windows like giant silent fish.*

"I'm here if you need me, Danny. But you know what to do."

Why didn't you let me die, Jace? *I opened my mouth to ask again, but a soft sound cut me off. It was the whispering drag of oiled metal leaving the sheath, and I jolted up to my feet, realizing in one horrified second that I was unarmed, I wore only rags, and I was human again, my pulse pounding thinly in my throat and wrists. The sunlight dimmed, clouds drifting over the sun—or something huge settling over the house, perhaps.*

Jace cocked his head. His sword was still in his lap, but I heard a soft creak. A footstep, bare flesh against wooden floor. Was it in the hall, or was I hallucinating?

"You're not finished yet. Better go, Danny girl."

The sunlight dimmed even further, and I heard something else: a rushing crackle, flame devouring something. The smell of burned paper and another deeper stench turned the air orange, and I whirled, my hair fanning out as I—

—was underground. The lack of psychic "static" told me I was underground. It was dark until I opened my eyes, and candlelight flowed like gelid gold into my brain. The spurred, twisting heaviness was gone, but I felt tender and savagely stretched all over.

"You will live." The white-haired demon bent over me, claws pricking my wrist as he felt for my pulse.

What the hell?

A rock wall rose up to my right. I lay on something unforgivingly hard, cold seeping into my skin. The weight of my rig was gone, and my clothes were stiff with the decaying-fruit stench of my own blood. My shoulder pulsed reassuringly, another bath of Power sliding down my skin.

I wet my lips. The demon's face was inches from mine. Long thin nose, long thin mouth, cheeks scraped down parchment-thin over high cheekbones, and those suffering, suffering eyes like shots to the gut. A fat white snake of his hair slid over his shoulder, dropping down to brush my cheek and slide off the edge of whatever hard surface I rested on.

Okay, I'll admit it. I screamed like an unregistered hooker caught holding out on her pimp. I also surged up and tried to hit him in the face.

He avoided the strike gracefully, dropping my wrist and stepping aside. I scrambled away along the platform, my back hitting a hard pebbled wall. I clutched the ragged edges of my shirt together and realized my jeans were unbuttoned and stiff with dried blood all the way down to my ankles. The scream died on a sucked-in gasp as my head cleared.

"I had forgotten how fragile they are," the white-haired demon said, meditatively. "*Avayin, hedaira.* You are well and whole."

He was right. Thin traceries of scar crisscrossed the bowl of my belly, golden skin marred with threadlike white. It looked like my guts had been run through a badly set laseslicer. I flattened my hand over warm flesh and realized my breasts were hanging out, clutched the shirt closed over my front, and stared gape-mouthed at him.

What the hell? One second my innards are falling out, and now . . . what?

"Do you know who I am?" He didn't retreat, pitched forward at the edge of the rough stone rectangle I braced myself on. The walls crawled with color—little bits and chips of stone, plasteel, plasilica, and other hard shattered things, in every conceivable shade. Figures whirled and swam in the mosaic, a wash of screaming art covering the dome above dark wooden bookshelves stacked with scrolls that smelled like rotting animal skins, stuffed in no apparent order. The only space not taken up by the shelves was broken by a low wooden door and the stone I perched on.

The dome itself was no slouch, a ribbed chamber easily thirty feet high. At its apex, a mellow sphere of something that looked like gold glowed, flickering. It had the breath of alienness that meant something demon-made, as did the arches of the vaulting.

My breath hitched in again. I searched for something to say. What ended up coming out of my mouth was almost as mortifying as it was comforting, because it sounded just like me.

"I'm pretty sure you're not Father Egyptos, sunshine. You look like a sk8 with a bad hair fetish." The words hit the mosaics, my voice a thin husk of its former throaty self, and I glanced frantically around for Japhrimel. He was nowhere in sight.

I was alone, underground, with a dreadlocked demon.

You should have known you'd end up like this, Danny. I mean, you really should have known. This is par for the course.

My sword was nowhere in sight either. But my bag, faithful companion that it was, lay at the end of the stone rectangle. It was open, and my rings spat an angry shower of gold sparks. Someone *else* had been going through my goddamn messenger bag. Would it ever end?

As if he'd read my mind, the demon held up a book-shaped object. I knew what it was as soon as my eyes lighted on it. *Hedairae Occasus Demonae,* the ancient demon-written book given to me by Selene, consort of the Prime of Saint City. I hadn't had a quiet moment to look at the goddamn thing since she'd handed it over, being busy hunting down a conspiracy that killed my best friend.

Funny how that works out.

"You are too young to understand this." His mouth turned down for a moment, as if he tasted something so bitter his entire body revolted against it. "You are too young to even begin. I will explain to you, in detail, what it means. If you will do me a service."

Just like a demon. Quid pro quo. My right hand curled into a knot, looking for a vanished swordhilt. No rig, no weapons, no Japhrimel.

Great. Just when I could really use him.

"I don't bargain with demons." I felt faintly ridiculous saying that, with my shirt torn open and my weapons gone. "I'm not a Magi."

"You are *hedaira,* beloved of a Lord of Hell, and under sentence of death wherever you roam." The demon's gaunt face twisted in on itself, then smoothed. "I am Sephrimel." Of all things, he held out his skinny hand, like we were at a dinner party.

I eyed his fingers like they might bite me. You never know, with demons.

After a few long moments he dropped his hand back to his side. His frayed robe whispered. "I am also called accursed, Fallen, *A'nankhimel.* I did what no demon dares to do."

My mouth had no trouble keeping up, even while the rest of me frantically tried to figure out what the hell was going on. "There's a lot of that going around these days." I began to feel even more ridiculous, which was a stretch. What was I doing with my clothes all opened up?

That question sent a bolt of sheer panicked nausea through my abused stomach. "What did you do to me?" *And where's my sword?*

His mouth compressed itself even thinner, his scraped-down face pulling itself into a parody of distaste. "I rid you of an unwelcome guest."

It is so easy to break a human—Memory rose inside my head, was pushed away, retreated snarling. I grabbed for the only thing I could. "Where's Japh?"

"Your Fallen is above, holding the temple against any intrusion." Sephrimel's eyes flicked down my body, once, and away. The book dangled in his other hand, tempting. Everyone seemed so damn interested in the thing. "I could, possibly, stay you here until the Prince's dogs—or some other of my kind, with a grudge—arrive. The Kinslayer will fight to his last breath, but the Prince's minions are numberless even when weakened, and even a killer such as yours may eventually fall. When he does, you may find yourself without protection."

A thin thread of panic wormed its way through me. He looked like he meant it. My sense of direction didn't work so well underground. Where the hell *was* I?

I decided to start with the most important questions first. "Who are you really? And what the *fuck* do you want?"

His shoulders dropped, and he opened the book with spidery dry-claw hands. The paper rustled thickly against cavernous silence broken otherwise only by my increasingly harsh breathing. Finding the page he wanted, he offered it to me with both hands and a slight bow, as if presenting a gift to royalty.

"You cannot read this, of course. But the picture is clear enough."

I glanced down, meaning only to take a tiny sip of the pages. But my eyes locked themselves to an illustration, as finely colored as a holostill, with snakelike demonic glyphs on the page facing.

In the picture, a slim golden-skinned woman with a glory of long blood-colored hair held her hands up in supplication, her white robes cut like a holomag film star's to show a twisting mark painted into the right side of her belly. She wasn't screaming, but the lines of her face expressed horror and pleading, mixed with terrible resignation. She had no weapons, and her back was to a white wall.

Filling a third of the page in front of her was a demon with a long narrow nose and thin lips, winged eyebrows, and laser-green eyes under short military-cut dark hair lying like ink against his skull. His clothing was a long cassock-coat with a high collar, feathered as it flared behind him and dripping with something dark. The glyph over his head was familiar, because it was scored into my own skin. His hand was raised, a slim curved blade rising in a wicked slash that had just finished, because the arc of the blade's passing was shown with a swipe of bloodspray.

The lower right quadrant of the picture held a demon

curled into a ball and flying backward from a terrific blow, fat white snakes of his hair writhing in agony no less than his face. The glyph over his head, announcing his name, was the same as the symbol on the hapless woman's belly.

Just the three of them in this picture, and the white wall behind the woman. The breath left me in a rush. My gaze stuttered back up to Sephrimel.

He nodded, the dark grieving holes of his eyes gathering the soft luminescence and turning it into pain. His hair slithered against itself as he moved. "Her name was Inhana." All the insectile rage had left his voice, and it held the same weary kindness I'd heard before. His lips shaped the name lingeringly. "She was my *hedaira,* and the Kinslayer slew her in the White-Walled City on a day of blood and lamentation. I have been bleeding from the wound ever since, diminished and alone." The book shut with a convulsive snap, dust puffing from the pages. "I have spent longer than you can imagine wishing for his screaming death, with all the torments Hell could possibly offer. And yet, he brings his beloved to me, and he asks for my help."

Boy, bad luck for you, sunshine. Only a sheer effort of will stopped the words in my throat. His eyes met mine, like a knife to the gut. I couldn't shrink back against the wall any harder, chips of color pressing into my back and touching my tangled hair.

"I will grant you what I can of the means to kill Lucifer, *hedaira.* But in return you will perform me a service, and if you do not I will strike you down to revenge myself on your lover." His thin lips stretched in a death's-head grin, showing old, strong, discolored teeth getting longer by the second. "That is our bargain. I suggest you accede."

I was fairly sure we were still below Sofya, since the Power throbbing in the stone was soaked with belief and pain. I hadn't known the temple was built on a honeycomb of passages in dank crumbling stone, somehow kept free of the water table but musty all the same. It smelled of demon. No—it *reeked* of demon, the fragrance of one of Hell's children rising through tunnels with curved roofs, their walls decked with mosaic. Repeating geometric patterns wove borders between scenes of gardens and blue skies; the sun repeated over and over in a strange golden metal giving out a pulsing of spiced musk, lighting the passageways.

The style of the art was odd, an echo of Egyptianica in the way figures were stylized, a touch of the Byzantin in the placement of the chips. Fantastical birds straight from Sudro Merican folk art mixed uneasily with Renascence lions and Assyriano griffins, gamboling on sealike lawns of green plasilica.

The woman with blood-colored hair was everywhere. She peered from behind trees in the gardens, stood with her face lifted to the sun, gazed inscrutably at the tunnels with sad dark eyes lovingly made of obsidian chips. It must have taken unimaginable years to cover all these walls with such tiny little pieces, each arranged for maximum effect.

It was obsessive, and just a bit frightening.

I'd buttoned up my jeans and edged behind Sephrimel, wincing each time my eyes found the woman again. She was *everywhere,* in the same white robe. It was like being stalked by a ghost, and after a while I began to feel dizzy as he led me down, and down, through a tangle of tunnels that messed up my internal navigation even more.

How long had he been here? Because it just didn't seem likely that anyone *else* had done all this.

No time like the present to ask. "How long have you been down here?" *Since I might as well get some information out of you.*

His shoulders hunched, but his even tread didn't falter. "A short while. Before that was a city they called eternal, but no city of mortals is. I was in Babylon once, too." He paused, before choosing a right-hand fork that led us even further down. The woman—Inhana—peered from behind a fig tree with a shy smile, the twisting mark I'd bet was her Fallen's name worked in lapis down the sweet curve of her hip.

Japhrimel killed her. I'm looking at pictures of a woman he killed. Sekhmet sa'es, how many people has he killed? Do the other demons count?

I'd never thought of it quite this way before. But her smile, replicated endlessly through these tangled passages, was like a padded sledgehammer blow each time. "So you . . . she died. And you survived." *Great, Danny. Remind him of what has to be the happiest event in his widdle demon life.*

"You call this survival?" Sephrimel's sarcasm bounced off tiled walls, fractured like the small pieces clinging to stone. "I bleed out through the wound left by her death, *hedaira.* I wander through a darkening world, falling toward a mortal death. Lucifer left me alive as a warning, and to punish me all the more."

"I thought there hadn't been any Fallen for—"

"I was the third." Sephrimel reached out one thin hand, brushed the wall the same way he'd touch a lover's breast. I had to look down, heat rising abruptly in my cheeks. "Certainly not the last, and I was counted not the least among us. I helped in the making of the Knife, and thought my theft had gone unnoticed. How much has the Kinslayer told you?"

Knife? I shifted the strap of my messenger bag uncomfortably on my shoulder. I'd finally settled on pulling up the shreds of my shirt and tying them like Gypsy Roen's midriff-baring hoochie costume. Every few steps I'd start and nervously rub at my belly, feeling the thin white raised scars. *Told me? He's told me damn near nothing, and right now I'm starting to think I should thank him for it. I'm starting to think I should buy him a holocard.*

As idiotic as it sounds, I was feeling better. The sick pulsing in the middle of my head had faded a bit, locked behind iron doors and safely held at arm's length. I had more important things to concentrate on. I could almost forget the aching nakedness of my left cheek, where my emerald should have been spitting and sizzling, alive with the double gift of my god's presence and my faith—instead of merely glowing numbly. I *should* have been two steps away from screaming and beating my head against the walls until my skull split and released me.

Instead, I felt lighter. Cleansed. As if something unholy had been ripped out of me, and I was no longer tainted.

The scars on my belly twinged, a heatless reminder. I almost faltered, but the demon in front of me stopped, his dreadlocks dragging on the worn stone floor. I wondered if there were parts of this labyrinth where the floor wasn't scraped smooth.

How long had he been recreating her in little bits of broken things? If something happened to me, what would Japhrimel do? The thought of him reduced to something like this gaunt shuffling creature was . . .

Terrifying. That's the word you're looking for, Danny. You've spent all this time doubting him, accusing him at every goddamn turn. My heart lodged in my throat, bitter and pulsing.

Sephrimel put his wasted hand up. His claws clicked as he trailed them lightly, lovingly, over a door made of old, dark stained wood. The metal holding it together was corroded bright green, and the wood was scored with angular crosshatch strokes that looked intentional, though I couldn't for the life of me figure out if I'd ever seen them before.

"Child. I asked you a question." He sounded like my old *sensei,* Jado, whenever I was being particularly dense. "What has your cursed *A'nankhimel* told you?"

My right hand curled into a fist, aching for a swordhilt. "Nothing. I mean, very little. What's this about a knife?" *It would really help if you gave me a clue here. Just one, that's all I'm asking for.*

"I do not blame him." Thin fingers tightened on the door's creaking wood, glassine claws easing free of his fingertips. I watched, fascinated, as they made fresh scars in the door's surface. "I would not tell you either."

Well, that's a vote of confidence, isn't it. I kept sarcasm back by sheer force of will. Huzzah for me.

"Let me teach you a few things, before we open this door." His claws slid free, and he turned to face me. I backed up four nervous steps, ending up bumping into a wall made of shattered edges, pressing myself back as if it could hide me.

The Fallen demon advanced, step by slow step, his horror-stricken eyes great holes above his starved cheek-bones and twisting mouth. He looked like a vox sniffer approaching his next high, face contorting as the nerves fired randomly, twisting and bunching muscles in ways no face should. I had no weapon but the blessed items in my bag, and they weren't clinking and shifting.

Of course, I was no longer sacred, was I? My faith had broken. There was no longer a god living in my bones and breath. I was wholly a demon's creature now.

Should I have been so grateful that Japhrimel's mark on my shoulder turned tense and hot, Power straining against the surface of my skin and shields? And why, when I felt so utterly alone, did the emerald on my cheek spit a white-hot spark of defiance?

Sephrimel stopped. His hand shot over my shoulder, claws sinking into solid rock with a screech like a hover slamming through a fiberoptic relay tower. For all the lunacy of his dark-burning eyes, his tone was cool and pedantic.

"Why does a demon Fall, beautiful one? Answer me." Hot cinnamon breath touched my cheek. The prickle of my accreditation tat writhing under the skin intensified.

I braced myself, weight settling into the balls of my feet. He could rip my throat out in a millisecond, and his teeth looked just strong and yellow enough to do it.

"I d-don't really know." For someone with a possibly insane Fallen demon breathing right in her face, I sounded almost calm.

Sephrimal gave a short galling laugh. His eyes didn't blink. They just *stared*, and each moment his gaze threaded itself though mine was another fresh burst of grief so intense I wanted to crawl away from it.

"For only the simplest of reasons, child. In Hell there is power, and primacy, and glory. There is pain and vassalage and exacting obedience. But when humanity crawled up out of the mire—and despite what Lucifer says, he did *not* extend a helping hand—we found there was one thing we did not have, a thing mortal creatures are blessed with." His eyes narrowed, their force undiluted, pinning me to the wall. The scar on my shoulder writhed against my skin, turning hot, a mass of warning spikes spreading from its twisting black-diamond fire marring my aura.

I never thought I'd be *happy* about that. I knew I could pull Power through the mark. Could I pull enough to strike at Sephrimel before he opened me up like a sodaflo can?

"The first of us to Fall knew it would not be long before the Prince moved to strike us down. In secrecy, with his *hedaira,* he created a weapon."

This part I could help out with. Just call me a mentaflo genius. "The Knife." The words eased past my lips. I couldn't stand looking in his eyes anymore. I dropped my eyelids, every fiber of my body screaming at me to *look at him look at him how will you know what he's going to do if you don't LOOK at him?*

"Exactly. The Knife of Sorrow." Tension bled out of the air like heat. Stone creaked, and I realized something fantastic, something utterly wonderful.

I could calculate this demon down to the last erg of Power he possessed. And it was conceivable, with a whole lot of luck and some fast thinking, that I could somehow hurt him.

Which led me inexorably, logically, on to a different thought. *Bleeding out through the wound. He's been slowly losing bits of himself, or his Power, since . . . when? Before Stamboul was built? That's a long time. Since Japh killed his* hedaira.

Just how long ago was that? Is he even "demon" anymore?

The only thing worse than having to ask a question like that is the possibility of having it answered for you.

"The Knife rests in two parts," Sephrimel whispered. He leaned so close the wiry snakes of his dreadlocked hair swung forward to touch me, and a fainting horror swam up through my head, rising like bad gas from the memory locked behind its reinforced door. Backed up against the wall. Again. "The Kinslayer took one half from the body of the first Fallen's *hedaira.* The other half, kept in the great temple in the White-Walled City, *I* stole, and have been glad of it ever since. I thought the Kinslayer did not know, since my portion would be swift death, no matter how much Lucifer wishes to keep me as an example."

Two parts? What the hell? "Wait a second." I forgot myself and looked up, just as quickly averted my gaze as it glanced across the edge of his. "Two parts?"

"The Knife is twain as the *A'nankhimel* are." Sephrimel's claws squeaked against stone and plasilica dust as his hand flexed. "Either shard will wound beyond measure a demon, even one of the Greater Flight. Together, there is no demon they cannot kill." He paused. Repeated it slowly, insistently. "No demon they cannot kill, no matter how powerful."

A shock went through me like lightning striking, and the thunder behind it was a familiar feeling. It was the first arc of intuition that told me a hunt was underway, the same feeling I got working bounties for Hegemony law enforcement. The first click of instinct always takes the longest.

After that, everything speeds up.

It's just a hunt like any other, Danny. Only now you're hunting the thing that can kill Lucifer. That's what you're doing here. So quit flinching and do what you have to.

I raised my eyes again. Stared at his almost-lipless mouth, drawn tight over those strong yellow teeth. He'd probably been beautiful, once. To *her.*

The same way Japh was beautiful to me.

"Where's the other half?" I whispered. *And what do you want from me in return?*

"It was given to our cousins the Anhelikos to hide, for they brought more than one *hedaira* to grief. Sneaks and spies, with their gardens and pretty faces." His lips curled in a bitter sneer. "The Kinslayer probably knows its route, and will collect it. If Lucifer does not do so first."

A shiver slid from my crown to my soles. I remembered the Anhelikos in DMZ Sarajevo, with its pretty sexless face and sticky, clinging web of euphoria. I wouldn't put it past that thing to eat someone whole, if they wandered into its nest. "But he figured he had a better chance of getting one half from you, rather than chasing after something Lucifer already knew about. Because Lucifer thinks the Anhelikos have both halves." *And so does Eve, I guess, or why was she in Sarajevo? Or did she even know there were parts to the thing?*

Does Lucifer?

Sephrimel stepped back, freeing his claws from the wall. I stayed where I was, shaking despite setting my jaw and internally reciting every filthy term I knew in Merican, Putchkin trade-pidgin, and any other language I've heard the blue words in. His hair dragged on the floor. I wondered if it had done its part to scrape the stone so smooth, the tunnel bottoms worn concave by repeated dragging footsteps. He paced back to the door and opened it with a simple push. Dappled light touched the ceiling, golden radiance reflecting off water making crazy patterns against the mosaic.

I glanced back over my shoulder. The woman's sad face peered back at me, the mark of Sephrimel's claws cradling it tenderly, as if he had been trying to feel her skin again.

I was shivering from more than the cold. But when the Fallen demon stepped down through the low door, ducking a little, I followed. Cold water lapped at my boots, ankle-deep and smelling of salt. I blinked against sudden dazzlement and found myself in a long low oval chamber, its walls blessedly free of mosaic. I didn't think I could stand to see Inhana's face one more time.

9

In the middle of the chamber stood a low wet obsidian plinth, and a plain wooden box lay open on its top. The water wasn't more than a few inches deep anywhere in the room, over a floor of rough blocks. It was clammy-cold, and steam lifted in lazy curls from my skin and his, demon metabolisms working overtime.

"Take it," Sephrimel said, and moved aside. He glided silently through the water, but I made wet noises every time I stepped. I hoped the boots were up for this kind of abuse. I *hate* wet shoeleather.

Great beads of sweat dewed the walls. I stepped forward cautiously, feeling gingerly each time I set my foot down, not committing my weight until I was sure I was on safe ground. When I finally reached the pedestal, the lid of the box quivered like one of those plants that eats unwary flies.

It moved because the box was rotting to bits, crumbling into a pile of slime. Velvet that had probably once been blue filled its interior. The cloth's decay sent a sharpish-sweet note through clean salt and a thread of demon scent. And there, on the bed of soft swelling corruption, the Knife lay.

It looked complete within itself, its geometry just slightly off like all items of demon make. The hilt was flattened and curved first toward me, then away, and the blade was the same. The guard was oddly shaped, finials reaching out for something but clasping only air. It hummed with malignant force, and now that I was close enough I saw a taint of black-diamond flame in the glow of Power it gave off. The world warped and shimmered around it, announcing *here's something that doesn't belong.*

I stared at the thing for a long ten seconds, water lapping at my boots.

"It's made of *wood*." I finally announced, hearing the same tone I'd use to announce it was fucking raining during a slicboard match. It was made of an old, dark wood, oiled and pristine. Its edge looked too sharp to be a tree's flesh.

"You are unnaturally observant," Sephrimel piped up, dryly. "Take it in your hand, *hedaira*."

"Why is it made of wood?" I persisted. I'd cut Lucifer once—with good old-fashioned steel. This thing didn't look like it could trim a demon's claws, let alone kill the Devil.

That is what we're talking about here, isn't it? Killing Lucifer. If it's possible.

"Ask your Fallen." The demon stirred restlessly, and water lapped against the walls. "For now, simply take what is yours by right."

By right? I don't think I want this thing, but thanks ever so much.

I stared at the thing. Wood or not, it looked deadly wicked. Did it throb with its own dark glee, or was I just shell-shocked and ready to believe it after all this drama of tunnels and a dead woman's dusky eyes? My bag clinked and rattled against my side.

Just pick it up, Danny. You touch that thing, and you're committed. You'll have to kill Lucifer. There's no way around it.

Still . . . I hesitated. I reached out, and saw the shape of my forearm, my fragile-looking wrist, tough golden calluses on my fingertips from almost-daily fighting or training. If I was going to kill the Devil, this was the hand I'd do it with.

My other hand rested on the thin raised scars crisscrossing my belly. I was suddenly, mortally certain Sephrimel had pulled *something* out of my cramping midriff.

I had a good idea of what that *something* was, too. If I'd had anything in my stomach I might have heaved until I was dry.

If I kill Lucifer, I can feel clean again. It was really that simple. Everything else, even protecting Eve, was taking a backseat to that one imperative. How shallow was that? I should have been more worried about protecting my daughter.

If she really was my daughter. It bothered me. Would Santino have worked with a contaminated sample? Doubt circled my brain again.

But still, her face. The little half-smile she wore, so like mine it could have been my twin.

I was doubting everything now. The world was a collage of lies and half-truths, everyone with their own agenda. Even Japhrimel.

Even me.

My hand hovered in midair. Who was I fooling? It had

been too late the moment Japhrimel had knocked at my front door.

Do you believe in Fate, Dante?

My standard reply was ringing ever more hollow. *No more than the next Magi-trained Necromance.*

Pretty soon I was going to have to start saying *yes*.

I picked up the Knife. It was obscenely warm. Or was I just chilled by the idea of what I was about to do? The wood was silken, like warm skin. The black fire of its aura socked home against mine, for all the world as if it recognized the taint of demon in my personal cloak of energy. My shields, battered and broken, blazed with a river of wine-dark Power.

Instinct born of bounty hunting for most of my life warned me, a prickle against my nape and the sound of water splashing suddenly married to chill certainty as the scar on my shoulder flamed into hot agonized life.

I stepped back from the pedestal, a cry wrenching itself from my throat, and spun in time to see Sephrimel extended in the air, claws outstretched, his face contorted as he leapt for me.

How can I say what it was like?

The Knife rammed home in his chest, his arms flung wide at the last possible moment, claws whistling as they clove sickly, salt-filled air. We hit the pedestal with a sickening crack, and slivers of glassy obsidian exploded from the physical and psychic force of that sound.

Flying shards of obsidian whickered through the air, peppering stone walls and pocking into thrashed salty water. I skidded, lost my footing, and went down hard, screaming until my voice broke. Sephrimel collapsed on top of me, twitching heavily, thick snakes of white hair spilling down to brush my face with woolen fingers.

I choked on a mouthful of salt water and *shoved*. Black demon blood bubbled between his lips, foaming. The Knife twitched in my hands like a live thing and made a greedy keening noise. Between the thin high moans was another sound, one I didn't understand until the first wave of energy spilled through me.

The Knife was gulping. It slurped like a toothless man inhaling a bowl of wet noodles.

Sephrimel made a low choked sound. "Inhana," he whispered, black blood dripping down and dewing my left cheek. He was close as a lover, and the weight of his body against mine was enough to touch off panic in the darkest corners of my head. *"A'tai, hetairae A'nankimel'iin. Diriin."*

My back, against cold hard stone, ran with prickles. It was a phrase Japhrimel had spoken to me, one I recognized even though I couldn't translate it. Something about a *hedaira* and an *A'nankhimel*.

But in return you will perform me a service, and if you do not I will strike you down to revenge myself on your lover.

He hadn't wanted to kill me. I realized it only now, too late to pull back. He'd attacked me so I would kill *him*. Tit for tat. Japhrimel had killed his *hedaira*, and here I was, finishing up the job.

Ogods I've killed him. Oh gods.

Sephrimel's eyelids fell. His gaunt, starving face relaxed. I heard a sobbing noise, realized it was mine, repeating the only prayer I had left.

"Japh . . . *Japhrimel* ohgods *help* . . . "

The gulping sound ceased. Ash trickled through veins of darkness running through the demon's golden flesh. Like porcelain, his skin cracked and broke, larger shards crumbling into fine cinnamon-scented dust. The veins of dryness even spread to his hair, threading through the clotted white.

The Fallen demon exploded into ash that ground itself finer and finer as a heavy silken tide of pleasure slammed through me. My heart drummed against my rib cage like a hummingbird's wings, the space where something had been ripped from my belly throbbing in response. My hips jerked up as I tasted the remainder of ash, vanishing until no trace of spice or musk remained on the air.

I gasped, got another mouthful of salt water, and scrambled to my feet. I wasn't losing my balance, the dome trembled. A chunk of stone fell from the vault, landing with an ominous splash. *Ohgods. Oh, dear gods.*

My knees almost gave out on me. I backed away from the spreading fine film of ash on the water's chopped surface. *Is the whole place shaking, or just here? Great. I'm underground and I just killed my only guide. Just wonderful, Danny.* I backed up, hardly caring where I stepped at this point, and my shoulders hit the wall with a thump. I stared up, only dimly aware of pleading. "Please don't fall, don't fall, *don't fall*—"

The dome shuddered once. Water trembled. Two things became apparent to me at once. The first was that something else was causing it to shake, some event communicating itself through stone like the squeal of overstressed hover dynos cuts through concrete like jelly.

The second thing was that the water was rising, lapping at my knees instead of my shins.

Move, Danny. Move now.

I bolted for the door as another huge chunk of stone tore free of the dome, falling with a whistle and sending up a sheet of foaming, ash-laced seawater. My fingers clamped around the Knife's satin-smooth, warm wooden hilt, and even in my adrenaline-laced terror I didn't want to drop the goddamn thing. If it could kill Lucifer—or even *wound* him—the last place I wanted it to end up was buried under tons of rubble.

Though it just might end up there anyway. Run, Danny. Run.

I ran.

10

*M*y sense of direction underground isn't the greatest. Fortunately, my Magi-trained memory had been busy taking in the mosaics, and Inhana's sad, lovely face pointed me the right way.

I hoped like hell that Sephrimel hadn't repeated the patterns over and over again down every passage.

That's a thought you don't need, sunshine. Just keep moving.

I did, because the air was moving with me, a cold exhalation of salt brushing my hair as I pounded down stone worn concave by a demon's dragging, grieving feet. I hit the door to the room I'd awakened in at full tilt, smashing it back against the wall, and shoved it shut with hysterical speed. Then I halted, my ribs flaring and flickering as I gasped, looking around for some clue of how to get *out* of here. The bookshelves looked too flimsy for anything, and the scrolls stacked on them were no help either, their smell a blind weight in my nostrils.

Up. Got to get up. When my breathing evened out, the low groaning coming through the stone became audible again. I turned in a full circle, searching for another door, and realized my folly almost immediately. Just because I'd woken up here didn't mean this room had an escape hatch.

Think, Danny. Quit fucking around and think!

I cast around again, trying desperately to force my brain to gear up and get me out of *this* one. Then the thing I was afraid of most happened.

Water trickled under the door, a few innocent little streamlets sending thin questing fingers over the dry stone.

"Shit," I hissed between my teeth. *Trust you to end up like this. Going to drown like a rat in a sewer if you don't*—"Shut up. Shut *up*. Think, damn you! *Think!*"

I would never have seen it if I hadn't hunched down, clapping my hands to either side of my head and thwacking myself a good one with the Knife's hilt against my temple. I'd almost forgotten I was carrying the damn thing.

When my eyes cleared, smarting and stinging furiously, my attention snagged on the wall directly over the chunk of stone Sephrimel had laid me out on. The mosaic there was blues and greens, and it stretched up in a passable imitation of a door, a round wheel of yellow right where the knob should be.

The edges of the pattern shimmered, just like a psion's glamour once you've slowed down to take a really good look at it. Illusion rippled, and my heart leapt up into my throat, pounding there like it intended to tear free of my ribs and dance.

I didn't stop to think. I scrambled across the room, wet feet skidding in the rivulet of water coming under the door, leapt up—

—and smashed into the wall full-tilt, knocking myself half-senseless back down onto the rectangle of stone.

I shook the stunning impact out of my head. *Dante, you idiot.* And with the utter lunacy of the desperate, shell-shocked, and insane, I reached up, my claw-tips scraping against polished bits of stone, and touched the yellow circle.

It felt round, firm, and real, under the screen of demon illusion. I used it to pull myself to my knees, hearing the soft insidious lap of water against the base of the stone chunk. It was rising fast.

I twisted my wrist. The shell of illusion on the door—a perfect piece of demon magick, either a cruel mockery or an aesthetic utterly divorced from practicality—folded aside as the door swung open, the golden orb at the apex of the dome beginning to dim as its light spilled through . . .

And touched stairs. Going *up*.

I let out a relieved sob and began to scramble on hands and knees, the worn edges of the risers biting into my flesh. The Knife made a little clicking sound against each step until I managed to get my legs under me. I ran, heart exploding with pain inside my ribs and the fear of the caverns behind me, filling with cold stone water mixed with Sephrimel's ashes, in my mouth like bitter wine.

The stairs were narrow and dark, golden light from below fading as water mouthed and lapped behind me. If I could have stopped, I probably would have lain down despite the hard stone edges and tried to at least catch my breath.

As it was, I had a hard enough time trying to keep myself upright, slipping on slick stone.

I ran, my fingers cramping around the Knife's warm pulsing hilt. Sick fever-warmth spilled up my arm with each pulse. Whatever it had taken from Sephrimel it was feeding into me, in controlled bursts like an immuno-hypo's time-release function. I'd been hurt bad enough, once or twice as a human bounty hunter, to slam painkiller-cocktails from a first-aid kit. This was the same feeling—knowing the pain was there, that I was functioning on borrowed time, that soon I was going to push my body past its limits, muscles tearing free of their moorings and my brainpan filling with blood from burst vessels—

Danny, you're running blind. Slow down.

I couldn't. Darkness was rising with the water, soft squelching sounds behind me that I *knew* was just the water sucking at the steps but my imagination had no trouble making into soft padded feet. Before the last glimmer faded and the dark wrapped close and soft as cotton wool over my eyes, the clutching of claustrophobia began in my chest. There wasn't enough air. If I didn't drown in the flood I would in the darkness, the weight of how many tons of earth and rock pressing down to crush the life out of me.

Focus. You have to focus. You have *to.*

I knew I had to. I tripped, barked both knees, and fell, my head hitting the wall with a sickening crack that made phantom stars swirl in front of my starving eyes.

Dammit, Danny, quit rabbiting! Get hold of yourself!

I lay on the stairs, panting, my shallow gasps echoing against the narrow stone hall. I sounded like an animal, exhausted from struggling in a trap. Just waiting for death from shock or blood loss, or for the hunter to come and put a plasbolt in me.

Claustrophobia descended on me, sheer terror wringing out what little sanity I had left. This was like Rigger Hall again, like the Faraday cage in the basement, where I had learned to fear dark closed spaces. It was ever so much worse than an elevator, because there was no escape.

My left shoulder flared with soft heat. It was so warm I expected it to glow as I stared up at the ceiling, stone edges digging into my hip and the back of my head.

Wait a second. I can see.

I shifted, and the light moved too, dappling the stone as soft wet sounds drew closer.

Just like a demon to die and leave his house to flood. The hideous, panicked amusement in the thought was a thin shield against rising hysteria. The light moved again as I tilted my head.

It was my emerald, glowing fiercely. Green light danced as I moved my head, slowly, watching the play of color against the stone. Spectral illumination—far too much to come from the one tiny gem in my cheek—bathed the steps. My tat writhed madly on my cheek, an itching so familiar and so comforting tears pressed hot against my eyes. I blinked them away. With the light came a little air past the clutching in my chest.

Get up, Danny.

I didn't want to. I wanted to lie there and rest.

If you stop moving you'll drown. Get up. Move.

I couldn't. I just wanted to rest. Just for a moment, until I could find enough breath to move. Until the terror went away.

Then Lucifer's already won. The deep voice was pitiless.

Merciless. It wasn't someone else's voice used to prod me into action, unconsciously using a familiar tone so I could pretend someone was here with me, that I wasn't alone. *Are you going to let him win?*

"Shut up," I whispered. "Shut the fuck *up*."

You might as well admit it, Danny. You've only got so much left in you. You're only human. There's no shame in admitting you're beaten. He's the Devil. He'll win. All you have to do is lie here and wheeze. There's plenty of air. Get up.

The soft lapping drew closer. How far below the water table were the mosaics, Inhana's dark eyes now watching blackness instead of the slow dragging passage of time and the shuffling of her *A'nankhimel?*

The thin moaning sound, I realized, was mine. I was lying on the steps groaning while the water rose. Like a beaten animal cowering in a corner.

Just stay there. The deep voice sounded disgusted. *I* sounded disgusted at myself.

The Knife hummed in my hand. Squelching, lapping sounds moved closer, teasingly.

"Get up," I whispered. "Get *up,* you bitch." *If I can talk I can breathe.*

I tried. My legs refused to move. The muscles were shaking, quivering as nerves rebelled, drunk on terror.

Just lie there, sunshine. Choke a little bit when the water reaches you. It will all be over soon, and you can rest.

Here in the dark. Forever.

It was amazing. Laughter rose inside me, from the wrecked place where I used to be human. It bubbled up past my lips, a dark rancid howl, and my eyes rolled up inside my head as I *strained,* the chilling little giggles broken by a long *hunnnnngh!* of effort.

I twitched.

Just lie there, sunshine. The voice was so reasonable, so calm, and so fucking disgusted with me. *It's all over.*

"Like . . . *hell* . . . it . . . is!" The pauses between the words filled up with howling, insane laughter.

Something cold touched my boots. Moved up, slowly, along the outside edge of my shins, my soaked jeans turning colder as fresh fingers of water caressed them.

I jerked away from those caressing fingers. Scrambled, finding fresh strength as the Knife hummed in my hand like a high-voltage cable. The world turned gray, light from the emerald set in my cheek bleaching stone. Strings of damp hair fell in my face. I was sweating, great drops of unhealthy water standing out on my skin. Salt stung my eyes as I gasped, heaving for air against the constriction around my ribs.

I made it up to my knees.

Well, look at that, the disgusted voice remarked. *You* can *move after all.*

"Shut up." Then I saved my breath for moving. The mark on my shoulder spilled a wave of strength down my skin, working in, barely enough to keep me upright. I choked on something hot rising from my abused, empty stomach, and stumbled along.

Each step was torture, working against the weight of childhood fear like a lead blanket. My knees felt shattered, my thighs on fire, my neck steel-strung cables drawn tight by a demented dwarf. I climbed up, swearing at myself with each step, curses that spilled past my lips the longer

I moved, until I was gasping both for breath to move and to keep up the string of obscenities.

The sound of water faded. I kept going, until the stairs vanished and I emerged into a long, low corridor lit by orange orandflu strips, long-burning firesafe illumination. My breath returned with a whoosh, claustrophobia easing. I stared at the shapes on either side of the hall, not believing what I saw.

What the hell?

Stacked on either side of the hall were bones. Great pyramids of skulls over neatly piled femurs, pelvic bowls stacked like bread bowls, the arched shapes of what I realized were ribs arranged aesthetically, fingerbones mortared into the wall, smaller bones sticking into crumbling concrete.

Sekhmet sa'es. Catacombs. The word swam up through layers of shock and exhaustion, and I let out a short bark of relief. My lips were cracked and stinging with salt. My clothes were ruined, blood and seawater drying as they plastered against my fevered skin. I itched all over. Skulls leered at me, their empty eyes holes of madness.

They're dead, Danny. They can't hurt you. Going to stand there and gawp all day?

"Anubis—" The prayer began, but I stopped it short. *On my own again.*

But the emerald, and my tat—

Don't think about that now. You have other credits to fry right now.

The walls trembled. I put out a hand to steady myself, touched a stack of bones that spilled from their careful teetering and puffed into dust on the way to the floor. The splinters that reached the stone broke with a dry whispering sound. How long had they been down here?

What was that? I braced myself against more crumbling bones.

The scar on my shoulder rippled with heat. And not just that—a sudden certainty bloomed just below the smoking surface of my mind, losing any conscious semblance of thought. It felt like a grassfire inside my skull, like I'd once seen on the rolling savannah of Hegemony Afrike. Smoke and crimson and dull gray dust, as far as the eye could see, the air too thick and hot to breathe, chunks of charred stuff visible even from a hover's-eye view— animals too slow to escape the burning.

I blundered down the aisle of bones as Hajia Sofya tolled in distress overhead, her walls singing a long sustained note, like a real crystal wineglass stroked by the lightest of touches.

Japhrimel. His name rose from the smoke in my head. *He's in trouble. He needs me.*

I didn't argue with the certainty. I just stumbled forward, wearily, with all the speed my exhausted, aching body would allow.

11

The long hall gave onto another bigger chamber, an ossuary with old stains showing against patched crumbling mortar where bones had dissolved into mineral streaks. There were more strips of orandflu lighting and a few dim bulbs burning out overhead, hanging from long cords. I got the idea nobody had come down here for a while except a mad dreadlocked demon.

The temple kept crying out as I stumbled through other passages, following a faint indefinable pulling against my bones. I no longer questioned it, I knew Japh was nearby and he needed me. I had the Knife now. I was going to save the day.

Well, at least half the Knife. Better than nothing, wouldn't you say, Danny?

I told that voice inside my head to shut up and almost ran into a dead end, a blank wall barring my path. I turned back, retraced my steps, and found a long sloping corridor going up, with decent lighting and—thank the gods—signs in Merican, Pharsi, and Graeci.

I'd somehow found my way into the part of the temple

set aside for tourists. I could have laughed at the irony, decided to save my breath.

The letters blurred and ran together, but I glimpsed enough to tell me the main part of the temple was down this hall and to the right, behind a massive blue-painted door that loomed up, quivering in its socket.

I started down the hall, dragging my right leg a little. It didn't matter. Nothing mattered except the fact that Japhrimel was on the other side of that door.

Unholy screechings and thuddings resounded as the door shook again. The entire temple flinched.

The Kinslayer will fight to his last breath, but the Prince's minions are numberless, and even a killer such as yours may eventually fall.

Had Sephrimel done what he had threatened?

The door rocked as something hit it from the other side, a long bloodchilling howl shivering it against its maghinges. They let out a distressing squeal, and the door sagged, no longer looking quite right. The massive sheet of blue plasteel, decorated with the Hegemony sunwheel, looked like someone had slammed it with a plascannon bolt on the other side.

I kept moving, finally within touching distance. *Last thing I need now is the damn door to fall on me. Hurry up, Valentine.*

I reached out with both hands, intending to shove. If the maghinges were damaged they might not open, and I'd have to think of something else.

Doesn't matter. The cold disgusted voice spoke up, the one that only showed itself when simple endurance was the only thing left. *Japh's in there and he needs me.*

The Knife let out a shuddering, bloodchilling howl,

one that burst out of my own lips as I coiled myself, compressing demon-elastic muscles until I exploded forward, hitting the doors with tired flesh and unhealthy, feverish Power both. My heart stuttered under the strain, a blinding flash of pain searing between my temples as mental muscles stretched, straining.

I landed on both feet, the door flung away like a ball of trash. It soared in a graceful arc across interior space, and I was driven down to one knee as my legs almost failed me. The Knife vibrated in my hand, force pouring into me, beating back exhaustion.

The inside of the dome was soaked with bloody light. McKinley, his face a mask of effort, drove a winged hellhound down to the floor, his left hand clamped in its throat as Vann unloaded plasbolt after plasbolt at it, missing by a hairsbreadth each time as it twisted, cartilaginous spine crackling. Lucas skipped to the side and fired on an imp, its greasy sick white skin stretching as it chattered, its bald, hairless babyface twisted around the syllables of Hell's mothertongue. Other imps writhed on the floor as rotting fluid gushed from mortal wounds.

Japhrimel stood before the high altar, his hands clasped behind his back as he regarded the demon in front of him. The left side of his face was black with mottled bruising, something I had never seen before. Behind his slim dark shape, Leander crouched, his katana an arc of brightness held in the guard position, spitting blue sparks as runes twisted in the steel's heart.

My arrival halted everything except the hellhound's gurgle as it died under the lash of plasbolts. The demon crouched in front of Japh was mantled in darkness like feathered wings, a shadow of black flame and diamond spangles. Corpses littered the inside of the temple, stinking and running with brackish fluid as demon flesh decayed. Hellhounds with and without wings rotted as I glanced at them, my attention centering on the feathered demon as it turned fluidly to face me, drawing itself up, and up, and *up*. It had to be at least nine feet tall.

I'd interrupted a hell of a fight. Twisted shapes of dead demonflesh were everywhere—some with a mass of hideous legs and others vaguely human-shaped, but with a grace and alienness even in death that humans couldn't match. There were also imps, their claws blackened and their faces grotesquely puffed.

I stayed on one knee, trying to get in enough breath as the demon in front of Japh turned its piercing silvery eyes on me. Feathers ruffled, each one edged with a dark steel gleam.

It had a slim, ageless face, built like Japhrimel's—lean and saturnine, long nose and thin mouth, winged dark eyebrows. The hair feathered into wisps so fine they lifted on uneasy air as everyone froze.

All eyes on you, Danny.

Or maybe they weren't looking at me. Maybe they were looking at the Knife, its finials stretching out and clasping empty air, my hand fitting against its hilt as if it was made for me.

The wooden weapon keened, a low hungry sound.

Get up, I told myself. *Get up, you stupid bitch. That thing is threatening Japhrimel.*

It worked. Fury poured through me, a rage red and deep like hot blood from a ragged hole. My legs straightened. I gained my feet in a stumbling rush and threw myself forward, the Knife held in the way my *sensei* taught me,

flat against my forearm for slashing, the pommel reversed
with its claws digging into my wrist.

Burn, a half-familiar voice whispered inside my head.
Burn them. Make them pay.

Shapeless shouts rose, Lucas yelling my name, Leander screaming, McKinley letting out a cry that shivered
the air. Everything vanished but the enemy in front of me
and the need to make him—whoever he was—*pay*.

In blood.

My left shoulder woke with a crunch of agony, Power
flushing along my aura and hardening. Japhrimel's
strength filled me like a river in a burning bed; the demon
and I collided with a sound like all the jars of the universe
smashing at once. The Knife rammed through muscle
and bone, shrieking with satisfaction as the entire world
stopped, crackling flame filling my ears and running
through my veins. I was made of it, this fire, and if it escaped me the world would burn.

The only thing scarier than not caring was how *good*
it felt.

I held the silver-eyed demon on the Knife, ignoring
the sudden blooming of pain as it clipped me a stunning
blow on the head with one taloned fist. A soft breath of
satisfaction slid past my lips, ruffling the pin-fine black
feathers along its high cheekbones. We were close enough
to kiss, its teeth champing as it writhed, held away from
me by the humming force of the demon-made weapon in
my aching, bruised, battered hand.

I found I didn't mind. Not with the flame pounding
behind my heartbeat, thumping in time to a song of fury
and destruction.

I had called upon Sekhmet, the Fierce One, and She had answered.

Burn, I thought, and the heat passed through me as the Knife gulped. The demon writhed, its mouth contorting in a scream of pure agony. But still, it reached for me, its claws flexing as it prepared to kill, even with the blade buried in its ribs.

I knew I couldn't kill a demon, I thought, and braced myself.

Japhrimel arrived.

He tore the demon off me, the Knife pulling free of my fist with an unholy screech. The world snapped back into its normal pace, chaos descending out of the stillness of concentration. I went flying back, the heavy shield of Japhrimel's aura over mine blunting the force of my fall as I collided with Vann. McKinley skidded to a stop while Vann and I went down in a tangle of arms and legs, I struck out with fists and feet, screaming.

The sound was incredible, howls of anguish and agony meshed with thudding booms and tearing like limbs pulled from their sockets. Vann had an arm around my throat and McKinley descended on us, trying to hold me down as I thrashed. The noise reached an amazing crescendo, felt more through the body than heard. My own scream was lost in that wall of clamor.

Sudden silence, sharp as a sword, sliced through blood-drenched light. I sagged in Vann's hands, smelling the dry demon-and-*other* reek of Hellesvront agents. McKinley was repeating something over and over again, and it took a while for the echoes to shake out of my head so I could hear what he was saying.

"Christos," he kept saying. "Jesu Christos. Mater

Magna, Jesu Christos. Is she all right? Tell me she's all right."

I'm fine, I wanted to say, *get off me.* But my mouth wouldn't work.

"Get over here." Lucas's throat-cut rasp was as hoarse as ever. "He's bleeding, *bad.*"

"Leave me be." Japhrimel sounded as dangerous as I'd ever heard him, the edge of his voice sharp enough to cut steel. "I am well enough. *Dante?*"

Vann's grip on me fell away. McKinley settled back on his heels, his dark eyes not leaving my face. "She looks okay." Every line of his body screamed weariness. His hair was wet with sweat, hung dripping in his eyes. "Valentine? Are you all right?"

"Get the fuck away from me." I erupted to my feet, or tried to. My limbs failed me, heavy and leaden, and I spilled back onto Vann, driving my elbow into his ribs. He let out a curse and Japhrimel appeared, leaning on Lucas.

That bothered me.

What bothered me more was the terrific bruising blotching Japh's face. He slumped wearily, black demon blood dripping from his right arm, which hung useless and limp at his side, his long elegant golden fingers clasped gingerly around the Knife's hilt, almost flinching away from its touch. His hair was wildly mussed, and his eyes burned almost wholly green, spitting and snapping with laser intensity.

Lucas looked like hell too, shirt torn and bandoliers missing, his pants ripped and bloody, garish streaks of gore painting his face and torso. He was wet to both knees with fluids I decided I didn't want to think about. McKinley was oddly pristine, but his fishbelly paleness was marked by dark bruised circles under his aching eyes.

I stared. I didn't like McKinley, I had *never* liked him, but the unguarded pain on his face was enough to make me pause.

He wore the same expression Sephrimel had, only diluted by his essential humanity. His silvery hand twitched, falling back down to his side, and the Hellesvront agent and I shared a moment of profound communication.

You don't know what I've lost, his eyes said, and I knew it was true.

Japhrimel went down heavily to one knee, with little of his usual economical grace. "Dante. Are you hurt?"

Am I hurt? Look at you! I struggled to hold back a rusty scream. What ended up coming out was a mangled sob as I reached up. His left hand came down, and he pulled me up, hugging me as best he could one-armed. I shuddered into his shoulder, burying my face in the warmth of him.

"Are you hurt?" He moved, probably trying to get a better look at me, but I clung to him.

Am I hurt? Sekhmet sa'es. Let's see. I was dragged through Hell, betrayed by my god, left in Jersey, and finished up nearly being drowned by a demon with a bad haircut and a hobby that makes freight-jumping seem sane. A high squeaking sound quickly melted into muffled giggles. I laughed as if I'd been told the world's funniest joke.

Laughed, in fact, fit to die, while the steady pounding of rage inside my veins retreated under Japhrimel's touch.

12

*H*ades." Leander was pale, his shirt soaked dark with sweat and various types of blood. He slumped against the hover's hull, the dusky glow of Konstans-Stamboul falling under night's wing receding over his shoulder through the porthole. "*Hades*. I never want to do that again."

We'd just managed to escape the temple before the aid hovers arrived, drawn by the noise and ready to dump plurifreeze to put out the fire.

Our hover was still at its landing pad under a carapace of demon shielding, and as soon as we approached it a tall shape with a mop of dirty-blond hair had melded out of the shadows, greeting me with a wink and a grin that exposed the tips of his long canines.

Tiens, the Nichtvren Hellesvront agent with the face of a holovid angel, was in the control booth, piloting us like a vast silent fish. "We do not appear to have been followed." His calm flat tone was shaped by the song of an ancient accent. I wondered where he came from and how old he was, but not nearly enough to ask him.

Go figure, I'm getting almost used to demons, but a suckhead scares me silly. Everything seemed hilarious right now, in a darkly morbid sort of way. I had my sword and my new creaking rig back, Fudoshin shoved through a stiff loop on the rig's side. I couldn't settle enough to sit down, so I stood restlessly near the hatch, turning the heavy wooden weight of the Knife over and over in my hands. It hummed happily to itself, a low moan sending steady pulses of unhealthy warmth up my arm.

If using the thing makes me feel like this, I'm not sure I want to. I considered this, staring at the gleam of oil against its carved grain, too close and fine to be of any tree growing in the real world.

What kind of trees grew in Hell? Or was it from somewhere else?

"God's wounds." McKinley finished bandaging Leander's arm, rattling an empty disposable hypo of glucose into a wastebasket bolted to the floor. "Winged hounds out of Hell. And one of the Greater Flight. Christos. We would have been toast, if you hadn't been there."

"Then it is well I was." Japh sounded tightly amused. His eyes glowed fiercely.

"Yeah, well, I don't want to die *just* yet. Vann owes me for our last round of vidpoker." McKinley's gaze skittered across the room toward me before he looked back at Leander's arm. "But what does it *mean?* Is it *him?*"

"I do not know if we can blame the Prince for this event." Japhrimel's hand was still clamped over his bleeding shoulder. I had tried to bandage it, but he'd simply, gently pushed my hands away and pointed me toward the largest cabin for fresh clothes.

I was hard on laundry nowadays.

"Who else?" Vann lay flung on a plasteel-and-canvas couch, one arm over his eyes. He seemed none the worse for wear, even if he wasn't nearly as neat and unmarked as McKinley.

"He is not our only concern. The Prince has lost his hold on egress from Hell, and the Greater Flight are settling scores. The one now dead had a grievance with me, and rather a large one." Japhrimel peeled his fingers away from the bloody mess of his shoulder and peered at it. His coat was shredded, and the bleeding wouldn't stop.

Why won't it stop? My hands ached, clenched so tightly claw-points prickled into my palms.

"So which one was that?" McKinley fished another hypo out of the aid kit. "Immuno," he told Leander, who nodded, his jaw tight and his eyes dark with pain.

Japhrimel's eyes half-lidded. It looked like his shoulder hurt. "He is dead and it matters little. Suffice to say I spoiled one of his toys some time ago, and he sought to return the favor. Our task now is to reach the Roof of the World."

"Why won't the bleeding stop?" My voice dropped like a stone into a placid pond.

McKinley pressed the hypo against Leander's arm, and the human Necromance sucked in a breath as the airpac discharged, forcing happy immunity-bolsters and a jolt of plasma into his veins. Vann shifted restlessly, a plasgun's butt clicking against a knifehilt. Lucas had settled himself on the floor, weaponry spread on a ratty blanket in front of him as he cleaned, oiled, and checked his gear. It was the closest to a nervous tic I'd ever seen in him.

Japhrimel merely considered his shoulder, his sensitive fingers probing at the shredded material of his coat. To see the bloody mess made me feel unsteady in a whole new way. He had always seemed so invulnerable, before. "It will stop soon enough." He visibly caught himself, glanced up at me again. "Some of us have poison teeth as well as claws, and I had those more fragile than myself to defend."

I choked back my irritation. After complaining so often that he didn't tell me anything, it was nice to see him trying.

The Knife's humming slid into a lower register. I lifted it up and stared at it. The finials were still writhing like a live thing, frozen in time. It was heavier than it had been, too. "I need a sheath for this," I muttered, and my eyes stuttered back to Japhrimel's face. "Are you all right?" *I should have asked before, shouldn't I.* Sekhmet sa'es, *Dante, you selfish bitch.*

Yep. Feeling more and more like myself all the time. Whoever "myself" was.

"I will be well enough. See?" The seeping had finally stopped, thick black blood sealing away the wound. But so slowly, far more slowly than usual. "There is no need for concern."

What if I'm concerned anyway? I looked back down at the Knife. My belly twinged, the mass of thread-thin scarring on the surface of my skin responding to the plucked-string hum of the wooden weapon.

I hardly recognized my own voice. "He tore that thing out of me, didn't he."

It wasn't a question.

Silence turned thick and dangerous. The hover rattled a bit, wallowed, and began to climb, probably to avoid traffic streams. I didn't want to know how we were avoiding the notice of federal patrols. Traffic to this sector was probably under heavy watch, since Sofya's interior now looked like something thermonuclear had hit it.

I raised my head again. Japhrimel looked at the floor of

the hover as if it was the most interesting thing he'd ever seen in his life. His hair shielded his eyes, falling forward in soft ragged darkness. It looked like bits of it had been charred away.

"It is customary for a Fallen to care for any *hedaira* in distress." His fingers tightened on his shoulder, digging in, tendons standing out on their back. If it hurt, his voice gave no sign. "Especially in . . . such distress as yours."

I realized my left hand was rubbing at my fresh shirt over the scarred tenderness of my belly. Revulsion swept through me, followed by a swift bite of nausea that faded as I took a deep breath. The rage running through my bones rose, flushing my cheeks with heat, and the inside of the hover rattled.

"Just what distress would that be? I'm only curious, Japh. What did . . . what was in me?" I tried hard to sound disinterested, failed miserably. The burning in my throat turned the words even hoarser than usual.

"Something to bind you—and your Fallen—to Lucifer's will." Each word delivered with care and finicky precision. "Sephrimel was adept at treating *hedaira* who suffered from . . . "

I shut my eyes, opened them again. *Well, everyone here saw it except Tiens. I suppose it can't hurt to say it out loud. Get it out in the open.* "You can say it," I whispered.

He did, the word cutting off the end of my sentence like a slamming door shutting away the sound of an argument. "Miscarriage. Only in this case, it was somewhat different. It was *a'zharak*. The word means *worm*."

Worms. I've been dewormed. The black, yawning hole in my memory expanded, ran up against the wall of my will. Retreated, snarling, back down into its hole.

What did I have matched against that void? Just my sorcerous Will, holding up fine despite my betrayal of my sworn word. My Fallen, who seemed to be holding up fine as well, despite my betrayal of *him*. And the fire in my blood, the song of destruction that was a goddess answering my prayers—but not my god.

My god had asked me to betray myself, and I had acceded. I'd had no *choice*. Yet His gem on my cheek had lit me out of darkness.

Had He abandoned me, or could I just simply not bring myself to go to Him?

I stared at the fall of hair curtaining Japh's eyes from mine. He studied the floor, his shoulders down but tense, waiting. The inside of the hover was as quiet as the rare texts room in a federal library.

A'zharak. The word means worm, *but he treated me for miscarriage.* I shivered.

I was an adult. I was tough. Right? One of the top ten deadliest bounty hunters in the Hegemony, a combat-trained Necromance, an all-around ass-kicking wonder.

So why were my knees shaking?

Japhrimel continued, each word deliberately placed. "Had your body not rejected the . . . rejected it, Lucifer would have a means of controlling you. You would become a vessel for his will as well as one of his . . . least-attractive progeny. The separation, when it bursts free of incubation, is . . . energetic."

Nausea slammed hard and fast against my breastbone, burrowed in and finished with acid at the back of my throat. I forced it down, swallowing sourness. "So that's why he did it." The queer flatness of my tone was surprising. I sounded like I was discussing the latest Saint City

Matchheads gravball game. "To control me, use me for bait. Use me against Eve, and probably against you."

I heard the faintest of sounds, like feathers ruffling in the wind.

"Yes." The hem of Japhrimel's coat moved restlessly. Under the whine of hover transport, it was the only sound. Was everyone holding their breath?

If I turned just a little, I had a clear shot to the bedroom door. My boots moved independently of me, squeaking ridiculously as I tacked out across industrial flooring for that harbor.

"Dante." Japhrimel's voice was raw, the bleeding edge of something smoking and terrible.

"I'm all right," I lied, still in that colorless flat voice. "I just want to be alone for a little bit. Call me when we get where we're going."

He said nothing more, but I could feel his eyes plucking at me. My shoulder ached with velvet flame, his name on my skin crying out to him.

My sword's scabbard creaked slightly as my fingers clenched around its safe, slim sanity. I didn't want the goddamn Knife. Just thinking of that satiny wood touching my palm again was enough to make the nausea triple.

I made it to the bedroom door. Pushed at it blindly. The sound of it shutting away the rest of them was not as satisfying as it could have been.

Lucifer wanted to use me as bait. I hadn't been fulfilling my purpose fast enough—in Sarajevo, Eve had left before the Devil showed up, and he hadn't really wanted me to kill any of the escaped demons. I was just a pawn, dangled out in shark-filled waters to see who bit, and if the bait isn't drawing your prey fast enough, you reel it in, readjust it, and throw it back out there.

He had put something *in* me. A worm in my body. In *my* body.

Eve.

My brain shivered, turning aside from what had been done to me and fastening on Doreen's daughter, like a shipwreck survivor latching onto a piece of driftwood. She'd been taken to Hell as a little girl. What had Lucifer done to her, to make her so determined to rebel?

Had it hurt? Had it scraped her insides out and made a black hole inside *her* head?

It bothered me. It bothered me a *lot*.

If I thought about what he had probably done to Eve— the closest thing to a child I might ever have—then maybe, just maybe, I could get away with *not* thinking about the violation of my own body.

My body.

Kill him. For Eve. For yourself. It whispered in my ears, tapped at the walls of my mind. Sweet hot flame, the undoing of the world.

"Make him pay," I whispered to the empty bedroom, as the hover ascended sharply. My stomach flipped one more time, and I slid down with my back to the door, my legs sprawled out in front of me, repeating it to myself. I could, if Japh was on my side. I could do this.

There was no way out now. The funny thing was, when I thought about it, there didn't seem like there had *ever* been any way out.

13

There's an old psion joke taken from a Zenmo koan. It goes like this: *Before they discovered Chomo Lungma, what was the highest mountain in the world?*

The answer, of course, is another Zenmo joke. *The one inside your head still is.*

Normals don't get it. But pretty much every psion who hears it cracks up. The laughter is bright and unaffected if you're a child, somewhat cynical and world-weary by the time you hit eighteen, and turns knowing when you're older. When you get to the combat-trained psions, the bounty hunters, cops, and government agents—we don't just laugh. We laugh as if our mouths are full of too much bitterness to be contained, because we know it's true. There aren't any geographical features that can stop you. It's the faults, fissures, and peaks inside your own skull that bring you up hard and short.

Chomo Lungma is the mountain's name—Great Mother Mountain. She rises in pleats and tooth-shapes from the rest of the Himalayas, a low thundering bass-note of Power throbbing from her rock and ice. She is more than a mountain. Generations of belief and thought have made her a symbol of endurance and the unconquerable, no matter *how* many climbers have climbed to her top unaided by hover technology. It's still an act of faith to scale her.

Our hover drifted through a night sky starred with hard points of brilliance, unwashed by any cityglow. The mountains around the Mother are a historical zone in the Freetown Tibet territory, no cities allowed, precious few hovers, the infrequent temples lit by torchlight, oil lamp, and candleflame.

I stared out the porthole, resting my forehead on chill slick plasglass. Hoverwhine boiled through my skull, rattled my back teeth, slid into my bones. Pleated gaps and gullies of stacked stone vibrated like plucked strings under the hover's metal belly. Starlight danced on snow and knife-edged crags. The air was so thin up here it sparkled.

A slim slice of waning moon drifted in the cold uncaring sky, shedding no light.

Japhrimel stepped into the room. I hadn't moved for a long time, watching the shapes of mountains as we circled the Mother of them all.

He shut the door and said nothing, but the mark on my shoulder hadn't stopped its distress-beacon pulsing. I searched the edged gullies and piles of rock below, my eyes not fooled by thin starshine. The mountains were hooded with snow, but it didn't soften their contours. Instead, it laid bare every grasping, razor edge.

My voice surprised me again. "I'm all right."

Another lie. They were coming fast and thick these days. I had always been so proud of keeping my word; I wondered if that pride was about to turn on me, cutting my hands as I tried to use my sorcerous Will. A Necromance uses her voice to bring back the dead; it's why we whisper most of the time.

We know what the spoken word can do.

He was silent for so long I closed my eyes, the darkness behind my lids comfortless. When he finally spoke, it was a bare thread of sound. "I do not think so, my curious."

The bitterness of my reply surprised even me. "I should think up a cute little nickname for you, too, you know."

It was something I might have said in Toscano, back when the world had still been on its course, not descended into insanity. I'd thought I was fucked-up then but beginning to heal. I hadn't had any idea of how fucked-up it could get.

A nasty little voice inside my head whispered that maybe I didn't have any idea now, either.

"You could," he finally said. "I would answer."

"You always do." The darkness behind my closed lids made it easier to say. "Somehow."

"I have not been kind to you." The words came out in a rush, as if he'd been sitting on them for a while and just now set them free. "What I have done, I have done with the best of intent. You must believe me."

"Sure." *Who the hell else do I have to believe?* "Look, Japh, it's okay. You don't have to."

Meaning, *I'm not in any position to throw stones when it comes to good intent.* Meaning, *you came for me, even when you didn't have to.* Meaning, *someone else hurt me, not you.* Meaning other things, too, things I couldn't say. There might have been a time when I could have opened up my mouth and spilled everything, but that time was long gone.

Besides, he probably wouldn't understand anyway even if I could say it. I had been reduced more than once to incoherence by his inability to comprehend the simplest things about me.

I didn't hear him cross the room, but his breath touched my hair. The warmth of him radiated against my back. "We do only what we must." Each word touched my hair like a lover's fingers, raised prickles on my nape. Precious few people got this close to me. "You more than most, I think. May I ask you something?"

Oh, gods. "If you want." The stone lodged in my throat coated itself with ice, froze the words halfway.

He paused. His fingers touched my left shoulder, skating over the fabric of my shirt. My chin dipped, shoulders unstringing, losing their tension.

Maybe I could relax for just a few seconds. I needed it. I was on the knife-edge of psychosis—too much violence, too high an emotional pitch for too long. It was a wonder I hadn't had a psychotic break yet. I just wanted to curl up somewhere and rest, close my eyes and shut out the world.

Trouble was, the world doesn't take too kindly to being shut out.

The hover lifted, gravity turning over underneath my stomach. We were in a holding pattern, drifting quietly over the tallest mountain in the world.

Except the one inside my head, that was. The one standing between me and any semblance of reasonable humanity. I heard Lucas mutter something outside the door, the sound of metal clinking—ammo, probably. Leander's muffled reply was short and terse.

Japhrimel sighed. It was a very human sound, stirring

my hair as a soft rustling began. When his arms came around me I didn't pull away, but neither did I lean back into him. His wings unfolded, rippling as they closed around me, heavy and silken. Spice and demon musk freighted the air, carrying the indefinable smell of maleness and the faint tinge of leather and gunpowder that was his, unique.

His wings draped bonelessly, the slice of starshine coming through the porthole closed off as they cocooned us, liquid heat painting my skin. He was always so warm.

A very long time ago I'd read a treatise on Greater Flight demons and their wings. It is a tremendous show of vulnerability, almost submission, for a demon of Japhrimel's class to close his wings around another being. The writer of the treatise—a post-Awakening Magi whose shadowjournal had been more difficult than most to decipher—hadn't used the word *trust,* but I'd inferred it anyway, fully aware of imputing human emotions to something . . . not human.

I just couldn't stop doing it. Not when I made a short broken sound, all my air leaving me in a half-sob, and relaxed, abruptly, all at once against him.

The darkness behind my eyelids turned kind and comforting. He held me carefully, resting his chin atop my head and occasionally shifting his weight as the hover banked. His pulse came strong and sure, one beat to every three of mine.

"I thought to ask your forgiveness," he murmured, his voice a thin thread of gold in the stillness. "I thought to ask if you regretted our meeting. I also thought to ask . . ."

I waited, but he said nothing more. *How am I supposed to answer either of those questions, Japhrimel? You hurt*

*me, manipulated me ... but you always show up just
when I'm about to get strangled by yet another demon.
And if I never met you Santino would still be alive, Doreen would be unavenged—but maybe Jace and Gabe and
Eddie would still be alive, too.*

*If I'd never met you the Lourdes hunt would have killed
me.* A thin shiver walked up my spine with tiny, icy claws.
Taking on a Feeder's ka birthed from the ruins of Rigger Hall would have been chancy at best for even a fully-
trained Necromance. Maybe I would have been strong
enough, maybe not.

Probably not. I would have been only human, after all.
If I hadn't met him.

If he hadn't *changed* me in so many ways. The physical changes were only the least of them.

How could I even *begin* to untangle it all? Lies and
truth and hate and need, all twisted together into a rope.
Even as it burned my hands and dragged me down, at least
that rope could be counted on to yank me back out of the
abyss. Every other safety net I'd ever had was gone.

*Tell him the truth, Danny, if you can admit it. Tell him
you wish you'd never seen his face. Tell him you wish he
and Lucifer had just left you alone instead of fucking you
up so bad you can't even think straight, so bad you can't
even talk to your god anymore.*

*Go ahead, sunshine. Deliver the bad news. It might
even hurt him.*

My fingers relaxed, my katana dangling from my left
hand. The rig was heavy, straps cutting into my shoulders,
weapons poking at odd places. In a while the leather and
hilts would conform to me, would be unfelt until I needed
them.

Tell him, Dante. You're always so proud of telling the truth and keeping your Word. Look where it's gotten you. Tell him.

"I'm glad I met you." The lie sounded natural. For once, I delivered an untruth, and I meant it while I said it, too. "Don't be ridiculous."

Japhrimel's weight pitched forward, resting fully on me for one heavy second. He straightened, a small sound escaping his lips as if I'd hit him. "Forgive me?" he whispered. It sounded less like a question, more like a plea.

What am I supposed to say to that? The answer came, and I was grateful for it. "If you forgive me." *We can be even, this once. Can't we?*

"There is nothing to forgive." He sounded more like himself, contained and even. His arms tightened, and for a moment his wings pulled even closer, warm scented air touching my wet cheeks.

I didn't know I was crying. I hadn't cried since Gabe's death. Not so long ago, really, but it felt like a lifetime.

The hover banked into a curve, Japh's weight shifting. He inhaled, his breath moving against my hair, and his body tightened the merest fraction. I knew that tension in him, had shared it so many times. It was a subtle invitation to have a conversation in the most intimate way, skin-on-skin, the only language we ever truly shared.

I flinched.

Japhrimel froze.

I struggled to contain the urge to flinch again. He had never hurt me in the private space of our shared bed. It was ridiculous to think he ever would.

Still, my body turned cold, the tears changing to ice on my cheeks, a black hole where something had been torn

out by the roots opening in my head, my body robbed
of its integrity. My own voice, breaking as I screamed,
echoed up from that well of darkness.

Don't think about that. Don't.

When he moved again, it was to reach up, smoothing
my hair. His fingertips were unerringly gentle, not even
a prickle to remind me of his claws. I remembered to
breathe again, took a deep steadying gulp of warm air full
of his goddamn safe-smelling pheromones.

"I'm sorry." Memory curved, overlapped—how many
times had I said the same thing to Doreen, to other lov-
ers? How many times had I apologized for my inability
to respond, my coldness, the echoes of trauma lingering
in my head blocking me from accepting even the smallest
gift of touch? "Japh, I—"

"No." At least he didn't sound angry. "Leave it be,
hedaira."

"What if . . ." *What if I can't ever go there with you
again? What if I can't ever stand to have anyone touch
me again?*

He inhaled again, smelling me, his ribs expanding to
make his chest brush my back. It was a relief to find out
I didn't want to cower away from that touch. "It doesn't
matter."

"But—"

"It *does not matter.* You will heal. When you're ready,
we shall see." His fingers combed through my hair, infinitely soothing.

I had to ask. "What if I'm never ready?" *What if I don't
own my own body, ever again?*

"Then we will find another way." The darkness changed
as his wings unfurled, slowly, flowing back down to armor

him even as his arms remained around me. He let out a short, soft sigh. "But first, we have a Prince to kill and our freedom to accomplish."

Just those two little things? Sure, we can get that done in an afternoon. An unhealthy, sniggering laugh rose up in my throat, was mercilessly strangled, and died away. "Japh?"

"Hm?" He sounded just as he always did. Except for the banked rage under the surface of his tone.

"I feel . . . dirty." *Unclean. Filthy, as a matter of fact.* I couldn't frame the question I needed answered most.

Does that *matter to you?*

He was silent for a long, long moment. Finally, he spoke into my hair, a mere thread of sound. "I did too, my beloved, when Lucifer broke me to his will. I healed. In time, you will."

His arm uncoiled from my waist and he stepped away, quickly. His retreat to the door was killing-silent, but I felt every step in my own body. I kept my eyes tightly shut. *Oh, gods.* "You mean he—"

"It is one of his preferred methods." The door opened, a slight click as he turned the handle. "We shall be landing soon. Bring your weapons, and especially the Knife. I regret there is not more time for rest, but we must move."

14

*W*ind moaned against antennae and landing-struts. The buffeting increased as Tiens held the hover steady. McKinley tapped a knifehilt, his metallic left hand clenching and releasing as he stared over the Nichtvren's shoulder at a wilderness of rock and snow. The air was thinner up here, so the hover had more bounce; even inside the pressurized seals the weight against eardrums made Leander and Lucas yawn in synchrony, their faces contorting. I could have found that amusing, but I was busy going through my rig one last time, making sure each projectile gun, plasgun, knife, and stiletto was in place. Vann had produced a sheath that fit the half-Knife, a nice bit of leatherwork with two straps for attaching it to a rig. The Knife's humming, malignant force was uncomfortable against my left hip, but better there than in my bag where I couldn't get to it if another demon showed up.

I'm not sure I like it. My skin chilled as Sephrimel's dying screech echoed in my memory, over the hideous sucking sound the Knife made. *Still, if it'll get the job done . . . but are we sure it will? It's only made of wood, for fuck's sake.*

I ducked through the strap of my bag and settled it on my hip, scooping up Fudoshin from the bolted-down table. *Add it to the list of things to think about later, sunshine. Right now there's a job to be done.*

Story of my life. Push it away so you can get it done, whatever *it* is. Worry about the cost later.

After a certain point, it's useless to worry about the debt you've built up. Just put your head down and go straight through, and hope it doesn't hurt too much. Just like a slicboard run through Suicide Alley back home.

"This is as close as I can bring us, *m'sieu.*" The Nichtvren's face was bathed in eerie blue from reflected starlight, the tips of his canines showing as his upper lip pulled back and he finessed the hover down to land. Leafsprings creaked and the hover kissed down as sweetly as a sheet settling over a tethered hoverbed, despite the tilt to the soft landing surface that had gyros whining as the craft stabilized.

It really takes a human touch to land a hover right, especially on a deep snowpack likely to shift and settle in unexpected ways. AIs just can't do it. Though how far I would go toward calling a bloodsucking predator *human* I don't know.

"Close enough." Japhrimel leaned down slightly, peering out the observation bubble. There was nothing out there but snow, rock, and a sheer cliff face going straight up. It looked damn cold.

"Someone is certain to be watching." McKinley couldn't contain himself any longer. "At the very least, let us come with you. Or leave her here with us. If they—"

"Nobody's *leaving* me anywhere," I immediately objected. "I've had enough of being left with you to fill me to the back teeth." *And then some.* Fudoshin rattled in his scabbard, sensing my readiness, I steadied myself with an effort.

"If the Prince catches her here, he'll kill her. Especially now that she's free of the . . ." Vann caught himself, leaning against the hull on the other side of the control bubble. Tiens's fingers flicked, going through procedural cooldowns to keep the hover landed but ready to take off again at the slightest notice.

He's already had his chance to kill me, kid. I shuddered. *Besides, he still needs me as bait, whether I've got that thing in me or not.*

Japh clasped his hands behind his back again. "She is *hedaira.* The Knife was made for a *hedaira*'s hand; demonkin cannot tolerate the thing. Even a Fallen cannot, for long. It is best she accompanies me for that reason alone." His tone was quiet and reasonable. "All is well, Vann."

McKinley spoke up again, running his hand back through his hair so it stood up in messy spikes. "My Lord? Who knew about Sephrimel?"

"As far as I am aware, I am the only one who suspected. The Prince left the matter in my hands." Japhrimel did not even glance in my direction. The wind screeched and fell off, stinging particles of snow rattling against the bubble. "That was of the time when he was certain of my loyalty."

"When did that stop?" I laid a hand against the chill plasglass of the nearest porthole. The hull vibrated, not with the whine of antigrav but with the force of the wind.

It looked *damn* cold out there.

"When I Fell." Japh's coat fluttered once in the stillness. "I shall need the item I left in your care, McKinley."

"Yes, my Lord." McKinley quit fidgeting and strode away, disappearing at the far end of the main cabin, heading for the cargo bay.

"M'sieu?" Tiens half-turned in the pilot's chair. "I may accompany you?"

"Thank you, Tiens. I require only my *hedaira*." Japhrimel half-turned, his gaze sweeping across the cabin and fetching up against Leander, who hunched in a chair, staring out a low porthole at a waste of ice and rock falling away from the narrow sloped shelf we were precariously perched on. The Necromance glanced up, and the flash of fear in his dark eyes was enough to make my breath catch.

I knew what it was like to feel that frightened of a demon. How could I ever forget?

Distract him, Danny. Let's get this show on the road. "It looks goddamn cold out there. Where are we going?"

Japhrimel's reply came after a long moment of considering silence, the color draining from Leander's face and his emerald spitting a single nervous spark.

"The entrance is very close." My Fallen still didn't turn to look at me. "The cold will not touch you."

Entrance to where? "There's nothing up here." I wanted his attention on me. "This is a Freetown Tibet historical zone. It's Chomo Lungma, for fuck's sake. They wouldn't let anyone build—"

"It is older than your kind, my curious." He turned away from Leander on one heel, a precise economical movement. "Come. If 'tis to be done, best it were done quickly."

I didn't know you were a student of the classics, Japh.
"If Lucifer doesn't know—"

"It is," he said, "always better not to underestimate *him.*"

The cargo bay was dark, lit only by orandflu and stacked with crates of supplies. I caught sight of a pile of ammo boxes while I shrugged into the coat Vann had handed me—an explorer's canvas number with plenty of pockets, slightly too big for me, and smelling too new to remind me of Jace's old coat with its Kevlar panels and the hole in one pocket. I'd lost that one, with everything else except my bag and jewelry, in Hell.

Strange that I should suddenly want, with surprising fierceness, a battered, sweat-stained old jacket. I'd worn Jace's coat at the end of the Lourdes hunt and for a long time afterward, while the ghost of his scent wore out of the tough fabric. I wanted it back.

It was only one thing in a long list that I wanted *back*. I stuffed two fresh ammo clips into the biggest right-side pocket, thought about it, and added another in the left. You never can tell.

McKinley handed over a small cylindrical iron container, darkly stained and reeking of demon. "Are you sure you want to use this?"

"What better time?" Japhrimel's tone was just amused enough to put me on edge. "Dante?"

"Right here." I flipped my bag closed, caught a whiff of Hell drifting up from its material. The strap was seamless, as if it had never been broken, the webbing reknitted. *It's a good thing he's so great at sewing, with the amount of laundry I bleed all over.* I caught McKinley's nervous glance at me and the reply died well short of my throat.

Feeling better, Danny? You're wisecracking again. Means you're okay, right?

Right?

"Thank you, McKinley. Inform Tiens and Vann that we shall only be a short time, and to keep our transport ready." It was a dismissal, Japhrimel's back was to me as he triggered the side-hatch from the cargo bay. The lens of the hatch opened, climate-control seals shimmering into life, and the sound of the wind got a lot closer. The seals bowed a little, stabilizing, and I clenched my jaw to equalize the pressure in my ear canals.

"Yes, my Lord." McKinley gave me one last dark look and hurried toward the ladder leading up to the main hall.

Japhrimel stared out through the seals for a moment, his face set as if he was contemplating a complex but not particularly challenging riddle. I'd never seen that expression on him before, equal parts demonic concentration and almost-human amusement, with a soupçon of seriousness thrown in to give it flavor and make his lambent eyes narrow slightly.

"It looks cold out there." I rolled my shoulders in their sockets, settling my rig a little more securely. "What's in the box?"

He shrugged, and just as I was about to take offense, thinking it was a dismissal, he spoke again. "Only a demon artifact. It will draw attention, but for a short time it is the best protection we can use. Do you trust me, Dante?"

My jaw threatened to drop. *You're asking me that now?*

Then again, what better time to ask? Did he need to know, the way I needed to know so many things?

"Of course I trust you." I tried not to sound irritable. Took a deep breath, smelled oil and the burnt-dust scorch of a difficult hoverlanding, the flat scent of climate control and the iron tang of snow. The wind howled, the seals bowing a little as they coped with the sudden change in pressure. "Why? Are you planning something that might change that?" I didn't add the *again* only through sheer strength of will.

"Perhaps. I must warn you, it is likely the escaped Androgyne will show her hand." He kept staring out the climate seals, where the windscream reached a fresh pitch and the darkness thickened as the hover's landing-lights switched off. Now there was only starshine and the orand-flu strips inside the cargo bay. He melded with the thick uncertain shadows, only his eyes firing to break the effect. "I may have to act without regard for your conscience."

You mean, you might have to kill Doreen's daughter, or take her back to Hell no matter what I have to say about it? Don't make me choose between you and Eve, Japhrimel. I can't. "Is Lucifer going to show up too?" I didn't expect myself to sound so calm at the thought. I *also* didn't expect the thick choking flare of panic that went through me, breath catching and pulse hiking, copper coating the back of my palate.

"I most sincerely hope not." He turned slightly, his eyes coming to rest on me, the light sliding over half his saturnine face, picking out the hollows and planes. He looked about to say more but stopped, his mouth thinning into a line that turned down at the corners even as his eyes paled, their glow less awful than Lucifer's but still . . .

My heart lodged in my throat, beating thick and quiet. *Focus, Danny. Just get through this. You only have to do this once.*

Even if it was a lie, I was grateful for it.

"Me too." I hefted my sword, its slim weight reassuring as it vibrated in the sheath, steel feeling my tension. "Let's get this over with. The sooner we have the other half of this goddamn thing, the sooner we can kill that bastard. That's the agreement, right?"

He nodded. "Then come. Stay close, and fear nothing."

I can do about half of that, Japh. I think. If Eve doesn't show up, and if the Devil doesn't know we plan to kill him. I didn't say it. I just shut my mouth and followed him.

15

The cold was immense, titanic, walloping all the breath out of me in one shocked second before Japhrimel's aura closed harder over mine, flushing me with heat. I shivered once, a short cry caught in my throat, and my body quivered, ice congealing in my lungs before I blew out a cloud that immediately flashed into ice and fell with a tinkle on the packed snow. I sank in powder-dry snow to my knees, stepping off the cargo hatch's open metal stairs, glad I hadn't touched the half-railing. In this kind of weather, skin could freeze to metal instantly.

A terrific spike of glassy pain sank through my head before my body adapted to the lower oxygen load in the air, a hazy stain of Power spreading out in the ambient atmosphere. Steam drifted away from the egg-shaped field covering us both, Japhrimel steadying me as I almost toppled, sinking in the snow. Iron-hard fingers closed around my upper arm, hauling me up, and I found myself balanced on the thin top crust just like Japhrimel, whose boots rested feather-light, leaving no impression.

It was a nice trick, but it dried my mouth out and gave my heart an all-new reason to start hammering.

I knew he was a demon. But such a casual use of so much Power was terrifying in an all-new way. *Just how many ways can a Necromance be scared to death?* It sounded like a stupid riddle.

I found I could breathe again, and looked up to find Japh studying me. The wind, pawing at the hover's corners and struts, hurling itself around rock edges with a sound like silk endlessly tearing, covered any sound I might have made. The scar in the hollow of my left shoulder flared with soft heat, stroking down my body just like a caress—one that didn't remind me of the blank black space inside my head, and the hideousness it contained.

Japh tilted his head slightly, and I took an experimental step when he did. My feet crunched in the snow and his fingers tightened, my boots leaving an impression a quarter-inch deep.

I took another step. Panic bubbled up, I set my teeth against it. Anyone coming behind us would look at my tracks and think I was alone, stepping lightly over powdery snow deep enough to swallow me even if it had afforded a soft landing to the hover.

Japh's hand on my arm gentled, slid up to circle my shoulders. He pulled me into his side, Power cloaking us both, and I had the sudden startling feeling of being invisible. The psychic static of a *demon,* spreading through the ether with black-diamond-spangled haze, cloaked and outshone me completely. It was the equivalent of not being able to smell my own pheromones, disturbing and comforting in equal measure.

He set off, shortening his long strides to mine, and we moved over the snow together, not bothering to talk. The sound of the wind would have overpowered anything I could shout, anyway. Steam turned to ice, cracking and tinkling as it shredded away from the small space of warmth he carried us in.

Could he have done this when he'd just been Fallen, not Fallen with a demon's Power restored? Add that to the list of questions I wasn't sure I was ever going to get answered.

We headed straight for the cliff face. I wondered what was about to happen—was he going to take us right up the sheer, ice-laden wall? *Could* he? What about spreading his wings and catching the wind? They were built more for gliding than actual flight, but he'd carried me before. Was he going to do it again?

There were people I might have wanted to share this with, tell them what it was like if I could find the words.

Unfortunately, they were all dead.

The cliff loomed, a trick of angularity making it wave-like, as if rock and stone might crest over and crush us. Japhrimel aimed us for a sharp spear digging itself into the side of the mountain, a slender black stone the wind had scoured clean, wet and glassy in the eerie snow-reflected light. I shivered, though I was nowhere near cold, and his arm tightened.

That type of rock doesn't belong here.

We drew closer, step by slow step. The wind stilled for a moment, howling elsewhere while a freak of drift deadened its force around us. My nape prickled, uneasy, and I tried to glance back to see the hover. Japh drew me on, either not noticing or not caring.

Next to the sharp black stone, a deeper darkness beckoned. *Is that what I think it is?*

It was a slim crevice in the stone, festooned with clear

sharp icicles. One of the ice-spears had broken and lay in shattered crystalline fragments on a rough-carved rock step. The aperture exhaled a low moan as the wind changed again, veering, and my ears protested at the pressure shift.

Japh kept going. The crevice looked smaller than it was, dwarfed by the massive bulk of the mountain. It was actually large enough for both of us to slide in, despite the sharp teeth. His stride didn't alter; he walked right up to the vertical mouth and maneuvered us in, one of the ice-daggers touching my shoulder and crackling as the heat of the shield touched it. I flinched, but nothing else happened, and with two more steps into darkness the wind fell off as if cut by climate seals.

The blackness thickened. *Japh, what are you doing?* I tried to hang back, slow down, but he pulled me forward, his arm gently irresistible. Another soft caress of warmth down my skin, a flush of Power against my nerve endings, and the skin of darkness lay against my eyes like a wet bandage.

"Japhrimel—" Claustrophobia filled my throat. *No. Not into the dark, it's too dark—*

"One more step." His aura hardened, slashing the blackness with diamond claws, and the night slid aside, crimson light spiking through its torn coat. Light struck across my adapted eyes. I flinched, and Japh steadied me as the shielding I hadn't even seen from outside snapped back out behind us, a wall of glaucous rippling black. Displaced air ruffled my hair, fingered my coat, and finally swirled away.

"Holy *shit*," I whispered when my eyes cleared.

"It is a sight, is it not?" Japhrimel sounded tightly

amused, but the bitterness in his tone robbed it of warmth. "No mere human has seen this, and precious few demons. Welcome to the Roof of the World, my curious."

We stood on a platform of smooth, glassy red rock. The cavern was so immense even the great bloody light couldn't fill its corners or its true height. A thin arching bridge of the same glassy redness poured away from our perch, its geometry just a fraction *off,* and that fraction hammered into my midriff, turning my stomach over hard. It was unquestionably demon work. Three other bridges slung inward from the circuit of the cavern, and their goal and apex was a massive crag of floating rock. Its bulk hung down like a shark's fin, and as I stared, trying to figure out the physics of something so vastly unreal, it drifted a little bit. It actually *moved,* like a whale will move slightly in the ocean's embrace, and when it did the bridge nearest us made a low sound that threatened to turn my bones to jelly.

The air was full of heat, sudden and shocking after the frigid waste outside. But this heat wasn't human. It mouthed my exposed skin with fierce chill, and my throat closed as I tried to backpedal, my body wiser than I was. Panic rose, beating in my head with jagged-edge wings.

Japhrimel's voice was lost in the terror filling my skull. I struggled to get free of his arms, because it was hot in here, so hot it *burned,* and I had felt a close cousin to that heat before.

In Hell.

"Stop!"

Down to my knees, teeth clicking together painfully as I jolted, Japhrimel's hands still at my shoulders. He shook me. "Dante. Stop. You will harm yourself."

I blinked up at him. For one horrifying second his face was a stranger's, only the green eyes searing and his lips drawn back as he said more, words lost in the roaring of memory.

I remembered. Claws snicking against my ribs, cradling the living beat of my heart, a sword of fire in my vitals. And a voice, deadly soft and oh-so-amused. *There are so many ways to break a human. Especially a human woman.*

I screamed, but it died halfway when Japhrimel clapped his hand over my mouth, the scar on my shoulder suddenly red-hot wire, digging into vulnerable flesh. The human darkness behind the green flame of his eyes returned, drowning me, and I struggled to *think,* to climb out of the sucking whirlpool of fear.

"You know me," he repeated. "You *know* me, *hedaira.* Come back."

I shuddered, teeth locking together and muscles turned to bridge cables, straining against his hold. Still, there was a curious comfort. I did know him. How many times had he repeated the same thing, over and over, while I shook and sobbed with the echo of psychic rape tearing through my head? The hunt for Kellerman Lourdes had left me with nightmares and reaction-flashbacks, none as intense as this but frightening enough.

I *did* know him. All the way down to my bones.

I broke the surface with a convulsive movement, almost tearing free of his hands. Even now, he was so careful not to hurt me.

I bent over, fingers locked around the slim comforting length of my sword, clenching around the terrible fist in my middle, lower than any nausea I'd ever felt before.

"Anubis," I whispered, the reflex of a lifetime hard to break. My lips moved against his palm. *"Anubis et'her ka. Se ta'uk'fhet sa te vapu kuraph."*

The prayer died on my lips. Hot water scorched my eyes, and I looked up to find Japhrimel still there, still holding me. His coat rippled, a small sound like feathers shifting as his hand fell away.

Tears trickled hotly down both my cheeks. "I'm okay." It felt like a lie. I was getting good at lying, finally.

Maybe not. Japh's silence was eloquent enough to pass for speech, and it was a relief to find I could understand, at least, this one little silence of his. It meant he didn't believe me in the politest of ways, and wasn't going to press the point.

His face was set, that human darkness very close to the surface of his glowing eyes. His mouth was a thin line, one corner slightly quirked, one of his winged eyebrows elevated too. My heart leapt, banging against my ribs and pulling the rest of my chest with it.

Gods above. I just had a panic attack and I think I'm having a cardiac arrest now.

"We should be quick." Half-apologetic, his mouth drawing down again and becoming solemn. "I would not ask it of you, but—"

"I'm *all right*." To prove it, I tried to make my legs work. I failed miserably, and was suddenly very aware of a hollowness inside me. I was *starving*.

Fine time to get the munchies, sunshine.

Japh pulled me up, held me steady, and indicated the floating rock. It shifted again, and another bridge sang as it took the stress. The vibration passed through me, from scalp to soles, the same way a badly tuned slicboard will thrum right before it dumps you. "Up there." The pulsation stopped as he spoke. "This is a place between your world and Hell, not fully of either. Tread carefully."

How careful can I be? I've got a head full of C19 and vaston, and someone's got their finger on the detonator circuit. Problem is, I can't tell who. I don't think it matters. I contented myself with nodding, my hair falling forward into my eyes. I blew it back, irritably, and Japhrimel smiled. It was a small, strained expression, but a smile nonetheless.

"Let's get this over with." I eyed the bridges and the chunk of floating rock, my brain struggling with the sheer *scale.* There was nothing to compare it to, so it seemed absurdly in proportion, but my eyes would snag on the delicacy of the glass bridges and recoil in self-defense. "Are you sure it's here?"

He didn't answer, just set off for where the closest bridge met with our platform, his arm settling over my shoulders again as if it was designed to. The bridges looked absurdly frail compared to what they held—were they really supporting that chunk of stone?—but they were wide as two hoverlanes and twice as thick.

Oh dear gods, do I have to? I've never been afraid of heights, but this—there were no handrails.

The bloody glow painting the cavern flared, a wash of crimson light like a silent explosion. Japh's steps quickened, soundless. My bootheels made small dry sounds against the rock as he led me onto the bridge.

It was a steep slope, and slippery. The surface was grainy, with a slightly oily-grit feel like granite steps after a hard rain. I blinked several times, furiously, because we didn't so much *walk* as almost . . . I don't know, *blink* along the curve, Japhrimel's arm steady and warm over my shoulders but everything else shaking and juddering, especially when the hunk of rock would shift and one of the bridges would cry out in pained stress.

It didn't seem to take very long to reach the sharpest curve of the bridge, and from there it was a matter of seconds before Japhrimel exhaled, a sound of effort, and we stepped from the glass onto something soft.

The surface of the central rock was matted with dark dryness, crumbling off the edges as the bridges sang. Awful icy heat touched my cheeks and my knuckles, white-clenched around Fudoshin's hilt and scabbard.

Screw the wooden Knife, if Lucifer showed up we were going to see how much steel he could eat.

The bravado made me feel better until I looked up from the maroon dirt disintegrating under my boots.

It was a ruined city. Jagged broken towers pierced the red sky, a cobbled road rising from the dirt in front of us, shattered walls scattered like broken teeth, glowing sickly-pale in the bloody light. They had probably once been beautiful, luminous white stones interlocked with care and precision, but now they leered and toppled like a drunken man.

Even broken as it was, the city held an echo of something lovely. The ruins sang, each with its own slow silent voice, a chorus of sorrow. *"Sekhmet sa'es."* I could barely breathe the words. "What the hell is this?"

"This?" Japhrimel's tone was so bitter it scorched my own mouth. "This is the White-Walled City, where the *A'nankhimel* would bring their brides. I was here once, long ago. I do not think the stones have forgotten."

16

I've been in plenty of places and seen lots of urban decay. It was still eerie to walk on a road with missing cobbles and see broken buildings with just a breath of demon oddity to their shape, dry blasted places that might have once been gardens, fluid piles of white stone that might have been fountains but were now only dry bones. Every building leaned hopelessly on its foundations, crying out for something lost. Every missing cobble was a hole in my own heart.

Japhrimel was silent, only removing his arm from my shoulders to help me scramble over piles of rubble. We were heading, near as I could figure, for the city's heart. He seemed to know his way, only pausing every now and again to look at a particular building as if taking his bearings.

Sephrimel's half of the Knife hummed in its sheath, the sound working through leather and into my hip each time the city shifted. I eyed each building nervously, every stone worked fluidly into its fellows except where some unimaginable force had torn them apart.

I kept glancing up at Japhrimel's face, set and quiet, and I began to wonder.

What was it like for him, to walk through here again? Were scenes of murder and screaming replaying in his head? Were all of them like the illustration in the book I carried even now in my battered, Hell-smelling messenger bag?

The strangest thing in the world happened. I began to feel *sorry* for him. I never had, before.

It took a while. The place ran with subaudible song, a long slow moan of stress that alternated between nostalgia like a sharp knife and memory like a fist to the gut. The psychic imprint of something horrible trembled in the air, and I was glad of Japhrimel's aura over mine. This physical space was *haunted;* had never been drained by a cadre of Hegemony-trained psions; and even though we've come a long way in the science of using Power and sorcerous Will I didn't know if there were psions alive capable of dealing with this kind of carnivorous reverberation in the ether. It could eat a Reader alive or tip a Skinlin dirtwitch into berserker rage. It might even drive a *sedayeen* healer mad. And a Magi? Forget it, the spice of demons hanging in the air would tempt them and the devouring grief singing from the stones would creep into their heads, replicating like a virus.

Like a Feeder's *ka,* devouring everyone in its path in its mad scramble to spread, a psychic cancer.

My battered shields, mending only because of the steady flushes of Power from Japhrimel's mark on my shoulder, quivered like the raw wounds they were. I was aware now of the extent of the damage soaking down through my psyche, huge gaping holes and fault lines, the terrain of my mind bombed-out like a city after the Seventy Days War. Like this city, in fact, still keening after an unimaginable tragedy.

We paused for a few moments by a waist-high wall. On the other side a blasted space that might have once been a garden lay, dead trees crumbling to dust. Japhrimel stared across it for a moment, his face settling deeper against its bones.

I put out my hand, blindly. Closed my fingers around his arm. "Don't."

His expression didn't change, but the hurtful tension in it eased a fraction. "It was so long ago," he said quietly. "Long and long. I still remember each of them."

"The *hedaira?*" The minute it was out of my mouth I regretted it.

"All of them. Each life the Prince ordered me to take. I keep them here." One elegant golden finger tapped at his temple. "We're very close now."

There was nothing to say. Still, I pulled on his arm. "Japh. Hey."

He didn't look at me. His eyes narrowed as they swept the crumbling garden. "We should hurry."

"Hey." I tugged on his arm until his gaze swung down, touched mine. "Come here."

"I'm here." His expression didn't change.

I pulled him close and slid my arm around his waist, a moment of awkwardness as my sword got briefly tangled up. I hugged him as hard as I could, squeezing until rewarded by his brief exhale.

He hugged me back, a slight careful pressure, before freeing himself with exquisite gentleness. His face had eased a little.

We set off through the ruined city again. I was beginning to get almost used to the sound the bridges made when the city shifted, and almost used to the vibration underfoot, sliding through the echo chamber of my body. I mean, as much as you *can* get used to being shaken like a bad sodaflo can every few minutes in a place that wasn't quite the regular world, drenched with a cousin to Hell's chillfire air.

The streets smoothed out, widening into an avenue that dumped us into a huge plaza floored with more red-glass stone. Here the light was brighter, but deeper in shade, heart's-blood instead of arterial flow.

In the middle of the plaza a massive building lifted, bone-white marble glowing along its pillared front. Its walls rumbled with grief and Power, and I stared, forgetting to move forward until Japhrimel, not unkindly, pulled me along.

"It's a Temple." The plaza threw the words back at me. Surely I didn't sound that horrified? The idea of a Temple here, in this twisted sorrowing place, filled me with unsteady loathing.

He waited four steps before he answered me. "It wasn't built for one of your gods."

The sound of my lonely footsteps echoed too, magnified by weird acoustics. I tried to imagine this place full of people and failed miserably. "A demon god?" *Call me a coward, but I don't want to know what kind of god a demon would worship.*

"No. This was a place to celebrate what we could become." He paused, thoughtfully, and the echo of my footsteps trickled away like running water. "The *A'nankhimel* spoke blasphemy, to the rest of us. This was where that blasphemy bloomed. When I came here, it was as a fire comes to cleanse." The words began to tumble out. "This was not just a place for *hedaira* and Fallen. Others were brought here, humans who showed promise, and taught. They were given many gifts, which they took outside to the world. Lucifer flatters himself that he *allowed* it, to bring humans up from the mud. *Shavarak'itzan beliak.*" It was obviously an obscenity; the air cringed away when he said it. "The first products of the unions between your kind and mine were born here. Later, an *A'nankhimel* would take a *hedaira* away to give birth in secret. They had good reason."

I knew about this. There was a chance that a *hedaira* could give birth to an Androgyne—a demon capable of reproducing. Which would pretty much destroy Lucifer's monopoly on reproduction in Hell. It was a big deal to demons—after all, the Devil had wound me up and sent me after Santino, who had merrily absconded with the means to experiment genetically until he performed the biggest hat-trick of all, making Eve.

Eve. The child I hadn't been able to save. Little girl all grown up and making trouble.

"Were all of them women?" I was curious, you see. This was the most information about *hedaira* he'd ever given me.

"There were stories about males—*hedairos*. I saw none."

You'd be in a position to know, wouldn't you. I was suddenly glad I hadn't eaten anything. "Okay. So why only women?"

The bloody light exploded again, soft crimson lapping at the air. I flinched.

"The human female breeds, my curious."

That's why Lucifer killed them, you idiot. "Oh." *You know, I'd give just about anything to go back to the hover now.* I tried to speed up, but Japh kept us to the same even pace. For a demon in such a hurry, he wasn't moving very quickly. Just steadily, our steps like clockwork measuring off eternity.

How long had it been since someone walked here? Did I want to know? There was no dust but plenty of the dry sterile red dirt, and the way the place shook every few minutes probably wasn't conducive to dust settling.

Another thought came hard on the heels of that one. *Where are all the bodies?*

Add that to the list of questions I could live without answering. The longer I lived, the more of those there seemed to be.

The Temple's steps sloped up, some of them broken and cracked. Another shudder and bridge-scream left the air shaking, icy hell-heat flapping at my new coat, reminding me of things I needed to forget if I was supposed to stay sane. I kept my sword in a white-knuckle grip, tried to ignore the way my hands were shaking. Maybe an onlooker wouldn't have noticed it, but I could feel the tremors, like an overstressed dynamo.

What if Lucifer shows up?

I told myself it was ridiculous. Japh wouldn't bring me here if he seriously thought the Devil would appear. He was just being cautious.

Yeah, right, sunshine. Tell me another one. I stole a look at Japh's face, its set lines, the perfection of his golden skin drawn tight against the bones. He didn't look as starved as he had. His hair fell over his eyes, feathering out in ragged bits.

"Up the stairs," he said, but he didn't look at me. The expression crept into his face, a look of *listening*. No matter how hard I strained, I suspected I wouldn't be able to hear whatever he was hearing—or *trying* to hear.

It was the same look he'd worn in Toscano, keeping to himself the fact that the Devil was asking for me, playing for time to let me heal.

Something's about to happen. I only have a touch of precognition; it's nowhere near my strongest Talent. Still, it's just enough to warn me when something awful is about to go down.

I wish it wasn't so well-exercised. I have just enough precog to warn me right before I step into quicksand up to my neck, not nearly enough to stop me from sinking.

Closer to the top, the steps were deep and riven. It looked like someone had taken a plashammer to them in several places, marble crushed and ground to pebbles by resonance-harmonics. I had enough to do in scrambling over broken stone, Japh's arm somehow never leaving my shoulders. He was impossibly graceful even now, as I slipped and slid.

We reached the top, and I hopped onto the porch. The pillars were chipped but otherwise whole, marching along the front of a building big enough to house a whole fleet of freight transports.

Typical demon. Build everything so huge it's unbelievable. Wonder what they were compensating for? The snigger caught me off-guard, echoes booming and shattering between the pillars, touching the doors. There were five of them, the central one largest and holding two shattered slabs of marble that once had been able to close. The last door on the left *was* closed, marble writhing with carving I didn't want to look at. The other three smaller doors were in varying stages of brokenness.

Knock knock. Who's there? Just me. Just me who?

Just your favorite demon assassin, that's who. I waved away Japhrimel's quizzical look. "Nothing. I'm okay."

"Keep the Knife ready." His voice fell flat, didn't bounce up from the hard edges like mine did.

No worries about that. The panic died. My left thumb caressed the sword's guard, ready to click the blade free. I could draw, drop my scabbard, and yank the wooden Knife free of its sheath if I was given half a chance.

There was no way I was facing a demon without good honest steel in my hand, no matter how powerful the demon-wrought thing at my hip was.

Sharp repressed anger stained the world for a moment, as if the bloody light had crept inside my eyes. I took a deep breath, shoved it down, and found the trembling in my hands had receded just a little bit. Just enough. "Which door?" *Sounds like a goddamn holovid game show. "I'll take the demon behind Door Number Three, Martin."*

"It matters little." He indicated the largest with an economical gesture. "If we were here before the City was broken, this would be the door I brought you to, at least the first time. There would be a celebration, and sacrifices to mark the occasion."

How the hell do you know? "You were here?"

"*Know thine enemy* is not only a human proverb, my curious." The listening look deepened, and he cocked his head. The city moved again, a huge restless stone animal accompanied by screams. "Some few demons came here to learn, and to watch."

"Learn what?" What could a demon possibly learn from humanity? Hadn't they been the ones to teach *us*? Or at least, that was the suspicion enshrined in academia.

"How to Fall. Come." He stepped over a rivulet of broken stone and dust, his arm leaving my shoulders. His hands flicked and two silver guns appeared, held low and ready as he edged forward. That's when I finally realized what I should have known all along.

Japh wasn't hoping trouble would pass us by. He knew trouble was about to happen, and had tried to keep me from worrying about it as long as possible.

Great.

17

The Temple's roof had either been nonexistent in the first place or destroyed so completely it didn't matter. The inside was such a mess either was a fair guess. Great chunks of masonry were gouged up and scattered around, and unlike the outside, dust lay in a carpet up to my shins, whispering against my jeans as I waded in. The massive rectangular space focused on the far end, where a bank of glowing nacreous steps crouched under a long winged shape I had to blink at before recognizing as an altar.

The walls ran with a riot of color unsmirched by damage, and I had to swallow hard when I saw it was mosaic. Fantastical creatures with wings and fins leapt and cavorted against jungle green, and everywhere there were slender graceful golden women, all with glyphs worked into their flesh, white robes cut aside to reveal the marks proudly. After the desertion of the city outside, it was an assault, and the echo of Inhana's dark sad gaze was enough to make me wish I'd never seen this place.

"Anubis." I sounded choked. "The mosaics."

"It was traditional." Japhrimel lowered his guns slightly. "Hurry."

Hurry? There's nobody here. Still, I wasn't about to argue. "Where?"

"Where do you think?" He tipped his head toward the altar, red light bringing out odd highlights in his shaggy hair. "Up the steps, while I make certain no other intrudes."

"It's up there?"

"If the Anhelikos brought it, the casket is there. Please, *hedaira*, as you love life, hurry." He backed away from the doors, covering them in standard position, something I might have learned at the Academy. Still, he did it far more gracefully than a human could. His coat rustled, its long edges rippling and settling.

He must be nervous. His wings wouldn't do that otherwise.

I waded through the dust, picking my way around beached hunks of stone. When I glanced up, there was nothing but the red light. I couldn't see the roof of the cavern, and it was probably a good thing. I didn't want to see what was glowing fiercely enough to drench this entire place with light. I *also* didn't want to be reminded of how far we'd fall if the bridges quit screaming and started breaking. It would be just my luck to have centuries-old demon glasswork fail just as I got here.

My boots slid on a hard pebbled surface under the shed skin of centuries. More mosaics? Probably. The thought made me feverish, the icy heat tearing at the edges of Japhrimel's borrowed Power over my aura.

I'm in a temple. What if I start feeling like my insides are being ripped out again?

I told myself not to worry. There was nothing sacred left here. The gods had fled, if they'd ever been invited in the first place. My cheek sizzled as my accreditation tat shifted under my skin, inked lines twisting.

Besides, I've been dewormed. The black humor in the thought almost helped.

Almost.

There was a long unbroken sea of dust, the stairs rearing out of it like spines. Oddly, no grime had settled on those white, white planes. The altar crouched, its shape less rectangular and more sinuous now, carved with deep scored lines I recognized as angular demon writing, their peculiar rune-alphabet. My shoulder twinged, the mark settling deeper into my flesh, nestling in the hollow of my shoulder like a bird with its own heartbeat.

I wanted to fix each rune in my Magi-trained memory, but settled for swimming my boots through the dust and struggling cautiously up onto the steps, testing the first one with my boot before trusting my weight to it. Other-Sight was almost useless here, between Japhrimel and the haze of grief in the air it was even difficult to see my own aura. It was like being blind, being unable to see the interplay of forces under the skin of the world.

The altar's main portion had a curved back, and something I stared at for a long moment before making sense of it.

Manacles made of silvery metal lay tangled across each end of the main part. On the winged sub-altars on either side were deep lines—*blood-grooves,* a long-ago memory of an illustration in a textbook rose to supply the term. The chains looked thin, strands almost hair-fine twisted together in complex patterned knots, but I would have bet every credit I ever earned doing bounties and quite a few I never laid hands on they would have held just about anything down.

In the middle of the tangled mess of metal, a rectangle of darkness sat. I recognized it immediately.

It was the twin to Sephrimel's wooden box. Only this one looked oiled, well cared for, and was closed, with a dainty little silver padlock shaped like wings.

For now, simply take what is yours by right, Sephrimel whispered inside my head.

I reached out for it, stopped halfway. What about those chains? Who had they chained here?

Hedaira? Or demons?

"Dante?" Japhrimel, his voice falling oddly away. He didn't echo here like I did.

"There's chains." I couldn't get enough air in. "What were they for?"

"For a *hedaira*'s safety. Is it there?" Impatience snapped the end of each word off.

"There's a wooden box. It looks like—"

"Pick it up. For the sake of every god of your kind *and* mine, *hurry.*"

The premonition hit so hard my chin snapped aside, as if I'd been punched. If I could relax, it would swim up through dark water and swallow me, and I would see a bit of the future. Not much, never enough, but maybe something useful.

The trouble was, *relaxing* wasn't anywhere close to what I wanted to do. I stared at the box, my eyes unfocusing as the premonition circled, drew closer . . . and passed me by, close enough that I felt a brush like thousands of tiny feathers through the air around me.

"Dante." Japhrimel's tone brooked no disobedience. "Take it from the altar."

Just as I leaned forward to do so, another voice slid through the Temple's shocked quiet. It was clear, and low, and definitely a demon's.

"Yes. Take up the Knife, Dante Valentine. Let us see what you can cut with it."

18

I jerked around in a tight half circle, Fudoshin clearing the scabbard with a low rasp of oiled steel. Blue fire woke along its edge, runes from the Nine Canons twisting on its curve, the heart of the blade burning white. Rage woke in a blinding red spray and I took two steps, my body coiling, compressing elastic demon muscle preparatory to explosive action.

The breath left me in a sharp sigh. I stopped, my rings spitting a cascade of golden sparks—no spells left in them, just pure Power accumulating in the sensitized stones and metal.

Eve stepped out of the shadows of wreckage at the far left side of the altar, her pale hair catching fire and lifting a little, framing her sweet face. She was beautiful in the way only demons can be, wearing her exotic golden skin like a silk glove, her wide dark-blue eyes—*Doreen's* eyes—meeting mine with the force of a hover collision. Above and between those eyes, an emerald glowed, set into the smoothness of her forehead. Just like Lucifer's.

I flinched at the thought.

She had Doreen's triangular face, Doreen's mouth, and

a wary little half-smile that was all mine, under the supple carapace of demon beauty.

On Lucifer, beauty looked deadly. On Japh it was purely functional. On Eve, it was . . . magick. And under it, I saw the shadow of the child I had rescued from Santino's lair, the child Lucifer had taken as I watched helplessly under the bright hammerblow of Nuevo Rio sunlight.

The only child I might ever have.

Behind her, resolving around a pair of bright blue gas-flame eyes, was Velokel the Hunter, broad and powerful as a bull, his large square teeth closed away behind lips that thinned as they took me in.

I twitched. But Eve's eyes met mine, and she smiled. It was a genuine smile, not the little half-grimace we shared, the armored expression I faced the world with. "You've come so very far." Her voice was soft and restful, and the smell of her—bread baking and demon musk, a power-fully comforting scent—boiled out from behind a screen of dust and age.

"How . . ." I had to clear my throat. "How did you get here?"

"Kel has tracked more tricksome beasts than the An-helikos, Dante. It was not quite child's play to follow the Knife, but it was close—and still, so much depends on you." Her smile widened. "Now here we are, and we have little time. Stay where you are, Kinslayer."

Japhrimel halted midway across the sea of dust. Both his guns were trained on Eve. "If you touch her—"

Eve shrugged. She wore black, a merino sweater and loose elegant slacks, a pair of what looked like handmade Taliano boots. Kel made do with buff-colored canvas slacks and a blouse under a leather doublet, something like a Renascence illustration of a woodsman, complete with a pouch and a curved horn hanging from his broad leather belt.

They called Velokel *the Hunter,* and I wondered if he'd seen this city before. When he was hunting *hedaira.*

That's exactly the least comforting thought in the world.

"There is no need for threats, Eldest." Eve took a step toward me, measured Japhrimel with a single glance, and took another. "We are not at cross-purposes here."

There were two slight clicks—Japh, pulling the hammers back on both silver guns. It was an absurd bit of theater, since I wasn't sure what they fired, but it was at least effective. The city screeched again as it wobbled in its setting, but his voice sliced through the low basso grumbling. "I will not serve *you.*"

"I have not asked for your service." Eve's voice, soft and restful, stroked the air. I stared at her face, transfixed. She looked so much like Doreen. "I have offered myself to my mother." Her smile was wide, white, and so forgiving I could have bathed in it.

My mother. She said it like it meant nothing, like she was talking about the weather. My heart leapt inside its cage of ribs, pounding high and hard until it settled in my throat. A worm of unease turned inside my battered brain.

Danny, something's very wrong here. Grab the box and let's go.

I hesitated, my sword dipping just a little. If Japhrimel moved on Eve, I would have to try to protect her. He was too damnably quick, and I was tired, starving, my head full of broken connections and even my shields incapable of protecting me from a direct hit. Maybe I could slow him down enough for her to escape.

Why was she here? I was supposed to meet her in Hegemony Franje, in Paradisse. Uneasiness bloomed into full-blown suspicion. What game was being played now?

I didn't care. She was safe, Lucifer hadn't caught her yet. Relief scored through my chest. At least I hadn't betrayed her. I'd taken the worst the Devil had to dish out, but she was safe.

Thank you, gods. If there are still gods who want to hear my prayers. Thank you.

"What nonsense you speak, even for one so young," Japhrimel replied. "Stay *back*. Dante, move away."

It wasn't a request. It was an order. I swallowed, my dry throat clicking in the charged silence. Fury turned sharp and cold in my veins, rising with the low keening of a swordblade cleaving air. "No."

I didn't have a free hand to pick the box up with. My eyes flicked to Velokel. His lip lifted as he caught me looking at him. He wasn't as powerful as Japhrimel; I could calculate him down to the last erg of energy.

I was getting good at doing that to demons. They could all kick *my* ass, but Japh was another thing entirely. Still, Kel might be able to buy Eve enough time to escape if my Fallen moved on her. Which left me with getting the other half of the Knife and helping hold Japh, if I could.

Once I had the whole Knife I had a chance. If it could injure *any* demon . . .

I felt sick at even thinking it. I didn't want to hear its disgusting little gulping noise ever again. And how could I even think of using the thing on Japh, now that I'd seen what it could do?

Eve. Think about her. You promised you'd save her, you couldn't before and Lucifer took her. Now you have a second chance. You'd better use it, Dante.

It took every scrap of courage I possessed to slide my sword back into its sheath and clutch it tight, a practiced, almost-silent movement I didn't need my eyes for. I edged back two steps, put down my other hand, and touched the altar.

The stone was warm, resonating under my fingertips like a plucked string. I snatched my hand back, and found all three pairs of demon eyes on me.

The city held its breath. Its low thrum of grief and agonized shuddering stilled. The dust around Japhrimel's boots stirred, little vortices rising as if tiny dancing feet dimpled its top layers.

"We should go." Velokel's voice, low and full of restrained thunder, broke the hush. I caught a breath of his scent—musk and torn-open oranges, demon spice and blood.

I felt behind me to my right again, searching for the box without touching the altar's stone. *Please.* Sekhmet sa'es, *please. This is beginning to get ridiculous.* My emerald spat a green spark, my accreditation tat running under my skin with sharp little insectile feet.

Eve folded her arms. Her emerald shot a dart of bright green, and looking at it made me feel sick all over again. "The next move is yours, Dante. When you take up the Knife, you will become the Key to the throne of Hell. *He* will have to come to terms with you, and so will the Eldest."

I'm the Key. Great. That makes so much sense now. Thanks for telling me. "When did you guess it was me?"

And why didn't you say something before? I kept feeling for the box. *She doesn't know the Knife is in pieces. So maybe Lucifer doesn't know either. That's either very good or very bad, depending.*

"Your coming was foretold." She indicated the altar with a sketch of a polite gesture, stopping when Japhrimel moved forward another two steps, his boots suddenly making soft shushing sounds in the dust.

"Nice of someone to tell me." My questing fingers touched oiled wood. I hooked them down and pulled the box toward me, cautiously. My hip brushed the altar.

A thrill like fire shot through my bones, blooming from my hip like an unfolding flower. The altar let out a piercing note, like plasglass right before a harmonic shatters it. I scooped up the box and whirled, faced now with carrying it and getting the hell out of here somehow.

Japhrimel stood, his guns vanished. I blinked. The long slim iron cylinder McKinley had given him was in his narrow golden hands, and his attention was fixed on Eve. I snapped a glance in her direction, but she'd already seen my eyes widen, and her gaze flicked to my Fallen, the color draining from her face, leaving an unhealthy pallor under the even goldenness.

"No—" she began, panic roiling under the smoothness of her voice, cutting the city's expectant silence like a lasedrill. *"No!"*

"Veritas in omni re." Japhrimel pronounced each syllable distinctly, his fingers curving over the iron box's lid. "Now we shall see your true face."

What the bloody blue hell? "Japhrimel—" I didn't have idea what I was going to say to stop him.

He tore the lid off, tossing the contents of the cylinder

from him with a convulsive movement. It *roared,* shattering the stillness, and my body reacted without thought, crouching and bringing the box to my chest, almost braining myself with my swordhilt in the process. It was a good thing, too, or I might have been knocked across the altar instead of into it.

The entire city woke in a cacophony so immense it was almost soundless, felt in the bones instead of heard, and hot blood gushed painlessly from my nose, rivulets of warmth sliding down my neck from my violated ears. I must have screamed, because my mouth was open, and I damn near dropped my sword.

Combat instinct pitched me to the side, rolling, and I bumped down the stairs in a flurry of arms and legs, gaining my balance in a crouch at their foot. I lurched to my feet unsteadily, just before Japh collided with me, rib-snapping force pulled just at the last second, and both of us went sprawling as a flare of black-diamond Power tore the air apart and left it bleeding.

Eve! I was struggling against Japh's hands almost before we landed, a chance twist of my torso breaking me halfway free. He caught me again, fingers digging into my nape just as a mama cat will hold an unruly kitten, and somehow he was kneeling next to me, his fingers irresistible as he forced my head up.

Eve had gone down, but Velokel was still standing. The Hunter's flesh blackened, running on his bones as he screamed, the cry tearing more stone loose and kicking up great gouts of choking dust. His shape *changed,* like ink on wet paper, and horns lifted searing-black from his forehead, curling back around his ears. He was even more squat now, corded with muscle, his legs sprouting fur and ending in massive hooves that cracked the stone steps as he leapt back to avoid whatever Japh had thrown. It was a smear of hurtful golden brilliance, rolling like an apple, with odd bounces as it leapt up the stairs in merry defiance of physics.

Only Velokel's eyes were the same, bright blue above a blackened ruin of a face that mutated even as I watched. I had to gasp in a scorched breath, having wasted all my air screaming.

Eve leapt to her feet. Her shape was still the same, slender and female, but a shell of Power clung to her in tattered streamers, painting streaks of green on the air as her emerald spat spark after spark, each a point of hurtful brilliance. Her eyes lightened, a blue to match Velokel's, and her haggard face was no longer a copy of my dead lover's.

I stared. Japhrimel hauled me up as the massive sound drained away into the subsonic, and the ground underfoot began to vibrate like a freight hover's deck.

"—go!" Japhrimel shouted. But I couldn't tear my eyes away from Eve.

Her shape changed like clay under running water, shards of illusion plainly visible to OtherSight now that it was broken. It was a glamour, a sorcery meant to feed the eyes a lie.

She was beautiful, still, as only a demon could be. Her eyes were blue and her hair ran with snow-white flame. But there was no echo of Doreen in her face.

And no echo of me.

Then who the hell is she? It can't be, she has to be Doreen's, she has to be!

Japhrimel hauled me up, his fingers biting into my

neck. My ears twinged with pain as they healed, twin
nails driven into the sides of my head. The noise was still
massive, but not enough to burst tender membranes. The
wooden box almost squirted out from under my arm. I
clutched at it, and my bag banged against my hip as Japh
dragged me aside just in time, a chunk of stone nailing the
floor right where we'd been standing. He whirled aside,
yanking me into a lunatic spin like a dance move, ending
with us both somehow facing the door. *"Run!"* he yelled
through the noise.

I'd lost all my air again, screaming, adding my thin
voice to the crashing and rending. *Think about it later.
Now* run, *run like hell and hope you get out of this alive.*

I got my feet under me and pelted for the door, leaping
a pile of rubble and almost slipping as I landed on unsteady ground, my unruly body once again going too fast
for me. Disturbed dust rose choking-thick, and behind
me, Velokel roared something in the demons' unlovely
tongue that I didn't need a dictionary to translate. The
other piercing cry was from the demon who had claimed
to be Doreen's daughter, *my* daughter.

The demon I was going to kill Lucifer to defend.

Japh's fingers closed around my left arm instead of
my nape. He pulled me aside, the doorway we'd entered
through crumbling. Its massive marble slabs teetered and
swung before crashing down. I flinched, and the entire city
shuddered again, a gigantic cracking noise like the world's
hugest egg broken against the side of a red-hot city-sized
skillet echoing through both physical and psychic space.

What the goddamn motherfucking hell is going on?

We made it through one of the smaller doors just in
time. The ground quaked, and I had nasty, uncomfortable

ideas about what exactly *was* going on. If one of those bridges had failed and we were even now falling—

Then, between one moment and the next, it stopped. The sudden cessation of noise was shocking in and of itself, but even more shocking was Japhrimel skidding to a halt, his fingers turning to iron and digging in mercilessly. He plucked the wooden box from me as easily as taking candy from a child.

I'll admit it. I screamed again. I was doing a lot of that lately. A complicated flurry of motion, his fingers lacing with mine, ended with me shoved behind him just as the one voice I never wanted to hear again broke the newborn stillness with its awful dulcet music.

"This is unlike you, my Eldest."

My ribs flared with starved heaving breaths. I blinked at Japhrimel's back, one of his hands behind his back holding *my* right hand with bone-crunching force, his knuckles pale under their goldenness.

He inclined his head, and I sagged. This was it. It was over.

Because in front of us, his very presence staining the air with black fury, was the Prince of Hell. Again. My entire body turned into a bar of tension, Japh's fingers squeezing pitilessly at mine, small bones creaking. Pain bolted up my arm, exploded in my shoulder as I backpedaled, trying to rip my hand free and escape. The scar writhed madly against my skin, and my Fallen's aura clamped down over me like a frozen kerri jar over an unlucky silkworm.

I *knew* it was Lucifer. I didn't have to see him and I didn't want to. Japhrimel held me in place, my arm stretched awkwardly as I twisted, my boots scraping against stone.

Japhrimel laughed. It wasn't the gentle, almost-human sound of amusement I'd heard from him so many times, or even the slight ironic *hm* he gave when I beat him at battlechess or otherwise surprised him.

No, this was a swelling demonic laugh, a harsh caw marrying delight to disdain, with a generous helping of pure hatred. He laughed like murder in a cold alley at midnight.

The sudden idea that I could probably tear my own arm off and escape didn't sound as laughable as it might otherwise have. There was a black hole in my head, dilating with terrible force, and at any moment I would *remember—*

"And this is unlike you, *Prince*." Japhrimel's tone was terribly, utterly cold. I had never heard him speak so. "I thank you for your care of my *hedaira*. Your hospitality remains ever the same."

The silence changed, pressure shifting and sliding as I struggled to free myself from Japh's iron fingers. When Lucifer spoke again, the coldness in his voice matched my Fallen's, and everything inside my skull trembled on the edge of insanity.

"I used her as I saw fit. What else is a Right Hand for?"

"We are all toys for your pleasure, my Lord." Accusation boiled under the words. Japhrimel made a small movement, and something clattered. Wood, striking the ruined stone. In the terrible hush that small noise punctured my heart.

"Of course you are." The Devil didn't even give it a second thought.

Ogods Japh let go what are you doing let GO of me—I swayed. It hurt, Japh's hand grinding mine into powder. The pain was a silver spike nailing me to earth even as the hole in my head widened, my psyche cracking under the strain like microtears in silk hovernets.

"*That* is what the rebellion was after, Prince. You should take more care with such trinkets."

Anubis, someone, help me. I bent back, my entire body a stretched-taut bow of longing, aching for escape; I could leave the arm behind if I had to, I just wanted *away*.

I have never, before or since, understood so completely an animal's struggle to free itself from the trap that bleeds it.

Lucifer said nothing, but the pressure of his rage was a storm front moving in, an eyepopping strain. Even the icy heat of this place between earth and Hell felt warm and fuzzy by comparison. Japhrimel drew himself up. He was a good bit taller than me, but he seemed even bigger now, and I was suddenly deeply grateful he was between me and the Devil.

Shame boiled up hot and vicious under my breastbone. I'd always fought my own battles before, hadn't I?

Not against that. Not that again. I can't.

My aura trembled under Japhrimel's, on the verge of locking down hard and crystalline. If that happened, if I went nova, I'd implode right before I did something stupid. I would die.

But we'd see just what my half of the Knife would do to any demon in my way first.

I heard the Devil take in a long breath, as if he was about to speak. The air hissed past his teeth, and I felt those teeth in my own flesh again, tearing at whatever remained of my sanity. They speared deep as I screamed, the world turning into shutterclicks as my eyelids fluttered, and Japhrimel's fingers gave one last terrible squeeze, the scar on my shoulder burning, *burning*.

Whatever Lucifer would have said was lost in a blur of hoofbeats and a cry rising from a demon's throat.

I slammed back home in my body, my head whipping to the side just in time to see Velokel the Hunter pound out of the Temple and across the dead plaza. He stuttered through space with the eerie graceful quickness of demons, his aura blazing. Blue fire veined his hooves and crackled between the points of his horns, and as he ran time stopped, slowed, and crystallized into a lattice of action, reaction, and sudden explosive motion.

Japh *moved*.

Kel collided with Lucifer.

The shock of that impact would have knocked us both sprawling if Japh wasn't already down, his body folded over mine, my scream lost in the noise and his own tearing more blood from my ear as we tumbled, the world turning upside down and inside out. Streaks of rancid light tumbled past, and a warm wall of displaced air shoved us even further.

Crunch. Japh let out another short cry, a flying needle of debris stinging my cheek. The breath knocked out of me but I struggled up, my left hand still weighed down with my sword, singing a thin note of distress inside its sheath. Dust scorched the back of my throat, a fume like the kick of hoverscorch while slicboarding through fast traffic, and the most amazing thing happened.

I realized I'd survived seeing the Devil again.

So far.

Japhrimel gained his feet in a leap that might have surprised me once. His eyes blazed, casting shadows down his gaunt cheeks, and his hair was caked with dust. His mouth moved, but I couldn't hear whatever he might have said. I was deaf from the noise of the world ending. He grabbed my arm again, the prickle of his claws sinking in through tough fabric, and *pulled*.

I went willingly. He didn't bother to slow down, just dragged me over a pile of broken house-sized stones jittering in place like marbles tossed by an angry giant. It was a good thing, too, because the snarling mass that was two demons in combat hit the pile right behind us, stone grinding into powder and flying aside, another shockwave hitting me in the back with an impact so massive it was almost painless. Japh's boots touched down and he leapt, his wings coming free with a convulsive fluid tearing, and the world turned over again because he'd tossed me, my arm almost pulling free of the socket, tendons screaming savagely as they stretched and I had to gasp in air flavored with heat, dust, and the sweet rotten-fruit smell of demon blood.

I tumbled weightless for what seemed like eternity. He'd flung me free of the blast zone, just like tossing a gravball for the hoop. Awful nice of him.

This is going to hurt. Body twisting on instinct, my legs might shatter if I landed on them, there was not time to look for a landing no *time* and I hit, hard, shoulder driving into stone and my head hitting something that might have cracked it like a melon if the hard shell of Power over me hadn't deflected most of the force. It still rang my chimes pretty good. I blinked, laying dazed and pinned to the floor of a nightmare, before being jerked to my feet once more.

A new vibration poured through the overstressed fabric of reality. I reached up, trying to smear the blood out of my eyes, and my hand hit Japh's shoulder. He pulled me down a narrow alley floored with quaking white stones, earth shifting below our feet as the city moved again. Not like an animal turning over in its sleep—no, this time it shook itself like someone had just poked that animal with a big sharp stick.

Danny, how do you get yourself into these things?

Don't answer that, Jace's voice whispered in my ear. I was too busy to care, for once. *Just run. You're running for your life, sunshine.*

As if I didn't know.

The alley twisted like it wanted to throw us off its back. I caught flashes of gates made of sculpted rosy metal, crimson light gouting from stab wounds in the walls, courts behind screens of carved stone full of blasted trees slowly turning to dust.

The dead tree gave no shelter. Panicked hilarity ran through my head in time with our blurring footsteps. *And no bird sang.*

I still could not stop screaming, though I needed all my air. My lips moved, soundless because I was still temporarily deafened. Light ran and blurred because my eyes watered, trying to cope with the caustic dust blowing everywhere.

Japhrimel dragged me aside, and we ran down a long avenue receding into infinity, rows of fantastical statues marching down either side. The shapes were hybrid—cats with wings, serpents with paws and manes—and each one was faceless, the features clawed off. It was like running in a bad dream, feeling the monster's hot breath on your back, the air turning to quicksand.

One of the statues uncoiled, streaking across the avenue and leaping for us. It was a long black sinuous shape, its eyes glowing green, and I was still screaming breathlessly when Japhrimel struck the hellhound down, the heat of its obsidian hide exploding around us. He shot it twice without breaking stride, shouting something sharp and heated in the demons' unlovely language, and runnels of decay poured through its body before it finished its leap. He yanked me past so quickly my head snapped back, and the bloody dust-choke light filled my streaming eyes.

We burst out onto the fringes of a long field of dry black crumbling dirt, and my hearing began to come back. Echoes ran and dripped like water, running feet, screeches, howls, and the great glassy snarls of more hellhounds. There was a streak of flame lifting to our right— one of the bridges, twisting like taffy and bouncing in ways nothing that looked so fragile should.

I stumbled and might have sprawled headlong if Japh hadn't given my arm another terrific yank, and my shoulder gave way with a crunch of agony. The field flashed underfoot and I let out a small hurt cry. My lungs burned, a live nuclear core dropped into my stomach, my dislocated shoulder crunching with furious agony each time Japh pulled, and he ran right off the edge of the world, carrying me with him. We fell, and the last thing I heard before a brief moment of merciful unconsciousness was the liquid sound his wings made as he spread them, his fingers slipping through mine as my abused shoulder suddenly gave way again. I fell free, cartwheeling through space, and a brief starry moment of darkness flashed over my eyes.

19

$\mathcal{H}$e was cursing. At least, it sounded like cursing, between steady thudding sounds, like a heartbeat. Gravity returned, and with it, the live fire in my shoulder.

I opened my eyes.

For a moment I thought I was flying. The vast cavern wheeled away underneath me, lit with bloody light.

Then there was a bump, fiery pain spilling through several parts of my body, and I saw with a great scalding wash of relief that my numb left hand was locked around Fudoshin. My right arm flopped uselessly, and I swallowed something hot and acidic as I jolted again, staring down past my dangling sword into a sea of waxy, directionless crimson.

The cavern went down for what looked like *miles*. But rising up underneath us was a thin thread of shadow. We hit the bridge hard and almost tumbled off, Japhrimel making a low sound of lung-tearing effort, and I found myself clinging to him, one of his hands tangled in my rig, my messenger bag's strap cutting into my shoulder, caught in his claws. His other hand flashed down, driving a silver-bladed knife—one of the short, slightly curved blades he sometimes used for sparring—into the bridge's surface. The sudden deceleration brought up a painless retch, and I started to feel a little pale. My legs hung out into space, the hard stony edge of the bridge right at my hips, and I would have thrashed if I could have moved, trying to get back up onto solidity.

Japh's eyes closed. His lips moved, still shaping words in his native tongue that hurt to hear. If I'd had a free hand I would have tried to stop my ringing, aching ears so I didn't have to hear that language spoken again.

He *pulled,* my dead weight sliding back from the abyss.

How the hell did he do that? We ran off the edge.

We lay there for a moment, tangled together, and I was mildly surprised to find myself still alive. Heart beating. Lungs mostly working. All original appendages mostly still there.

Hallelujah. I'd've shared my joy, but I was still shuddering with great gouts of unholy, uncontrollable panic. *I've gone mad. Wonderful. Marvelous. Great.*

The most horrible thing was that it didn't feel abnormal anymore. Insanity seemed the order of the day.

The bridge flexed underneath us. Japhrimel's eyes snapped open, their greenness a sudden relief in all that red. He pulled me into his chest, his other hand still on the knife, driven hilt-deep into stone. His lips pressed my forehead, once, so hard I felt the shape of his teeth behind them.

I'm happy we're alive too. Now can we go home and forget about all this?

His ribs heaved. He was gasping for air, too. I suddenly

didn't feel too happy about that. *Get up, we have to get up. Come on, sunshine. Move your ass.*

I twitched.

He seemed to understand, because his entire body tensed and he rolled to his feet. I struggled up to my knees, my dislocated arm flapping bonelessly, and he pulled on my rig. I barely managed, even with that help, and when I was finally set on my boots, I leaned against him, burying my face in his coat.

My ears buzzed. I realized it wasn't because I was deaf. It was an actual sound. The bridge flexed again, and if Japh hadn't moved we would have been pitched overboard.

"Can you walk?" He didn't quite shout, but his voice cut through the chaos. I heard hellhound snarls, their low coughing roars, and shuddered. Kel had sent hellhounds to chase me, and so had Lucifer. Maybe they were busy fighting each other now, and they would forget all about me.

Yeah. And wild hoverbunnies will fly out your ass. Get moving!

I tilted my head back. Tilted my chin back down to approximate a nod.

He wasted no more time, but set off down the snaking gallop of the bridge. It was hard going, trying to negotiate a road that either dropped out from under us or slammed up to shake us off with no discernable rhyme or reason. My head dropped forward, chin resting almost on my chest, and I concentrated on one foot in front of the other.

Lucifer. That was Lucifer back there.

I *should* have been screaming in utter panic. Instead, I

felt only weary amazement to still be actually breathing, however short the time remaining for that miracle was.

Go figure. I must be stronger than I thought. Then I wondered if that would be a challenge to the gods to prove it.

When we finally reached a broad shelf of rock anchored to the cavern wall, the sudden cessation of movement was shocking. Just as my feet landed on relatively solid ground, there was a cry unlike any of the previous hellish noise. It was a high keening ending on a throat-cut gurgle, and ice filled my veins.

That sounds like someone's dead. I hope it's him. If there's any justice in the world—

"Not much time." Japhrimel pulled me into his side. "Only a little farther, *hedaira*. Stay with me."

Not going anywhere. Sticking like glue. I wanted to nod, to tell him so, to make some sort of response. All that came out was a half-choked garble cut short by a longing gasp for air that wasn't full of dust. I sounded like I'd lost my mind.

Maybe I have. I hope I have. This would be so much easier to handle if I did.

"Not so far," he whispered. "Just stay with me, beloved. Only a little farther, I swear. I have not brought you this far to lose you now."

I would like to say I remember how we got out of the cavern, but I don't. Patches of darkness and the immense shock of the cold, the mark on my shoulder sending pulses of warm oil down my skin that couldn't touch the frozen inner core of me. I do remember the hover looming up out of the crystalline air and thinking, *How did he manage to get us back here?* I remember snow drifting up against the leafsprings holding the landing legs, icicles blooming on the moorings. The stairs were too much for me; Japh had to drag me up one by one, and he pushed me through the seals and into the blessed smells of humanity, oil, metal, and hover. I fetched up against a stack of ammo crates, my skin twitching with exhaustion and my dislocated shoulder settling into a deep unhappy throb.

I do not ever want to do that again.

The cargo hatch closed. A faint whine filled the stillness. I knew that sound, and it filled me with fuzzy alarm.

I looked up.

Leander Beaudry stood in the low orange glow of orandflu strips, the plasrifle socked to his shoulder and pointed right at me. A little in front of him and out of his fire angle stood a tall, slim demon with ice for hair and burning blue eyes.

The demon I'd known as Eve was still smiling, a rather gentle, childlike expression.

Japhrimel stood by the hatch control, dust ground into his hair and his eyes volcanoes of green. Metal popped and pinged, responding to the sudden flush of heat as his aura flared.

"Your agents have been overpowered, and the Prince will not long be delayed." The Androgyne's voice stroked soothingly, calming. The emerald in her forehead glowed, casting triangular shadows under her pretty, inhuman eyes. "I think it best we parley quickly, Eldest."

20

Japhrimel stared at her for a few long seconds, as if a new and interesting insect had crawled out of the drain. The laserifle whined, unholstered and primed. Even if Japh went for Leander, he'd still have to deal with Eve, or whoever the hell she was. Demons couldn't outrun a plasbolt.

I sure as hell didn't feel up to outrunning one either. The laserifle was pointed right at me, and I wasn't sure what a plasbolt would do to me if it was set to kill instead of stun.

I was Japhrimel's weak point. If I ended up dead, would he turn into another Sephrimel, bleeding away through centuries and obsessively recreating me in whatever he could get his hands on? Which brought up an interesting, chilling little question—just how would he go crazy? Did he ever think about it while I was sleeping? When he looked at me?

How did it make him feel?

I found my voice. Amazingly, I even sounded halfway coherent. "Beaudry. What the *fuck?*"

"Sorry, Valentine." Even, neutral, his dark eyes never leaving my chest. If I twitched, he'd put a bolt through me. His accreditation tat twitched on his left cheek. "I've got orders."

You bastard. Laying on the "I'm so scared" act. And I fell for it, just like a green kid. Loathing coated my tongue. "Working for demons now?"

He didn't shrug, but the way his eyebrow lifted was just as eloquent. "Hegemony federal, actually. Field agent. Running across you in New Prague sure made my life interesting."

"Charming." The blue-eyed demon's tone shouted she found our chattering anything but. "I am ready to bargain, Eldest. Or we can let *him* find us here."

"Speak." Japhrimel's lips barely moved. The single word coated the air with ice, made it tremble. I slumped against the ammo crates, trying hard to come up with something brilliant.

Nothing happened.

The blue-eyed Androgyne folded her arms. "Where is the Knife?"

He threw the other half at Lucifer. We're fucked. I kept my mouth shut. So did Japhrimel.

"Come now. I saw you. You would not have handed over the one weapon that could set you free of his games so easily. Ergo, there is something amiss." One ice-pale eyebrow lifted, and the grin she wore turned wolfish, a trick of a few centimeters changing in the landscape of her face. I couldn't stop staring, searching for echoes of Doreen, of the child Lucifer had taken so long ago.

It has to be Eve. It has to be. She just looks different because of whatever Japh threw at her.

Japhrimel's eyes flicked to me, his attention never wavering. "It is elsewhere. The box was a decoy. I did not think it wise to trust such a weapon to the Anhelikos."

What? "What?" I wanted to screech the word, but the only thing that came out was a pale whisper. "What did you say?"

"The box on the altar was one of three decoys. Meant to force both the rebellion and the Prince to show their hands."

Disbelief curdled in my throat, but I spit it up anyway. "A *decoy?* You . . . we . . . *I* . . ." *You mean I went through all that for a* decoy? I leaned against the crates, my right shoulder burning with deep drilling pain as it twitched. I hoped it was healing.

"The moment the Prince opens the box, he will know I am playing a new game. He may know now. When he does, he will be angry." He acknowledged the understatement with a slight lift of one eyebrow. "But it will also alter the playing field. He cannot afford to let me reach the Knife, but he also cannot afford to strike me down without knowing where it rests and holding it in his hands, to assure himself he is safe. This one—" His tone changed as he regarded Eve, or not-Eve, or whoever the hell she was, "he will slay on sight."

The demon shrugged. "I am his favored one, and the thing he longs to possess. He has sought to capture me, because he will not let me die unbroken."

"He may change his mind," Japhrimel observed.

I sagged against the crates. I was so tired. Even my hair hurt. Even my *teeth* ached, and burning dust still scorched my throat and lungs. *Let's just go. Can we just please leave?* The thought of Lucifer maybe still alive back in that city full of red light, smashed things, and Hell's cold

fire was enough to make the black hole inside my head
shiver like a cat shaking off unwelcome rain. The pain of
my dislocated shoulder was beginning to seem very far
away, and that was a bad sign.

"Such pretty things." The blue-eyed demon didn't look
away from Japhrimel, and her stance was just a little bit
too tense. "They are so very fragile. How is her health,
Eldest?"

*I'd be a lot better if people would stop dragging me
around. Oh, and if demons would stop trying to kill me.
I'd have a* much *better time. It would be a vacation.*

"How does Velokel the Hunter fare, Androgyne?" Japh
flung it at her like a challenge.

"Sometimes a piece must be sacrificed. You have
played such games."

"I hate to interrupt," Leander cut in, "but we're exposed
here. If there's a pissed-off demon heading this way, we'd
best conclude our business quickly."

"Cease your yapping, little human." Japh's tone could
not have held more contempt.

*Where's Lucas? And the agents? Not to mention the
goddamn Nichtvren.* "Japh?" My scabbard rattled against
the ammo crates as I shifted. "He's right. We should get
the fuck out of here."

"I am waiting to hear something of consequence."
His eyes glowed, and one corner of his mouth curled up,
slowly, dangerously. "I will not wait much longer."

"The Prince wants me." The blue-eyed demon's expression matched his, an eerily perfect mimicry. "I have
become the bait that will lead him to the killing field.
You are the hand that will strike. And *she* is the Key. We
should not linger here."

That's three votes for getting the fuck out of here now. I consider the motion carried. "Japh." My knees almost gave way. I propped myself against the crates. Prickles raced up my arms, the cold in my bones spreading out. Soon I would be made of ice. It seemed a wonderful thing. "We need to go now."

"Very soon, beloved." How could he sound so coldly murderous one moment, and so tender the next? I blinked, trying to figure it out, and the scar on my shoulder sent a hot torrent of Power through me, driving back the cold.

Still, even pure Power wasn't enough. I was too tired, too hurt, and the broken places in my head were too raw. I'd seen Lucifer again. Well, not *seen* him, because Japh had kept himself between us. But I had heard the bastard's voice again. I had survived.

I heard a noise that didn't belong. A slight, definite click. I froze.

Everything happened at once. The hover woke into humming life, acceleration pressing down on everything in the hold as Japhrimel *moved*. He did not so much blink through space as reappear, knocking aside the other demon's hands as she spat at him, his fingers sinking into her throat. The laserifle crackled, and McKinley's arm was across Leander's throat, dragging him backward. The Hellesvront agent's black hair was wildly mussed, his clothing singed and torn, and his aura flared with violet light that fumed like homicidal rage.

I spilled over, my muscles suddenly unable to cope with the task of keeping me upright. My sword clattered against the metal grating, my bag clinking and clacking as I curled over it, my wounded right arm twisting uselessly.

Chaos. My eyelids were terrifically heavy. As soon as I got one to peel up a little bit the other one would fall down.

Japhrimel? Will you please explain what's going on?

I got no answer, just the feeling of gravity pressing along my body as the hover pressed up, my consciousness lifting away, disconnected.

Gone.

21

There was a sickening crunch, and I let out a short, half-chopped yell. My eyes flew open, and Japhrimel caught my fist, the punch stopped as if by a brick wall. My right shoulder was back in its socket, throbbing with a high note of yellow pain before another warm bath of Power slid down my weary flesh.

He slid his arm under my shoulders and lifted me just a bit, held something to my lips. "Drink."

It was a sign of how confused and miserably tired I was that I didn't even think to question it. I simply filled my mouth with whatever was in the cup and swallowed. It was warm, thick, and gelid, and the spice of it coated the back of my throat, touching off a chain of memory like flashbulbs inside my aching head.

For a moment I thought I was back in Nuevo Rio, golden sunlight striping the bed as a demon held me in his arms, Power burning inside the channels of my bones just as his blood burned in my throat, reshaping me from the inside out while barb-wire pleasure slammed through each changing atom of my flesh. Since I'd awakened with a new body and a seriously screwed-up life, he had been the only constant.

Even dead and ground to cinnamon dust in a black lacquer urn, he had been my guiding star. The taste of his blood in my mouth brought it all back, memory strong as a lasecannon ricocheting through my aching head.

I gagged, but it was already down. "*Avayin, hedaira,*" he murmured. "Peace. All is well."

The lunacy of his assurance hit me sideways, and I almost choked again. He tipped the cup, and I had to swallow. I took it down in three long gulps. Japhrimel made a small sound of approval and set the cup aside. He sat next to me on the bed, his solidity comforting. His eyes were still glowing green, casting small shadows under his high gaunt cheekbones. He didn't look half-starved anymore, but he didn't look happy. The dust was still in his hair, stiffening the silk of it. A smear of something dark traced one high cheekbone, his mouth was set and thin. Still, I felt ridiculously relieved to see him. The relief was as deep and unquestioning as my trust in whatever he wanted to make me drink.

I was spending a distressing amount of time knocked-out lately. Did half-demons get brain trauma?

Would I live long enough to find out?

Warmth exploded in the pit of my stomach, a comfortably full feeling as if I'd just eaten my way through one of our old Taliano meals. I was able to sit up, finding myself still fully clothed. I was probably still able to wear my clothes again, despite them being dusty and dirty. At least they weren't torn to shreds and soaked with blood.

Not much blood, anyway.

My right shoulder throbbed before the pain vanished.

The only question I could ask, the one I'd been trying to ask all along, bubbled up. "Eve?"

He was quiet for a long few moments as the hover began a long slow descent. "That is not her Name."

I don't care. "But she . . . is she Doreen's? *Is* she?" *I have to know. I don't care about anything else.*

"She is Vardimal's Androgyne." The words were heavy. "You do not understand."

I wanted to set my jaw and shove down the sudden flare of anger. It flared anyway, the shout bursting past my lips. "Whose fault is it if I don't understand? You won't *tell me* anything!"

He actually flinched. I don't blame him. My voice rattled everything not bolted down and the hover shook like a nervous cat. The injustice boiled over, and I lashed out at the closest thing, the thing I could be sure of providing a good target.

"You keep lying to me! All of it, *lies!* You won't tell me what I am, you won't tell me what's going on, you just keep lying, lying, *lying!*"

"Yes." His voice sliced through mine.

Whatever I'd expected, it hadn't been simple agreement. It managed to shut me up so he could get a word in edgewise.

His eyes slid away from me, stared across the small cabin. Outside the porthole, faint dappled gray danced—clouds. Wherever we were, it was now cloudy, and still night. "I will lie to keep you safe. I will lie to save you pain. I will lie to ease your mind, and I will lie so you may be certain of me. Answer me this, my curious—if I, even *I* will lie to you, what might another demon who does not cherish you do?"

I think I have an idea. More than an idea, in fact. My new rig lay tangled at the end of the bed. My sword was propped against the nightstand, but Japhrimel was between me and its comforting slender length.

"Is she still alive?" The last thing I remembered was Japh's fingers in its throat. *Her* throat. Which was the true face—the echo of Doreen with my faint iron-clad smile, or the demon with her clotted-ice hair and blue, blue eyes? I wanted, *needed* to know.

"She is more useful to us alive. She is chained, and watched. The human is also alive, a gift for my *hedaira.* Does that please you?"

I'm all aglow, Japh. Why, that's just marvy. Sarcasm smoked inside my head and I restrained myself with an effort that left me shaking, my hands clasping together and biting down. "What did you do?" I barely recognized the raw, shocked whisper as my own.

"What have I not done? I set my trap and baited it, I played the Prince of Hell for a fool and lured him into showing his hand too soon. Today I have cost him a great deal, in pride, in Power, and in peace. The knowledge that he no longer has possession of the one weapon that could kill him has reached Hell, for I made certain of it when I invited him to meet me in the White-Walled City."

"You did *what?*" Open-mouthed shock was apparently the order of the day. The hover's nose tilted down a little more sharply. We were descending, and quickly.

"One of the Prince's marks of favor for his assassin was a certain item. When used, it strips the disguise from a demon, forcing him to take his true form. We are a tricksome species, and sometimes the veil of seeming must be torn. We have different weaknesses. If you know the form

of a demon, you may fight him." A single, elegant shrug.
"Using the Glaive, unfortunately, creates a disturbance that
can be felt in Hell, especially in a place where the walls between our world and yours are so thin. All of Hell knows
the Glaive was triggered in the city. The Prince could not
afford to stay away, as that is the agreed-upon resting
place for one of the decoys."

"Decoys." *Keep talking, Japh. This is the most you've
ever given me, and what do you know? It's too goddamn
late.* I was ashamed as soon as I thought it.

He rose like a dark wave, the mattress creaking slightly
as he did. I tasted dust and bitterness, added to the thick
spice of his blood. The room was narrow and curved,
squeezed under the hull and bare of anything that might
be considered a personal possession—that is, if I didn't
count my new rig. My sword. And my bag, now suddenly
visible on a table bolted to the wall near the porthole.

Japhrimel crossed to the porthole and looked out. His
back was perfectly straight, his shoulders drawn up. Dust
streaked along the curves of his coat, revealing subtle dips
and creases of musculature hidden in the liquid black.
"You must understand, Dante. I have served the Prince
for so long. Obedience became its own kind of trap, and I
buried the rebellion in my heart. I was not free to act until
you freed me. But still . . . I had dreams."

"Dreams?" I didn't mean to sound like an idiot. I just
couldn't seem to say anything applicable or even intelligent.

"The Prince was younger then, too; I was able to hide
the fact that I had only recovered *half* the Knife. He told
me what he wished—that the Anhelikos would hold the
Knife, for they care little who rules Hell as long as their
nests are not tampered with. That if a demon without the

proper signs and signals came to fetch it, they would send it along a route known only to Lucifer and myself, each Anhelikos theoretically knowing only the next stage of the route. I was to create two decoy routes as well. It was my only disobedience in longer than you can imagine, to make all three routes empty games and hide the half of the Knife we possessed . . . elsewhere. Even today I do not know why I did so."

"So you. . . . Is that why you helped Santino escape Hell, with the Egg? Because you were being disobedient?" *Don't interrupt him, Danny. Maybe he'll keep talking.*

"No. I was ordered to do so, by Lucifer himself." Each word was clipped and short. "I bless the day he did, Dante. It brought me to you." He turned away from the window, approached the table with two long steps, and opened my stained canvas messenger bag. The tough cloth made a whispering sound against his fingers.

I scrambled up out of bed, my legs finally obeying me, a hot knot of liquid warmth behind my breastbone. "Leave that alone!"

It was too late. He held up the book, its cover with leather too fine-grained to be animal skin shocking against the goldenness of his fingers. "What price did you pay for this, *hedaira?* What lies came with its presentation to you? I did not tell you of the *A'nankhimel* and their doom for a *reason.* To know that you would be hunted, sooner or later, reviled, suffering endless fear because of a crime you were innocent of—I tried to save you that! I have *tried* to save you from the knowledge of what you have been drawn into, what has been done to you. You hate me, and well you should."

I came to a halt less than five steps away from him, my hands curled into fists and shaking. "You should have told me." Quiet venom dripped from each word. "I don't care what you thought you were saving me from."

"Told you what? How could I have explained what I feared, to you? How could I burden you with *this?*" He tossed the book at me. It was a passionlessly accurate throw, and it landed on my feet with a tiny thud before it slid off to the side, spine-up and open, its pages pressed into the flooring.

We faced each other over a small space of crackling, pulled-tense air. I struggled to contain the rising tide of anguish and red fire inside me.

"Look at what I have done to you." It was his turn to whisper. "No wonder you hate me."

Sheer maddening frustration rivaled the bitterness of dust in my mouth. "I don't hate you." The words felt foreign against my lips. "I can't hate you. That's my goddamn problem." *Or at least one of them. I've got so many others now this one seems like a walk in the holopark.*

It was hard work to bend down, keeping my eyes on him, and pick the book up. The feel of the cover against my fingers was enough to make my gorge rise. I was getting so used to nauseated disgust, I wondered if I'd ever eat again. "Nobody gave me any information with this at all. Selene only knew it was a book on the Fallen. Eve never told me what was in it. Sephrimel showed me *one* picture and . . . gods, Japhrimel, if you're so fucking worried what I'll think of it, why didn't you just tell me yourself? I could have tried understanding, you know."

He actually *shrugged,* a complex eloquent movement. I *hate* demons shrugging at me. They do it so much, like the only thing humans are worthy of is a shrug. Or maybe we perplex them. I'd like to think it's the latter.

Call me an optimist.

"Fine." I gave up. My shoulders slumped. I was too tired to fight with him over this. I had other questions, other problems, and other things I needed to figure out before Lucifer got another crack at me. "Let's move on to something productive, at least. Where's the Knife?"

"Close." Silence stretched like taffy. "I have some other things to tell you, but not yet."

Great. More secrets. "I don't want to hear it." My fingers tensed, pressing into the leather. I struggled with the beast of pain tearing inside my chest. Tearing like glass-clawed fingers around my beating heart.

It took every scrap of self-control I possessed to hold the book out to him. "If it means that much to you, you can have it, and all your goddamn secrets too."

The hover evened out. We'd descended a long way. He didn't move, staring at my hand holding the book the way a mongoose stares at a cobra.

"Just take it," I persisted. "Just fucking take the thing, Japhrimel."

He slid it from my hand gently, as if afraid I'd change my mind. The hover bounced a bit, atmospheric pressure rippling around it. His hand fell back to his side, carrying its cargo. Whatever the goddamn book said, I no longer wanted to know. He couldn't tell me what I was.

Nobody could.

I was broken, I knew that much. I was a wreck in the shape of a woman, and I had something to get done. But most importantly, I was who I decided to be. Hadn't my life taught me at least that much?

I am Danny Valentine. Everything else was just noise.

"Now." I drew myself up in my dusty, bloodspotted

clothes. "You're going to answer a couple questions, and then we're going to get this goddamn thing done. I'm tired of Lucifer fucking around with my life. Fucking around with *me.*" *You can't even comprehend how tired I am of that.* The black hole in my head shivered and retreated under the sound of rushing flame. I pushed both things away, bottled the rage and covered over the horror. "Where's Eve?" I almost said, *where's my daughter?*

I couldn't let the words past my lips. I was keeping my own secrets from him. I couldn't throw any stones on that account, could I.

But oh, how I wanted to.

He actually answered me directly, for once. "Chained, and watched. In the hold."

"Great." I turned on my booted heel and stalked back to the bed, scooped up my rig, and began buckling it on. "Where are we flying to now?"

"Sudro Merica. Caracaz." In Japhrimel's voice was something new—a hoarseness, as if there was something in his throat.

The rig was none the worse for wear, and it creaked much less than it had. I guess that kind of hard use will take the starch out of any gear. It was all to the good as far as I was concerned.

I scooped up my sword. The sound of fire in my head abated, a thin red thread at the bottom of my consciousness. Waiting.

What do we do next, sunshine?

"All right." I rolled my shoulders habitually, settling the rig. "Let's get this run started."

I left him standing there and stamped for the door.

22

I was getting pretty sick of the cargo hold.

McKinley leaned against a stack of plasteel crates, his aura flushed a weird violet, matching the purplish light running over his metallic left hand. My eyes wanted to slide right over him, helped by the smooth shell of *seeming* that wasn't quite a glamour, since it didn't carry any stamp of personality like sorcery or psionic camouflage would. He was like a chameleon, blending motionlessly into his surroundings. His dark eyes met mine and flicked away, and I recognized the hair-trigger tension in him.

Past him, in a space cleared of all gear and boxes, sat a small, slender shape with a flame of pale hair. Her arms locked around her knees, and it became apparent she'd had a hell of a fight. Her sweater was torn, her slacks singed, and she was missing a boot.

I stepped forward. Eve's face was buried in her knees, that pale sleek cap now subtly wrong, ropes instead of the silk of Doreen's hair. I couldn't even *smell* her, and that was wrong too.

"Valentine." McKinley's voice, oddly respectful. "Don't get too close."

Don't tell me what to do. I took another step. I'd shoved my sword into the loop provided on my rig, not trusting myself with edged metal right now. "Eve." All the things I might have said boiled through my head, and I settled for just one. "I know you're not asleep."

Her face came up slowly, a pale dish on jeweled bearings. Doreen's daughter looked at me, and there was nothing human in that blue-fire gaze.

My eyesight was keen even before Japh changed me; thanks to genesplicing it's hard to find anyone with bad sight anymore, except Ludders. I can't see like a Nichtvren, in total darkness—even demon eyes need a few photons to work with. So I stared at Eve, searching the demon's face for any shadow of what she'd looked like before.

Running along the floor between us was a thin silver strip, humming with malignant force as it circled her. It matched the brutally thick cuffs around her ankles and wrists. The silver seemed a part of the metal grating, despite its fluid movement. It was a piece of demon sorcery I'd never seen before and should have been surprised at.

Nothing seemed surprising anymore.

"Why?" I barely had the breath for the word. "Why lie to me?"

One corner of her perfect lips tilted up. She acknowledged the question with a slight, wry smile. "Would you have believed me, if I looked like this?"

"But when you were small—"

"That was humanity. It burned away from me. In Hell." One shoulder lifted a little, dropped. The silver circle responded with a change in pitch, its low evil hum stepping up a half-note and dropping back down.

Damn demons, always shrugging at me. But something else crossed her face—a swift flash of vulnerability, gone in less than a moment. The look of a child caught with her hand in a jar full of candy, incongruous on a demon's face.

I kept forgetting how young she had to be, even if time moved differently in Hell than it did here.

I felt Japhrimel arrive, though he was soundless as Death Himself. His hand closed gently over my shoulder, and I didn't know whether it was to offer support or because he wasn't sure if I'd pitch myself at the circle to free her.

Eve's gaze flickered up past me. She studied Japhrimel intently for fifteen long seconds, the color draining under her golden skin, and dropped her face back into her knees. The air subtly changed, and I got the idea she was ignoring us, very loudly and pointedly.

And very desperately.

Good for you, kid. I couldn't find it in me to blame her. I turned and headed for the end of the cargo bay, brushing past Japh. His hand fell away from my shoulder.

The ladder leading up to the main deck was solid cold plasteel. I rested my hands on a crossbar, staring at my wrists. It occurred to me that they were like Eve's, seemingly frail and made of demon bone. We'd both started out human, hadn't we? Partly human?

Was I still? I felt human where it counted, inside the aching ruin of my heart. "Japh?"

He made no sound, but I felt his attention. He was listening.

"Is that . . . what she really looks like?"

Why was I even asking? I had seen the glamour shred

away from her with my own eyes, I saw her now. I *knew.* But I still wanted to hear it. I needed to hear someone say it.

"We are shapeshifters, my curious." His breath touched my ear; he was leaning in close, the heat of him comforting against my back. I hadn't been this aware of his closeness in a while.

My breath caught in my throat. I leaned forward, rested my forehead on the plasteel. "So what do you look like?" *If you're wearing a glamour, I might as well just get it over with now. Horns? Fangs? Hooves? Let's take a peek. It can't hurt.*

After all, I've shared a bed with you. Does a demon glamour fool the skin as well as the eyes?

Japhrimel considered for a long moment. "What would you like?"

I swallowed so hard I was surprised my throat didn't click. I turned to face him. "No, I mean it. What do you really look like?"

The dimness of orandflu lighting painted the hollows of his face. The hover started to descend again, pressure pushing against my eardrums.

"What would you have me look like, *hedaira?* If it would please you, I can wear almost any shape you can imagine."

You know, before I met you, I might have had trouble believing that statement. Now I don't have enough trouble believing it. I wonder which is worse. "But what are you underneath it? What's the real you?"

A shadow of perplexity crossed his face. "This is the form I have worn most often," he said slowly. "It does not please you?"

Just when I thought I had a handle on this, something new managed to wallop me. "Never mind." I swung back toward the ladder and put my boot on the first rung. "We've got work to do." *I can't believe I'm even having this conversation.* "When are you going to let her out of that circle?"

"When I am certain she is more a help than a threat." His hand came up, touched my shoulder. "Dante—"

I shook him off and began to climb.

23

$\mathcal{W}$e entered Caracaz as morning rose steaming over the city, the hover dropping down into a haze turned rosy. Tiens had given the controls up to Lucas, who guided us down through freight lanes and streams of regular commuter traffic. The Nichtvren had vanished, and I wondered—not for the first time—where he spent his days. If there was a spot for him to sleep during daylight on the hover, it was well hidden.

Vann pushed a battered, bruised, and bandaged Leander out into the main cabin, not very roughly. The Necromance half-stumbled, but the Hellesvront agent made no move to help. From where I sat, straight-backed in a chair magsealed to the flooring with my sword over my knees, I could clearly see the damage done to Leander's face. It turned my stomach.

"Bring him." Japh stood, staring out a porthole dewed with condensation. We'd been flying through high clouds, and the drop into Caracaz's muggy breathlessness would make the hover's exterior stream with water before long.

Vann escorted Leander across the hover's length. I hoped we were going to shift to a smaller craft. Flying around in this barge was enough to paint a big target on us.

Lucas glanced over his shoulder, turned back to the controls with a shrug. The message was clear. Leander was on his own.

Japhrimel let the Necromance stew for a bit. I kept staring at Leander's accreditation tat, his emerald sparkling and singing with the presence of his god. Was he praying?

Would it do him any good? Even I had no idea what Japh was likely to do next. I wasn't complaining much—I was hoping Lucifer couldn't predict him either—but still.

Finally, his profile harsh and clear in the returning light of dawn, Japhrimel moved slightly, clasping his hands behind his back. "Do you know why you are still alive?"

Leander couldn't help it. He shot me a glance, his dark eyes widening. He looked almost naked without his katana and weapons rig, his broad shoulders uneasy without their cargo of leather straps.

"Exactly," Japhrimel said, as if Leander had spoken. "You are alive because it pleases my *hedaira* to see you so, and because it does not matter. There is no compelling reason to remove you. Still, it is a marvelous turn of events, that one such as you would help a demon in rebellion against the Prince."

My ears perked. *Does Japh just mean that he's human and helping out a demon, or does he mean something else? Hegemony federal, which means Leander's domestic internal affairs. Field agent, which means his Matheson score was over the moon to tip him into the domestic-defense program as an active instead of an analyst.*

I sat up a little straighter, and watched the Necromance

turn pale. The sharp smell of human decay under the screen of healthy male pheromones hiked in response to the fact that he was sweating, now.

I didn't blame him. Japhrimel turned away from the porthole and let the full force of his glowing eyes rest on Leander. Vann stepped back, a move calculated to make the Necromance subconsciously aware he was alone.

He handled it well, shrugging and folding his bruised arms. He wasn't cuffed or magtaped; the habit of years of bounty hunting rose under my skin. That was *wrong,* he was a combat-trained psion, a Hegemony field agent, and if I'd been hauling him somewhere I would have made *damn* sure he was trussed up tighter than a Putchkin Yule turkey.

But really, what could he do?

"I'm a sucker for bright-eyed girls with cute smiles." The Necromance actually flashed Japhrimel a cocky grin. His pulse thundered audibly, and a chemical tang of fear spilled through the air.

I had to give him points for sheer brass. I couldn't help myself. A laugh jolted out of me, the soft husky sound broken by the permanent damage done to my throat by the Devil's fingers.

Japhrimel's eyes flickered toward me.

I regained control of myself with an effort that made my hands shake just the tiniest bit.

"You are an agent of the human government." Japhrimel's tone hadn't changed. "You are Lucifer's tool just as surely as a Hellesvront vassal. Why would you, a human, aid a demon in rebellion against the Prince?"

I blinked, replayed my mental footage. Yes, he'd just said that.

"Wait a second." I took a step forward, my boots making a slight creaking sound. "The Hegemony—"

Japh's tone was kind but utterly weary, as if I'd overlooked something so stupid-simple even a child could see it. "Do you really think Lucifer would allow it to remain in power if it was not thoroughly subject to his will?"

"The Alliance—" It occurred to me that surely, if the Hegemony was controlled, the Putchkin Alliance would be as well. And they were the only games in town as far as governments went, unless you were a Freetown with an independent charter—and sometimes, even then. The Hegemony and Putchkin often function as one world government with two major departments rather than rivals. With thermonuclear capability and the freedom of information traffic nowadays, rivalry doesn't make sense. "Oh."

I'd never bothered to think about just how deep the net of financial and other assets demons held on earth was. *Hellesvront,* Japhrimel called it, and he'd used it before while hunting Eve. But to think that those resources reached up into the government itself, that the Hegemony might be infested with Lucifer's influence . . .

Is there anything around that demons don't control?

"Hades." Leander stared at me. "I never thought you were such an optimist, Valentine."

Oh, shut up. The trembling went out of my hands as I took a deep breath. "You're working for Lucifer?"

"I work for my division. We get orders from higher up." Leander rubbed gingerly at his bruised face, stubble rasping against his blunt callused fingers. "You came to New Prague while I was following an arms-trafficking ring. I'd almost gotten in, too. Eight months of work down the drain as soon as I got word you were in town and I was to try and make contact if I could. Seventeen agents in the city got that message, but I was the only one unlucky enough to stumble across you. I was supposed to ID, keep a lock on you, and call in a strike. Orders from high up— they didn't want you dead, just something noisy enough to draw attention to you. I was waiting for the teams to get into position when a hover falls out of the sky and some idiot lets off a plascannon."

I shuddered. The reactive paint on the bottom of hovers and a plas field—*that* had been uncomfortable. Only a moron mixes reactive and plas; the resultant molecular-bond-weakening explosion is enough to give even the most hardened criminals pause.

Plot and counterplot, everyone having an agenda, and me blundering through the middle of it all, trying to keep my head above water. Bait intended to draw Eve out so Lucifer could close his filthy paws on her. All my struggling and striving had been next to useless.

And instead of treading water, I'd finally drowned. "So who dropped the hover on me?" Go figure, everything happening and me fixating on the one unimportant detail.

"You were not the target." Japhrimel hadn't moved his attention; it was still on Leander. His tone wasn't combative, merely flat. "Though the strike was aimed at you, it was me they intended to kill. I have other enemies, *hedaira,* and your death would be a prize to any of them. Lucifer cannot control the avenues from Hell to your world any longer. We are on the brink of chaos."

Tell me something I don't know. The steady hissing whisper of fire under the surface of my thoughts surged; I fought to keep it back. Now was not the time to explode in homicidal rage. *Save it for the next fight, Danny. There's bound to be another one, after all.*

"I got a directive after that, while we were in Saint City." Leander dropped his hands. The hover dropped, water streaming down the porthole. Lucas whistled, a low tuneless sound of concentration as we banked, a wide shallow turn that meant he'd probably spotted our landing area. Vann leaned over his shoulder, murmuring something. "I was supposed to hook up with Omega—that's what we call her, Project Omega—and liaise to neutralize *him.*" A quick sketch of a movement, his chin jerked toward Japh.

"Project Omega?" *Hello? The Hegemony knows about Eve? Did they know about Santino too?*

I had the answer to that one, a cynic's answer. Of course. Trying to hunt Santino down after he'd killed Doreen was just one closed door after another, no help from law enforcement ostensibly because the murdering bastard had incorporated under the Mob laws and those files were sealed, unable to be opened for a simple homicide no matter how hard Gabe and I tried to link him to the other serial murders. You'd think they would have cooperated.

Now I was beginning to see why they hadn't.

The memory of Gabe and me working together, frustration and grief making us both walking time bombs, finally giving up but never really stopping to pick at the scab of Doreen's death, sent a pang right through me. The mess inside my skull twinged, turning over. I owed Gabe; I'd promised to look after her daughter.

Broken promises, a trail of deceit and manipulation.

Just throw Danny Valentine into the snakepit and watch her jump.

"She was supposed to be the Hegemony's way of slipping loose of Lucifer. If we had access to her, we could have experimented. There was a whole division ready to do testing. A real live cooperative demon to study? It's the fucking Holy Grail. The scientists went gaga. Then something happened, she vanished, and the goddamn demons had her." Leander made a slight restless movement, an abortive shrug. "And we couldn't figure out what *you* had to do with it, and how you'd ended up involved with *him*." Another jerk of his chin toward Japh, standing motionless and unblinking. "It was decided to just keep you under surveillance and see if the demons would bite again. They did, and I got sent in."

"Gods." I swallowed. "So that's why you were so intent on sticking around." *And I let you. I even tried to protect you.* Bile rose in my throat, was repressed, retreated. If I threw up now, the only thing that would come up was demon blood, and the thought made me feel even sicker.

"Got a job to do. You know how it is, Valentine."

The worst thing was, I did.

Behind him, the water began to lift off in globular droplets as the temperature equalized. Our descent evened out. Lucas muttered something, and Vann murmured right back.

They're Hellesvront agents too, Vann and McKinley. Why does Japhrimel trust them? Did he lie when he told me they were agents?

I didn't know what to believe anymore. "So what's your job now?"

"Right now I'll settle for staying alive. I've missed

four call-ins. They probably think I'm dead. No big loss, just another agent down in the crossfire." His shoulders hunched, the crossed arms more of a defense now. "We're expendable, even the psions. You get to knowing that for a while and it does funny things to your head."

Was he fishing for sympathy? I didn't have a whole hell of a lot left over for anyone but myself, and even that was in short supply.

The hover juddered a bit as landing gear unfolded. Japh's glowing eyes met mine, and I could have sworn he was asking me for something. I couldn't understand what. I simply stared, my brain shivering between past and present, a monstrous design coming clear. The Hegemony, Lucifer, Japhrimel, Eve . . .

Was there anyone still alive who *hadn't* wanted to use me? When had I become such a game piece? Just pick me up, put me down, shove me from one place to the other. Even what Lucifer did wasn't directed at me—it was a way to hurt Japhrimel, catch Eve. I wasn't even worth personalized violence. No, it was all about who he could hurt *through* me.

Even my god, my safety in times of trouble, my refuge, had used my obedience to His will to spare a murdering *sedayeen* who had killed my best friend. Slaying a defenseless healer was a violation of who I was, but still . . . there was no way, standing over her with my sword in my hand, that I could have kept every vow I'd made, to my god, to my friend, or to myself.

And now this. Gods, demons, the government, everyone had their finger in the pie.

Even Japhrimel, who probably wasn't telling the whole truth either. He was conducting his own war against Lucifer, a war that sounded like it had started before I had ever been born. I might just be a convenient excuse, no matter what affection he felt for me.

Affection? Call it what it is, Danny. He loves you, but he won't tell you the whole truth. Nobody will.

By every god there ever was, I hate being *used*.

My left hand tightened on Fudoshin's scabbard. Were there any more lies waiting to be discovered?

I'll bet there are. You'd better start thinking how you're going to get out of this one alive, Danny. And once you do, where in the world will you be safe? Nowhere. There's going to be game after game as long as Lucifer's alive. The Devil doesn't give up easily.

That left just one option. Playing *back*.

I'd lied too. My sorcerous Will was still strong, despite my betrayal of my sworn word in circumstances beyond my control—but still inexcusable. It was an article of my faith that my word was my bond. That I used my words, my voice, to control and shape the Power necessary to bring a soul back from the dry land of Death, so it was best to speak softly and do what I said I would. Wasn't that who I was, who I had *decided* to be?

How far could I lie and still keep my own soul?

It was another article of faith that Japhrimel loved me, would always come for me, and would do his best to see me through this alive. Was that enough to excuse the lies? How much could I weigh each part of that equation?

Yet another article of faith: that my god would never abandon me by asking me for more than I could give. My right hand crept up, touched my naked right cheek. On my left cheek, the emerald sang a thin piercing note before it spat a single spark, my cheek prickling as the tat moved, a thorny caduceus twisting under my skin.

Not Anubis. Sekhmet. You should swear by Her, now. Who answered when you lay bleeding? Who has not broken faith with you?

Who have you *not broken faith with, Necromance?*

"Dante." Japhrimel, softly, as if he didn't want to disturb me. "It is your decision. I will spare him, as a gift to you. Still, he is a liability. This dog's loyalty is to his masters."

The color drained from Leander's face. It would have been funny, if I'd been in a humorous mood. Why anyone was scared of me while Japh was around was beyond me.

Still, I considered Leander, holding his dark eyes with mine, my left thumb caressing the lacquer of the scabbard. The sword rang softly inside his sheath, just aching to be drawn.

Compassion is not your strongest virtue, Danyo-chan. My teacher's voice when he handed the sword to me, a warning I hadn't known the depths of.

Compassion. It kept fucking me up every time. Staying my hand when I should strike. Being honorable. Submitting to my god, or my ethics. Doing the right thing.

What the hell was the *right thing* now? Had there ever been one right thing?

I used to be so certain. Didn't I used to know what to do, no matter what?

"Leave him alone," I said, finally. "Give him back his weapons. If he needs killing, I'll do it." I held Leander's gaze with mine, and whatever he saw on my face could not have been pleasant. "If they've given you up for dead,

Beaudry, I suggest you start rethinking where your loyalty lies."

With that, I turned on my heel and stalked for the cabin, just as the hoverwhine crested and we touched down on Sudro Merican soil.

24

Caracaz was a center of resistance during the last third of the Merican Era, digging in its heels as the Evangelicals of Gilead rose and the Vatican Bank scandal began to unfold. When the Republic reached its height of power, Caracaz and Old Venezela were a major clearinghouse for supplies to be sent to Centro Merica, where Shamans and others fought the desperate guerilla battles against the Republic's tide. Psions flooded over the borders during the Awakening, joining in the fight against the Gilead fanatics who considered us subhuman, worthy only of extermination—just like anyone else who got in their way.

In pretty much every language now, *Gilead* is a dirty word. *Republic* isn't far behind. You can only fight the whole world for so long before the world starts fighting back, a lesson the Evangelicals didn't learn while they choked on their own blood after the Seventy Days War. But then, fundamentalists aren't bright thinkers. Fanaticism tends to blind people.

Caracaz is built with plasteel and sandy-colored preformed concrete. The ambient Power tastes like coconut oil, hot spicy food, and sweat, with the bite of petroleo underneath it. The crash of petroleo as an energy source had hit here hard, but the War and its buildup provided the city with the chance to become a major trade hub, which the entire country grabbed with both hands. Or it should be said, which the anarcho-syndicalist collectives who had taken over day-to-day running of the country after the crash seized with all hands. The Venezela territory is still administered by those collectives, which make it the nearest thing to a Freetown in the Hegemony.

The old proverb is, *In Caracaz you can make ten fortunes in a week—and lose fifteen.* Just about anything can be bought or sold here, and head on its way in less than an hour to another port. Only in Shanghai is turnover quicker.

In short, it's so busy it's easy to hide a hover. Which was great, since we weren't inconspicuous, in a freight transport the size of a small building.

We landed in a deep transport well, the hover powering down. It was an anonymous berthing, at least until someone started running registry traces. How many people were looking for me now? How many were looking for Eve?

There was a knock on the door, very polite. I turned away from the porthole, where I had been staring blankly at strips of reactive and double-synaptic relays, feeling the familiar urban wash, the surfroar of many minds squeezed into square miles. Japhrimel's borrowed Power kept the screaming chaos away. If he withdrew it, my shields were in no shape to cope, even with the repair work going on. And forget about taking a direct hit, sorcerous or psionic.

I was as vulnerable as it was possible to be, without

him. It was a wonder the connections inside my head hadn't fused, turning me into a mumbling idiot.

Should I call that good luck, or bad?

Vann opened the door, his face set and composed, shades of brown overlapping and the whites of his eyes startling. A brief glance, then he stared at the floor. "Jaf wants you." A pause, letting me absorb the fact that they used the shortest version of his name, when they weren't calling him *my Lord*. Just like I had when I'd first met him. "If you would like to come, that is." So excessively polite.

I wonder what new parade of heartstopping excitement he's got planned next. Another decoy? I rolled my shoulders back, settling the rig more securely, and gave Vann my best *fuck you, sunshine* glare. "Am I really all that necessary?"

The Hellesvront agent didn't even blink. He moved into the cabin, smoothly, freeing himself from the door. "To *him*. So, to us." Another pause, letting me digest an all-new cryptic comment. "Hellesvront is the Prince's toy, but McKinley and I—and some others—were recruited by Jaf. We're his shadow organization, his vassals inside. Something happens to him, we're left without protection. Sometimes the only thing keeping a demon from unzipping your guts is fear of the other demon—the one you belong to. So we'd like to keep you breathing. For *his* sake."

Well, that's a nice bit of news. "Glad to hear it."

"You should be." Vann's thin mouth stretched into a mirthless grin. "If we didn't, there'd be no place on earth you could hide."

I stared past him, at the slice of the main chamber, the

shape of the hull giving it an odd distortion. "You know, that sounds an awful lot like a threat." My throaty whisper, a Necromance's voice with an overlay of demon seduction, turned cold. The small flaming thread running through the bottom of my head paused, swelling slightly.

It would be so easy, even if he was armed to his shiny bright teeth. Even if his stance shifted slightly, shoulders coming up a fraction and his weight pitching a little forward, ready to move in any direction if I exploded.

I didn't blame him.

"Not a threat. The truth." He stepped back, aiming for the door, and edged out, not looking directly at me. It was the way he might ease out of the cage of a not particularly tamed or predictable animal. His soft shoes made no noise against the grated flooring. He didn't even *breathe* loud enough.

Go away. Just go away. I unfocused my eyes and stared at his moccasins, the way his feet moved inside supple thick leather.

He vanished. I let my vision stay hazy for a few moments, breathing deep and soft until the rage retreated, folding back down into its bright ribbon.

"I don't like it," Lucas muttered darkly, glancing back over his shoulder at me. "Leavin' him there is just an invitation for ol' Blue-Eyes to get loose."

"It matters little." Japhrimel walked with his hands clasped behind his back, his long dark coat moving fluidly. The heat painted every surface, a wet Sudro Merican heat smelling of tamales, rice, beef cooked in spices, and the ever-present coconut oil. I'd gone from Chomo

Lungma's deep-freeze to this, and I wasn't unhappy. This weather was purely, blessedly human.

Vann and McKinley flanked me, McKinley hanging back on my right, Vann close enough to touch me on my left. Between them, Japhrimel, and Lucas, I was beginning to feel hemmed-in. They surrounded me like Mob bodyguards around a Family Head.

I shot a look back myself at the hover, drifting gently in its berthing. Leander was locked in the cabin I'd just vacated, and Eve was in the hold, surrounded by a thin silver line.

Japhrimel pressed the button for the cargo lift. "If the Necromance sets her free, where will she go? Lucifer will not care what prey is snared in his nets, and will not treat her kindly now. I am her only chance, and my *hedaira* is her only chance for mercy. No, I think the Androgyne will remain our guest for some time."

I eyed the metal grating. There was an elevator not thirty steps away, along the curve of the platform. A hot wind blew steadily up from the depths of the well, air buffeted by reactive and antigrav.

Thank the gods we're not taking the lift. I couldn't stand it. The thought of being trapped in such a small space made prickles race up my back, spreading down my arms. The claustrophobia was getting worse. I wondered if it was stress.

In fact, I wondered so hard I didn't hear the conversation, slapping myself back into awareness as the cargo lift shuddered to a halt. *Pay attention, Danny. Don't wander.*

I'd been doing more and more of that, lately. All through the hunt for Gabe and Eddie's killer. Staring off into the distance, thinking about the past.

As a coping mechanism, it sucked.

The cargo lift was open plasteel meshwork, no walls to close the air out. I was grateful for that, at least, even though the agents pressed closer and Lucas eyed me speculatively.

We spilled out onto a Caracaz street, all hot sunshine and bright colors. They paint the sandy concrete in primary colors, outside. Under that sun it's an assault, the head reeling and the breath suddenly stopped by a riot of color. The crowd wasn't bad, but we were still outside a transport well. Hovers lifted off every few moments, their rattling whine cycling up as they rose to take their places in the complicated pattern overhead, run by an AI in realtime and watched over by failsafes. Others landed, a stream of blunt reactive-painted undersides feeding into the well.

Japhrimel looked up, taking his bearings. He looked suddenly out of place, a tall golden-skinned man in a long black coat under the oppressive yellow weight of sunlight. The world spun underfoot. I blinked against the assault of light, the unfamiliar weight of Japhrimel's shielding over mine restrictive, bearing down and squeezing me into my skin.

Japh finally tilted his head back down. He reached back with one hand, his fingers open, and I didn't think twice, just stepped forward and laced mine into them.

"Walk with me," he said, as if there was nobody else around. It was suddenly like every other time I'd ever been beside him, close to the not-human heat from his skin.

Even my rage retreated from him.

"Where are we going?" I finally thought to ask.

"To see a Magi. It's not far."

25

It's not hard to hide in cities. That is, in the right *parts* of cities. As a bounty hunter, you get the feel for a place where nobody asks questions—the red light districts, the bordellos and hash dens, the places where a drink makes you friends and another drink makes you liable to get killed one way or another. Places where the air is thick with sex and violence, psychic static to hide even the stain of a demon on the ether.

Unfortunately, we were in the wrong part of Caracaz. It was a quiet, upscale neighborhood, and we walked down a sidewalk in the shade of giant genespliced palms, broad fronds fluttering and drenching the sidewalk with relative coolness. There were no crowds and precious little cover.

So we walked along, two Hellesvront agents, Lucas in his worn boots and bandoliers strapped across his chest, his shoulders hunched, and one tall demon with eyes that glowed even through Caracaz's hot sunlight.

And me. I was beginning to feel more and more conspicuous. Almost naked.

The houses were large, high sand-colored walls surrounding gardens that peeped through iron gates. Several had shimmers of shielding over them, each with its particular tang—a Shaman's spiked honey-smell, another with the earth-taste of a Skinlin. At least Japh's shielding didn't stop me from Seeing here.

Welcome to the psionic district. I wonder who's peering out the curtains, seeing us coming for dinner. The thought of psions running to their windows, peeking at us like old grannies, drew a sharp bitter humor up in my throat.

"Do you think he's home?" Vann stepped carefully, amazingly quiet for someone with so much metal strapped to him.

"He'd better be," McKinley replied, shortly.

Japhrimel didn't even slow down, though his steps were shorter to compensate for mine. He strode right up to a low, pretty villa behind a scrolled-iron fence, the walls blocked in red and yellow, harlequin paint screaming in the heat of the day and covered with a nervous, shifting mass of energy. I catalogued it before I could stop myself—Magi, with the subtle spice-tang that meant both *active* and *demon-dealing.*

Japh broke stride only once, to wait for the gates. They were already opening on silent maghinges, the curtain of energy parting to let us through.

Someone's expecting us. Knock knock, demon calling. I kept a straight face with difficulty. The front of the house, pillared to within an inch of its life and covered with yellow and blue mosaic—I suppressed a shudder—yawned sleepily and regarded us with falsely closed eyes, each window blind with polarized glass.

The door was a concrete monstrosity hung on maghinges and reinforced with shielding so strong it sent a weak glimmer even through the vicious sunshine. *Some-*

one's paranoid, was my first thought. And, *I wish I'd had shielding like that when Japh came to my door the first time.*

Too late, sunshine.

Japh didn't even knock. He simply stepped close to the door and stopped, regarding it with a narrow green gaze.

He didn't have to wait long. The door creaked, the shielding's shimmer pulsing. A slice of cool darkness grew as someone pulled it open, frictionless hinges working slowly with the mass.

A breath of cooler air slid out, fragrant with musk, spice, and the thick sweetness of *kyphii.* The Magi in the door was well over six lanky feet tall, with large paddle-fish hands and skin shaded a rich dark cocoa. His chiseled lips set themselves in something less than a grimace, despite the laugh lines bracketing his mouth and fanning from his chocolate eyes. He wore a loose indigo tunic and a pair of blue canvas pants with enough pockets and loops to make any plasteel worker proud. Bare feet resting gently against the floor, placed just so, told me he was combat trained. The scimitar riding his back, its hilt topped with a star sapphire, told me so as well, quietly and with no fuss.

He watched Japhrimel the way I might watch a poisonous snake hanging on a tree branch right before it's hurled at me.

"Anton." Japh got right to the point. "Your services are required."

The ripple of fear spiking through the smell of dying human cells plucked at my control. My lips parted, the fear scraping against raw edges on my shielding, taunting. My Magi-trained memory gave a twitch, sending a hook through dark waters, fishing for a name to match the familiarity of his face. His tat, fluorescing with Power and inked with dullglow to make it visible against his skin, was a Krupsev, its spurs and claws fitting nicely on his cheek.

Then I had him. I'd seen the newspapers and holostills, not to mention the retrospectives. "Anton Kgembe." I was too shocked to whisper. "But you're *dead!*"

The Magi's eyes flicked to me, their irises so dark the pupil was almost indistinguishable. "So they tell me." His voice had the crispness of Hegemony Albion, each syllable precisely weighted. "My Lord. You are welcome in my house, and your companion as well." He stepped aside, and Japhrimel moved forward, taking me with him.

"You have not lost your courtesy." Japh's tone veered from politeness toward amusement, settled somewhere between. A cool draft folded around us, and Lucas made a slight tuneless whistling sound as his worn boots touched the floor.

Inside, it was dark before my eyes adapted. The floor was bare stone, the interior walls mellow wood hung with loose linen hangings and a few priceless, restrained pieces—mostly masks, none prickling with life or awareness but still gorgeous and worth a great deal to any Shaman for their aesthetics alone.

The Magi padded in front of us, his back very straight and the sandpaper perfume of fear roiling off his aura. He didn't *look* like the most powerful Magi in the world, and he further didn't look like a man who had died years ago in an industrial accident. He looked healthy and unassuming, just like any other combat-trained psion wandering around. He didn't even seem all that twitchy.

He also didn't look like the most dangerous Left Hand theorist around, the one who had single-handedly revised the entire canon of those who worship the Unspeakable. Kgembe's Laws, four principles of dealing with Left Hand magick, had been standardized only because they were so effective the Hegemony and Putchkin Alliance needed some way of dealing with practitioners who used them for purposes outside the law. In other words, he was responsible for one of the biggest cover-your-ass moments in Hegemony psionic-affairs history.

All things considered, I figured he had a legitimate reason for wanting to be dead.

He's a Left Hander. That means dangerous *and* not particularly careful about casualties *all in one pretty package.* I suppressed a shiver. Japh's arm tightened around my shoulders. The scar sent another warm oil-bath down my skin.

"Might I inquire what I'll be doing for you, my Lord?" Kgembe's tone hadn't altered its crisp politeness. The Hegemony Albion stiff upper lip at its finest. The doors closed with a click, sealing us in coolness and quiet, the walls thrumming with shielding that felt familiar because it was demon-laid.

I was beginning to suspect I knew which demon.

Japhrimel glanced down at me, his face unreadable. "You will be opening a door into Hell, and keeping it open long enough for one demon to pass through."

I slammed the Knife down on the tabletop. Glass cracked with a sound like projectile fire, a single well-placed shot.

I didn't even feel bad for killing someone else's furniture. *"No."* My voice cracked too, like a young boy's.

The small room was lined with bookshelves, its polarized windows looking onto a central courtyard teeming with lush green. A bird feeder stood on a graceful curve of iron just outside, and a fountain plashed musically, audible even through the glass.

"There is no other way." Japhrimel's face was set and drawn, his eyes veiled as he stared at the Knife. "Creating a scene does not help."

I folded my arms, mostly to disguise how my hands were shaking. The Knife hummed inside its new sheath. "You hid the other half of this thing in *Hell?*"

"It seemed a fine idea at the time. Lucifer is not at home—he is traveling the wide world, dispensing his own justice and hunting for both us and his wayward Androgyne. I may very well go unnoticed."

"Lucifer's looking to finish me off. What am I going to do if he finds me and you're stuck in Hell?" When I got right down to it, *that* was what worried me most.

Lo, how the mighty have fallen. And I used to be so tough.

Japhrimel clasped his hands behind his back and inclined his chin, slightly. "Vann and McKinley will protect you. If need be, they will sacrifice themselves for your safety."

"Oh, that just makes me feel *so much* better." Sarcasm. The last refuge of the doomed. Not to mention that I didn't trust either of them. I was getting to the point where I didn't trust *anyone.*

"We have little time. At any moment, Lucifer may find the other two decoys are merely that—empty boxes. Then he will know how far my betrayal extends. When that happens, it will be war. He will scour the earth with his minions, those he can afford to trust. They should be few, but they are powerful. And he has an endless supply of the Low Flight to work his will."

The rock in my throat swelled. The Knife's finials writhed silently. It was a hideous feeling, staring at the inhuman geometry of the thing and feeling that it had *just* moved, and that I wouldn't necessarily notice or remember if it moved again. "This isn't helping."

"I would take you with me, were it possible."

The thought of going back into Hell dried my mouth. So much for hiding my shaking hands—my fingers bit into my arms and my rig creaked slightly. What could I say? *Gee, thanks, but the last two times I've been I haven't enjoyed it a bit.* I shook my head, actually feeling all the blood drain from my face. Something occurred to me, then. "That's why you went back into Hell while we were in Toscano. You went to see if you could get a chance to get your hands on the other half."

His mouth tilted up at the corners, a rueful expression. "All the hosts of Hell save me from your ideas, my curious. Yes, I thought it might be possible to retrieve it. The Prince kept too close a watch on me."

"Which meant you suspected something."

"I suspected a time would come when my potential value to Lucifer was outweighed by my status as *A'nankhimel*. After all, Lucifer left you alive." A single, short nod. "When I returned to myself after dormancy, I thought it very likely, so I waited. When he called for us again, I knew half the Knife of Sorrow would perhaps afford me an edge, and you some protection. Then I could collect Sephrimel's half at leisure before anyone discovered my plan."

"When were you going to get around to telling me *this?*"

"We have had little time, of late, and we have even less now." He reached down, touched the oiled wooden hilt with one golden finger. Pulled his hand away, as if it had pricked him. "I need your help, my curious."

Funny, you seem to be doing all right on your own. Why don't you, Eve, and Lucifer fight this out, and leave me alone? The Knife hummed, a low dangerous sound. "Nobody in this thing needs my help," I muttered.

"I do. You freed me from Lucifer, you mourned my dormancy, you brought me back. If anyone can be said to own one of my kind, I am yours. Give me the freedom to act in this matter."

Give you? "You're going to act whether I *give* you anything or not. You always have."

"Give me some credit for seeking to change, even at this late hour." It was his turn for a sardonic tone.

Why is it that as soon as I think you're a complete bastard you say something like that? "Credit given, Japh. Fine. If this is what we have to do, let's do it." I turned on my heel and stalked away from the table, leaving the Knife in its spiderweb of broken glass.

"Dante."

I stopped.

He approached me silently. "This is yours."

I turned my head a bit. He gingerly proffered the Knife, hilt-first. In his hands it actually looked normal, the alienness of its geometry matched by the subtle difference of his bone structure.

It would be idiotic not to take it and use it, especially if Japh was going to make a suicide run into Hell.

Story of your life, sunshine. You're on your own.

I took it, its unholy satin warmth sliding into my palm, rattling the bones of my fingers with its low hum.

Either shard will wound beyond measure a demon, even one of the Greater Flight. Sephrimel's voice. He'd proved it, too. So had the bird-feathered demon.

Japh shook his hand, a quick short movement, as if ridding his skin of the feel of the thing. "I will return." He made it sound like a fact instead of a promise. "As quickly as I may. Time moves differently in Hell."

Don't I know it. "If you're going to do it, do it." For once I sounded steady, and strong. "Let's not wait around."

26

The walk back to the hover was too short for serious brooding and far too long for me to feel anything other than horribly exposed and completely vulnerable. I wanted to stay and watch, but Magi don't practice in front of other psions . . . and as Japh had pointed out, a doorway to Hell was not anything I wanted to be around.

Because if something can go in, something might be able to come *out*. So we all stepped merrily out Kgembe's front door.

Without Japhrimel.

Ten minutes later the scar in the hollow of my left shoulder went numb, a varocained prickling that probably meant he was nowhere in the normal world. I'd felt that before, and it was miserable to have confirmation of what it meant.

Vann spoke once. "Don't worry. He'll be back before you know it."

When I said nothing, he shut up. The rest of the walk was accomplished in complete silence, except for Lucas swearing under his breath, a steady monotony of obscenities mixed in different languages, a song of nervousness.

That certainly didn't help my mood. Wet heat lay thick and clotted against every surface, the shadows knife-edged and drenched with color. I carried my sword, wanting it to hand.

Just in case.

Sirens boiled through the air as we drew closer to the transport well.

That doesn't sound good. Precognition tickled my nape under tangled hair. Still, why assume that every disturbance in Caracaz had to do with me?

We rounded the corner. *Because it probably does, Danny.*

There was a snarl of hover traffic in holding patterns and a column of black smoke lifting from the depths of the well. I stared, Vann cursed, and McKinley pushed me back around the corner. "Stay back. Lucas?"

"On it." The yellow-eyed man unholstered a plasgun and set off down the street, moving quickly but smoothly. He looked bleached, surrounded by blocks of primary color.

Who the hell put McKinley in charge? I swallowed my protest and tried to peer around the corner. McKinley pushed me back, his metallic left hand glittering. A fine sheen of sweat covered the Hellesvront agent's forehead. "Just a minute, Valentine. Let's not be hasty."

"Leander. And *her.*" *Eve. Or whoever she is.*

"Lucas'll see what's going on. We don't want to risk you." He exchanged a worried look with Vann, one I could decipher all too easily. This changed things a little. It was faintly possible the column of smoke had nothing to do with us.

Faintly.

The semi-industrial district butting up against Kgembe's quiet neighborhood provided no cover at all. I felt like a huge neon-lit sign. *Tasty demon treat, just come and take a bite.*

"Mac." There was a long, low, sibilant hiss—Vann had drawn a knife.

"I know." McKinley let out a short sharp breath, and I smelled sudden peppery adrenaline from both of them under the dry stasis-cabinet smell of Hellesvront. "Valentine?"

"What?" My right hand almost-cramped, and I squeezed my swordhilt and felt every nervestring pull itself taut. This suddenly began to feel normal. There was violence approaching.

I didn't mind a bit.

"If this gets ugly, you'd better run. As fast and as far as you can. We'll take care of the rest."

We'll see about that. "What is it?" *A demon, all right. Which one, and where, and what the hell are you two going to be—*

I didn't even get to finish the thought. They boiled out of the daylight, low unhealthy shapes with skittering legs, and I swallowed a scream before McKinley shoved me so hard I stumbled. *"Run!"* McKinley screamed.

My sword cleared its sheath, and the rage woke in a blinding red screen.

Oh, no. I have had enough of running. I rocketed forward past Vann, who had gone into a crouch as one of the things leapt, an uncoordinated fluid movement twisting its flexible two-part body. It looked like a nightmare of a spider, with the off-kilter grace of something demonic. It was also sickly-hot, a feverish icy heat cutting through the sunshine and raising my hackles. A coughing roar exploded, either from my throat or from someone's projectile gun.

No. It was me. It was the cry of a hunting cat.

I ducked into a crouch, sword whipping in an arc, blue flame painting the air behind it in a sweet natural curve as the scabbard clattered to the concrete and my left hand closed around the hilt of the Knife, ripping it free.

Tchuk. Fudoshin split demonic flesh, and the spider thing made a screeching hurtful sound. I rose from the crouch, the long muscles in my legs providing impetus, and leapt, twisting with the follow-through of the slash. The Knife whipped out, following the arc, and the hellthing screamed again.

I hit the ground before I'd finished my yell, my throat scorching with the sound.

And *fire* bloomed. Red-yellow flames coughed into existence, running wetly over the thing's bristling, glassy black hide. The scar hummed with Power, flushing along my skin and armoring me in liquid heat.

Had it always been this simple? The world was no longer a garden of threat and fear. Instead, it was a clear, shimmering web of action and reaction, violence and death. All I had to do was *look* to see the shining path of killing that would free me from this.

It had never felt so right to destroy everything in my path.

"Valentine!" McKinley, screaming. I pivoted on the ball of my left foot, bringing the sword around again, and engaged the second spider. Plasfire crackled around me, the air seared with a stinging smell of something dry and

bristled, its mouth stuffed with silk, flicked into a candle-flame and shriveling.

Something ripped along my calf, but I paid it no heed. Short thrust, pivoting again, boots scraping the concrete, and the Knife let out a high keening as I plunged it into the spider's back. The horrid gulping noise cut short, a flood of hot sickening Power jolting up my arm before I pulled the blade free and ducked, venomous black blood flying.

More whining plasbolts. There were so many of them, the spiders clicking and hissing, moving to flank me. Rage smoked and strained as the reflex of a lifetime spent bounty hunting calculated the odds and came up with something I didn't quite like.

They were about to surround me.

Don't care, the rage whispered. *Kill them. Kill them all. Make them pay.*

It hit me hard and low, driving me down as a laserifle whined. I landed hard, twisting, and almost drove the Knife into McKinley's throat before I realized he wasn't one of *them.*

It was harder than it should have been to stop myself.

The spiders screeched and writhed, black rotting blood steaming on the concrete. The aftermath of a repeating laserifle isn't a pretty sight, and these creatures seemed even more vulnerable to lasefire than the hellhounds. The smell was incredible, but even more incredible was the sound of little bristled demon feet scratching, scratching, *scratching.*

More of them, and they're massing. I gulped at stale, fetid air. The heat was incredible.

"Get *up!*" McKinley hauled on me, I scrambled to my feet. "Now *run, goddamn you!*"

I didn't wait to be told twice. Still, every muscle in me resisted for the first few steps, wanting to turn back and kill until there was nothing left. He shoved me again, right between the shoulderblades, and it took every vanishing thread of control I had left not to spin and plunge bright steel into the man's body.

I ran.

His footsteps followed mine as we flashed through wet sunlight and sharp-edged shade, harsh heaving breaths echoing in my straining ears. I heard more lasefire, and the chattering of projectile fire. On the far end, another explosion rocked the transport well.

They're certainly going all-out, aren't they. Whoever they are. I wonder if I'll ever find out. Does it matter?

I can move very quickly, especially since Japhrimel taught me to use the demon-born strength he'd given me. McKinley kept pace, having enough breath to yell when I instinctively bolted left at the next intersection, impelled by the idea that I had to find some cover. The city thrummed, a deep well of ambient power at its core beckoning. There was enough static in those depths to hide me, maybe.

Except for the sudden ravine cutting across our path, a waist-high railing and hover traffic whizzing by. A major traffic lane, an artery feeding the city's throbbing heart.

Oh, shit. I was moving too fast, dug my heels in, and skidded to a stop.

McKinley almost ran into me, gasping for breath. He snapped a quick glance down into the hovertraffic. "Do you trust me?"

What? "What?" I looked over my shoulder. The street seemed clear, but the shadows warped in a way I suddenly didn't like. As I looked, one of the shadows developed legs and skittered out into the hot sun, sending up a high piercing cry.

"Do you *trust* me?" McKinley repeated. He still held a knife, the blade reversed along his right forearm, his metallic left hand limned with pale violet.

I had no time to lie. "No." *I don't trust you. I don't even like you.*

"Fine." He grabbed, his left hand tangling in my rig's straps, and *hauled.* The railing hit me at hip level, he yanked again, and we tumbled over the edge.

Instinct pulled my arms and legs close, I twisted like a cat in midair and almost crunched into the side of a freight hover, its wash of warm air stinging my eyes. Gravity eased for a heart-clenching moment, McKinley fell free, and we landed *hard* on a moving surface, the breath driven from my lungs in a *hungh!* of effort that might have been funny if it hadn't hurt so goddamn much.

"—ow—" My voice was very small in the rushing wind.

He'd aimed us for a hovertrain, bulleting along at the bottom of the trough. If I'd been human, the fall would have killed me. As it was, I shook the stun out of my head and made it to my feet, sword in one hand and Knife in the other, miraculously mostly unharmed. Wet warmth dripped into my eyes before black blood sealed the hurt away. The top of the train was dimpled from my landing, lines of force clearly showing in the plasteel.

Hope we didn't scare anyone inside.

McKinley was on all fours, coughing up bright crimson

blood. He looked terrible, and his ribs on one side were malformed, hammered in by the force of our landing.

Oh, lovely. This is ever *so much better.* I opened my mouth to say it, but a motion further down the flexible snake of the hovertrain caught my eye.

Shit. I spared another glance at McKinley, whose eyes had rolled back into his head. The violet glow around his left hand flashed, getting brighter, and crackling noises punctured the wind-sound as his ribs snapped out, mending.

He'll live, the voice of experience inside my head whispered. *But not for long, if they get to him in this state.*

Loping on all fours up the hovertrain's bouncing back, their bald heads glistening in the golden light and their eyes firing when they passed through brief shutterclicks of shadow, were imps. Their long, waxen-white flexible limbs bent in ways no human's would, and they snarled and chattered through the roaring wind as the train took a sharp bend, my knees flexing to keep me upright. My sword came up, blue flame streaming and dripping from its keen edge, its heart burning white-hot, visible even through daylight.

I could just leave him here. I really could.

I launched myself over McKinley, who blurted out something through his coughing and choking for breath, and ran headlong for the imps, not realizing I was screaming in defiance until I ran out of breath and slammed into the first imp with a sound like hovers colliding. The Knife rammed into the thing's chest, and its screech was sweet music as rage took me again, the inside of my skull turning into a grassfire, smudges of charcoal and dull stained crimson taking the place of thought.

Front foot planted, yank the Knife free and swing back foot around, whirling to extend in a lunge as effortless as it was deadly, a roar of speed-laced wind stinging my eyes, my hair rising and obscuring my vision. It didn't matter, I wasn't using my eyes to track them anyway. They were smears of black-diamond fire on the landscape of Power, interlocking cascades of intent and threat. I lost track of myself in the clear light of what Jado called *mind-no-mind*, moving with a speed and clarity I had rarely achieved in my human life and never since—until now.

The enemy vanishes, Danyo-chan, and all you face is yourself.

The leap uncoiled, my knees coming up, and I *kicked*, my boot meeting another imp's face. The sound of a watermelon with glass bones dropped on scorching pavement was satisfying, to say the least, but not as satisfying as carving the thing's arm off on my way down, landing splay-footed and bouncing again, the train's rollicking passage suddenly a rhythm I had no trouble catching.

Just like riding a slicboard, eh, Danny?

The flood of feverish Power up my arm from the Knife was almost natural. Gritty ash exploded, demonic flesh sucked clean of vitality, and the sound I heard—a falsetto giggle, high and clear as ringing glass in an empty room after midnight—was my own insane laughter. I was *laughing* as they swarmed me, jaws champing and sharp teeth clicking through foam, maddened by daylight or by my presence, I couldn't tell.

I was still making that sound when McKinley grabbed the back of my rig again. The train halted for one vertiginous second, and I realized what was happening as it fell away from underfoot and we launched out into

space again. The hovertrain was heading down a sharp
almost-vertical slope to plunge underground, probably a
commuter line, and we were in freefall again as one imp
leapt the sudden distance, slavering and champing, for my
throat.

Landed, *hard*, breath driven from my lungs again and
something snapping in my right leg, a sudden sickening
sheet of pain bolting through the clarity I'd just achieved.
McKinley was cursing, low and steady in a hoarse broken tone. My hair stung my eyes, whipped into a tangled
mass by the wind. I fetched up on my side, trying to get in
enough breath to scream as the freight hover we'd landed
on bounced, a sudden application of force controlled by
its whining gyros. The imp vanished into the slipstream,
not lucky enough to catch our trajectory.

Oh, ow. Ouch. Agony rolled through the rage, sharpen-
ing it like a shot of vox sharpens a sniffer's senses. Pulling everything into a different kind of clarity. *"Sekhmet
sa'es,"* I moaned, the words filling my mouth like hot
copper blood. *Why does it take getting the shit beat out of
me before I feel human again?*

"Don't *ever* do that again!" McKinley yelled. "Goddammit! I'm trying to *protect* you!"

*You didn't look in any shape to take on those guys,
buddy boy.* My right femur crunched with pain as the
bone swiftly healed itself, demon metabolism running
fiercely, heat blurring out from my skin. It actually felt
cold with the wind howling as us, the freight hover moving at a good clip away from the trainline.

Caracaz wheeled above and below, skyscraper spires

piercing hot hazy sky, stretching down to pavement crawling with crowds below. Ambient Power stroked my skin, interference rising like steam to cloak my aura. *This is better.*

This, I can work with. I coughed, swallowed a mouthful of something too warm and nauseatingly slick to be spit, and tested my right leg. It hurt like hell, but it was better. I made it up to hands and knees, the hilts jarring against my palms as the hover bounced again. The Knife hummed, a low satisfied sound that suddenly made me feel like emptying my stomach.

Quit it, Danny. Puking won't get you anywhere. I snapped a glance over my shoulder—the hovertrain had vanished. I wondered if the imps had survived.

I got my feet underneath me, made it up. My right leg ached fiercely, the bone assaulted and unhappy. The scar sent another warm pulse of Power down my skin, and I was suddenly glad Japhrimel's repair work on my shields had held up.

And glad that neither imp nor spider-thing had been able to use Power against me.

McKinley grabbed at my shoulder, and I controlled the twitch that could have buried the Knife in his guts. *Twitchy, twitchy, Necromance. Mellow down easy.* I came back fully into myself and felt suddenly . . . what was it?

Whole. Cleansed, the fire of rage having burned something sticky and viscous away from me. I'd fought them off. I'd *won.*

I liked the feeling. I wanted it to last.

I tore myself out from under McKinley's hand. "Watch it."

"We've got to get off this thing." He checked the sky,

his black hair lifting on the wind of our passage, cut now because the freight hover was in a downtown holding pattern.

My eyes followed the loops and curves, hovers delicately woven into streams of unsnarled traffic. *This one's remote from the realtime AI controller, probably, since it didn't change course when we thumped into it. At least, let's hope so.* My eyes stung, whipped by wind and hair. I should have tied it back, but how was I to know I'd go jumping off hovers?

You should have guessed, Danny. Isn't that how these things always go?

"There." McKinley pointed. A residential high-rise, with the hoverlane going directly over it. The fall was bad but not immense, and there was plenty of room for error.

"You want me to break my leg again?" I sounded delighted, the remainder of the chilling little giggles spilling through my voice.

"Better than the alternative," he snapped. Dark circles had bloomed under his eyes, and he was chalk-pale. The violet glow around his left hand had subsided.

"Guess so." The Knife slid back into its sheath. "What about Vann and Lucas?"

"They can take care of themselves. They'll provide a distraction, it's part of the plan."

"Plan? What *plan?*" *There was a plan?*

"Standard for bodyguard duty. If we get separated, Vann goes low and fast and loud, drawing everyone away. I get the package and we rendezvous." He coughed, a racking sound, and winced. His ribs didn't look staved-in, as they had before. I wondered just how fast a Hellesvront agent healed.

"Where?" *I would have liked to know this, you know.*

"Where else? Hegemony Europa. Paradisse, actually. We've got a safe place there. That is, if it hasn't been blown. That town's always crawling with demons." His lips pulled back from his teeth, a sharp delighted grin. "Don't worry, Valentine. We're going to keep you in one piece for our lord, whether you like it or not."

27

*P*aradisse started out as a Roma Taliano colony, back in the mists of time. During the era of the Religions of Submission Franje became a country, and the city grew like a pearl around the muddy banks of a river now running deep underground. Layer upon layer of history added itself to each street, each house, each tower.

During the Awakening the Old Franje government—still not folded into the nascent Hegemony—threw open the city as a sanctuary for the emerging psionic community, sheltering them from the ravages of the Evangelicals of Gilead. Kochba bar Gilead had pronounced psions abominations, and the beginning years of the Awakening were marked by death camps and persecutions, rising to a fever-pitch during the bloodbath that led to the only tactical nuclear strike of the Seventy Days War, the bombing of the Vegas Territory. Paradisse, however, was shelter for any psion who could reach it, and the Awakening accelerated even as the Evangelicals choked to death on their own fanaticism, their vestigial gift to the social fabric the Ludder party and their xenophobic hatred of psions and paranormals—not to mention the lingering distaste of normals for anything psionic or paranormal.

While her daughter Kebec is pearl and shimmer, Paradisse *shines*. The city throbs with light, glowing spires crisscrossed with moving walkways, hanging gardens, open-air cafés with climate control, each zipping hover gilded and each slicboard leaving a glittering trail in the effervescent air. Paradisse has been built on for centuries, and even though everything is Hegemony Europa now still the Old Franje shines through, in all its aesthetic and chauvinistic splendor. Aboveground, on the Brightside, Paradisse is often used in holovid representations of nirvana, and artists have wandered its upper byways for centuries, sketching and immortalizing.

Underground, under the centuries of accumulated human habitation, is something else.

The Darkside of Paradisse isn't like the Jersey Core. It isn't even like the Tank in Saint City. It's Chill-fed urban blight, true, but down in the Darkside the rule is assassination, stealth, and debauchery. Some parts of the Darkside are mostly safe for regular citizens to go slumming; in those slices the bordellos and hash dens are strictly policed by Hegemony police regulars, Hegemony federal marshals, and a contingent of freelancers known as the Garde Parisen.

The rest of the Darkside isn't somewhere you want to go, even on a bounty. I wondered if the running sore of urban decay would begin to heal now that there was a cure for Clormen-13—Chill, the drug that caused so much death and destruction. It would have been nice, but if history has taught us one thing, it's that people *want* to get high. The pharma companies would come up with more drugs to be abused, and the Mob would sell them. As Old Franje says it, *plus ce change . . .*

That's the problem with studying history. It will make even the sunniest optimist a cynic. For someone with my pessimistic bent, it gets downright fucking depressing.

Two days after escaping Caracaz during a bloody sunset—as stowaways on a trans-ocean freight hover, no less—I sat very still on a chair in the middle of a dark little hole of a room, my sword across my knees. There hadn't even been a chance to find a scabbard for the blade, despite the fact that wandering around with naked steel was likely to draw notice.

Outside the curtained window, the Darkside seethed.

McKinley twitched the curtain aside, slowly, and peered out into a narrow street lit only by sodium-arc lamps. Down here under the rest of the city, it was always night. The immense press of centuries and dirt overhead threatened to trigger claustrophobia with every breath I took.

I closed my eyes and breathed. The wards I'd put on the walls and window—subtle, gentle wards, meant only to warn me if someone was looking at the room—shivered uneasily. I wished I could shield the room like Japhrimel did, but that would have been like advertising my presence on the local holoboards.

My shoulder was still numb. Now I knew that feeling. It meant Japh was in Hell, somewhere far away from the normal world. If anything could be said to be *normal* nowadays. The ban on Magi practicing hadn't slowed down the ferment one bit, psions being notoriously edgy when denied the chance to practice their gifts. Magi were still showing up dead or going missing, and the Hege-

mony had its hands full with the confusion *that* was causing. Industrial espionage and theft was at an all-time high.
The holonews was full of chaos and destruction.

There were other whispers too—of *things* glimpsed
on the street in broad daylight. Things not seen since the
Awakening, when psionic and sorcerous talent flowered
and the world was turned on its ear again, taking a collective jump into the future and struggling free of the Era of
Submission.

The underworld of bounty hunters and mercenaries
was alive with the news that I was out there somewhere,
and worth a fantastical sum dead or alive, if you could just
figure out who to deliver me to. Information on my movements would fetch a fine price too.

Since I hadn't moved from this room since we got
to Paradisse, I could only imagine what was going on.
McKinley had made one run for supplies, not bringing
back a scabbard, and returning pale and shaking just a
little, smelling of demon and adrenaline. He brought back
food, several bottles of distilled water, and two medikits.
And he didn't hold it against me when I met him at the
door with a projectile gun, my finger tight on the trigger—and the Knife in my other hand.

I was liking him more than I had, which still wasn't
much. Still, I slipped the sheathed Knife inside my bag.
The throbbing whisper of the thing set me on edge, and I
didn't need more of a reason to lose my temper.

I had plenty of reasons anyway, and a naked sword as
well.

I held on to the armrests. The room was in a rundown
little boarding-house deep in one of the worst sections of
the Darkside, enough pain and despair—not to mention

illicit sex, spikes and eddies of violence, and just plain psychic noise—to almost cover up the stain of my aura on the landscape of ambient Power. It was barely furnished, just a cot and this chair, and a ramshackle table made of splinters and glue. McKinley had taken to sleeping on the floor, his hand on the hilt of a knife and his eyelids lifting whenever there was the slightest noise.

I didn't sleep.

Instead, I closed my eyes and breathed, the red ribbon of flame sliding at the bottom of my conscious mind comforting. It was the same comfort I used to associate with the blue glow of Death, the rising crystal traceries of my god's attention. My sword rang softly, and the Knife hummed in its sheath, responding to each twist and curve of rage. My fingers sometimes lifted and touched the back arc of the katana, warm metal responding to me like a purring cat.

Waiting is the hardest part of anything, bounty hunt or combat run. The circular mental motion can be maddening. Add to that McKinley pacing, peering out the windows, or dozing lightly with one eye open, and you had a recipe for wearing my nerves down to bare threads.

Not that there was much tread to wear off.

I slid out of the chair, settling down cross-legged on the floor. My bag was flung near the chairlegs, a forlorn little canvas pile. I opened the top flap, laying my sword aside but within easy reach, and dug for a familiar hank of blue silk, knotted tightly.

The fabric smelled of *kyphii,* gun oil, and faint nose-tingling human sweat, as well as the ever-present taint of demon spice. I had to pick at the knots for a while before they finally gave way, and my worn deck of tarot cards with their blue-and-black crosshatch backs lay in a nest of silk.

I scooped them up, smoothing the silk out, and shuffled them with quick gunning snaps. McKinley tensed, turned his head to watch. His profile was almost ugly, a narrow nose and the bruising of exhaustion under his eyes, his mouth set like he tasted something bitter.

I hadn't touched my cards in a long time. When I'd been living with Japh in Toscano, there didn't seem much need. And since he'd broken the news that Lucifer wanted my services, I hadn't had time for any quiet reflection, let alone divination.

I snap-shuffled them again, the sound very loud in the empty room. Echoes whispered off the walls. McKinley said nothing.

The cards almost laid themselves out. *Two of Blades. Death,* with a skull's grimace looking pained instead of its usual saucy smile. *The Tower,* screaming faces and shattered stones. The *Devil* card fluttered as I laid it down, despite the absolute stillness.

The next card was blank.

Well, that's useless, Danny. It only tells you something you already know. My rings sparked, snapping as Power swirled in the charged air, something about to happen.

"What is it?" McKinley's soft whisper almost hid the low sound of a knife sliding from its sheath.

I've seen these cards before. My eyes flicked toward the door just as it resounded with three hard knocks, shivering in its frame.

I froze. Memory curled over inside my skull, past sliding seamlessly into the present. McKinley ghosted between me and the door, his left hand suddenly aglow with violet light. My right hand curled around the sword's <u>hilt</u>, yet I didn't try to push myself up from the floor.

I smelled musk and baking bread, and I thought I knew who it was. I didn't reach for my bag and the Knife's almost-audible pulsing.

Another cascade of knocking, fast light polite raps. McKinley glanced back at me, black eyes narrowed.

Suddenly I heard a rapping, as of someone gently tapping, tapping at my chamber door. I swallowed, hard. The Knife's humming rattled against my hip. "You might as well answer that." *If they're knocking, they haven't attacked yet.*

He eased forward, weight balanced catlike. "Be ready."

For what? But I only nodded. My hair fell forward into my eyes, I blew it irritably away with a sharp exhale.

McKinley edged toward the door. He was four steps from it when the knob turned, the locks groaning sharply before they flipped, one by one. It creaked theatrically as it opened, slowly, revealing the dirty hallway outside and a slice of weak golden light from one unshattered bulb.

There, in the doorway, stood a demon.

28

You'd better come in." Wonder of wonders, I even sounded steady.

Eve stepped over the lintel delicately, like a stray cat. Her pale hair caught all the available light, a torch in darkness. Behind her, a strange-familiar face swam out of the darkness of the hall. Anton Kgembe's hair was damp, beads of water clinging to it, and the star sapphire in the hilt of his scimitar winked. My cheek burned—his tat moved under his skin, the faintly fluorescing dye adding a highlight to the gleam of his eyes.

McKinley lifted his left hand, the violet light streaming in weird geometric patterns from his fingertips. His knees loosened, and if Eve had come for me—or so much as pitched her weight forward at the wrong moment—I think he might have actually tried to kill her.

I never liked you much before, sunshine. But I'm beginning to change my mind.

They came fully into the room, step by step, and I almost wasn't surprised. "McKinley. Close the door." Who was the person using my voice? She sounded almost prim. She *also* sounded like someone you didn't want to fuck with.

He gave me a look that suggested I was a few bananas short of a full sundae. "Valentine—"

"Shut the *door.*" I made my hand unloose with an effort of will. He moved, the geometrics streaming from his fingers, and the door swung slowly closed. "Kgembe."

He bowed slightly. The knives strapped to his rig looked well-oiled and loved, and he eschewed plasguns for a pair of serviceable 9 mm projectile Smithwessons. Just my type of gun.

I braced myself. "Eve."

"Dante." She tilted her head a little, and I got the idea she would have curtsied. Her hair rubbed against itself, much rougher than the silk of Japhrimel's. She was cool, calm, and clean, in a long deep-indigo Chinese-collared shirt and tailored khakis. Low blue Verano heels clicked slightly as she took another two steps forward, seemingly not noticing McKinley's immediate move to put himself between us. "Mother."

The word itself was salt in the wound. I shook it away and rose, not quite as gracefully as a demon, but at least I didn't fall over. "How did you find me?"

"We share a bond." Eve's smile broadened, just a little. It was difficult to look at her.

I couldn't look away. *And I suppose having that Magi right there, the one that opened a door for Japh, didn't hurt.* "Let's just get to the point. What do you want?" *And do you know I have the Knife? Or half of it, anyway?*

A shrug, her shoulder lifting and dipping gracefully. "What I have always wanted. To survive. And not so incidentally, my freedom. Surely you can understand."

"Even if you have to lie to me to get it." I tasted bitterness with the words. The room rattled a bit under the lash of my tone. Her smell wrapped around me, cajoling, teasing, and I found with a burst of relief that I didn't respond to it. The black hole in my head stirred uneasily.

Her bright-blue eyes actually dropped. She looked, of all things, *ashamed.* Like a kid caught cheating on a mentaflo test.

Was it another trick?

"Would you have believed me if I looked like this?" Eve spread her hands, long supple fingers hiding her claws. "What could I have done? Tell me."

Guess we'll never find out, will we. I didn't say it. Instead, I studied her face, searching for some echo of myself in the lines of demon bones, the suppleness of her skin, the gaunt beauty.

There was no human left in Eve. Had there ever been?

It was burned away. In Hell.

I could have hated her for it, except I knew what it felt like. I'd felt that burning myself. Did she ever regret it?

Was she capable of regretting it, now?

How long would it be before I was incapable of regretting the same thing?

No. Stubbornness rose up inside me. *I decide. I'm human. Wherever it counts, wherever I have enough of me left to make it, I'm human.*

Hollow words or not, at least it sounded good. "Where's Leander?" I didn't shift my weight, but I might as well have. The words were ready for war, my tone a lot less than conciliatory.

"I don't know. I had enough to do rescuing *this* human." Eve took a half-step back, avoiding McKinley and keeping an avenue of escape open. Her gasflame-blue gaze flicked toward the darkened window, the Darkside pressing against dusty plasglass. Kgembe didn't look in the least discouraged, or even afraid. The smell of his fear was muted under the screen of Eve's perfume. Still, his gaze settled on McKinley, and I could have sworn the Magi was daring the Hellesvront agent to look at him.

Did you abandon Leander, Eve? Did you even stop to think before you did? What about Velokel? I discarded the questions as useless. Wherever the Necromance was now, I couldn't help him. I had my hands full.

I'd feel guilty about it later. Later, later, later. "You're here, you must want something. What do you want me to do?"

"The Eldest?" Her tongue darted out, smoothed her shapely lips. If I'd still been dazzled by her resemblance to Doreen, I might have been distracted.

That's what you're actually after, I bet. My shoulders dropped a trifle. "You can find me, but not him? Oh, that's right. You've got a pet Magi there. Which side of the street is *he* working?"

The Magi tensed, but still didn't speak, his liquid dark eyes on the hand clasping my swordhilt. Why was he looking at *me* like that? He was hanging around with demons far more dangerous than I ever would be.

Then again, he was a Left Hander. The thought that maybe I'd end up worshiping the Unspeakable myself if I kept breaking my Word was chilling, to say the least. Could he tell?

"We share a link, Dante. I did not lie about that." Eve almost seemed to shrink, a little girl in a demon's body. McKinley moved restlessly, straining against a leash.

Dust shifted against the room's plain, dirty surfaces, reminding me of the choking grit in a city full of shattered white walls.

I'm not even going to dignify that with a response. "Get to the point, Eve. What do you *want?*"

I didn't think it would make any difference. But she opened her mouth, and she told me.

Silence like dark wine filled the room. McKinley's eyes widened, a ring of white around the dark irises like a spooked horse's. I didn't blame him.

"You want me to *what?*" If we'd had any neighbors in the adjoining rooms, they might have heard my shriek.

So much for dignity. Fudoshin rang gently, the steel responding to my voice. It hadn't lit with blue fire yet, but the quiver in my wrist spoke volumes.

Kgembe folded his arms, one eyebrow lifting. Like he didn't believe I was making such a big deal about it.

Eve still looked very small, and very young. And very much like a demon, her eyes the brightest thing in the drab, dull room. "I need time, both to gather my allies and plan. You can provide me with that time, and enough confusion to distract anyone we need to. No Magi has your power, by virtue of what you are—enough Power to do what must be done. I *need* your help, Dante."

Oh, ouch. The way into my psyche, the key precious few of my human friends had known about. *I need.*

Not *want.* *Need.*

I am a sucker for being needed. Jace had known that. Doreen had too. And so had Gabe.

Did Japhrimel know? It was unlikely. He didn't have the first clue about what made me tick. Maybe that was why he loved me.

Maybe that's why I loved him.

The realization hit me between the eyes like a projectile bullet. Eve needed my help, certainly. But I could help Japhrimel, maybe, too. By *doing something,* not just waiting like a lost suitcase, yearning to be picked up and rescued.

Play their games back at them, Dante. See how well you can.

Besides, no human Magi could do what Eve needed. It would take plenty of sheer Power—the same Power that thundered through the mark on my shoulder. Maybe it was time to use it instead of moaning about how different it made me.

I took a deep breath, filling my nose with the musk-sweet spice of Androgyne and the dry demon-tang of Hellesvront agent. Eve might need me, or she might be using me as a distraction—just as Lucifer had.

But Japhrimel definitely needed me right now, for once. If this would create a little chaos to cover his path, I was all for it. I was all for taking back some control in this mess.

"All right." My swordblade dipped, my wrist relaxing. "Tell me how. Use small words so I can understand."

McKinley actually choked, his pale cheeks turning crimson; I glared at him and he shut his mouth over a protest I didn't want to hear.

"Anton can explain much of it, I can fill in any gaps in his knowledge." A flash of something hard and delighted bolted through Eve's eyes, almost too quickly for me to identify. "It is not so difficult, once one knows *how.*" Her hands relaxed, and she smiled, a thin small cruel curve of her sculpted lips.

She still looked nothing like Doreen, and just a little like Lucifer. But that tiny smile, fleeting as it was, was still so familiar a chill touched my spine.

Maybe she was my daughter after all.

McKinley stared at the empty hall for a few moments, then swept the door closed. The hinges squealed in protest before he locked it. He stayed where he was for a moment, his left hand braced against the knob. "Are you insane?" His shoulders dropped, shaking under his torn shirt.

Do you really want to know? I looked down at the tarot cards scattered around my booted feet. My heel rested on the Devil card, my weight pitched forward in combat-readiness. I sank back down from the balls of my feet, my boots creaking as I shifted, and my heel ground sharply into the floor. "McKinley." *Dear gods. I sound like Japhrimel.*

"I'd really like to know what the *hell* you're thinking, Valentine. Jaf should have been back by now. He's gone and we're fucked, and you just made it worse by agreeing to openly throw down the gauntlet." He leaned into the door, wood groaning sharply. Outside our bolt-hole, the Darkside inhaled, catching its breath before the plunge.

The gauntlet? Like the cuff I used to wear, saying I was Lucifer's errand-girl? I ground my heel down even more sharply as the thought made my stomach twinge, the darkness inside my head revolving on oiled bearings, silent and deadly. *Okay, Danny. Think your way out of this one.* My brain began to work again. "Please tell me you have a way to get in touch with Vann."

29

The Il deCit is now underground, and the spires of Notra Dama melt into the landfill top of the cavern of Plásse Cathedral. Unlike most of the Darkside, the Il deCit runs with crimson light—from low-heat sublamps during the night and the sublamps plus incandescents during the "day," or whenever the city's central AI tells the lamps it's between dawn and dusk on the surface. The Il is also one of the bigger thoroughfares, so mini-airbikes and slicboards are popular, the air unsteady and trembling with antigrav wash from reactive paint on the boards and bikes.

The sk8s in the Darkside are different than slictribes in most other parts of the world, being lethal and filthy instead of just clannish and unhygienic. A gang of Darkside slictribers can strip a corpse in seconds or a live victim in under a minute; citizens are just lucky the organ trade isn't on fire in Hegemony Europa like it is in, say, Nuevo Rio.

We crouched in the shadows of a refuse-strewn alley. There's really no smell like a main street in the Darkside. Maintenance 'bots come through at regular intervals, but the constant ambient temperature and the volatile hoverwash make it a breeding ground for all *sorts* of smells, including the effluvia of humanity.

We melded out of the shadows and crossed the street, McKinley flanking me. The crowd was thick but not overly so, and nobody went up the steps of the Notra Dama without having serious business. As soon as it became obvious we were heading for the old temple, the milling pedestrians—Darksiders and regular Paradissians out for a night of slumming fun—suddenly avoided contact with us, a path opening without comment.

I wished it didn't feel so depressingly normal.

Notra Dama rose broken-toothed and slump-shouldered but still beautiful, vibrating with uneasy energy. If Paradisse had a heart, it was probably the Floating Arc Triomphe, retrofitted with hovercushions and a popular tourist destination.

But if the Darkside had a pulsing heart, it was the Lady, as the Notra Dama was known, an ancient Christer temple slumped into the rubble and wreckage, waiting for the next turn of the great wheel. She'd seen pagan sacrifices and the rise and fall of the Religions of Submission; she was where a small group of psions had barricaded themselves during one of the last battles of the Seventy Days War. Old Franje had tried desperately to shield paranormals and psions, granting them sanctuary and parrying both the diplomatic and the military maneuvers of the Evangelicals of Gilead, who demanded the return of any escaped North Merican citizens for internment in the death camps.

I shivered. Hegemony Albion and Old Franje had both been horrifically bombed during the War. The first and last nuclear strike, resulting in the Vegas Waste, had been

in North Merica . . . but in Hegemony Europa, people had
long memories. Notra Dama had taken a direct hit, and
sometimes, it was said, you could hear the screams of the
dying.

I didn't doubt it. An old temple built at the juncture
of five ley lines feeding energy into the city's gravita-
tional center was a prime place for ghostflits. She really
deserved her own collegia of Ceremonials to drain her
charge and restore her, but down here in the dark it wasn't
a good idea.

Psions tend to go a little nuts underground.

My boots clicked gently on the steps. At the top the
great doors hung, creaking slightly on their ancient hinges
as currents of Power threaded through the physical structure of the building. The Lady was restless tonight, maybe
reading my intentions—or perhaps just restless because
the presence of demons made the entire city shiver like a
hooker watching a knife in a pimp's hand.

Like a Knife made out of wood, Danny? The voice of
strained hilarity had a particularly jolly tone tonight. *The
Knife in your bag? Not going to do you much good in
there.*

I pushed the doors open, scanning the interior of the
temple through a haze of Power. To OtherSight, white-hot
snakes crawled and writhed over the floor, crackling up
the columns and walls, dripping from the ruined choir-
loft and the magnificent chipped stonework and fading
frescoes.

It was even better than I'd hoped, the magickal equivalent of a fallout zone. It would keep me hidden in the
first stage of the work I intended to perform, and when I
drained the ambient Power to fuel the spell it would make

a huge stinking noise—a noise noticed by every psion and probably every demon in a good three-hundred-mile radius.

"It just doesn't get any better than this," I muttered, shoving my sword into the loop on my rig. My voice rang off stone, fell back at me, given fresh echoes by the buzzing vibration of Power.

Small shuffling noises edged around us as pale transparencies of ghostflits rode the currents of Power, some of them silently screaming, others just drifting, wearing out their chains until they found by accident the way into the clear rational light of What Comes Next. The flits were a good sign, gathering here where there was enough Power to bathe them in something approximating borrowed flesh, even though my skin chilled to See them, cold breath on my back and wariness rising to my nape.

Necromances don't like flits much. They congregate in nightclubs, some old uncared-for temples, anywhere there's enough Power, instability, and heat to give them a simulacrum of life. Back in the days before the Awakening, those gifted with the ability to see the dead were often pursued by flits, and battered into insane asylums and suicide by the harassment. It technically isn't *harassment,* since flits are just confused and can't understand why normals can't see them . . . but it's still pretty damn uncomfortable, and before the Awakening the training to keep mental and emotional borders clear and firm to ward off the confused dead wasn't available in any systematic way.

I had to breathe through my mouth, trying not to smell the ripe fresh odor, hitting the back of my throat like a kick of Crostine rum back when I was human, spilling through my bloodstream in a hot wave. Power stroked along my ragged shields, almost matching the soft numbness in my left shoulder. I pushed the door closed, scanning the entire place. Not a soul except the rats in the walls and the flits, a few of them taking notice of the glittering sparkle in my aura that meant Necromance.

Do you know what you're doing, Danny?

I ignored the voice of reason and made a slow circuit of the whole place.

I checked the door in the east quadrant, behind a screening pile of rubble and garbage that smelled unwholesome in the extreme. It opened up into a narrow alley excavated between Notra Dama and the sloping tenement next door. At the end of that alley, at the bottom of a well that went up to the third level—that is, three discrete levels down from the surface, if the Darkside could be said to have actual official *levels*—the slim shape of an airbike was a thin metal gleam. It hadn't been touched, the thread-thin warding I'd laid on it undisturbed.

"All right," I whispered. Turned to McKinley. "It's still there. *Now* are you happy?"

He nodded. "Ecstatic."

I had to suppress the urge to snort. "I wish we'd been able to find Vann and Lucas." *Not to mention Leander. I hope he's still alive, federal agent or not.*

He pulled his lips in, his shoulders tensing. "They can take care of themselves. You're who I'm worried about."

Maybe you should be. I'm about to do something insane. "You might want to take notes. You're going to see a Greater Work of magick performed tonight." *And if it doesn't work, maybe we'll both die in here.*

"Are you really going to do this?" He took up his position by the door, his hands shaken out and loose. The violet glow around his left hand brightened, maybe in response to the ambient Power. I wondered just what exactly that metallic coating on his flesh meant, decided I didn't want to know.

"I said I would. Eve's right—this will buy us some time and create enough confusion to keep us in the game a bit longer. Not only that, but Japhrimel needs some cover." My throat went dry, my heart picking up its pace against my ribs. "If it doesn't work, at the very least it'll make a lot of noise and distract a bunch of demons."

"Or the Prince will find you." His pupils had swollen in the dim light, crimson-tinted from the sublamps outside. He sounded like I'd just informed him of my intention to put on petticoats and sing the entire score of *Magi: The Musical*. With sound effects. A rancid giggle rose up in my throat, was strangled, and fell back down.

Thanks, McKinley. You know, I might have forgotten about that if you hadn't reminded me. "Which is why Eve can't do this. If Lucifer or one of his stooges grabs her . . . " I swallowed the rest of the sentence. I wasn't about to let that happen.

"If he shows up we might both die. I'm supposed to look after you."

I know. But we're both out of our depth here. It's only a matter of time before someone other than Eve finds me. I shrugged. "I'm going to help Japh and Eve at the same time, McKinley. You want to try to stop me, all you'll get is a bellyful of steel. You want to test me on this?"

His pause was gratifying, at least. "Jaf can take care of himself. And *she*—"

Quit stalling, Danny. "This isn't under discussion,

sunshine. You want to leave, there's the door." I turned away, my bootheel scraping the ancient stone of the floor. There was a clear space in front of the altar, and I flipped open my bag as I strode away, around the mound of rubbish that would give us some cover if we had to retreat firing. My fingers rooted through the chaos—spare ammo, leather-wrapped wood pulsing with its own obscene life, a plasglass container of cornmeal still miraculously unhurt, and the small jar of salt.

What I really needed was the chunk of consecrated chalk. My pulse began to hammer, my mouth tasting sour, and I inhaled a long deep breath as I stepped back out into the soaring space of the ruined temple and surveyed the mounds of garbage.

It isn't the location that matters, Danny. Magick is a state of mind. Get moving.

"Fuck," I whispered in lieu of a prayer, as my fingers closed on the chalk.

The sorcerer's circle is an invention of seventeenth-century magick, but it's still a useful innovation. A psion has to be ready to deal with nasty things outside the charmed border of a circle, but as a *container* for magickal force, the circle is without equal.

I didn't precisely hurry, but I didn't take my time either. I'd bought a bottle of Crostine rum at a tiny Darkside shop run by an anemic-looking normal woman, and the pack of synth-hash cigarettes sat with it at the north point of the circle. I made it double, runes from the Nine Canons sketched between the outer and inner rings, each drawn from Magi-trained memory sharp and crisp against cracked stone. Between them, the twisted fluid glyph scored into my flesh writhed, doodled so many times I could have traced it in my sleep.

I should have had incense, and divination to pick the proper time, and a ritual robe. I should have had a consecrated cup, expensive wine instead of cheap liquor, and a week or so to pattern and prepare myself. I should have meditated for an hour or so to clear my head.

Instead, I finished the circle and stood inside it, then dropped the chalk back into my bag with a faint uneasy click. Ever since the climax of the hunt for Kellerman Lourdes, the thought of consecrated chalk raises my hackles just a little.

The leather straps of my rig creaked. I'd fastened my sword to the backcarry, hilt standing up over my shoulder; I'd need both hands for this and possibly for piloting the airbike in a hurry if this worked the way I wanted it to. I settled my bag against my side, breathing deeply, cinnamon musk rising to combat the odor of garbage and the sour sharp smell of stagnant Power.

Danny, what are you doing?

I pushed the voice of reason away one more time. I was trying to stay alive, same as usual. The game was rigged, sure—but I was going to make it a little more difficult to rig. Hopefully.

The hollow place under my ribs, pulsing with my heartbeat, whittled itself deeper as I stood in the middle of the circle, checking its confines. The salt, the rum, the cigarettes . . . all present and accounted for.

If I pull this off it's going to be one of the finest Greater Works I've ever seen performed. And I'm not even a Magi.

Most Magi would kill to have a demon tell them even half of what Eve had told me. Kgembe had handed over his shadowjournal, something Magi *never* did, with the steps to break open the walls of the world clearly delineated. I wondered what kind of hold she had over him, or if he was one of Japh's people, playing along with her for an unspecified reason. Games within games, plot and counterplot, and me with the benefit of a successful Magi's magickal diagrams and explanations. "Yeah," I muttered, my right hand caressing a knifehilt. "Lucky me."

I was still stalling.

I sank to my knees, facing the north. Shut my eyes and tried to breathe calmly.

Rage bubbled and boiled under my breastbone. It was never far from the surface these days, and it was good fuel.

I uncapped the rum, took a swallow, and let it burn the velvet cavern of my mouth. I tore the package open and arranged the synth-hash cigarettes in a wheel, all pointing outward. The salt made a fine thin noise as I tossed it straight up, letting it sift down, kissing my hair and face.

I let Power bleed out, fueled by my rage. It slid free with a slight subliminal hiss, filling the chalk marks and turning them silvery. Power soaked into the runes marked between the rings, each one named as I drew it, a sudden subsonic note beginning to thrum as I chanted silently, my lips moving, burning with rum. Alcohol has no effect on me anymore, but the fume of it still brought back memories. Bounties, drinking sessions, celebrations, the ceremonial sharing before a fast dirty suicide run or a slicboard duel . . .

Jace. Was he watching me? Were all my dead watching?

Enjoy the show, everyone. I'm about to make my mark.

McKinley shifted nervously behind me, his aura a drawing-in, a point of tension in the sea of Power. Notra Dama shivered again, like a sleeper rolling over in bed, struggling toward waking.

If this doesn't work right a whole hell of a lot of people in Paradisse are going to have a very bad day. For a moment my conscience pricked at me. What was I *doing?*

But needs must when the Devil drives, and the Devil was driving this engine. Besides, the damage would be contained—I hoped.

You're playing roulette with other people's lives, Danny.

I knew it. But if Lucifer caught Japhrimel *or* Eve, how many other people would suffer? All of Japh's agents, however many he had salted away. All of Eve's rebellion—demons, sure, but still. Was the enemy of my enemy worth what I was about to do?

If Lucifer keeps playing these games, more people are going to suffer. Here's your chance to end it, Danny.

I shut all the arguments away. I needed all my concentration now.

The last rune shimmered. *Uruthusz,* the Piercer of Veils, with its two downward-spiking teeth. I let the Power slip through my mental fingers, filling the rune like a cup. The circle clicked into completeness, a sound felt more in the solar plexus and teeth than heard.

Moving air mouthed my tangled hair, pushing it back. The ghostflits rode closer, drawn to the circle's humming tautness. None of them approached me yet, but they shimmered, taking on false substance. Eyes glittered, hands of tinted smoke reaching out and curling away, their mouths opening. If I listened, I could hear them chittering, pleading, squealing.

Touch me. Feed me. Give me life.

Not tonight.

Heat bloomed in the center of the circle, in a space behind the physical. It was a good sign, the walls of reality thinning here under an onslaught of centuries of Power. The point of heat became a flame, wavered, and held.

The cigarettes trembled like spokes of a wheel about to roll into motion. All it needed was a little push.

"Valentine . . ." McKinley didn't sound too happy. Maybe he was having second thoughts.

Too late. I centered myself, the pattern of what I was about to attempt rising through the surface of the world.

Then I jacked into Notra Dama's ambient Power and sent everything I could reach pouring into that small, nonphysical flame.

The cigarettes lit, fuming, synth-hash smoke rising in angular shapes. The runes froze, sparking with blue and crimson light, then settled into a golden glow and began writhing against the floor, running between the two circles in a smeared streak. The temperature rose. My voice was suddenly audible even to me, chanting.

It wasn't a Necromance's power-chant, to bring a soul over the bridge and allow it a voice in the world of the living.

This was something else, a harsh sliding tongue that bloodied my lips even as I spoke it. It roiled the air and tore into the circle, the words taking weight and form, streaming into a vortex of *absence* blooming like a camera lens away from the flame, now visible as a pale colorless twisting.

I had no idea where the words came from but I went with it. Once you start a Greater Work like this, the magick takes its own shape. It rides you, for good or for ill, and you are a passenger on its tidal wave. If the Work miscarries you can get backlash sickness, or drained down dangerously far as it tries to complete itself even through its flaws. Which is why preparation, planning, divination, and good old-fashioned luck are key to surviving your own Greater Works.

Ghostflits began to peel away, their smoky forms shredding. Their mouths opened in silent crystal screams and the Power rode me, a riverbed in its channel. I was actually draining Notra Dama, the floodtide of energy directed at weakening the walls of the world, already tissue-thin but made of strong, resilient stuff.

The Knife vibrated in my bag, harmonic resonance aching in my teeth and bones. Fudoshin answered with his own scabbarded hum, echoing the runes in the circle, now moving so fast they were a golden ring, a hoop of fire, a thin thread of crimson running through the warp and weft of the spell, drawing it tight, tighter, tightest.

McKinley shouted something, but I didn't care. I was too far gone in the spell. There was more and more Power, forcing itself through my shredded shielding, tender scarred patches in my psyche smoking under the strain. I was a glove too small for the hand forcing its way in, the magick uncaring of my human limits, the fabric of my mind bending and ripping under the strain—

—just as the cloth of reality tore, a vertical slit opening

with the sound of parachute silk tearing under too much stress.

McKinley yelled again, a shapeless noise. The second half of the spell locked down, anchors driven deep into the temple's floor, stone groaning and the entire city ramming through my unprotected skull for one endless, horrific moment. The anchors held, reality warping and skewing at the edges of the hole I'd just torn in the world.

Through that long tunnel, a weird directionless red-orange glow bloomed. The icy heat of Hell boiled through, cracking the floor and straining against mortal chill. But it *held,* the circle shuddering and pulling Power through the temple—and from the city's deep, sonorous heart with its acres of pain, fear, and the psychic sludge of a whole population jammed together, living cheek-by-jowl and boiling for centuries.

The door was open.

I'm not even a Magi, I thought in stunned wonder. *Any Magi worth their salt would pay to have me do this; I've done what it takes them years to do.*

Damn. I'm good.

I fell backward as they boiled through, the temple groaning in distress, and McKinley grabbed me. Consciousness narrowed to a thread as the rushing tide of darkness took on lambent eyes and horns, feathers and long arms, chuckling and chittering in their unlovely language as the denizens of Hell grabbed their opportunity and *escaped.* Chaos smashed against the temple's walls, and Notra Dama woke in a blinding sheet of Power and thundered against the violation.

McKinley dragged me. Psychic darkness washed against the temple's walls, coated its refuse-strewn floor, and no few of the demons paused in their headlong rush to eye me as my bootheels scraped against the floor. The Hellesvront agent swore, pulling me behind a pile of garbage, cutting off my view of the circle and the escaping Lesser Flight demons. "What the *hell* is wrong with you?" he screamed in my ear, just as the temple shivered again. The snap of connection breaking between me and the circle was blessed relief, my mind contracting behind the borrowed weight of Japhrimel's shielding.

Yet another time my brain should have turned to oatmeal. Lucky lucky me.

The door would stay open as long as the taplines feeding it Power could handle the strain before slamming shut, the fabric of reality reasserting its structure. Demons would flood through, and since Lucifer's big thing was controlling which demon went where, he'd have his hands full.

I'd just altered the playing field and hopefully created enough chaos to cover McKinley and me for a little bit, until Japh could get back—he would also, hopefully, find it a little easier to sneak around Hell now that I'd thrown the dice again. I'd given Eve the time she asked for.

For my first toss of the dice in the game, it was a doozy.

I'd also just unleashed who-knew-how-many demons on the world. *Gods forgive me.*

The Hegemony would also have its hands full dealing with this eruption, and that meant they wouldn't be sending any more field agents after me.

Welcome to the game, Danny.

The temple's side door yawed, and McKinley hauled me through, greasy crud scraping against our boots. He swore, filthily, in every language I had the blue words in and quite a few I didn't.

We made it to the airbike, Notra Dama tolling in distress. Little scrabbling sounds behind us didn't sound human *or* animal, and McKinley thumbed the starter. Antigrav whined. I threw my leg over the bike's saddle and looked back to see imps boiling over the trashheap, their bald heads gleaming and their naked limbs moving in ways nothing of this world should move. Nausea rose, I almost pitched off the bike and retched—but McKinley bent over the handlebars and kicked the maglock off. I grabbed at his waist, the antigrav woke with a rattling whine, and we rocketed away even as the imps ignored us and scattered like quicksilver.

Notra Dama surged behind us, psychic stress becoming physical, masonry creaking and squealing as the first surfroar of crowd noise began. I clutched at both McKinley and consciousness, hanging onto each by the thinnest of threads. My cheek ached, the tattoo shifting madly under the skin. We raced for the surface of Paradisse on the expanding edge of a circle of chaos I had just unleashed on an unsuspecting world.

30

The rooms were beautiful, singing arches pierced with shafts of golden light that wasn't daylight but well-placed full-spectrum bulbs. It was a nice touch, even if the air swirled and trembled with the tang of spice and musk that said *demon*.

Priceless antiques, mostly vases, sat on fluted plasglass tables, each one humming with magickal force. Demon warding was anchored to the walls, but straining bits of demon magick were also set in each knickknack and curio, sending up waves of interference into the atmosphere. Someone was taking a great deal of trouble to make this place invisible, protections woven over every inch of wallspace, triplines and protective wards showered over the flooring and furniture.

It was uncomfortably close to the way things looked in Hell, and the shivers juddering just under my skin didn't help. I kept expecting to glance in a corner and see a pair of level burning-green eyes in a lean golden face, a straight mouth and the long black Chinese-collared coat of my Fallen. Or a pair of green eyes and a shock of golden hair, burning like an aureole.

I sat in Eve's hideout, the air buzzing and blurring with demon musk, McKinley by the door to the suite she'd shown us to. This tower rose among hundreds of others, a forest of glowing spires watching as dawn rose over the world.

The city trembled. Up here on the Brightside it wasn't too bad, but the ambient Power tasted like burning cinnamon. The holonews was full of weird occurrences—a street on one of the Darkside's lowest levels turned to a sheet of glass, a wave of fights breaking out in taverns, a "paranormal incident" at Notra Dama calling Hegemony containment teams from around the globe. People were uneasy. Even the normals feel it when the ambient Power of a city is drained or altered.

I was hungry.

McKinley sighed, leaning his head back against the wall. "You okay?"

He kept asking me, about once an hour. Normally it would have dragged irritation against my bare nerves, my shoulder still prickle-numb, my eyes sandy and aching.

But right now I was glad of the company. "Peachy." I shifted, and the chair squeaked. Little sounds came through the walls—footsteps and faroff voices too strange to be human.

"Tell me again why we're trusting her. Jaf won't like this."

"He said himself that she has a reason to keep me alive and him happy. We need more backup, McKinley. This is safer than being on our own." *In any case, it's too late now.*

"It's not like Vann. He's never been late before."

And he has Lucas with him. "I'm not happy about it

either. I bought us some breathing room, at least." The hollowness of my belly taunted me. I needed food. What I wouldn't give to be able to walk down the street to a noodle shop, or even grab a heatseal packet of protein mush.

Too bad, Danny. You've worked hungry before.

"Guess so." The electric light ran over his hair, glittered in his black eyes. The windows were polarized; we would be invisible from outside—if anything but empty air was this high up, sandwiched between hoverlanes. Nobody would think to look for me in a tower in the poshest slice of Paradisse.

I found myself rubbing at my left shoulder, pushing cloth over the twisted, numb scar. *How long is this going to take, Japh? I've about run out of delaying tactics.* "What do you think is going to happen?"

The agent shrugged. "Jaf will come back. He always does, sooner or later."

Now there was an opening. "How long have you been . . . working . . . for him?"

"Long enough to trust him." He shifted his weight, peeled himself away from the wall. "You don't have to like me, Valentine. I just do my job."

Sekhmet sa'es. "I was just *asking.*" I pushed myself up to my booted feet. My hair felt filthy, tangled with dust and dirt, reeking of Notra Dama, spent magick, and demons. At least I hadn't had my clothes blown off me this time. "He never tells me anything."

"Not known for explaining himself."

Could you sound any more dismissive? "What *is* he known for? Or is that classified information, too?"

McKinley sighed. "He's a demon. He's the Prince's Eldest and the assassin."

The city glowed, fingers of gold reaching through the streets as the sun lifted itself up over the rim of the world. The Senne glittered in the distance, a river of molten stuff coming up from underground amid the sprawl of the suburbs, and I could just see the column of light that was the plasglow beam atop the Toure Effel fading as the sky flushed with rose instead of gray. I could feel the plucked string of the Toure vibrating as it channeled the city's distress. "Fine. I get it."

"What can I tell you that you don't already know?" McKinley moved behind me, not quite silently, and my back prickled. "Jesu Christos. He's risked *everything* for you."

I didn't ask McKinley what he thought *I'd* risked for Japh.

It would take a few days for Paradisse to get back to itself, its population feeding back into the ambient well of Power. The psions around here were probably having headaches and nausea, their bodies getting accustomed to a lower level in the energy flux.

Congratulations, Danny. Making friends everywhere you go, aren't you?

My psychic fingerprints were all over the work at Notra Dama. That was the trouble with the use of Power, it was so highly personal. I was going to be very famous once everyone figured out what had happened.

If, of course, word got out. The Hegemony had a reason to keep this under wraps, if they were Lucifer's toy. Plot and counterplot; nobody was what they seemed.

Not even Japhrimel. Not even me, playing the Devil's game now. My breath fogged the glass, a circle of condensation. "You know, I'm getting a little tired of everyone assuming I made Japh Fall."

"What exactly *did* you do?"

What did I do? "I was just trying to stay alive. All of a sudden the Devil wanted me to kill someone, and I had a reason to do it. Then things just got out of hand, and before I knew it I had a demon all over me and a serious case of genesplicing. Then he up and dies on me and . . ." The circle of breath-fog spread. I rested my forehead on the cold, reinforced plasglass. It was thick enough to be projectile-proof, humming slightly with the shielding applied to it and the everpresent sound of a river of high-altitude air shifting around the tower's walls. The words curdled in my throat. Why was I trying to explain myself to *him,* of all people? "It wasn't my fault." *There's enough that is my fault.* "Forget it. I was just trying to find a few things out."

"Why don't you ask *him?*"

The stupid man. As if I hadn't been trying to do just that for so long now. "He won't answer me. Or he lies. Look, McKinley, I'm sorry I fucking well asked you. Just shut up."

Mercifully, he did. I rested my forehead on the glass and bumped Fudoshin's hilt on the window. Once. Twice. Three times. For luck. Eve had even come up with a scabbard, a lovely black-lacquered curve of reinforced wood. "I don't like this," I muttered. "Don't like it at all."

McKinley held his peace. I swung away from the window, my rig creaking, and cast a sharp glance over the room. Bed fit for a princess, choked in blue velvet. Fainting-couches in the same blue velvet, lyrate tables holding knickknacks humming with sleepy demon magick.

The pale cream carpet was thick enough to lose credit discs in. Electric light grew paler, compensating for day rising in the east.

Fine hairs on my nape rose. Premonition ruffled past me, icy fingernails touching my cheeks. Whatever was going to happen was coming soon, rolling toward me like ball bearings on a reactive-greased slope.

The black hole inside my brain shivered. The same sounds chuckling up from its depths were coming through the walls—the muffled evidence of things not human walking around, making themselves at home, doing whatever it was demons did.

Keep moving, Danny. If you stop you'll drown.

That was rabbit-talk. Right now I was safest with my head down, staying in a protected location. The more I moved around, the more people would see me, the more chance someone would get word of where I was.

I had just acted on my own, for once since this whole thing started not just being pushed from place to place. I was pretty sure nobody would have expected this from me. The thing to do now was wait for the countermove, just like in battlechess.

I let out another long, soft breath. My stomach twisted unhappily. Finally, I peeled myself away from the window. "You hungry?"

McKinley had picked another wall to lean against, where he could see both me and the door. He glanced up, the bruised circles under his eyes harshly evident in the new light. "I could eat," he said, as if it had just occurred to him.

"There's bound to be a kitchen in this pile. We'll find something."

If I can't move around out in the city I'll settle for poking around here. If I have to stay in one room for very long I'm going to go insane.

I wished I was exaggerating.

We didn't have to go very far—at the end of the short curving hall outside the suite's door, there was the hoverlift we'd come up in and a small kitchen, stocked with the usual Paradisse hotelier fare—cheese, bread, fruit, coffee, a wide array of gourmet freeze-reheat stuff like individual pizzas and packets of beef pho with noodles like brain wrinkles pressing against plaswrap. Human food, which made me wonder about this place. I knew demons *could* eat—sometimes Japh ate with me, for example, and seemed to enjoy it—but I wasn't entirely sure if they had to. Was this just Eve planning for me, or did it come with the tower? Who was paying for all this?

Then again, demons have no problem with money.

McKinley settled down with a hunk of yellow cheese and a baguette, taking bites off an apple in between. I popped one of the individual pizzas into the microwave and hit the button. Everything was new, top of the line, and unused.

This is weird. Then again, sunshine, weird is your middle name these days. "Why would she have human food?"

"They like it. It's not nourishment to them, it's an accessory." McKinley cracked a bottle of mineral water open with a practiced twist of his wrist. "Plus, any demon is going to have human retainers. It's how it works. They like to stay behind the scenes unless there's killing to be done."

Just a fount of useful information, aren't you? When you're not sneering at me, that is. "Oh." I watched through the plasglass door as the pizza heated, cheese melting and bubbling, the smell of marinara and cheese, not to mention crust, suddenly filling my mouth with water. "Retainers. This is so very feudal."

"Guess so. Like the Mob, only not so nice." He was perking up, eating in great starving bites, barely stopping to chew. His eyes never stopped roving the room, and he'd picked the seat between me and the door.

Exactly where I'd sit, if I was doing bodyguard duty on someone.

My nape prickled again. The microwave dinged, and I retrieved my little pizza. I settled myself in the safest spot, my back to the blind corner holding a mini-fridge and the disposal unit. McKinley shifted a little in his seat, his metallic left hand lying discarded on the blondwood tabletop.

"How did you end up working for Japh?" I didn't think he'd tell me, but it was a way to pass the time. I waited for the pizza to cool down, eyeing the gobbets of melted cheese. It smelled like real cheese too, and I was suddenly reminded of the first meal I'd ever eaten with my Fallen.

My, how the world turns.

"I was almost dead but I'd put up a hell of a fight. He was impressed, and offered me either a quick passing or service." McKinley shrugged. "I wasn't ready to die yet."

I peeled a precut slice out of the golden wheel. Blew across the piece to cool it. "You know, you could give a demon lessons in not really answering the goddamn question."

"My former lord wanted to kill the Eldest. We tried like hell, but we were only human, even with . . . modifications." He lifted his left hand slightly, laid it back to rest on the tabletop.

I held the pizza, my mouth hanging open, for what seemed an eternity. Then I took a bite. *Huh.* "We meaning you and Vann?"

"And a few others." His face changed, and he laid down the hunk of cheese. "They should be looking for you too. That's another reason why I'm worried."

"Looking for me?"

"Just like guardian angels, Valentine." He took a long pull of mineral water, washing some taste out of his mouth. "We had a perimeter set up in Toscano, keeping you under wraps."

I was getting tired of my mouth hanging open in astonishment, so I took another bite. Hot tomato sauce, melted cheese, a little heavy on the oregano. The food helped, made me feel more solid. "I never knew."

"That was the *idea*," he replied in a stunningly good *you are an idiot* tone.

I'd suspected something, of course. But I'd never had a whisper of anyone watching Japhrimel and me while I did my best to settle into a boring regular life, shopping for shadowjournals and antique furnishings, going for walks in the afternoon sun . . . and waking up screaming with Mirovitch's *ka* whispering inside my head, ripping and tearing as fingers of burning ectoplasm tried to claw down my throat and rape my mind.

I shivered, dropped my pizza back down to its nest of

plaswrap. The black hole in my head widened, echoes spilling through my skull.

The scar in the hollow of my left shoulder twinged, warningly.

"You okay?" McKinley eyed me.

My shoulder twinged again, like a fishhook in flesh, plucking as it twitched. "Fine." I scooped up the pizza again and began wolfing without tasting it. I'd need fuel, no matter what happened next. "You know," I said between bites, wiping tomato sauce away from my lips, "I don't think I should stay up here like a princess in a pea, or whatever. I think we should wander around this place and peek at what the demons are doing."

McKinley choked on a bite of baguette. His black eyes got very wide. "Why not just get the hell out of here?"

I settled down to the rest of my pizza. "Because without Japhrimel, you and I are *both* dead out there. This isn't just a papercut to Lucifer. I threw down a challenge big-time. I'm sure the Hegemony would love to get their hands on me too. I'm too hot to handle now—but I don't trust demons either, even if they have good reasons to protect me. I'm getting to where I don't trust anyone, not even myself. So I want to look around where I've landed."

Besides, I can't take being cooped up in this tower.

I felt horribly naked, even with all the demon shielding on the walls. I also felt filthy, messy, ugly, and the slightest bit shaky. I itched for some kind of action—sparring, or a hard clean fight. Something to get rid of the bright red ribbon of rage under the surface of my thoughts, growing in increments, pressing against the confines of my temper.

A shadow fell over the kitchen door, and I knew who

it was even before she appeared. I *smelled* her, a smell that was quickly growing unique, impressing itself on my sensitive nose.

McKinley's chair scraped as he bolted to his feet, the color draining from his cheeks and turning him whey-pale as the scorch of a demon filled the air. I finished the last two bites of crust, and Eve folded her arms, smiling that imperturbable smile. Her clotted-ice hair touched her shoulders, almost writhing with life, and her gasflame eyes passed over me in a long arc.

"I see you found your provisions. I thought it best not to ask you to dinner with our other guests."

I licked my fingers. "Charmed. I could probably eat my way through here in an hour or so. But I was thinking of looking around, seeing what your setup is here."

A slim shoulder lifted, dropped. She wore blue, again, an indigo cable-knit sweater and slacks that had to be de-signer, the same pair of low Verano heels. Nothing but the best for this demon.

I found myself searching her face again for any echo of Doreen, comparing her to what she had looked like, the glamour that had fooled me into . . . what? Going up against the Devil? I'd've done it anyway. It wasn't like Lucifer was going to leave me alone.

"If there is time," she finally answered.

I deliberately didn't reach for Fudoshin's hilt. The Knife hummed against my hip. "What's going on? Where's Kgembe?" The scar twined again, and began to tingle—not the numb prickle of Japhrimel *elsewhere,* but a waking-up feeling.

I hoped it was what I thought it was.

"The Magi has disappeared—wise of him, I think. We

have planned a council of war, and I thought to request your presence. Several of my allies have found themselves recently freed from Hell." A slight tilt of her head, like a servomotor on jeweled bearings, a graceful oiled inhuman movement.

"Fancy that. War, huh?" *Well, what else would you call this, Danny?* "When?"

"Tonight. At dusk. It's traditional. May I count on your presence?"

I nodded, my hair moving uneasily on my scalp. I was suddenly aware of how I must look—dirty, bled on and air-dried, and probably just two short steps away from crazed. "You can."

"Very well." She turned on her heel, sharply, without even deigning to look in McKinley's direction.

"Eve." *If that's even your name.*

She halted, her narrow back to me.

"You can put that face back on. If you want. The one that looks like Doreen." *I might even find it easier.*

She paused for just the barest of seconds. "Why? This is what I am, Dante."

I might find it a little easier to look at you. Or then again, I might not. "You were human. At least partly." Not just human. She'd been a little girl.

A child I had been unable to save.

"Nothing of humanity survives Hell's fires." No shrug, just a simple statement of fact. Fresh dawning light ran along the snakes of her hair, touched the supple curve of her hip under the sweater's hem, and cringed away from something that didn't belong in this world.

I let her kiss my cheek, once. I got so close to her I could smell her, feel her heat. The thought sent a shiver

through me. Had it just been that she looked like Doreen?
Was there any truth to her claim that I was part of the genetic mix used to make her?

How else had she found me? "What about what you
got from me? Doesn't that count?"

"It matters as little or as much as you want to make it
matter. You're still the only mother I have."

McKinley made a restless movement. Maybe he
wanted to argue.

"I can't hold a gun to your head and make you human."
I can't even do that to myself.

"If you could, would you?" She still didn't turn around,
and her tone was excessively gentle.

"No." It came out immediately, without thought. "I
wouldn't."

"Why?"

Because that's not the way I play, goddammit. "Just
because. It wouldn't change anything."

She turned back, slowly, letting the light play over each
feature, each hill and valley geometrically just a little *off,*
altered. "I cannot afford to be *too* human. Not with *him*
to slay, and all of us to save—and your lover, ally or not,
to reckon with." As usual, her face twisted slightly when
she referred to Lucifer, her lip lifting and nose wrinkling.
I watched, fascinated. It was a curiously immature movement, like a teen sucking on bitter algae candy.

My right hand fell limp at my side, no longer aching
for the feel of a hilt and a blade cutting flesh. The ribbon
of rage shrank, just a little bit.

"But as human as I can be, I will be in your honor, my
mother." A slight little bow, her icy hair falling forward
over slim shoulders, and then she was gone, the sunlight

falling through where she'd stood as the sound of her footsteps—too light and quick to be human, and faintly wrong in the gait as well—retreated down the hall.

The scar began to burn, faintly at first, heat working through its numbness. A candleflame moving closer and closer to the flesh, a spot of warmth.

I found my right hand hovering over my dirty shoulder, fingertips aching for the feel of the ropy scar twisting and bumping under my touch.

"Valentine—" McKinley began.

"Shut up." I sounded strained and unnatural even to myself. "Just eat. I'm going to get cleaned up."

31

*D*ying sunlight turned bloody in the west, and the room was long and wide, windowless, and full of movement that stopped the moment I stepped over the threshold. Plain white walls vibrated with demon warding, and the long, slim, highly polished table running down the center was full of demons.

I froze.

At the head of the table Eve straightened, pushing back her pale ropes of hair. The plunging inside my stomach turned into a full-fledged barrel roll with dynos straining.

The room full of demons turned still and trembling as a pool of quicksilver on a level surface, twitching with Power as each of them turned their lambent eyes on me.

Tall or short, most slender and golden-skinned, but each with that aura of *difference* demons carry. They are not beautiful or ugly, though some of them are bizarre in the extreme. It's that breath of alienness that makes the human mind shiver when looking at them.

They were all of the Greater Flight. There was no mistaking it. To my left, dozing in a corner, two hellhounds slumped together, sleeping, their obsidian limbs splayed in a caricature of relaxation. From under one eyelid, a sliver of orange peeked—not sleeping, then.

A prickling shiver ran through my entire body, and I was suddenly very sure that I wanted to see Japhrimel again.

Right fucking now.

"Dante." Eve's voice stroked each exposed edge, from the table to the ceiling, and a breath of baking bread and fresh musk reached me. The smell of an Androgyne.

Like Lucifer.

My stomach heaved, the black hole in my head pulsing and straining until I could push it down, lock it away. I swallowed with difficulty and met her eyes again.

I found myself relieved she hadn't taken on Doreen's face again after all. There was no denying the demon in her. Even the way she held herself, completely still, as if liquid grace had frozen itself at one particular point in a dance.

"Gentlemen," she continued, "I present to you Dante Valentine, the Eldest's *hedaira*, and the Key to the throne of Hell."

I wondered if I should take a bow.

"What nonsense are you speaking?" This voice, from a demon with dappled, mottled skin like the side of a painted pony, was a knife against the skin after the soft restfulness of Eve's. "This is the Eldest's whore, and our hostage."

A ripple ran through the assembled demons. One at my end of the table, a tall sharp-faced male with a shock of black thistledown hair, tensed as if to rise to his feet. He wore white, rags fluttering as his fingers curled around the edge of the table, and my awareness centered on him, my hand itching for the swordhilt again.

When Eve spoke I almost twitched.

"Zaj." The single word was loaded with gunpowder threading through the softness of her tone. The shortening of a demon's name sounded like a weapon in her mouth. "Our plan requires the Key. Without the Key, we could not retrieve the Knife. Without the Knife, there is no challenge we can make to Lucifer that will not end in our death or capture. With Dante's help, we can rob Lucifer of the greatest support of his regime—the Eldest's loyalty. And *with* the Knife, there is hope for us to topple Lucifer, or simply reach a treaty with him that he dares not break."

"You are a fool. No demon can wield the Knife." The mottled demon's chair grated along parquet as he rose slowly to his feet, his bright blue burning eyes fixed on me. My skin chilled, my throat going dry, and I was vaguely aware of McKinley moving closer to me, his peculiar null aura contracting.

"She is *not* demon. What does the riddle say? *The hand that can hold the Knife has faced fire and not been consumed, has walked in death and returned, a hand given strength beyond its ken.* So spoke Ilvarimel's *hedaira,* in the Temple of the White-Walled City, before she died at the hands of the Kinslayer." Eve turned away from the table, passing the high-backed chair, pacing to the wall and staring at its smooth white gleam. The warding sunk into the walls trembled under her attention, my knees echoing that tremor.

Well, that's bad poetry. Why didn't anyone ever tell me about this before?

"Who fits this description, Zaj?" Eve's voice was soft. "Who has escaped fire, walked in Death, and been given strength beyond a mortal's ken by the first Fallen in millennia? If you have another candidate who fits the bill, feel free to produce them for our study and illumination."

Zaj dropped back into his chair, still staring at me. I didn't like the look on his broad face. Neither did I like the increasing sense of motion threading through the other demons present. Their faces ran like ink on wet paper, because I couldn't make my eyes focus on one of them—too busy trying to watch them all.

You'd think this sort of thing would seem almost normal to me by now. Dark hilarity welled up in my throat, was shoved down with hysterical strength.

"You think she can wield the Knife." This demon, halfway down the table, was dressed all in fluttering red, long sleeves and a minstrel's dreamy face marred by the thin crimson lines of what looked like tribal tattoos swirling across his cheeks. His eyes were scarlet drops with black teardrops painted over them, I stared at the sharpness of his white teeth against golden skin and scarlet markings. He looked oddly familiar.

I am not thinking clearly. I am not even close to thinking clearly.

Increasing heat mounted through the lines of the scar on my left shoulder. I touched the Knife, buzzing in its hilt strapped to my rig, and the demons went still, each pair of lambent eyes fixed on me.

Maybe taking it out of my bag hadn't been such a great idea, after all. On the other hand, if any of them came at me . . .

Another demon, with a veil of gold tissue over its head

and the shadow of something under it I had no desire to
see, let out a slow hiss, like an adder swelling with poison.
"I applaud our leader for her show of strength." Its voice
loaded the sibilants with toxic strength. "What precisely
are we discussing?"

"Rebellion, and the death of the Prince of Hell." This,
from the crimson-painted demon. Its voice was strangely
sexless, a high clear tone like glass under moonlight.
"That *is* what we are speaking of, is it not?"

*With a whole bunch of you guys for backup, it might
even be possible.* My entire body was a block of numb
ice. My stomach filled with uneasy, unsteady loathing.

I hoped my eyes weren't the size of plates. "Sounds
great." I spoke before Eve could, my mouth bolting the
way it always does. "I'm all for it. When do we start?"

"You see?" Eve whirled away from the wall, her hair
swinging in a heavy pale wave of ropes. "A *hedaira* does
not fear him. Why should we of the Greater Flight fear
him, when we have the means to make the Eldest behave—
or at least remain neutral? If we are allied with the holder
of the Knife of Sorrow, we have the upper hand."

"None have ever successfully challenged the Prince."
A demon with fat yellow tentacled dreadlocks leaned
slightly aside in his chair, his fingertips drumming the
tabletop in one smooth arc. He had eight fingers on his
right hand, and I stared at the muscle working in his slim
forearm. "Still, we have come this far. It is logical for us
to pursue our course." He paused, his fingers drumming
down again, eight beats marking off time. "After all, *he*
will not forgive us. Are we resigned to death?"

"He will suspect our intentions, and send someone to
collect the Knife." This from a tall, thin demon whose

face was hidden under the hood of a gray cloak, the material shifting oddly as it twitched.

Eve's eyes met mine. "He did. But we had our own viper in the heart of that mission. Any other demon he sends will meet a harsh fate."

"Our own viper?" Zaj's eyebrow didn't lift, but he sounded skeptical. "This little thing?"

I could not look away from Eve's face. My heart thudded thinly, and I was suddenly aware of sweat prickling under my arms and at the small of my back. It took a lot of effort to make me sweat, a half-hour of hard sparring at least—or a room full of demons.

Go figure.

"She has been far more successful than any of you, has she not? And as long as we hold the allegiance of this Necromance, we hold the allegiance of her Fallen. If you do not respect her might, I should hope you are not stupid enough to disregard his." Eve's voice was very soft. "We do have your allegiance, do we not, Dante?"

Silence. Every eye in the place on me. McKinley shuffled slightly, near the door. I wondered if the coppery smell of fear riding the air was from him—or from me.

It came from that black place in me, the thing I didn't want to remember. The rush and crackle of flame filled my veins, a lioness's head lifting behind my eyes, Her face full of bloody light.

The world turned over, ramming me back into myself with a concussive internal blast. I almost staggered, caught myself. Air scorched my lungs as I let out the breath I'd been holding, returning to my skin with a rush of certainty. "You told me you wanted me to set myself up against the Prince of Hell. Here I am. That son of a bitch has messed with me for the last time."

"And your Fallen?" Eve persisted, but she looked pleased. A slight cruel smile lifted the corners of her mouth, and my face felt so numb I couldn't tell if I was copying the expression—or if she'd stolen it from my face.

"He's with me." My throat was dry, but the words were soft, husky, laden with promise.

"You are certain?"

Don't ask me that. I'm pretty certain, but he's pulled fast ones on me before. I searched her face, finding only the taint of demon overlaying her skin with a high gloss, covered with the dark hood of my own guilt at not being able to save her from Lucifer in the first place. There were so many I had failed to save—Lewis, Doreen, Jace, Eddie, Gabe . . . the list stretched on. My arms and legs were frozen, my face a stiff mask.

All that remained was to say the words. "I'm sure," I husked. "What do you have in mind?"

She opened her mouth, but my scar turned molten, sending a soft wave of Power down my skin. I shivered, my right hand empty without a swordhilt. A susurrus ran through the assembled demons.

The sun turned into a bloody eye, low in the sky. Paradisse glimmered, slim plasteel towers each vetted by an aesthetic committee before the first hoverload of dirt was lifted. They pierced the gathering twilight, shimmers resolving near their tops, lights blurring along each graceful arch.

"Ah." Eve lowered herself into the iron chair at the

head of the table, its high spiked back spearing the air. The demons all turned still as statues, waiting.

Usually when demons are this still, they're conserving their energy, compressing the elasticity of their bodies so they can unleash that spooky blurring speed of theirs when the time comes. This was a different immobility, almost tranquil except for the razor-edge of nervousness under it, like hounds scenting blood and waiting tensely for the leash to slip.

Crimson painted the windows, and if I hadn't been so nervous and just plain exhausted I might have enjoyed the once-in-a-lifetime view of Paradisse stretching out beneath us, the buildings beginning their nightly dance of illumination, streams of hovertraffic winking with reactive paint, the towers also beginning to let loose scarves of synth-perfume that glittered crystalline as the lowering sun shone through them. Walking in Paradisse is an olfactory experience as well as visual.

I should have been having the time of my life.

Darkness gathered along the floor, and I felt the quivering that ran through the building. It felt like a padded hammer tapping at my left shoulder, and I let out a small sound between my lips. Every demon in the room turned his gaze to me, except Eve, who settled down languorous into the chair.

"It begins," she murmured. "Semma?"

A demon at the far end of the table—the one with a long shock of blue hair woven with glittering gold charms that tinkled as he moved—rose and padded to the hover-lift door. I heard the lift machinery beginning, the whine of hover transport and a swoosh of displaced air. I didn't look, staring down the table and off to the left, where the windows framed a cityscape just falling under night's cloak.

Steady now, Dante. I edged along the table, passing behind demons so still they might have been statues, and finally paused, almost to Eve's chair. To get there I had to pass the mottled demon, and I didn't want to. The mood of the room turned dark, Power spilling against my nervestrings like warm oil, a sizzling bath.

The lift arrived, and the doors opened with a soft chime. Silence, three soft steps I knew as well as my own heartbeat, and he came into the room.

Dear gods. Thank you. He's out of Hell. The scar on my shoulder turned live, singing against my skin, a burst of Power working its way down through flesh and racing through my bones.

Another silence, this one managing to convey shock and growing apprehension. He tipped a room full of scary-ass demons into fear just by walking in.

Japhrimel. My Fallen.

My very own demon. *I am so happy to see you right now, Japh.*

I let my eyes swing over to him. He'd come alone, and stood in front of the hoverlift doors, his eyes burning green under winged dark eyebrows. His hair was longer, too; he hadn't cut it. It fell in his eyes and shadowed the first shock: the gauntness of his face.

He looked *starved,* perfect skin drawn tight over bones that revealed demon architecture as surely as my own. There were hollows under his cheekbones, and dark smudges under his eyes, just as piercing and laserlike as Lucifer's, but just a shade less inherently awful.

It was still too close for comfort. Little whispering

fingers chuckled nasty things inside my head, taunting me. McKinley let out a sigh that didn't bother to conceal his relief.

The second shock was the threads of paleness in Japh's hair, silvery gray strands in the rough dark silk. I took all this in with a glance, met his eyes again. A burning prickle started in the scar, like a limb waking up. Like my entire body, a swift pulse slamming through me and shouting his name even as remembered screams boiled up, as the Devil chuckled and whispered in my ear.

Oh, gods. There was a lump in my throat. It was my heart. *I am so glad to see you. You have no idea.*

Eve spoke first. "Welcome, Kinslayer." The softness and conciliation had dropped from her voice. It was almost as sheerly, nakedly powerful as Lucifer's. The only thing saving me from flinching was the mounting discomfort as the scar turned hot on my shoulder, molten liquid spreading out from it in intricate pathways.

Japhrimel's eyes didn't leave mine.

He didn't even acknowledge Eve's opening salvo. Instead, he spoke to me, as if we had just met on the street. "You are well?" Just the three words, but the air cringed away from them.

He was *furious.* His rage circled the room lazily, gathering itself, and the bottom of my stomach dropped out. I had never seen this in him before. I'd seen him calm and I'd seen him lethal, I had seen him languid and I'd seen him tense with danger, but I had never seen him look so much like he was going to start killing and he wasn't particularly picky about who he began with.

My shirt fluttered a little, though the air was still. His

aura crackled, and the other demons shifted uneasily in their chairs, darting bright nervous glances at Eve.

Who looked completely unaffected. She tilted her head slightly, as if giving me permission to respond.

"Never better," I lied, my mouth moving independently of my brain again. I closed it with an effort—the words *you look like hell* were just dying to come out.

And right after them, *why do I get the feeling you're not happy to see* me?

Japhrimel studied me for a long few moments. Immovable, a sword of darkness against the glow of Paradisse leaking through the plasilica behind him. The sun died, sinking below the earth's rim, and the city suddenly blazed.

"Make your offer," he said finally, tossing the words like a challenge. His eyes didn't leave mine, and his hands tensed slightly at his sides. Fudoshin hummed inside his sheath, a single low tone of dissatisfaction. The Knife's hum slid up another notch, rattling my bones.

Before I could ask him what the hell he meant, Eve spoke in the harsh, consonant-laden language of demons, a long string of rolling words that tore the tattered air even further. The mood of the room was beginning to tip again, the fine hairs on my nape rising. It felt like a riot was going to break out, or a thunderstorm.

It *also* felt like I was standing right in its path. Normally I'd have been looking for a wall to put my back to.

There's no easy way out of this one. Little invisible tremors twitched through my muscles. *Fine time to start coming down with the shakes, Valentine. Focus!*

Japhrimel spoke briefly, pointedly keeping his eyes locked with mine. Eve responded, her tone softening—if anything can ever be *soft* in the language of Lucifer's children. Even her voice couldn't make the hard sounds any prettier, and Japhrimel's short reply shivered the plasilica windows in their mounts.

"Let's ask her, shall we?" Eve spoke Merican, but the shadow of demon language lay behind it. I shivered. "Who do you prefer, Dante? Him, or me?"

Prefer? Both of you are pretty goddamn scary right now. I peeled myself away from the chair, my legs suddenly weak and shaking. Some kind of letdown from all the adrenaline I'd been soaking in, at the worst possible time, as Japh's mark on my shoulder pulsed, burning away the veil of numbness.

I took two steps back from the table. The demon Zaj tensed, and so did McKinley, twin movements I could feel like a storm-front against a sensitive membrane. "Japh. We're all on the same side here, and Eve—"

"I did not come here for *her*." He answered so quickly the words bit off the tail of my sentence. "The Prince has pronounced doom on every *Ifrijiin* in this room." His eyes still didn't flicker away from mine. "You are all under sentence of death, for treason to the throne of Hell. I am here to execute that sentence."

The way he said it, it sounded like a done deal.

What? The reality of what he'd just said hit me square in the chest. *Hey. Wait a second. When did this happen?*

Betrayal, sharp and pointed, hit me just afterward. *Sure, Danny. Let me go into Hell and get the Knife. You idiot. He probably went to have another little tête-à-tête with Lucifer, and you let him! You fell for it!*

It was the last straw, the last betrayal. A small, quiet part of me was asking why I was jumping to conclusions, but the rest of me shouted that little voice of doubt down. How many times would Japh have to pull a mickey on me before I got the idea?

I was *justified* in thinking he'd turn on me. How could I not be?

Sentence of death. That meant he wanted to kill Eve.

Not while I'm breathing, bucko. "Japhrimel." My right hand closed around Fudoshin's hilt. The blade left the scabbard with a short singing note, and I settled into second guard, a movement so habitual and natural it seemed easier than standing upright and feeling the shaking work its way into my bones. Light ran like oil over honed steel, blue flame waking along its sharp sweet curve, and I tossed the words at him. "You can start with me."

Are you kidding, Dante? You know how fast he is. You don't have a chance.

It didn't matter. Nothing mattered now. And if nothing mattered, everything was permissible.

Everything was *possible.* So it was glancingly possible that I might hit him if he came at Eve.

Reality made one last stab at my consciousness. Sekhmet sa'es, *Danny. You at least could have drawn a gun.*

Eve's laughter rattled the table, blew through the assembled demons like a hard wind through a field of wheat. "You see, Kinslayer? Come for me, and she will do what she must. If I am a traitor, so is she. Will you kill your own leman?"

That brought his eyes to her for the first time, and I felt faintly ridiculous, standing there dressed in air-dried wrinkles with drawn steel and nobody paying any goddamn attention to the fact.

"It matters little," Japhrimel returned equably. "Neither you, nor Death, nor even the Prince may have her, and I have time to teach her manners. Which is none of your concern. Yield and return to your nest, Androgyne, and you may yet be forgiven."

I sensed Eve's chin lifting. When she spoke, it was the soft finality of a declaration of war. "Come and take me, if you dare."

The trembling air was riven again, demon Power spiking and tearing. A low glassy growl started.

I knew that sound. *Hellhounds. Oh, gods.* This was rapidly getting out of hand—if it had ever been manageable in the first place. The growling was coming from right behind me, and McKinley let out a short low curse he must have picked up in Putchkin Near Asia.

"Game," Zaj said. He rose slowly, his chair scraping, and I was suddenly conscious he was far too close to me. "And set."

Japhrimel actually smiled. It was one of those slow murderous grins I'd seen him use during the hunt for Santino, only it was dialed up to ten instead of two on the scary scale.

The urge to dive for cover collided with the need to back up, both fighting with the sudden desire to turn around and see what was behind me.

Right behind me, breathing heat into my hair. My mouth went dry, and the strength left my legs in a liquid rush. Only the locking of my muscles kept me standing, the scar suddenly blazing with spiked iron wire, driving into my flesh. Burrowing in.

Japhrimel's right hand came out from behind his back. Gold glittered in his palm.

It was a wide round golden medallion, demon runes

scored deeply into its soft surface and writhing madly, beginning to burn with clear crimson radiance. Chairs scraped as the assembled demons scrambled to their feet, a collective growl raising itself, plasilica cracking as the windows finally gave up under the onslaught.

"Game. Set." Japhrimel's tone did not alter. "Match."

His hand came forward with a sweet economy of motion, and he tossed the gold medallion toward the table. An extension of the motion brought him into an effortless lunge, and I threw myself down and past Zaj, colliding with the iron chair bruising-hard, tipping it over and going down in a tangle of arms and legs with Eve as Japh met the hellhound with a sound like freight transports crashing together.

The beast was low and sinuous, heat smoking off its glassy obsidian pelt, its eyes a flaming carnivorous orange. It wasn't like the other hellhounds I'd seen, those smooth basalt creatures with fiery snouts. This one had a longer, pointed muzzle with viciously curved teeth made of volcanic glass, and wings with sharp daggered feathers half-spread as Japhrimel struck it down, gunfire blooming in the sudden screaming chaos. He had both silvery guns out, and *twisted* in midair, somehow landing lightly as a cat on the table as I made it to my feet, McKinley's hand sinking into the skein of my hair and doing more than anything else to pull me up. The agent's fingers slid free as he yelled, the noise swallowing whatever he wanted to say.

The world turned sideways. The medallion flared with a thundercrack of sound, demon protections laid in the room shattering. It tore through the careful layers

of warding like the whine of hoverfreight thrums in the
bones, a deep undeniable sound.

I made it to hands and knees and launched myself, rolling. Fudoshin's hilt socked into my hand as I struggled
up. The blade sliced air, a small sound lost in the swelling
chaos.

Eve rose like a wave from the wreck of the iron chair,
spun on her toes, and bolted for the stairs. I whirled and
sprinted after her, hysterical strength filling unruly limbs
suddenly weighted with scrap plasteel. I heard McKinley
yell something else short and sharp behind me.

*Sorry, sunshine, but you work for the demon that just
threw a wrench in the works.* My priority now was getting
Eve *out* of the fire zone. The past had looped over and
touched the present again—Doreen in front of me, pale
hair swinging as she ran; my heart in my mouth, tasting
of copper and bile—and the sound behind us of demons,
and a hell of a fight breaking out. My katana blurred down
in a half-circle, ending up with the blade tucked behind
my arm; it would do no good to spit myself on my own
sword if I fell.

It felt goddamn good to have the hilt in my hand again,
to have a fight in front of me, everything becoming clear
and sharp as only the last desperate battles are. It felt so
stupidly good my breath caught on a half-sob I couldn't
afford, I needed all my lung-strength for running.

The stairs spiraled up, and Eve outdistanced me.
I lagged under the weight of effort, my breath coming
harsh and tearing, and saw the door just as she neatly
nipped through it.

*Roof access. Good plan. Hope she has a hover
stashed, or this could get real ugly.* McKinley's footsteps

pounded on the stairs behind me—at least, I hoped it was McKinley.

I was fairly sure I could outrun *him*.

I tumbled out of the door into the moaning wind of a high-altitude platform. I almost ran into Eve, whose golden hand shot out and caught my upper arm, digging in with fingers like steel claws. The sudden stop almost tore my arm out of my socket and my stomach from its moorings, and I was suddenly very sorry I'd eaten.

The landing-platform spread out like the petal of a flower, glowing a pale amber to match the rest of the tower. My hair lifted on a wave of sweet synth-perfume. I caught my balance just as McKinley plowed through the door behind us, and I brought my sword around in an easy semicircle, blade cutting air with a low whispering sound into the ready position. My scabbard was in my left hand, and I turned my wrist to brace it, using it as a shield and potential weapon. My sleeves flapped, pulled by the freshening breeze.

"Eve." My voice cut through the whine of the wind. "You go. I'll take care of this."

Because there on the platform, with a laserifle and two plasguns pointed at us, were Vann and Lucas Villalobos. Of course they hadn't come to meet up with me. They were on Japhrimel's side.

32

Eve's fingers fell from my upper arm as I moved forward, blocking their firing angle. Vann was on one knee, laserifle against his shoulder and his other weapons glinting. A bruise spread up his neck, mottling the left side of his face, dried blood clinging in his hair.

Lucas stood, disheveled and threadbare and dangerous, his yellow eyes focused past me on Eve. His guns glittered too—SW Remington 60-watt plasguns. Not even a demon can outrun *that*.

Lucas, on the job and working overtime. Only he'd forgotten he was working for me.

Which made him an enemy.

Great. It's me against the world now. Why am I not surprised? I felt almost like myself again, with the unholy urge to laugh rising under my breastbone.

"Eve. I mean it. Go." I took another step forward, and Vann twitched.

"Give it up, Valentine." The wind flirted with his hair, his eyes were narrowed and professional, cool and distant in the bruised mask of his face. "Don't make us hurt someone."

He sounded like it would be so *easy*. And Lucas's finger tightened on the trigger, his entire body tensing. There could be no question about it. He'd betrayed me too.

I. Have. Had. Enough.

My temper snapped behind my breastbone, and welcome wine-dark rage flooded me. It scorched through tender burned channels where psychic scars still smoked, courtesy of whatever Lucifer had done to me and the strain I'd put on myself since then. A roar filled my throat, flame springing up from a deep burning well of rage. I dropped my scabbard, both hands closing around the hilt and bringing the swordblade high.

Fucked with me for the last time, it whispered in the sudden silence of utter berserk rage. *Kill them. Kill them all.*

I flung myself across the intervening space, a sound I barely recognized bursting from my throat. It was a cat's scream, fury and terror rolled into a pretty package wrapped with barbed wire and ignited with nuclear force. Eve ran for the edge of the bare empty platform as I brought the sword down, blue-white flame streaking along the arc of the strike, light stuttering because I was moving with berserker speed, the crackle and hiss of flame filling my ears.

Time slowed down. The streak of red down low was Vann, firing at Eve. I crashed into him first, the katana making a high shivering note as I followed through with the strike, a perfect downsweep. The laserifle split asunder, a burst of plas splashing out and underlighting the scene with bloody glow. I pivoted on my front foot, hearing faintly my *sensei*'s habitual admonition from the soup of memory inside my imploding head.

Move, no think! Fight, no think!

My knee met Vann's face with the sound of a melon dropped on a hot sidewalk. He flew back like a rag doll, and my leg paused, cocked now for the strike back, which pitched the top half of my body forward under Lucas's fire. He was shooting over my head, aiming at Eve.

At *my daughter,* at the only piece left of my dead demon-murdered lover. Human or not, she was mine.

She was all I had left.

I snapped my leg back, my heel hitting something soft and crunching. It snapped like a flag in a high breeze. Another pivot, heel sliding out, and my katana blurred as my wrist turned, everything gaining momentum by the spin, and I struck not to injure but to kill.

If Lucas hadn't flown backward from the kick, I would have cut him in half. As it was I completed the movement, stamping down with what was now my lead foot, the blade kissing only air.

The building swayed like a plucked harpstring, and I heard the whine of a hover engine, close. Very close.

"Valentine!" McKinley screamed, his voice breaking. *"Stop it!"*

Oh, no. I am not nearly finished here. They're still breathing—and so are you. A hover rose up to the landing pad, sleek and black, and I saw a hatch in its side dilating as a pilot or AI held it steady. I also saw Lucas dragging himself up to his feet, blood painting his face into a mask of yellow-eyed rage as Eve paused at the edge of the platform, her pale hair whipped by the wind.

She leapt.

I forgot all about Vann, who lay gasping and choking some ten feet away, his ribs battered in. I forgot about

Lucas, painfully hauling himself upright. All I could think of was that pale head, vanishing straight down. *Eve!*

I flung myself after her, my boots grinding in broken bits of laserifle, and was just gaining momentum when the entire side of the tower shattered and the hellhound landed with a thud on the platform, which was swaying in earnest now. Demon warding sparked and fizzed, fluorescing into the visible range as *something* huge and powerful as a magickal tornado exploded below somewhere in the tower, like a freight hover looming up out of nowhere under a slicboard. It was that explosion that saved me, the tower bucking at the precise moment the winged hellhound leapt for me; the heaving of the entire edifice knocking me off my feet and sending me rolling toward the edge, my sword hammered from my hand and skittering along the platform's floor.

Sword get your sword that thing's coming for you, it's coming for you, get up and kill it and go after her—My fingers closed on the hilt as I scrabbled, and chaos boiled behind me. The whine of plasbolts mixed with a high squealing roar told me the hellhound had been hit; I rolled to my feet, body moving with inhumanly precise coordination as my mind struggled to keep up, to control the motion. I skidded, gained my feet, snapped one glance back, and saw the hellhound crouching as plasgun bolts peppered the platform around it. It leapt again, this time thankfully not aiming for me, and Lucas rolled aside as the thing crashed into where he had been standing a moment before. There was too much plasfire in the air to be accounted for, but I didn't care.

I turned back to the edge.

The air became molten and my scar turned to clawed

fire, nailing my feet in place. I almost overbalanced, wind screaming up and pouring over the platform in a wash of burned plas, hoverscorch, and the musky fume of demons. My shirt flapped in the wind, my whipping hair stinging my eyes.

"Stop." Japhrimel's voice sliced through chaos.

Poised on the brink, I looked back over my shoulder again. He halted, too far away, and his wings settled, the edges of his coat ruffling. His eyes burned, and behind him the hellhound snarled. More plasgun bolts whined. The streaks of silvery gray in his hair, new and shocking, threw back Paradisse's light.

Japhrimel took another step forward, his hands out, palms cupped. Demon blood smoked along his sleeves and the hem of his coat, and there was a spatter of it high on one gaunt cheek. "Dante," he mouthed, and the world stopped its rolling inevitable course.

His boots were wet, and he'd left dark bloody prints on the shattered floor of the platform. The tower heaved again and I heard a massive belling note of rage from below, a howl that chilled my blood and lifted every fine hair on my body. I could even feel the individual hairs on my scalp trying to rise.

Demon. That's a dying demon. Which one? I exhaled, the breath lasting forever.

I no longer cared.

"Dante." Again, Japhrimel did not precisely speak, but mouthed the word. Or was there so much noise I couldn't hear him, though a great silence had settled over the world?

His voice bypassed my ears, smashing directly into my brain like carbolic flung across reactive. *Come with me.*

You must come. Now. Sheer naked command in the words, wrapping around me and yanking.

Demanding. Controlling me.

Forcing me.

Gods above and below, how I hate to be forced.

My fingers loosened, and my sword chimed on the platform, Japhrimel's will wresting it from my hand as easily as an adult might wrench a toy away from a small child.

It is so easy to break a human. Especially a human woman. Claws buried in my chest, and the sound of my own screams as someone hurt me, invaded me, *hurt* me—

I had thought nothing else inside me could break. But something deep-buried in my mind snapped and rose up like a shattered cable suddenly free of weight, a sheet of flame blinding me. My lips shaped one single word, the only thing I could say.

No.

The alpha and omega of my epitaph, what they would lasecarve on my urn when I finally was forced kicking and screaming into the dry land of Death.

But not yet. I wasn't finished yet. The hardest, most stubborn deep-buried core of me ignited even as my body betrayed me, already starting to shift its weight to obey him, to accept the inevitable and *submit*.

To give in.

No. The word boiled through me. I am not sure if I screamed, or if the roar was merely psychic, locked behind my rictus-grin of a face. The curtain between me and a black hole of something too terrible to be spoken or thought of pulled aside for a single heartstopping moment, and I remembered what had been done to me.

Who had done it.

And how much it had *hurt*.

No. The single word filled me. I would *not* give in. I would not endure another rape of my body or my mind. I would not go gently into any dark night of submission. I would not be *forced* any further.

I would die first.

I tore myself free, and hurled my traitorous body out into empty space.

The roar of the wind cradled me as I fell, arms and legs pulled close. A streak painted the air—my rings, boiling with golden light, their gems and silver screaming in defiant rage as I narrowed my welling eyes against the stinging hurricane.

Looking for that pale head, the spot of brilliance I could aim for. What did I think I was going to do? I couldn't survive a fall like this, and Eve had vanished. Paradisse wheeled crazily under me, hovertraffic reaching up to swallow my falling body, the buildings turning to streaks of amber, silver, and anemic gold.

I couldn't see her anywhere. Eve was gone, disappeared.

A curious comfort spilled through me. I was going to die. None of it mattered anymore. I was done, and once in Death's arms the Devil couldn't harm me or involve me in any more games.

A swift, piercing pain lanced through my heart. *Japhrimel.*

He can't save you, Danny. Nobody can. The truth whispered in my ears, in my fingers, in my heartbeat, which stupidly kept plowing ahead, not understanding or stubbornly ignoring the fact that I was *dead,* finally dead, that I was falling and it was over.

Finally, blessedly over. My left cheek burned as the emerald embedded atop my accreditation tat spat a glowing-green spark, a high sudden fracture-pain as if I'd been punched hard enough to crack my cheekbone. The flash of green dyed the entire world for a timeless second before it was swallowed by the rip of torn air.

Flying, a bubble of something hot behind my lips, my clothes fluttering and snapping as my body relaxed, tumbling through space and time, synth-perfume filling my nose—apples, musk, peaches, fresh-mown grass.

If you have to die, Paradisse is a good place to do it. Why is this taking so long?

Then, the impossible. Tumbling in freefall, completely free for the first time in my whole miserable existence—

Fingers closed around my wrist and a jolt of arrested motion popped my shoulder from its socket with a sickening crunch.

I screamed. Wings beat, filling the air with crazy mixtures of synth-perfume tainted with the dark musk of demon, familiar to me as breath. I hung pinned between the point of no return and the absolute freedom of death, the world spinning frantically as the sound of straining wings and a long howl of effort smashed through my head. My arm stretched like elastic, tendons creaking and popping as the rooftop loomed below us, flowing nacreous pearl. It was another tower, and I flinched away from the impending shock, screaming again until the bubble behind my lips broke and sweet spicy black demon blood filled my mouth.

Impact. A crunching, hideous shock drove me out of myself, ribs snapping, the force of the fall broken just enough to keep me from dying on impact. Something in my other arm snapped too, and I was flung across the rooftop like a doll, rolling limp as a rag. Plasteel buckled and bent, an invisible layer of force closing around me, cushioning, a flexible shield stopping me just short of a climate-control housing shaped like a whipped confection of spun plasteel and plasglass.

Warm wetness dripped into my eyes. I lay against the housing, blinking, my breath stuttering out in an abused howl.

I saw him rolling too, shedding momentum as his wings gracefully bled the force away from his body, rising in a perfectly coordinated movement and whirling, a familiar curve of steel in his hands. He drove my sword into the rooftop with one economic movement, shaking his hand out as blue sparks popped and snarled between him and the hilt. He turned, his wings beginning to flow back down to armor him, a flash of his narrow golden chest heaving as he filled his lungs—

—and the winged hellhound streaked down from the sky and hit him with a bone-shattering crunch.

Japhrimel! Agony roared through me, preternatural flesh stretched to its limits, bones struggling to reknit themselves, a tide of black demon blood smashing through my lips as I coughed, creaking sounds spearing through my chest as my ribs snapped out, mending themselves. The scar turned into a red-hot drill, and if I could have breathed through the convulsions I would have screamed again, pointlessly, as the flurry of motion disappeared, driven past my line of sight by the collision.

My arms boiled red-hot with pain as I made it up to elbows-and-knees, realizing I wasn't healing fast enough. Black blood should have been welling up and closing the wounds, sealing them away—but more blood pattered on the rooftop as I scrabbled, my fingers slipping in slick hot wetness as the air closed around me, suffocatingly heavy. Material ripped as my claws extended, shearing through plasteel and fabric alike. Gunfire echoed behind me, and the snarls of the hellhound made the whole building shake like a flower on a slender stem.

Get up! Get up and fight! Stark terror boiled up through my mouth as I coughed more blood.

Every cell in my body rebelled. I forgot his betrayal, I forgot my own, I forgot everything but the need to get to my feet and fling myself at the thing that was going to kill him.

I don't know why. It was an instinctive response, like jerking your hand back from a red-hot stove.

Power smashed through the scar, flaring down my skin and sparking into the visible range, black-diamond flames twisting through the trademark sparkles of a Necromance's aura. My shielding, smashed and rent, cracked open, and for one dizzying eternal moment the entire city of Paradisse shattered through my skull again, as if I had once more opened the taplines in Notra Dama and ripped a hole in the world.

The assault smashed me flat onto the floor of the roof, blood sizzling with the heavy odor of decaying fruit. My shields closed, mended by the thunderbolt of pure Power spilling through me. I heard my own voice from very far away, an animal's howl, breaking in the higher registers as it spiraled into a deathscream.

Still I tried to get up, to *make* my body respond. Beating darkness closed over my vision—whether my eyes were shut or I was just blind with effort was anyone's guess. A great glass bell of silence closed over me as my body twitched, little moans escaping my mouth between sips of air.

"Be still." The voice was hoarse but utterly familiar. "*Shavarak'itzan beliak,* woman, be *still.* Calm yourself. Stop. *Stop.*"

Hands on me, familiar hands. I lay limp as clingfilm as he pulled me into his arms, my ribs still crackling as flexible demon bones tried to heal themselves. Yet more Power roared into me through the scar, coating my skin and working in, filling the hollow channels of my nerves and skeleton, I coughed one last time and convulsed, my heels slapping the rooftop.

I collapsed.

Something against my forehead—I realized it was his mouth just as he began kissing my cheeks, my temple, my hair, anywhere he could reach. He almost crushed me, his arms like steel bars, holding me to earth as my dislocated shoulder howled with pain.

I didn't care.

They had to be obscenities, whatever he was saying in his native tongue. Curls of steam threaded away from us both, heat bleeding off through his aura as his shielding closed over me, a touch almost as intimate as his wings pulled close, enfolding me in a double layer of protection.

Sobs came fast and hard, breaking me open. I wept

against his chest, his skin against mine again, as he kissed every part of me he could and cracked his voice saying, over and over again in a language that I for once needed no translation for, that I was safe. That he had plucked me from the sky, because not even Death would take me from him.

33

I lay on my side, in a bath of delicious heat and softness. It was like sleeping on clouds, and the heat burrowed into me, all the way out through my fingers and toes. Flushing away the last remaining traces of pain and injury. Soothing.

The entire world was a gray smear. I wanted it to stay that way.

Along with the warmth and the softness was Japhrimel's hoarse voice, another constant. He spoke, sometimes calmly, sometimes not, but I didn't listen to the words. Other voices intruded, but I paid no attention. I simply curled in on myself, shutting them away as best I could. My mind shivered, psychic wounds raw and smoking, all careful work to heal them undone. Quivering on the edge of insanity, not even the blue crystalline glow of Death's country to break the darkness.

I came back in bits and pieces, drifting for a while. Then I lunged into consciousness, jolting off the table, my hands around a hilt and the blade making a low whooshing sound as air split.

Warm irresistible fingers closed around my wrist. Hoverwhine drilled through my back teeth. I opened my eyes, and Japhrimel twisted my wrist—not hard, but enough to lock it and keep the blade down and to the side.

I still had my boots on. They scraped grated metal flooring as I shifted my weight, left hand coming up in a flat strike, meaning to break the nasal promontory and drive it up into the brain. It was a reflex action, snake-quick, and Japhrimel avoided it gracefully, his streaked hair ruffling as he ducked aside and caught my left wrist. The room was narrow, very small, and smelled of hover-wash and oil.

He drove me back, pinned me to the wall, I brought my knee up and he avoided that too. My breath caught in my throat, my shoulders suddenly against the hull. It was a hover, we were traveling, and the entire ship shuddered as I struggled with flesh and Power both. His aura clamped down over mine, the pressure excruciating for a long infinite moment.

"Calm," he said, softly. "I am here. Calm, my curious."

He looked just the same, except for the streaks in his hair and the shadows under his burning eyes. His face had hollowed out, but it was still essentially his, and the same essentially human darkness lay under the green fire of his irises.

"Let go." I didn't recognize my own voice, low and flat, with the terrible weight of fury behind it. "Let go *now.*"

"No." He didn't even bother to dress up the refusal, his fingers clamping home. Leather creaked, the rig responding to pressure. I tried shifting and sliding away, struggled until sweat broke out along the curve of my lower back, pressed into the metal hull. My hair fell in my eyes. "You do not understand."

"I don't *want* to. You *lie*." Still quiet, as if every shade of inflection had been washed out of my throat.

"I have the other half of the Knife, Dante. We are so very close to being free." He sounded so reasonable. Over his shoulder I could see the rest of the narrow room, a shelflike bed and plasglass-fronted cabinets. "I have returned from the very depths of Hell, and I have—"

I know what you did. You sold me out. "Shut up." I didn't know if it was possible to care less. "Where's Eve?" *If you've hurt her I'll—*

"Vardimal's Androgyne is safely confined. Lucas and McKinley restrained her." His fingers softened, but not nearly enough for me to slip free. The hover settled into a rhythm, short choppy bounces as if we were just above rough water, gyros straining as antigrav slipped and slithered against waves. "Her supporters are scattered. It was *necessary.* I had to, Dante."

I finally slumped against the wall, leather and hilts digging into me as Japhrimel leaned in. His eyes were inches from mine, filling the world until I closed my eyelids, shutting out that green fire. Fudoshin's bladetip clattered, my shaking hand pushing forward against a vise-grip. "You were going to kill her," I whispered.

"If it would serve my plans, I would."

Great. I suppose that's one statement I can unequivocally believe. The deep, sarcastic voice inside my head showed up again, right on time. "Your *plans.* Do I serve your plans?"

If the words had carried any steel they could have cut. They could have shattered the hull and left me free. I would have tried to struggle free, but it would do no good. Instead, I gathered myself, harsh hurtful tension building in my muscles.

"You do not serve my plans. You are what I engage in planning to keep safe. Look at me."

"No." Other people might have a witty saying or a pretty epitaph. Not me. I will have only sheer, stubborn refusal. He was still forcing me, still demanding.

"*Look* at me." The softest of his voices, the most careful. The most human. "Dante. Please."

My eyes flew open.

He leaned in close, lashes veiling the green burn of his gaze. His hair fell, thick choppy streaks of silvery contrasting sharply with wet blackness. Fine lines bracketed his mouth, fanned out from the corners of his eyes.

After so long unchanging, he seemed to have aged. But demons don't age. Was it another mask?

"What happened to you?" My traitorous heart pounded inside my chest.

"I made a fresh bargain with the Prince." He overrode my sudden surging struggle. "Our salvation is so very close, do not doubt me now."

"Eve—"

"That is *not her Name*. She is Lucifer's Consort, not a human child. You *fool*. Did you open a door into Hell at her bidding? Do you have the least comprehension of what that means? A large portion of her allies, her precious resistance, escaped into the free air. Lucifer will make war upon them himself, he cannot afford to do otherwise—but she was my bait in a trap I laid with care, a trap you almost made unusable. I *had* to kill her gathering once you broke the walls between your world and Hell."

How could I even begin to explain? "I was giving you time," I whispered. "And staying alive. It was the only way I could—" *Do something, instead of waiting for you!* I was going to finish, but he didn't let me.

"McKinley was more than capable of hiding you."

"Not from *her* he wasn't." *She's mine, Japhrimel.* The words trembled on my lips, the secret I had not opened my mouth to tell him directly. My own small private deceit in this snakepit of lies and clashing agendas. I couldn't tell him now. "I had to, Japh." I sagged against the wall, going limp in his hands, but my fingers were tight on Fudoshin's hilt. If he let go of me now—

He sighed, a sharp dissatisfied sound. "It matters little now. We are on our way to a meeting with Lucifer. I will deliver the wayward Androgyne and—"

I brought my knee up, sharply, he countered the movement, and we almost spilled to the floor. He regained his balance, fingers biting in cruelly. *"Stop."* Did he sound breathless? The scar turned to molten metal on my shoulder, another warm pulse of Power filling my nerves and veins.

My skin crawled. I opened my mouth to scream at him, but he overrode me.

"Once she is delivered to him, she has agreed to distract his attention. I will strike him down even as he gloats over her. *Will you stop?*"

I went utterly still, a clockwork spinning inside my head pausing for just a moment. *Don't trust him. Don't listen. Plot and counterplot, Danny.*

When I did speak, it was a low, gravelly whisper. "How can I trust anything you say to me?"

"I have gone into Hell for you, not once but several

times." He let go of me in a sudden convulsive movement. "That should be enough. Even for you."

"You think I've been on a fucking holiday cruise? Where do you think *I've* gone?" My arm fell to my side, Fudoshin avoiding a stack of crates strapped to the floor.

"As far as necessary. As I would for you." His hands dropped. His coat was just as black as ever, but that shock of silver-threaded hair . . . he was different. Too different.

We had both changed out of all recognition. What was left?

"Let me get this straight." I swallowed, my dry throat clicking. "You expect me to stand there and trust you while you hand Eve over to Lucifer—the very thing he's *always* wanted out of this game." *He wanted me to tell him where she was, and when I wouldn't I was a Judas goat, meant to lure her in. He used me, you used me—what's the god-damn difference?*

His left hand came up. In it, satiny wood gleamed, and the sheathed Knife at my hip gave a slow sonorous ring-ing, like crystal stroked just right. The finials of its other half cradled Japh's hand, moving slightly, yearning out of his grip and toward me. His fingers trembled as he held it, as if he wanted to drop it.

He took two slow steps forward as the hover's gyros stabilized, the bounce telling me we were ashore now. We'd just made landfall.

Where the hell were we?

Off the map, sunshine. You've just gone off the fucking edge of the world.

Japhrimel offered me the Knife. "Take it."

My heart thumped against my ribs. I eyed his hand,

eyed the other half of the Knife. So he *had* retrieved it. Where had he hidden it in Hell?

Would I ever have the time or the courage to ask him?

He cupped the blade in his right hand and released the hilt, offering it like a goblet of wine to thirsty gods. If it hurt him, his face showed no sign. Time ticked by as the hover began to climb, the earpopping of altitude a heavy auditory weight.

If you take that, Danny, you'll be able to kill him. He's fast and strong, but you saw what it did to Sephrimel. You'll have some power in this relationship. You'll have a little control.

And if he pulls a mickey on you one more time, you can bury the thing in his guts.

My tat shifted on my cheek, diamond pinpricks under skin. My emerald lit, a spark popping in the gloom. Japhrimel waited, half of the Knife trembling in his hands, aching to clasp its twin and be whole again.

"It's yours." Very softly, his mouth its usual straight line after it had given the words to the air. Still, he didn't look at me, his eyes hidden behind that fringe of hair. A muscle in his cheek flickered. "It was made for a *hedaira*'s hand."

Go ahead, Danny. Take it. You've got to finish this game anyway. You dealt yourself in at Notra Dama. Time to pick another card.

I didn't realize I'd moved until I closed my fingers over the hilt. It hummed in my hand, happily, and the memory of the sick gulping noise turned my stomach over hard.

Japhrimel raised his eyes, shaking his hair back. He shook both his hands free, flicking his fingers. "Will you trust me?"

Four little words. I weighed half the Knife in my hand, its mate vibrating against my hip like a slicboard rattling before it dumps you. *I don't know if I should. I don't know if I want to.* "I don't know if I can."

His shoulders dropped. My stomach rattled and flipped, as if I was tumbling in freefall again. Roaring wind in my ears, prepared to leave all this struggling and striving behind. The look on his face was like being stabbed, and all the broken places inside my head gave a flare of devouring pain.

Why was I such an idiot for him? Just when I thought I had no reason to trust him, he went and did something like this. Like giving me a weapon.

My mouth opened. "But I can try."

We stared at each other. The hover groaned and rocked as the angle of ascent sharpened. I stood there gripping half the Knife with white-knuckle fingers, my head suddenly full of the rushing noise of Paradisse wind sliding past as I prepared to splatter myself over the pavement below. I'd been so ready just to give up.

Again.

Japhrimel nodded, a short sharp movement. The silver in his hair glittered. "Thank you." Gravely, as if he hadn't just handed me the only weapon in the world that could possibly kill him.

The scar flamed with soft heat, and his aura over mine settled, thin fine strands of gossamer energy binding together rips and tears, healing the rent tatters of my shielding with infinite care. Was he doing it consciously?

Did it matter?

I searched for something else to say, another question

to keep him standing here and talking to me. "What happened to you? In Hell?"

One shoulder lifted, dropped. Goddamn shrugging demons.

"Nothing of any account." Dismissive.

The sharp bite of frustration whipsawed through me, drained away. "Come on, Japh. Your hair."

"It doesn't please you?" He tilted his head slightly, letting the dim orandflu light play over its shagginess.

Goddammit. "That's not the point. I just wondered what happened." *You're not going to tell me a damn thing, are you? Especially not now. You just want me to trust you blindly. You want to control everything about this.*

But the weight of half the Knife in my hand said differently.

"Tell me why you almost killed yourself fleeing me." His hands spread slightly, expressive. I glimpsed dark shadows across his palms—from the touch of the Knife?

I wondered.

The edges of his coat ruffled as the hover shifted, settling at a new altitude.

You really want to know? "I . . ." How could I put it into words? Because he'd tried to force me. Because Eve was the last shred of Doreen left walking the earth, and I had to believe there was some humanity left in her—because if there wasn't, there was none left in me either. Because I could no longer pray, because the Devil had robbed me of myself, because Eve was sticking it to Lucifer where it hurt—for any number of reasons, none of which I could explain without a half-hour, absolute silence on his part, and a whole lot of luck. Or maybe a demon-Merican dictionary, if such a thing existed.

"Exactly." He clasped his hands behind his back, his feet placed just precisely so. "There are some things that cannot be explained, even between us. Whether we founder on them or learn to leave them unsaid, I leave to you." He turned on one heel, his long black coat flaring with a sound like feathers rippling. "You should gain some rest. We will be there sooner than you think."

"Where?"

"Where else would Lucifer meet us? Where he can see us coming." With that, he was gone through a hatch door, a brief slice of daylight outside stinging my eyes.

I let out a sharp breath. The shaking in my arms and legs circled like a beast waiting to pounce.

I drew the first half of the Knife from its sheath. It was awkward, but I hitched one hip against the shelflike med-bay bed and compared the two wooden weapons. They both looked complete, but after a few moments my brain started to work and I saw how they could be fitted together, by tangling the finials and twisting just so. They hummed, my hands drawing together as if I held two powerful electromagnets, thrumming their attraction almost audibly.

I slid them together with infinite care, my almost-translucent fingernails still bearing chips and flecks of black molecule-drip polish. They matched the mellow glow of the wood, and the humming intensified until I gave the final twist, locking both halves of the Knife into place.

Power drew heavy and close in the confined space. The hover bounced, and the Knife's hum dropped below the audible. The world warped around it, the same kind of seaweed drifting I remembered around the edges of a door torn in the fabric of the world. The geometry of the Knife was slightly off, for all its grace, yet it looked at

home in my grasp, the finials caging and protecting my
slim golden hand. The blade, now leaf-shaped and slightly
curved, looked wicked enough to do some damage just
sitting there, and I suddenly had no trouble believing this
thing could kill any demon it chose.

*Still, it didn't do the other women any good. Don't get
cocky, Danny.*

Had Sephrimel's *hedaira* ever held this thing? If I
tried, could I find any traces of the women who might
have thought they could wield it locked under its glossy
surface? Psychometry wasn't a skill of mine; I was no
Reader.

And it was only made of wood, from some unspeakable tree I couldn't imagine.

The Knife hummed. It was power, and control, and
a way to end this madness so I could breathe again. So
I could think again, without the black hole in my head
threatening to drive me insane, without the hole in my
heart that kept crying Japhrimel's name. Without the
weight of sick grief and guilt I couldn't let myself feel if
I was to function.

"It doesn't matter," I whispered to the empty air.

Because it didn't. It didn't make a damn bit of difference whether I could trust Japhrimel or not. We were
locked into this course, like an AI locking in a freight
hover. Like a Greater Work of magick completing itself,
snapping home and driving a change into the fabric of the
world, reshaping reality according to its own laws.

He would either hold up his end of the deal or he
wouldn't. Either way, a demon or two—or more—was
going to die. I was going to see this thing finished.

Nothing else mattered.

34

There's no pretty way to describe the Vegas Waste.

The nucleus is an immense slag-crater full of radiation and thin glass where silica sand fused together, broken by twisted screaming shapes of ferrous metal. On the outside edges, the Ghost City slumps and crawls. Even from the air bones are visible, buried in drifts of sand that ride up and fall away so the entire place shifts. Moaning wind is the only sound left.

Once, the city stretched into the desert, full of gambling, liquor, and the peculiar Merican Era duo of fleshly urges and frantic penance for those urges. The Gilead government was like every other totalitarian regime—the ones in power wanted a playground, and Vegas was nothing if not accommodating.

Maybe the hard-line Republic thought it was being tricky by moving its StratComm into the city once it was pushed out of DeeSee by opposition forces after Kochba bar Gilead's assassination. Maybe they had nowhere else to go, having been blown out of the Coloradin Bunkers in massive firefights. Maybe it was just sheer disorganization.

Whatever it was, their threat of nuclear strike was met by an *actual* nuclear strike. Nobody after the Seventy Days War took responsibility for actually giving the codes to drop the bomb. Whoever did it saved plenty of lives—the hard-liners weren't going to go out quietly, and they had enough fanatics and material to wage war for a while, especially in the mountainous regions.

But whoever did it also slaughtered a million civilians if not more, not just in the first bomb-blast but also in radiation sickness and pure misery in camps afterward as the provisional government struggled to figure out who was a Gilead guerilla and who was a civilian.

McKinley was in the cockpit, guiding the hover over the shallow dips and crests of desert. Acres of broken ruins stretched in every direction, old crumbling concrete and real steel too twisted and heavy to be salvaged, crusted with rust. Glaring light reflected from sand in shimmering dapples wherever there was a porthole, casting weird shadows into the interior. The hover was slim, much smaller than our previous version, with no extraneous chambers. The cargo bay was open, a deep narrow well bare except for one pale-haired demon trapped again in a silver-writhing circle, her face tilted back to look at me above her.

I had my scabbarded sword in my left hand and the Knife in my right, its hum rivaling hoverwhine. Behind the cockpit, Vann leaned against the hull, occasionally exchanging soft words with McKinley. Japhrimel loomed behind them, his hands clasped behind his back, his hair gleaming. And, wonder of wonders, Anton Kgembe, his springy hair wildly mussed, shot an indecipherable glance at me before leaning toward Japh to whisper, very fucking familiar, into Japh's ear.

Plot and counterplot, double agents and deception. Where was Leander? Had he survived whatever had happened to the last hover?

Lucas, arms folded and a scowl settled over his thin sallow face, stood at the railing at my right shoulder. "You shouldna done that."

You shouldn't have pointed a gun at me. You're working for me. Or at least, you said you were. "I already said I was sorry." I sounded unhelpful even to myself. "I'm having kind of a bad week, Lucas."

"Not used to my clients tryin' to kill me. I've put rabid bounty hunters down for less." He shifted his weight as the hover tilted, wind pressure moving against its skin.

My back prickled. I swallowed my temper with an almost sweat-inducing effort. "You were firing on her." *And on me, come to think of it.*

"Orders. Your boyfriend's got better sense than you." The sneer loading his whisper was almost visible.

"So you're working for him now?" I stared at Eve's pale head, the ropes of her hair stirring as she crouched immobile in the empty cargo bay. The humming line of silver tautened as her shoulders came up, as if she felt my gaze. "Just so I'm clear on this, because I thought *I* hired you." When he didn't respond, I considered the point carried. "Fuck you, Lucas."

"No way, *chica.* You too high-maintenance."

"Now is not a good time to bait me." *I just might do something silly.*

He was unimpressed. "Not a good time to try to kill me, either."

"You *welshed* on me!" I rounded on him. "I'm *warning* you, Lucas. Don't ride me. I'm not in the mood."

"I been watchin' this whole thing play out." His yellow eyes narrowed, and despite his slumped shoulders and crossed arms Lucas was on a hair trigger. If he twitched for a knife or a plasgun, what was I going to do?

The engine of chance and consequence inside my head returned the only answer possible. If he moved on me, we were going to find out if he was as deathless as everyone claimed.

Once, before Japh changed me, I stood in a Nuevo Rio deadhead bar with a demon in my shadow, facing down Villalobos, almost too terrified to talk. And now there was only the calm, almost-rational consideration of how I'd kill him before he could return the favor.

My, how times change.

He continued, and I forced myself to pay attention. "I gotta admit, you were smart when it started. But you gettin' dumber and dumber. Wind you up and watch you knock down everything in your way's kind of fun, but it don't get the job done."

"Where's Leander?" I didn't want to hear how stupid Villalobos thought I was. I didn't care if I was stupid or not. All I wanted right now was a chance to kill a demon, and I was getting to the point where I wasn't too picky which one.

Lucas stared through me. His lean sallow face was the picture of contempt. "You just gettin' around to wondering? Glad you didn't get a crush on me, or I might be in even more trouble."

That was uncalled-for. I couldn't drop my eyes, trained reflex resisting the urge to look away. "Keep your goddamn commentary to yourself, Villalobos." If Leander hadn't been able to keep up, would Kgembe be any different?

Was it horrible that I didn't care? The thought was a pinch in a numb place. He was *human.*

But he'd taken his chances.

You sound just like a demon, Dante. He took his chances, so sorry, too bad. I shifted, restlessly.

"What if you need to hear it? You've fucked this up six ways from Sunday and it's only goin' to get worse. I always see a job through, but—"

"Lucas." Japhrimel's quiet word sliced through our rising voices. The hover rattled. "Enough."

As if we needed any reminding who was actually in control of this situation. We stared at each other, Lucas Villalobos and I, and my sudden desire to smash his fucking face in made the Knife quiver in my hand. It was a weapon meant for demons, but I wondered just how much damage it could do to the man Death had denied.

"Are you thinking about it, Valentine?" Very softly. If Lucas had ever had a lover, he might have whispered to her in just this deadly quiet tone, almost-tenderness over razor-sharp rage. "Come on and try me. It'd be a fight worth having. Before you do, though, you'd better think about who was on that hover with Leander. D'ya think *she* stopped to cover his retreat? You think she gave a rat's ass about him? You bein' *used,* and if it wasn't so pathetic it'd be goddamn hilarious to see you barkin' up whatever tree ol' Blue-Eyes there points you at—"

I pitched forward, but Japhrimel arrived, his fingers locked around my wrist. I had started to bring the Knife

up, its humming in my hand a sudden siren call. *Strike.
Kill. Make someone bleed.*

"Lucas." Japhrimel matched his quietness. "You have
a contract with me."

"I lived up to it so far, ain't I?" Villalobos's teeth-
baring grimace wasn't a smile. "You an idiot too, demon.
You shoulda done what had to be done when you had the
chance."

"I did not ask for your opinion of my methods."
Japhrimel's hand tensed and released, his coat ruffling
slightly along its wet lacquered edges. "I asked for your
skill in killing Hell's citizens. Any more is not your
concern."

"Your funeral." Lucas wheeled and stalked away, the
effect of his retreat ruined by the close quarters. He ended
up near the cockpit, reflected desert light stippling his lean
face. I wondered if the flesh between his shoulderblades
was prickling because of *my* nearness, now.

Japhrimel did not look at me. Instead, he clasped his
hands behind his back and stood very still, gazing down
into the well of the cargo hold. Eve still crouched, motionless, and my heart gave a sudden pang. She was trapped
down there without even anyone to talk to, alone in a bare
hold.

Not a very human way to treat someone, is it, Danny?
"Can I go down there?"

Japhrimel appeared not to have heard, staring fixedly
at the demon's pale head. I drew in breath to ask again,
but he stirred. "Why?"

Sekhmet sa'es. "Do I have to get a permit?"

"You hold the Knife, my curious. I can hardly stop
you." A single shrug, his shoulder lifting, dropping.

It hung heavy in my hand, curved, obscenely warm wood. My rings sparked and sizzled in the uncertain air. Out here in the radiation wastes, static would build up, discharging in blue-white sparks. I could almost feel the silent killer against my skin, lethal power unleashed by the splitting of an infinitely small piece of the universe.

Should I be worried? I'm part-demon; will I get radiation sickness? Will I care if I do? "When were you going to tell me about this prophecy thing?"

"Meaningless gibberish." No shrug this time, but a slight tension in the straight line of his shoulders. "I suppose the Androgyne made it sound tailored to you."

The hand that can hold the Knife has faced fire and not been consumed, has walked in Death and returned, a hand given strength beyond its ken. "It sounds pretty specific."

"Ilvarimel's *hedaira* did speak before her death. She spoke her *A'nankhimel*'s name, and cursed me. The prophecy is simply noise." Each word was so bitter it was a wonder it didn't dye the air blue. "I suppose you will not believe me."

I don't know what to believe. My eyes snagged on the Knife's finials, clasping my hand. *Revenge. Kill the bastard and stop him playing around with me.*

But what then? Could I even imagine anything past that? If the gods smiled on me and I was lucky enough to kill Lucifer—by no means certain, even with Japh's help—what the hell would happen *then?*

There was Gabe's little girl in Saint City, playing in a House run by a sexwitch transvestite. I'd promised to raise her, to look after her and protect her.

I'd also promised to protect the demon crouched in the

cargo hold, the child-demon who held bits of both me and Doreen in her genetic matrix. Who set me barking at trees in a way Lucas found so fucking amusing.

Who I would have killed for—or died for—atop that Paradisse tower. If Lucas or Vann had been human still, would I have slaughtered them in the name of keeping Eve safe?

Who was I really trying to save? Eve, or myself?

My teacher's voice drifted out of a cracked memory vault. *Compassion is not your strongest virtue, Danyo-chan.*

I could not keep every promise I made. I'd broken my vow of vengeance on Gabe and Eddie's killers; I had left that faithless murdering *sedayeen* bitch alive. Because Anubis, my god, my patron, had asked.

More than that, though. Because she was incapable of fighting back, because she was a healer. Because I could not murder an unarmed woman and retain any tattered shard of my honor. Because I had lived my life with no shortage of killing and violence—but always directed at someone who *deserved* to die, by any standard. Someone who had chosen to fight without honor, broken the law, or attacked me first. It was who I was.

Or who I used to be. Who was I now? A Necromance who couldn't stand to face her god. A half-demon with a head full of reactive fumes, liquid fury in place of blood, and a weapon that could hopefully kill the Devil in my fist.

Nobody's ever tried this Knife on Lucifer. You don't know if it works or not.

Still, I had Japhrimel, didn't I? He had declared war on Lucifer. If I could believe him. If I could trust him to hand Eve over to Lucifer in one breath and rescue her with the next.

What then, Danny? What comes after this?

More lies and games? What would happen in Hell with Lucifer gone?

Kind of late to be thinking this over now, sunshine.

The hover jolted a bit, steadied. Silence crackled, and when I blinked, returning to myself, I found Japhrimel had half-turned. He looked at me now, the silver threading his hair dappled with reflected light and his eyes burning holes in the artificial dusk left by the sealed portholes.

The human darkness behind a screen of green fire sent another sharp bolt through me. Had he even paused before throwing himself off a high-rise after me?

Of course not. You know he didn't. Sounding disgusted with myself was turning into a full-time career by now.

I set my jaw and lifted my chin. I also lifted the Knife slightly, but he didn't look at it. "I need a sheath for this. The old one won't fit."

He nodded. My heart ached. There was nothing else to say; I couldn't tell him a quarter of what I wanted to, and he wouldn't do a quarter of what I needed him to do. Go figure, the love of my life, and I couldn't trust a goddamn word he said. I *had* to trust what he would do.

I turned away, breaking eye contact with a small sharp pain, a needle going into whatever heart I had left. There was a ladder leading down to the cargo bay, and I slid my sword into the loop on my rig, needing at least one hand free for climbing.

"Dante." Why did he sound so ragged, as if he'd just finished some huge task? "May I ask you one thing?"

I studied the blank hull on the other side of the open

cargo well. Deathly silence even managed to quiet the whine of hover travel. Vann and McKinley had stopped their murmuring. "Ask away." *All I can do is lie to you, you know. All I can do is betray you, keep things from you, manipulate you. Like you've done to me. Is turnabout fair play?*

"When Lucifer lies dying at your feet, what will you do?"

Good question. I swallowed dryly, closed my left hand over the railing, and prepared to climb down. Let out the breath I'd been holding. "I'll find out when I get there, Japhrimel."

I just hope that's the destination you really have in mind.

Sand swirled. The cargo hatch opened, a thin gleam bowing out as the airseals took on the load of oven-hot, evening desert wind. A flat glass field shimmered under a pall of fierce sunny heat, and even though I knew it was invisible I shivered, thinking of the radiation soaking that reflective waste. The hover would need decontamination and a plurifreeze wash on the way back, if there *was* a way back.

Eve still hadn't opened her eyes. She crouched in the very center of the thin silver circle, its taut drone an octave or so lower than the Knife's buzzing against my hip. Vann had produced yet another leather sheath, fitting the ancient weapon as if custom-made.

Airseals bowed again as the wind picked up, moaning between struts and sending fine sand hissing against the static containment field. I imagined radiation creep-

ing into my flesh and shuddered again. Long shadows
stretched away from the hover, made tall by the westering
sun. We'd spent the whole day circling the city, wastes of
twisted metal and old shattered buildings heaving under
the hover's metal belly.

Vann tried again. "At least let us accompany you. For
her protection."

Japhrimel shook his head. He checked a silvery gun,
sighting down its barrel, and made it disappear. "I am
all the protection she will require, and if I fail you could
hardly succeed. No, Vann. It ends here."

"My Lord." McKinley this time, even paler than usual.
"It'll be dusk soon. Tiens—"

"No." Japh's tone brooked no further argument.

Lucas slung a bandolier over his shoulder, buckled it.
"Goddamn sun," he muttered. "Goddamn Vegas. Goddamn everything."

I heartily agreed. At least my clothes were still mostly
in one piece and not too filthy. My hair tangled wildly,
and I ran my fingers back through it, wincing as I en-
countered matted knots. My heart thumped, skipped, and
settled into a fast high walloping run. Inside my head, the
thin red ribbon of rage smoked. My shields crackled, another flush of Power reinforcing the tissue-thin energetic
scabs. I was in no shape to take *anyone* on, let alone the
Devil himself.

My knuckles drifted against the Knife's smooth warm
hilt, the remainder of my left hand closed firmly around
Fudoshin's hilt. A hot burnished smell of cooking glass
and oven-warm sand filtered in through the seals, distant
wet mirage-shimmers on the curved, receding horizon.

The sword kills nothing, my teacher whispered inside my head. *It is* will, *kills your enemy.*

I hoped it was true. Old Jado had given me this sword, and it had already tasted Lucifer's flesh once without breaking.

Sekhmet sa'es. *Lady, I invoke You. You answered me once. Be with me, I pray.* The reflex of faith was too deeply ingrained for me to escape. I'd spent forty-odd years or more praying to the god of Death, my own personal shield against the vastness of whatever lies beyond human understanding.

Now I was praying to someone else, and I hoped She was listening. My right hand rose to my throat and touched the knobbed end of a silver-dipped baculum, Jace's necklace quietly resting against my collarbone, its weight a comfort. All the voices in my head were silent, for once.

Waiting.

Japhrimel stepped to the edge of the silver double circle. The glyphs between the inner and outer layers responded, their dance becoming a single solid streak of light, running through the grated metal flooring without a single hitch. "It is time."

Eve's gasflame eyes opened. She rose to her feet in a single fluid movement. She tilted her head back, the pale supple cervical curve gleaming. Demon-acute sight picked out the pulse throbbing in its secret hollow, vulnerable and strong.

"Consort. You are a piece in this game." Japhrimel's tone was flat. He stood in his habitual manner, hands clasped behind his back, head slightly cocked as if the demon he regarded was an interesting specimen in a kerri jar, nothing more.

Eve stared over his shoulder, her blue gaze finding mine. The Knife buzzed against my hip. "Merely a pawn, Eldest?" Her voice was familiar, and a thread of her scent escaped the circle. Baking bread, heavy musk, and the edge of some spice, purely demon. "Who is the queen?"

"None of us may move as we will." Japhrimel shrugged at someone other than me for once.

"Are you so sure?" She indicated the circle holding her captive. "I am to play the prisoner, very well. Will I be shackled?"

"I see no need for such theatrics." Japhrimel didn't move, but the circle's hum slowed, deepening. "Though were I to return your recent hospitality, we might learn the look of your blood."

I made a small restless movement. McKinley's shoulders came up, his metallic left hand flexing into a fist as he stared at me. No, not at me.

At the Knife at my hip, and at Japhrimel's unprotected back, turned to me. At Eve, looking over Japh's shoulder.

Did he think I was going to stab my Fallen in the back?

Wouldn't put it past me right now, would you. Can't blame you. Instead, I looked out the hatch, the airseals shimmering as sand rasped them. The vast bowl of the blast zone shed heat like liquid, the hover's climate control working overtime. Puffs of cool air touched my cheeks.

"It was necessary." Eve didn't sound regretful in the least. "Even your *hedaira* knows as much."

"I am not here to bandy words of what might have been. I am here for what is to be done now. *Should* I shackle you?"

"You say yourself there's no need." Eve's relaxed amusement filled the air with softness.

Impatience boiled under my breastbone. "I realize this is the usual roundabout demon way of doing things." The scabbard creaked as my fingers clenched, lacquered wood protesting. "But can we pretty please with sugar on top get *on* with this?"

"You're so anxious to see *him* again?" Eve spread her hands, a graceful movement expressing resignation. "I am ready, Eldest. We may as well accede to your *hedaira*."

Japhrimel was silent for such a long moment I almost thought we were going to have trouble. The world slowed down, hissing sand caressing the hover's plasteel skin, a thin film of sweat covering my forehead.

The circle's hum spiraled up and winked out of existence. Silver drained away, fading under the assault of actual daylight. The thought of radiation sickness returned again, circling my brain, and I shifted my weight back as Lucas holstered his last plasgun and sighed.

"I'm pretty sure I got somethin' more pleasant I could be doin'," Villalobos said. "We're not meetin' *el Diablo* until dark."

"I would prefer some necessary reconnaissance of the terrain, which will allow you the time to hide yourself should you so choose." Japhrimel turned away from Eve, who stood smiling at me, the tips of her white, white teeth showing. My Fallen's boots were soundless as he took three long strides away from my daughter.

I tensed. Premonition tickled my nape, swam through dark water, flowered in the space behind my eyes—and sank away, showing me nothing. Nothing except the dread of *something* unpleasant about to happen.

"I ain't gonna hide," Lucas said. "I want him to know I'm standin' with you. That was the deal."

What the hell? "What deal?"

Lucas coughed, rolled his shoulders back, and settled his bandoliers. "The one I made with your boyfriend, *chica.* The one that kept me in this game. What, you thought I was workin' for you?"

"That was my understanding, yes." *But Eve hired you before I did, and Japh paid you. So I suppose you were working for me until a better offer came along.*

"If I was still workin' for you I'd've killed you. After you tried to unzip my guts, that is." Lucas brushed past me. McKinley and Vann, wearing identical expressions of worry, stood like statues. Eve still didn't move, watching me with that unsettling smile.

You lying sack of shit. "I said I was sorry," I repeated, despite Japhrimel halting less than two feet from me, his head slightly bowed. The scar, softly burning against my shoulder, pulsed once. Another warm, soft coat of Power eased down my skin. Caress or last-minute bolstering, it cleared my head a bit.

The thin red ribbon of rage smoking in the bottom of my mind shivered, uneasy. Eve finally eased forward, stepping cautiously over the now-defunct borders of the circle. My nape prickled, the skin of the world suddenly too thin and full of whispers just beyond my auditory range.

I braced myself. Eve's smile widened, and her hands came up, elegant fingers spread. The thermagrenade bounced as she flung it, one deadly accurate throw, straight into the middle of the ammo crates Lucas had been digging in, stacked alongside the wall.

"Oh, *shi*—" McKinley never got time to finish the word.

The world turned over. Japhrimel spun aside and I dove for cover, oxygen hissing as fire bloomed, a hungry flower. I hit hard, rolling to the side, searching for something, anything, in the vast naked space of the cargo bay to hide myself behind.

Eve landed next to me, catlike, one hand tented against the floor for balance as the other curled around my upper arm and hauled. The scar gave a flare of spiked heat, Japhrimel's aura compressing over mine, and the desert invaded the hover as an explosion so huge it was soundless tore plasteel like paper.

What the he—This time it was me who didn't get to finish a word as my body left the grating, the shockwave and Eve's application of force conspiring to drag me through air turned hot and viscous. I went limp as a rag doll, the slim iron bar of Eve's arm now around my waist as she compressed herself, then let loose, flinging through space, my head jolting as we cleared the huge starfish hole torn in the side of the hover.

Bleeding. Nose and ears. Sand grinding underfoot as Eve landed hard, physics taking revenge as we both skidded. A cloud of grit rose, Power screaming, and I realized debris was raking the ground around us.

Eve leapt again, my sword almost jolting free before my fingers clamped shut, and I searched for a way, any way, to help her instead of just bouncing along for the ride.

Nothing came to mind. There was a brief starry moment of unconsciousness, desert heat mouthing my skin, and Eve dragged us both down a rocky incline scarred with detritus. We reached the cover of the edge of the blast zone, but even then she didn't stop, fleeing not just for escape but also for her life.

There was no water. We sheltered in the twisted ruins of what might have once been a tallish building, one side of it black and flash-fried from the blast centuries ago. Eve propped her back against the wall, gasping, and peered out onto the wasteland of Vegas. "Are . . . you . . . hurt?"

I shook my head, struggling to bring my own lungs under control. When I could talk, I still kept breathing, savoring the feel of air in my lungs. It was hellishly hot even in the shade, and something about this heat wasn't as nice as, say, the sun I'd basked in outside the boarding house in Hegemony Afrike. I'd always hated sweating before Japhrimel changed me; afterward I'd had much more tolerance of temperature variance. But this heat was something else—an oppression, helped along by the thought that thousands had died and crumbled to dust in these very buildings.

"You're bleeding," Eve finally said. Fine thin stripes of black demon blood on her own strange face glistened before they soaked back into golden skin. "My apologies."

"So were you." I braced my back against the wall and cast around, calculating fire angles. "Didn't know you had a grenade."

"Necessity being the mother of invention." She shook her head, the icy ropes of her hair providing no relief from the heat. "I could not warn you, either."

"Understood." And it was.

"I couldn't afford to let the Eldest chain me, or take the chance he might—"

I wouldn't trust him either, if I was you. "Understood, Eve." I sounded weary even to myself. The scar on my shoulder throbbed angrily, another bolt of pure Power flushing down to my bones and spreading outward. "Really. So what's the plan?"

"The best I can come up with is not very good." She slid down to sit cross-legged, scooching herself between a shattered chunk of concrete and something that might have once been a couch covered in faded tattered plaid. Shards of silica glass littered the building, sand-laden wind whistling on the other side of the wall. In this wilderness of cracked and dead buildings, cover was cheap and sight-lines a dime a dozen. If I'd had six or seven bounty hunters and was up against a human adversary, it might have been a good locale. "*He* is due to arrive at dusk." Her face twisted, blue eyes rivaling the heaving light outside. Every time she mentioned Lucifer, her expression held such pure loathing it almost covered up the fear. "We can either run and search for another opportunity to kill *him,* or take our chance now. Without allies—unless your Fallen decides, as I hope he will, that covering your attempt is the best way to keep you alive."

I tipped my chin down toward the scar. "I'm not exactly inconspicuous. He's going to come looking for me."

She nodded. "Dusk approaches. It won't be long, and we are not the only danger here. Listen."

I did, tilting my head in a parody of her graceful motion. My entire body ached.

Wind, moaning. The ever-present hiss of sand, and the sound of roaring distance without hovers or crowds.

And little, skittering noises. Too light or too heavy, too

fast or too slow to be mortal. Noises that hit the ear wrong and raised my hackles.

I breathed in softly, tasting the air. Dust, dry rotting things, decay and the faint odor of long-ago violence. Threading under that, a faint well-traveled hint of burning cinnamon and musk.

"This is not a human place," Eve whispered. "Even when it was a city, it wasn't a human place. Since the catastrophe here, a door to Hell has remained open. *He* will use it, if *he* has not already, either to issue forth from Hell or to return once *he* has won. At least, that is what *he* thinks." Her eyes glittered, her mouth twisting. She seemed not to notice her sweater was torn to rags, the firm golden slopes of her breasts peeping out.

Nausea rose hot and acid. I swallowed it, my rig creaking as I shifted. I had all my weapons and a serious case of sand-in-the-crevices; it's why I never go to the beach. "Okay." *You and me against the Devil? We're dead.*

"We know where *he* will be," she persisted. "And despite the Eldest, I am not without allies. Hell is in revolt. We have challenged *him,* you and I."

Exhaustion crested, washed over me. *Just shut up and show me where I can die, all right?* "Eve, there's no need for the speeches. Just tell me what you want me to do." My muscles trembled on the edge of cramping; I slumped against the wall and shook the ringing out of my ears.

She paused for a few of the longest seconds of my life. I watched the knife-sharp shadows, sunlight spearing through the temporary shelter of a building older than the Hegemony and still clinging, wrecked and broken, to the edges of life.

"Will you kill *him?*" She sounded very small, and very

young. But that smile was neither small nor young. It was the smile of a vidpoker shark holding a full hand of wonderful about to call your bet and take your firstborn.

Or maybe just your soul. Were demons even interested in souls anymore, now that they had all the government, sex, Power, and favors humanity could come up with?

"Sekhmet sa'es," I whispered back. "Why do you keep asking me? I'm sure as hell going to try."

35

It wasn't that long until sundown, and I spent most of that time not-thinking as Eve and I flitted from shadow to shadow, working along the edge of the bomb crater and the huge reflective glass pan. Purple veils of shade grew longer and longer, and once I crouched next to her in the lee of a huge pile of scrap preserved by dry desert air while a hellhound slid in plain view through a golden column of fading sunlight, its green eyes catching fire and heat shimmering from its pelt. The Knife vibrated against my hip so hard I expected the beast to pause and look for whatever was buzzing like a wasp, but the slitherings and skitterings of demons in the ruins must have drowned it out.

Or at least, so I hoped. My eyes, dry and heavy from the flying sand, kept welling with hot water. My shoulder pulsed with soft velvet heat.

This is a bad idea. You know this is a bad, bad idea, right? Even if Japh was planning to hand Eve over to him, he would have kept you alive. This is a bad idea.

I dismissed the thought as not even worthy of the craven bastard I was turning into. There was no shame in being afraid, but there *was* shame in hiding from it. So I was afraid. So what? I've been afraid most of my life, of one thing or another.

But I've never let that fear drive me. Spur me, maybe. But not drive me.

Eve circled our destination a few times before we worked our way closer, picking our way through piles of junk and broken concrete. The sun lowered itself into the west like an old man sinking into a bathtub, slow and aching. I tried not to feel the insistent tugging in my shoulder, a pulling against the ropes of the scar. Where was he? Had he intended to turn Eve over to Lucifer? He'd promised not to, asked me to trust him. Still, I could see how Eve might not want to take that chance.

It didn't matter. Nothing mattered now.

The sun turned to blood, and I thought I could see the haze of radiation crawling over every sand-scoured surface. Or maybe it was just the blurring in my eyes.

As the sun sank, Power rose.

It was coming from somewhere close, a diseased heart in the ruins thumping irregularly but gathering strength. One huge broken building, a massive structure that looked like it had once been a pyramid, loomed over a twisted unrecognizable statue. I guess humanity's never lost its taste for making things huger than they need to be.

A slight rise of rubble made a natural amphitheater, the mountains in the background and the edges of the blast zone spilling away, the glass fractured in crazy spiderweb patterns that reminded me of the deep angular scorings on the altar in the city under Chomo Lungma. I shivered as the baking wind, redolent of sand and demon spice, breathed up into my face.

I lay on my stomach and peered down into the bowl of rubble giving out onto the wastes. Eve crouched below the lip of the hill, dust grimed into her hair turning it the color of clotted cream instead of pale platinum ice. Both of us were tattered almost beyond recognition. I pushed matted, filthy hair out of my face and shivered again. My nervous system was rebelling like a Chill junkie's, out on the edge of control, ready to jolt away from under me.

Breathe, Danny. Just breathe.

There, in the middle of the wreckage, something that should not be . . . was. The dying sun gathered itself and plunged fully below the horizon, desert stars striking sparks as the wind veered again, the ground thrumming below. The paint of dusk bled down the vault of heaven, and as true night dropped like a curtain—because it does fall fast out here in the desert, with no streetlamps to hold it back—a slim figure with a shock of golden hair melded out of nothing and took his place at the focal point.

The ruined city cringed.

Other shadows gave birth. The spiderlike things clicked and scuttled, straining at leashes held by graceful, inhuman forms with burning eyes in shades of blue, green, and molten gold. Hellhounds, winged and flightless, snarled and jostled. Imps lolled, some chittering in the strange unlovely tongue of Hell, and the deeper shadows held eyes that had to be higher-ranking demons, not deigning to show themselves.

"Anubis," I breathed, then clapped my hand over my mouth.

Eve said nothing, but crouched tense as a violin string next to me. "Not so many of the Lesser Flight, and none at all of the Greater." The words mouthed my ear as if she'd placed her mouth next to it.

So what? They're still fucking demons. I spotted a way down through the rubble, an easy path.

A primrose path, Danny? Get it? Howling hysterical laughter rose up under my skin, was mercilessly choked, and died without even a gurgle. "I don't suppose we have a plan," I whispered back.

"Do you believe in Fate, Dante?"

Past turned into present again, looped and stuck tight, a gear-wheel sliding into place. Nothing to do but finish this, now.

"No." I wasn't sure whether it was a lie or the truth, but I said it.

Lucifer turned in a circle, the flame of his hair not replacing the sun. My hands shook. My entire body shook. The gaping hole in my mind struggled to open like a cancerous flower, the reality of what had been done to me fighting to break free and douse my sanity with black water. My shields shivered, one powerful burst of fear tinting them purple-red before I controlled myself again. Fudoshin sang as it cleared the sheath and I found myself on my feet at the top of the slope, clearly visible in the backwash of starlight.

Pebbles clicked and shifted, and I knew without looking that Eve had risen too, her lambent eyes glowing over my shoulder. For a moment my heart paused. It should have been Japhrimel standing there, watching my back as I faced down the Devil.

It doesn't matter. It won't matter in a few red-hot minutes.

My sword woke. Blue flame twisted along its edge,

runes of the Nine Canons spilling through the steel, its white-hot core singing its own silent song of destruction. I took three steps forward, and my fingers loosed themselves from the scabbard. It clattered to the ground, and my left hand closed around the Knife's warm, wooden hilt.

Lucifer slowly turned. The movement was exquisitely leisurely, light sliding down the line of his body. Gold lived, scorching, in his hair, casting a glimmer around him. He tilted his head back slightly, and the dish of his face rose to catch my gaze.

His face was a holovid angel's, sheerly beautiful and just as completely male. The emerald set above and between his flawless, burning-green eyes snapped a spark. The marvel of his mouth was set and unyielding. There were shadows under his flaming eyes, and his beauty was somehow worn but not diminished.

The Devil looked very tired.

My left cheek itched, the twisted-caduceus accreditation tattoo straining inked lines under my skin. My own emerald burned like a lase bonedrill, spitting a tearing-green spark fat as a teardrop.

His eyes met mine and I recoiled without moving, a scream tearing through the blank spot in my head, the one space where my Magi-trained memory mercifully failed.

Lucifer paused, the silk of his simple black tunic and trousers fluttering. A hood of darkness slid over his perfect features, a psychic miasma of hate made visible. His eyes slid past me as if I was a piece of furniture, coming to rest on Eve.

When he spoke, it was with the utter finality of a being who expects immediate obedience. The voice of the

Prince of Hell lashed every exposed surface of the wreckage and made it groan and tremble.

"Aldarimel, the Morning Star, most beloved of my consorts." Lucifer's mouth twisted down at one corner, rose again in a sneer. The thin white scars on my belly twitched as if something still lived in the bowl of my pelvis, a heavy heated stone.

The wall inside my head quivered, stretched—and *held,* my stubbornness sticking fast. I lifted the Knife and stepped forward again. The demons had frozen, hellhounds, spiders, and imps all alike crouched and staring like statues.

Lucifer took no notice. He *ignored* me, speaking past me to Eve. "I shall offer you one chance, and only one, to return to your nest and await your penance."

I'm not sure what she would have said. She never got the chance. I opened my big fat stupid mouth.

"Hey." My voice, cracked and husky, echoed all along the bowl of rubble. "Blondie. You two-faced lying sack of demon *shit.*" My face froze, lips stretched in a facsimile of a smile. "You've got business with me first."

"Indeed I do." He nodded, and I almost had no time to duck before the first hellhound leapt for me.

The Knife jerked in my hand. Fudoshin sang, and wood met demon flesh as I pitched forward, blade stuck to the hilt in the roasting hide of a hellhound I had barely even seen.

The sucking sound hit a high keening note, and Power slammed up my arm, exploding in my left shoulder and fluorescing in the visible range. Black-diamond fire burst in a perfect sphere around me, the edges of my ragged aura

clearly visible under the smooth carapace of Japhrimel's
borrowed Power.

A quick twist of my wrist, muscles flexing in my forearm, breaking the suction of muscle against the blade.
The finials scraped against my skin, caging my hand and
protecting it as a writhe of the hellhound's flexible body
almost tore the Knife free.

I kicked the body, fine ash already spreading in capillary-
patterns through the glassy shifting heat of its hide. I rose
from the half-crouch its attack had driven me down into,
Fudoshin sweeping down in a curve painted with blue
fire, slicing across an imp's face.

Clarity spilled through me, rage sharp and bright as a
new-pressed credit disc. They descended on me, the lowest of the scions of Hell, and the Knife screamed in my
hand as the world unrolled, strings of energy under its
surface showing me the path through. Step-kick, demon
bones crunching and the Knife sending another shock of
feverish Power up my arm, the sword halting in midair
and slicing down, the Knife's finials crunching against a
hellspider's face. They moved in on me, skittering and
chittering in their demonic language, or snarling and
clicking.

This is what I was born to do.

All thought vanished. My grip on Fudoshin's hilt was
gentle, like clasping a lover's hand. The sword responded,
steel flexing as it bent, whipping through forms coded into
the very lowest levels of my brain.

*Turn. Flex the wrist, back foot stamping down, front
foot turning out, bring the knee up, quickly, don't think
don't think, kill it, drive the Knife in, pull it free.*

It was a string of fire tied to my wrist, the Knife

humming as it settled into jerking my body like a mario-nette's, burning all the way down to the bone, the finials clasping tighter and tighter as the weapon took over.

And I didn't care.

The last hellhound fell at my feet with a thud, whim-pering as veins of ash threaded its flesh. It convulsed, and hissing whimpers sounded as the rest of them drew back, a circle of glowing eyes and heatshimmer in the dark-ness. The temperature had dropped, steaming sands losing the day's baking. My boots crunched on silica glass at the bottom of the hill, and I faced Lucifer over a rubble-strewn plain. Raised my eyes, the ribbon of rage widen-ing. It flushed my body, this clear clean fury, sweet in its single-mindedness.

I knew what he had done to me. I didn't quite remem-ber it, but I knew as if it had happened to someone else, some brutalized girl crouching in the corner of a bed-room, whimpering as she beat her head against the wall, the borders of her body violated, her mind no longer quite her own.

The Prince of Hell's green eyes narrowed. That was all. The emerald in his forehead ran with light as sterile as the radiation crawling through the ruins.

It occurred to me that I hadn't seen a single plant or an-imal since touching down. Just sand, shattered buildings, and trash. Pure destruction, so intense that after centuries nothing grew here.

Lucifer's hands were loose at his sides, elegant fingers relaxed.

I filled my lungs. Grit-laden wind touched my cheeks, fingered my filthy hair. My ribs heaved with deep gasp-ing breaths, but I didn't care. My heartbeat mounted behind my eyes, so quick and hard it threatened to burst out through my veins.

"Here I stand, Lucifer." My throat cracked with dry heat, but my voice was steady. "And not all the hosts of Hell shall move me."

In other words, you want Eve? Come and get her—but you're going to go through me first. And I have some pay-back for you.

The voices in my head stilled. My left shoulder ran with velvet fire, and the heat was building in my arms, my legs. It pressed against the thin film of my psyche, stretched over some unknowable bulge.

More lamps lit in the dark behind him. Demonic eyes, shadows resolving around slim graceful shapes. The air crawled and ran with Power, whispers, little tittering gasps of laughter. Those of the Greater Flight that still called the Devil "Master" gathered, just in time for the show.

I didn't care.

Lucifer stirred. "Not all the hosts of Hell are neces-sary, Necromance." His hair lifted, gold running along its edges. His Chinese-collared tunic ran with wet light as he lifted one graceful arm and pointed at me, the claw-tip at the end of his index finger lengthening. "Just one."

Fudoshin's tip described a precise little circle in the air before the hilt floated to the side, a natural movement settling in second guard, the Knife along my left fore-arm singing its high-voltage song of gathering murder. Stars ran overhead, their crystalline fires not choked by cityshine. Eve was still behind me at the top of the hill; I felt her attention, spark after spark crackling from the emerald in her forehead echoing Lucifer's. The gem on my cheekbone sparked too, my tat running wildly under the skin, a high sweet itching pain.

The world narrowed, shrank to a single point. Neither of us could back out now. Gauntlet thrown down, challenge accepted, and I was about to die.

I wondered if my god would take me in His arms, or if I would slide unnoticed into the well of souls I had crossed over so often.

Did it matter?

"Come on," I whispered. *Come and get me. If you can. If you dare.*

I had no warning. Before the words died he was on me.

The shock was like worlds colliding. My left arm was thrown aside, his bladed fingers striking my solar plexus, robbing me of breath as shocked lungs and heart struggled to function. Fudoshin jabbed in, hilt used like a battering ram to strike the Prince of Hell's fair golden face, now twisted with rage and horribly, inescapably still beautiful. It snapped his head back and he was flung down as I stumbled back, digging in my left heel to regain my balance, nausea rising and my bruised torso seizing up, cramping.

Nausea retreated as he flowed to his feet. A single dot of black blood welled at the corner of his mouth and I dropped into position as he lifted the back of one golden hand to touch his lips. Fudoshin described a bigger circle this time, the blessed blue flame along its edge adder-hissing.

I heard myself speak. "I remember."

I remember how I screamed when you put that thing in me, how you sliced me open like I was a sodaflo can—and how you laughed when I screamed. I remember what you

*said, and how you really seemed to enjoy yourself. I re-
member how you sent me out to betray my daughter and
my lover.*

"What do you think you remember?" Contempt loaded
Lucifer's voice, smoking land glittering like carbolic
tossed over reactive paint. "Where were *you* when I made
your kind? Where were you when I made your *world?*"
He drew himself up and pointed again, the holocaust glow
of his eyes so intense teardrop trails shimmered horizon-
tally from their corners. "You have interfered for the *last
time!*"

Oh, will you just shut up and kill me? I raised the Knife
slightly, its clawlike finials prickling against my forearm,
and felt the points slide into my skin. The sweet rotting-
fruit smell of demon blood hung cloying in the air. Was I
bleeding?

I didn't care. I brought my sword down and around, a
swordsman's move, hilt rotating in my hand as the blade
spun like a propeller, before he leapt for me again.

Impact. Bones snapping in my side, the agony immense
and useless, like everything else. Stars of pain shattering
across the surface of my mind, I brought the Knife up in a
sweep and felt the blade *bite,* a feedback squeal grinding
the rubble around us into dancing cascading dust—

—and the Knife, wrenched from my grasp, clawed
my hand desperately before flying in a high impossible
arc, up and *away,* the Power feeding up my arm jolting
to a stop as Lucifer backhanded me, smashing me to the
ground.

36

*R*olling.

Get up get up get up—Before the words faded I was on my feet, every ounce of demon speed I could use in one last desperate lunge, swordblade screaming as it split air and twisted, driving home in the Devil's chest. A spike of fire jabbed through my left lung, blood dribbling down my chin, muscles pulled out of alignment by smashed bones, I swayed on my numb feet and saw what I had done.

We stood like that, Lucifer pinned like a butterfly, the scream dying on my lips as the Devil, black blood griming his ivory teeth and his eyes inches from mine, *smiled.*

The world halted. Sick realization thumped home in the wasteland my shattered mind had become, smoking with fury. *That's not going to kill him.*

There seemed no shortage of time as I watched his hand come up, claws springing free. *This is going to hurt.* I shifted my weight to pull Fudoshin free, knowing I would never be able to cut him a second time.

The Knife I dropped the Knife ohgods I'm dead I'm dead—

It was hopeless. But I tore my blade free, metal howl-

ing under the abuse, Power raying out from the event
we had just created in spiderwebs of force and reaction,
rubble grinding to smaller bits and dust pluming, shaping
into mushroom clouds.

Everything inside me rose and halted, hanging in the
air above my skin. My left shoulder burned, a prickling
mass of hot ice and barbed wire flooding me with a desperate burst of Power, straining through me, trying to
shield me against the inevitable. Flexible demon-altered
bones crackled, and the relief and weightlessness I had
felt falling through the roof of Paradisse wrapped around
me again.

It's over.

Lucifer's hand began its descent, claws sparkling with
emerald flame to match the gem in his forehead. His face
was a mask of unholy rage, psychic darkness flooding
under its beauty, and my heart stuttered as the essential
inhumanity of the thing I saw beneath that screen of love-
liness was revealed.

And I *recognized* it. I recognized the twisted teeth and
burning eyes. I heard its echo in my own brain. It was my
own hatred.

How much more *like* the Devil was I going to have to
become to kill him?

No.

Time paused again.

No. I will not be like you. No. The only word I could
say repeated, gathering force in my eyes and arms and
lips, filling me. It was the only prayer I could utter.

Dante, you have been so blind.

And I *struck.*

Not with my sword. If I tried to cut with Fudoshin

again, it would be in rage, in anger. I already knew how useless that would be, fury turning back on itself, destruction for its own sake.

Compassion is not your strongest virtue, Danyo-chan.

How had my teacher known?

The red ribbon of rage in my head paled. It shrank to a thread-thin line. I did not want it to go. It was my only defense. I could not help what had been done to me, but I could fight. I could *kill*.

Couldn't I?

I can't hold a gun to your head and make you more human.

The dead rose about me, each of them a distinct shape of silver lattice and crystalline intent holding an imprint of the flesh they wore in my life. Lewis, with his smile and his steadfast love. Doreen with her gentleness; Jace with his stubborn refusal to give in. Gabe, who had known me better than I knew myself—and Eddie, always on the periphery but still necessary, who would have done for me what I did for him and not counted the cost.

All of them rose in me, a tide of love and obligation, the nets of duty and the lines of promises made, kept, broken, and kept again. The dead keened in my bones, spilled through my blood, and blazed through me as the red thread inside my head opened its jaws and *roared*.

Has a god ever used you to complete a circle? Have you ever been ridden by a *loa?* A vaudun Shaman will understand. The god or spirit spills into you, stretching you like a too-small glove on a hand, and the thin ecstasy of a bursting, too-ripe fruit shatters whatever you thought you were. Infinity recognizes you, and how can you help but recognize the infinity in your own soul?

My god woke in me, His slim canine head turning to look with its terrible eyes that became *my* eyes. For a dizzying moment Death filled me.

Compassion is not your strongest virtue.

Lucifer screamed. The force boiled out of me, my hand spread instead of locked in a fist. I touched the Devil's face, cupping his cheek as if he was a lover, my fingers gentle and delicate, the silk of an impermeable, invulnerable skin sending a heatless pang through my cracking ribs and bleeding meat.

Yes, it is, I replied. *Gods grant I do not forget it.*

They did not.

Married to Anubis's still quiet, Sekhmet woke. She took a single step, the stamping dance that would unmake the world moving on, creation flooding in its wake. It was and was not me who did the striking, at the last. It was *them.*

No, it was me too. I swear it was.

The scream was the world stopping. It was a death-cry, or the cry of love like a knife to the heart. The god I thought had abandoned me gathered me to His chest, comfort singing through my sobbing, broken body.

It was not Anubis who had turned away. It was me. He had never left me for a moment.

You may not take this, Anubis-Sekhmet said. *This is Mine, and you may not have her.*

Ash threaded through Lucifer's skin, the even gold and bright light dimmed by spreading veins of dusty dirty gray. The sound was a crackling. My other hand came up, met his face. His emerald cracked, sending out one vicious caustic flash. The gulping sound was very loud in the stillness. A dripping point speared free of Lucifer's ribs, and over the Devil's shoulders, a pair of yellow eyes dawned, meeting mine with a blow no less critical than the one I had just meted out.

Lucas twisted the Knife, and Lucifer screamed again. My breath jagged out of me, the gods receding like a tide full of wreckage, foaming and split.

The flesh under my fingers collapsed, runnels of dry decay replicating furiously. The twin pieces of Lucifer's emerald ground themselves into dust. The Knife keened, satisfaction in its chill, curling voice.

The explosion of dusty diamond grit blew my hair back, scouring my eyes and filling my mouth with dry sand. I coughed, choked, and stumbled back, my legs failing me.

Someone caught me, breaking the force of my fall. My sword clattered on the ground, my fingers spasming open. Power slid through the mark on my shoulder, detonated inside my bones, and Japhrimel folded himself over me, saying something I could not quite hear. It might have been my name. It could have been anything.

I convulsed. Footsteps sounded through the deafness of pain in my ears. My head tilted back, stars scoring the sky through veils of dust.

The ground tilted, desert shaking like liquid brushed with hoverwash. The pain was a diamond nail, driven through me from crown to soles. My body struggled against it, a fish on a hook.

Lucas said something, in a deadly-quiet whisper. Footsteps brushed a slope of wreckage, picking their way delicately down.

Japhrimel's arms tightened. He pulled me, once more, into the shelter of his body. My cheek burned, the emerald grafted into the bone red-hot. "The Prince is dead," he said quietly. "Long live the Prince."

Eve laughed, the sweet carefree giggle of a little girl. "It is the way of our kind, is it not?"

Demons drew close. I felt them against the raw edges of my broken shielding, Japhrimel's aura over mine smooth and seamless. Whispers and chittering, their voices tearing at the night. The smell of burning cinnamon turned cloying, dust-decay threading its sweet muskiness. Eve's smell—baking bread, vulnerability, pure sweetness—rose in my nose, slid down the back of my throat.

I gagged.

"Come any closer and I'll make you eat this thing." Lucas's tone was flat and utterly serious.

"Give me the Knife." Eve sounded like she was smiling. "It's what you were contracted for."

"Funny thing about that." Dust squealed under booted feet and a clicking sounded before the whine of an unholstered plasgun drilled the air. "I ain't never welshed on a contract before. All three of you tryin' to hire me away from each other, and all for a simple goddamn assassination."

I was just trying to stay alive, Lucas. The thought was clean, the shock of a god's touch falling away from my mind. The blank spot in my memory receded, Japhrimel murmured something into my hair.

"Lucas." Eve's voice held a warning now. "Give me the Knife."

"It ain't yours. Neither am I." The footsteps paused. Something nudged my shoulder. "Here, *chica.* You'd best hold this." Cold fingers touching mine. Something obscenely warm touched my palm, feverish energy jolting up my wrist, slamming into my elbow, and socking into my shoulder before spreading down through my healing bones. I tried to open my eyes. They obeyed, slowly. A slice of blurry light danced in front of me. *What the hell just happened?* Echoes of a god's touch drained away, swirling. Leaving me alone again inside my mind, the red ribbon of rage turned to ash, blowing away. Fine, cinnamon-scented ash, lifting on the confused wind.

My vision cleared. Lucas stood, threadbare and slump-shouldered, an unholstered 60-watt plasgun pointed at the ice-haired demon who stood, her emerald glowing. Dust danced as if the amphitheater was a hot griddle.

The Knife buzzed in my hand. Japhrimel kissed my forehead. "Merely breathe, *hedaira.* All is well."

"I hired you first," Eve said, silkily. "Don't make an enemy out of me, Deathless. You won't like the results."

He leveled the plasgun, yellow eyes narrowed. "I think you'd better get the fuck out of here, Blue Eyes. I already killed one demon today, and I might take it in mind to kill another. Besides, ain't you got some trouble back home to take care of?"

She shrugged. The movement was so uncannily like Lucifer's my heart jolted in my chest. "It makes little difference, anyway."

"J-J-Japh—" My voice wouldn't work properly. I finally managed to wrap my lips around a single syllable. "Eve—"

Her eyes slid away from Lucas, traveled over acres of burning air to look at me. Around the rim of the rubble-bowl, the paired lamps of demon eyes were winking out, stealthy scrapes and clawings retreating. *Show's over, folks. Nothing left to see here. Move along.*

"Goodbye, Dante. Thank you for your help." Her smile was the plastic grimace of a child's doll. "Though you were wrong."

About what? My throat was stoppered with dry dust. I could only stare, accusingly, from the shelter of Japhrimel's arms. His fingers closed around mine, sliding under the Knife's finials, his lips against my filthy hair. Still murmuring something, over and over.

"Any Key will do in a lock, with enough coaxing." Eve's gaze lingered on the Knife for a few moments. A calculation crossed her face, and another.

I almost cringed. Was she thinking how easy it might be to set me barking up another tree?

I had been so *blind.*

Japhrimel raised his face from my hair. When he spoke, the entire pan of rubble rattled, little bits shifting and sliding. "This stays with me, Androgyne."

"One day, I might come to reclaim it." The gasflame glow of her eyes dimmed slightly, a new color blooming underneath the screen of light.

Green. Like sunlight through new leaves. Like a laser.

Like Lucifer's gaze.

I shuddered. Japhrimel's hand was warm and steady, holding my fingers against a silken hilt of wood and grief.

"On that day, you will meet *his* fate. Rule Hell if you will; I care little. But us you will leave in peace." He sounded absolutely certain.

I found I could breathe again. *Eve.* I struggled to sit up, to shake free of Japhrimel's arms. What was happening to her?

My daughter tilted her head slightly as the last shades

of blue died out of her eyes. She was unmistakably female, the sheerness of her beauty maturing in breathtaking leaps, her face thinning a little and the gold of her skin flushing warmly. Had it been another glamour?

No, this change was something else. Something deeper. Any pretense she might have made at humanity was now laid aside, and I found myself lying under the hard brilliant sky of the Vegas Waste and watching something inhuman settle into its newest form.

The Prince is dead. Long live the Prince.

She turned away, her supple back under the torn dust-smeared sweater shining with its own grace. "My thanks for your aid, my friends. But now I have a whole world to conquer."

"May it give you joy," Japhrimel said softly, like a curse. But she was already gone, vanishing between one breath and the next. A sound like ripping silk assaulted the air, died away.

My Fallen let out a long, shaking breath. For a few moments, he held me, while the dust settled, silence returning and filling the amphitheater like liquid in a cup.

It was over.

I was still alive. But I had failed in every way that ever counted.

37

There was another hover, a long sleek new craft with a battery of mag-and-deepscan shielding that resolved out of the desert sky, landing with a bump and opening its side hatch like a flower. I didn't question it, even when Tiens greeted us all with a cheery smile that showed the tips of his abnormally long canines. Anton Kgembe, his head bandaged, didn't even look up from strapping down cargo containers. Vann looked a little worse for wear, bruised and battered and moving slowly as he brought a blanket that Japh wrapped around me before handing me and the Knife over to McKinley.

I felt nothing except a numb wonder that they had all survived.

All except Leander, that is. Was he dead? The numbness even covered that with a sheet of plasticine wrap, insulating me from the bite of guilt.

It was McKinley, oddly enough, who brought me up to speed on the long twilight journey back from the Waste. Him, and the holonews, because Japhrimel wouldn't speak to me and neither would Lucas.

The incidences of Magi dying had tapered off a little.

The Hegemony directive was rescinded and everyone got back to work. There were still . . . problems, of course. Plenty of demons had escaped Hell and would have to be dragged back kicking and screaming. But that was a job for the new head honcho, the brand new Prince of Hell, the leader of the successful rebellion.

Eve. Or more properly, Aldarimel, the Morning Star, Lucifer's youngest and most favored consort. The new toy he'd brought back to Hell, reverse-engineered from Doreen—a human descendant of the Fallen—and his own genetic material. Was it narcissism, or was the Devil just like a human with a new love affair?

In any case, she'd gotten just what she wanted. The Prince of Hell was dead.

Long live the Prince.

Hello? I said to the silence inside myself. *Hello?*

The holonews was salt in the wound. Picture after picture of shattered houses, Magi gone missing, weird occurrences all over the world as the jostling factions from Hell fought it out. I watched the flickering pictures through a heavy blanket of water-clear exhaustion, refusing to close my eyes, refusing to look away. They were comparing it to the chaos at the time of the Great Awakening, and expert holo-heads weighed in with utterly useless analyses.

"Here." McKinley handed me a thick china mug. It smelled like coffee, and I slumped in an ergonomic chair bolted to the floor with the blanket pulled tight around me, staring fixedly at the dark liquid. "You should drink." He even managed to sound kind.

"Why?" Shell-shocked, numb, and exhausted, I pushed away a curtain of weariness and tried to take a drink. My stomach closed, tighter than a fist.

He shrugged, rubbing at his metallic left hand. His fingers left no smudge behind on the smooth, gleaming almost-skin. "It's over. At least, for now."

What, you're expecting more? I set the cup down on a slice of table snugged into the chair's side. "What happens now?" I sounded like a kid again, breathy and scared.

"Now we pick up the pieces." He tilted his head slightly, indicating the front of the hover, Japhrimel in whispered conference with Vann and Tiens, Kgembe slumped asleep in a foldout chair bolted to the hull, Lucas leaning on the hull at the periphery of that conversation, his yellow eyes trained on me.

I swallowed hard. The hover bounced a little, the AI piloting since Tiens was now leaning closer to Japh, making some earnest point. The Nichtvren's gaze flicked to me and away, and he brought one fist softly into the palm of his other hand for emphasis.

My sword lay across my knees, the metal quiescent and shining only as much as ordinary steel. It had rammed through Lucifer's chest, and still remained intact. The Knife lay on the table, its slow song of grief and rage sounding more and more foreign.

My eyes drifted closed. The coffee sloshed. I drifted, my fingers and toes gone cold and rubbery. The broken places inside my head shivered, too tired to even try knitting together.

For a long time I rocked like that, my head lolling against the back of the seat, the bumps and jostles of the hover a cradle's soft movement. I heard raised voices, and Japhrimel's tone suddenly cutting through the cotton wool surrounding me. He said something short and sharp, and all discussion ceased.

Not too long afterward, someone touched my dirty, dust-caked hair. The fingers were gentle, and I opened my eyes to see Japh standing over me, his face drawn and thoughtful. My left shoulder twitched, as if a fishhook in the flesh had been pulled.

"Can you stand?"

He might as well have asked if I could fly.

I grabbed the arms of the chair. Braced myself, tensed, and managed to push myself up with a low sound of effort, my right hand scooping up Fudoshin's hilt.

Japhrimel steadied me with one hand, picked up the Knife with the other, using only his fingertips and wincing slightly. "I shall have Vann make another sheath for this."

I shook my head, the entire hover tilting as I did. "You keep it. I don't want it." *I'd say give it to Lucas, but I don't know if he wants it either.*

Japhrimel paused. He glanced over his shoulder. Lucas had closed his eyes, leaning against the hull and listening while McKinley said something to Tiens, the Nichtvren casting a dubious look at me.

I didn't care anymore.

His hand fell away from my arm.

I swayed. "Where are we going?"

"I thought you might prefer a bed. Such as it is." His eyes caught fire, but his face was merely set and thoughtful. "Dante."

I set my jaw. *A bed. Just one more thing, and I can sleep for a week. That'd be nice.* "Japhrimel."

Then I can start untangling the rest of this mess. All those things I swore I'd do once I finished. All those promises I made.

The pain wouldn't go away. It was right under my ribs,

my heart caught in a nest of splinters. All my friends were dead, and so was the Devil.

Why didn't I feel any better?

The hover bounced. McKinley finished what he was saying, and silence folded through the interior.

All eyes on you, Danny. Do something.

I took an experimental step. Swayed. Japhrimel moved restlessly, but I waved his hand away. I'd make it to the bed on my own, goddammit. One thing at a time.

Why don't I feel better? Tears rose in my throat, prickled behind my eyes. *Why?*

"Valentine." Lucas, his whisper half-strangled.

I stopped, tensed, and waited. *The hand that can hold the Knife has faced fire and not been consumed, has walked in death and returned, a hand given strength beyond its ken.*

Had there truly been a prophecy? Or was it just absurdity? He was the Deathless, but Eve had thought I was the Key.

Had I been? Would I ever know?

What he said next bordered on the absurd. "We even?"

Even? How the hell could we be even? I tried to kill you; you were working for everyone except me—but you killed Lucifer. And you gave me back the Knife. Even doesn't happen in this kind of situation.

An exotic thought stopped me. I considered it, in my exhaustion-fogged state. Thought about it for a long while, as the hover rose and fell, its gyros coping with various stresses.

"Valentine? Are we *even*?" Tension under his throat-cut whisper, I could almost feel his entire body tightening.

Amazing. Was Lucas Villalobos asking if we were still friends?

I never thought I'd live to see the day.

It didn't matter. Nothing mattered, now. If I could live without knowing some things, I could live with calling Lucas Villalobos something other than an enemy. "We're still friends, Lucas. If that's what you're asking."

Nobody moved. I barely even breathed.

"Good 'nough." Villalobos sounded relieved, and my heart eased, a sudden convulsive movement. "Get some rest."

Not all my friends are dead. I followed the hem of Japhrimel's coat, stumbling with exhaustion and clutching Fudoshin's hilt. When the door closed behind us and he took me in his arms, I found tears running hot and thick down my cheeks.

For once that didn't matter, either.

"Where are we going?"

"Santiago City, Dante. Your home. Ours, now."

Epilogue

The city lies under its pall of orange light and fog, sheets of white coming up from the bay. It pulses, from the depths of the Tank to the spires of downtown, the financial district to the suburbs. Against the skyline, lines of hovertraffic slide between buildings in patterns almost random enough to practice divination with. You can spend a whole night up here, the curtains pulled back and the bulletproof plasglass dialed to maximum transparency, the entire room dark except for the red eye of the nursery monitor. Each night the sound of human breathing soothes me, a child's deep trustful sleep in a room guarded by two agents.

They take turns at her door.

In our house, a little human girl sleeps. She does not ask, anymore, when her mother is coming back. I know better than to think she's forgotten the question.

She has Eddie's golden curls and Gabe's wide dark eyes, and dimples when she smiles. Oddly enough, it's the demon she likes best; he is endlessly patient with her, willing to spend hours reading brightly colored primary books or playing small games designed to teach her how to control her gifts. Of course, she is a child of psions, *and testing at birth returned a Matheson score almost as high as mine.*

Her mother's will is explicit; I'm named as guardian and trustee. Gabe, with her inherent precision, reaching from beyond the grave to hold me to my promise. Love and obligation, the net that holds me here, all boiled down to a child's laugh and scattered toys.

Did I break the other promises so I could keep this one?

Do I want to know, if I did?

Tell me what you want, *he says, and each time I shake my head. I take my sword into the long dimly lit practice room, its wooden floor smelling of workouts and its mirrored wall reflecting a body I no longer have to strain to control. The katas my teacher first taught me unfold, each movement precise and restrained.*

Sometimes that control breaks, and the blackness infecting my mind leaks out. It is most often at night, and I will resurface to find myself in his arms, my throat aching with unshed screams and my body tense, stiff and wooden with the strain of holding it back.

If I can't, if it escapes me and I struggle, there is another net to hold me above the abyss. It is the net of a demon's arms, his hand cupping my skull to keep me from battering it to pieces, the grip he keeps on my wrists so I cannot claw my own eyes out.

We do not speak, those nights. I cannot stand the sound of another voice.

There are whispers.

The net of human and financial assets available to demons on earth is strangling in its own blood. The only ones safe from vengeance and chaos are vassals of an-

other demon, one the new Prince does not control. They hear the whispers, and pass them on, safe in their scrupulous neutrality. Kgembe visits each month with a report, and each time he studies me as if I am the answer to a question never asked.

Hell has never been quiet. Lucifer ruled with fear and iron discipline, torture and trickery. Ousting him from his throne was the easy part; now the new Prince must solidify her grip on power. She is young, and there are older and mightier among the Greater Flight. There are also those who might not believe Lucifer is quite dead.

He was, after all, the Prime. The alpha of demonkind, if not the omega.

The whispers are mounting. Magi have never found it so easy to break the walls between our world and Hell. It's a Renascence in their branch of magick, and precious few are looking for a sting in the tail of the gift. Those who question its provenance are told they don't have to participate. Psions are uneasy, and violent attacks on those with Power are at an all-time high.

If it's a chemical reaction, it's nowhere near finished yet. Even the cure for Clormen-13, that great drug blight of our time, hasn't helped. There are new drugs, and rumors of a high better than any drug—a high available, for a price, from new sources. Inhuman sources.

There's one more thing.

The urn sits on the mantelpiece, over the nivron fire I never turn on, in the bedroom where I sit at night and watch the city glow. It's black and wetly lacquered, a beautiful restrained demon artifact. It is full of cinnamon-scented ash.

Japhrimel and I do not speak of it.

The broken places inside my head are healing, slowly. I have not spoken to a god since the moment of spillskin ecstasy when they filled me, denying me, body and soul, from a demon's grasp. I can't call my faith lost, precisely. It's just . . . quiet.

Dormant. If it ever wakes, I'll light my candles and speak to my god again. I think He, of all creatures, understands.

On the other end of the mantel, set on a twisting stand of glass, a Knife of silken wood and grief hums sleepily to itself. Its point spears toward the urn, and sometimes it quivers a bit, as if sensing . . .

But that's impossible, isn't it? Lucifer was not Fallen. A Fallen's dormancy doesn't apply to him, does it?

It matters little. The Knife was made to kill demons, no matter how powerful. While we hold it, the weapon guarantees us some safety.

If the new Prince manages to hold Hell, we're safe.

Or are we? Plot, counterplot, lies, and agendas.

If the new Prince doesn't hold Hell in check, what might happen? The walls between their world and ours grow thinner every day. And sometimes, when he thinks I'm not looking, my Fallen's face holds a familiar expression. Listening for a sound I can't hear, ready for a threat I can't imagine.

A Knife, and an urn full of ash. Right now the Knife is insurance, and the urn is . . . what? A token? A memento?

Tomorrow they might be bargaining chips in a new game. And I have a daughter to keep safe now. A promise I will keep, even if it means playing their games again. I'll be better at it next time.

Much better.

I wait, and watch, and raise my best friend's daughter. Already there's an idea growing in the back of my mind, a little tickle of precognition, a plan I might have to put in play. Whoever occupies the throne of Hell, I hope they have sense enough to leave us alone.

Because if they don't . . .

. . . all Hell will break loose.

That's a promise I'll have no trouble keeping.

Glossary

Androgyne: 1. A transsexual, cross-dressing, or androgynous human. 2. (*demon term*) A Greater Flight demon capable of reproduction.

Animone: An accredited psion with the ability to telepathically connect with and heal animals, generally employed as veterinarians.

Anubis et'her ka: Egyptianica term, sometimes used as an expletive; loosely translated, "Anubis protect me/us."

A'nankhimel: (*demon term*) 1. A Fallen demon. 2. A demon who has tied himself to a human mate. *Note: As with all demon words, there are several layers of meaning to this term, depending on context and pronunciation. The meanings, from most common to least, are as follows: descended from a great height, chained, shield, a guttering flame, a fallen statue.*

Awakening, the: The exponential increase in psionic and sorcerous ability, academically defined as from just before the fall of the Republic of Gilead to the culmination of the Parapsychic and Paranormal Species Acts proposed and brokered by the alternately vilified and worshipped Senator Adrien Ferrimen. *Note: After the culmination of the Parapsychic Act, the Awakening was*

*said to have finished and the proportion of psionics to
normals in the human population stabilized, though
fluctuations occur in seventy-year cycles to this day.*

A'zharak: (*demon term*) 1. Worm. 2. Lasso or noose. 3. A
hand fitted into a glove.

Ceremonial: 1. An accredited psion whose talent lies in
working with traditional sorcery, accumulating Power
and "spending" it in controlled bursts. 2. Ceremonial
magick, otherwise known as sorcery instead of the
more organic witchery. 3. (*slang*) Any Greater Work
of magick.

Clormen-13: (*Slang: Chill, ice, rock, smack, dust*) Addictive alkaloid drug. *Note: Chill is high-profit for the big
pharmaceutical companies as well as the Mob, being
instantly addictive. Rumors of a cure have surfaced.*

Deadhead: 1. Necromance. 2. Normal human without
psionic abilities.

Demon: 1. Any sentient, alien intelligence, either cor-
poreal or noncorporeal, that interacts with humans.
2. Denizen of Hell, of a type often mistaken for gods
or Novo Christer evil spirits; actually a sentient non-
human species with technology, psionic, and magickal
ability much exceeding humanity's. 3. (*slang*) A particularly bad physiological addiction.

Evangelicals of Gilead: 1. Messianic Old Christer and
Judic cult started by Kochba bar Gilead and led by him
until the signing of the Gilead Charter, when power
was seized by a cabal of military brass just prior to
bar Gilead's assassination. 2. Members of said cult.
3. (*academic*) The followers of bar Gilead before the
signing of the Gilead Charter. *See **Republic of Gilead**.*

Feeder: 1. A psion who has lost the ability to process

ambient Power and depends on "jolts" of vital energy stolen from other human beings, psions, or normals. 2. (*psion slang*) A fair-weather friend.

Flight: A class or social rank of demons. *Note: There are, strictly speaking, three classes of demons: the Low, Lesser, and Greater. Magi most often deal with the higher echelons of the Low Flight and the lower echelons of the Lesser Flight. Greater Flight demons are almost impossible to control and very dangerous.*

Freetown: An autonomous enclave under a charter, neither Hegemony nor Putchkin but often allied to one or the other for economic reasons.

Hedaira: (*demon term, borrowed from Old Graecia*) 1. An endearment. 2. A human woman tied to a Fallen (*A'nankhimel*) demon. *Note: There are several layers of meaning, depending on context and pronunciation. The meanings, from most common to least, are as follows: beloved, companion, vessel, starlight, sweet fruit, small precious trinket, an easily crushed bauble. The most uncommon and complex meaning can be roughly translated as "slave (thing of pleasure) who rules the master."*

Hegemony: One of the two world superpowers, comprising North and South America, Australia and New Zealand, most of Western Europe, Japan, some of Central Asia, and scattered diplomatic enclaves in China. *Note: After the Seventy Days War, the two superpowers settled into peace and are often said to be one world government with two divisions. Afrike is technically a Hegemony protectorate, but that seems mostly diplomatic convention more than anything else.*

Ka: 1. (*archaic*) Soul or mirrorspirit, separate from the *ba* and the physical soul in Egyptianica. 2. Fate, especially tragic fate that cannot be avoided, destiny. 3. A link between two souls, where each feeds the other's destiny. 4. (*technical*) Terminus stage for Feeder pathology, an externalized hungry consciousness capable of draining vital energy from a normal human in seconds and a psion in less than two minutes.

Kobolding: (*also:* **kobold**) 1. Paranormal species characterized by a troll-like appearance, thick skin, and an affinity to elemental earth magick. 2. A member of the kobolding species.

Left-Hand: Sorcerous discipline utilizing Power derived from "sinister" means, as in bloodletting, animal or human sacrifice, or certain types of drug use (*Left-Hander:* a follower of a Left-Hand path).

Ludder: 1. Member of the conservative Ludder Party. 2. A person opposed to genetic manipulation or the use of psionic talent, or both. 3. (*slang*) Technophobe. 4. (*slang*) hypocrite.

Magi: 1. A psion who has undergone basic training. 2. The class of occult practitioners before the Awakening who held and transmitted basic knowledge about psionic abilities and training techniques. 3. An accredited psion with the training to call demons or harness etheric force from the disturbance created by the magickal methods used to call demons; usually working in Circles or loose affiliations. *Note: The term "Magus" is archaic and hardly ever used. "Magi" has become singular or plural, and neuter gender.*

Master Nichtvren: 1. A Nichtvren who is free of obligation to his or her Maker. 2. A Nichtvren who holds territory.

Mentaflo genius: 1. An individual with a registered intelligence level above "exceptional," generally channeled into Hegemony or Putchkin high-level civil service. 2. A highly intelligent individual. 3. (*slang*) An individual who, while being "book-smart," lacks common sense.

Merican: The trade lingua of the globe and official language of the Hegemony, though other dialects are in common use. 2. (*archaic*) A Hegemony citizen. 3. (*archaic*) A citizen of the Old Merican region before the Seventy Days War.

Necromance: (*slang:* deadhead) An accredited psion with the ability to bring a soul back from Death to answer questions. *Note: Can also, in certain instances, heal mortal wounds and keep a soul from escaping into Death.*

Nichtvren: (*slang:* suckhead) Altered human dependent on human blood for nourishment. *Note: Older Nichtvren may possibly live off strong emotions, especially those produced by psions. Since they are altered humans, Nichtvren occupy a space between humanity and "other species"; they are defined as members of a Paranormal Species and given citizen's rights under Adrien Ferrimen's groundbreaking legislation after the Awakening.*

Nine Canons: A nine-part alphabet of runes drawn from around the globe and codified during the Awakening to manage psionic and sorcerous power, often used as shortcuts in magickal circles or as quick charms. *Note: The Canons are separate from other branches of magick in that they are accessible sometimes even to* *normal humans, by virtue of their long use and highly charged nature.*

Novo Christianity: An outgrowth of a Religion of Submission popular from the twelfth century to the latter half of the twenty-first century, before the meteoric rise of the Republic of Gilead and the Seventy Days War. *Note: The death knell of Old Christianity is thought to have been the great Vatican Bank scandal that touched off the revolt leading to the meteoric rise of Kochba bar Gilead, the charismatic leader of the Republic before the Charter. Note: The state religion of the Republic was technically fundamentalist Old Christianity with Judic messianic overtones. Nowadays, NC is declining in popularity and mostly fashionable among a small slice of the Putchkin middle-upper class.*

Power: 1. Vital energy produced by living things: prana, mana, orgone, etc. 2. Sorcerous power accumulated by celibacy, bloodletting, fasting, pain, or meditation. 3. Ambient energy produced by ley lines and geocurrents, a field of energy surrounding the planet. 4. The discipline of raising and channeling vital energy, sorcerous power, or ambient energy. 5. Any form of energy that fuels sorcerous or psionic ability. 6. A paranormal community or paranormal individual who holds territory.

Prime Power: 1. The highest-ranked paranormal Power in a city or territory, capable of negotiating treaties and enforcing order. *Note: usually Nichtvren in most cities and werecain in rural areas.* 2. (*technical*) The source from which all Power derives. 3. (*archaic*) Any non-human paranormal being with more than two vassals in the feudal structure of pre-Awakening paranormal society.

Psion: 1. An accredited, trained, or apprentice human with psionic abilities. 2. Any human with psionic abilities.

Putchkin: 1. The official language of the Putchkin Alliance, though other dialects are in common use. 2. A Putchkin Alliance citizen.

Putchkin Alliance: One of the two world superpowers, comprising Russia, most of China (except Freetown Tibet and Singapore), some of Central Asia, Eastern Europe, and the Middle East. *Note: After the Seventy Days War, the two superpowers settled into peace and are often said to be one world government with two divisions.*

Republic of Gilead: Theocratic Old Merican empire based on fundamentalist Novo Christer and Judic messianic principles, lasting from the latter half of the twenty-first century (after the Vatican Bank scandal) to the end of the Seventy Days War. *Note: In the early days, before Kochba bar Gilead's practical assumption of power in the Western Hemisphere, the Evangelicals of Gilead were defined as a cult, not as a Republic. Political infighting in the Republic—and the signing of the Charter with its implicit acceptance of the High Council's sovereignty—brought about both the War and the only tactical nuclear strike of the War (in the Vegas Waste).*

Revised Matheson Score: The index for quantifying an individual's level of psionic ability. *Note: Like the Richter scale, it is exponential; five is the lowest score necessary for a psionic child to receive Hegemony funding and schooling. Forty is the terminus of* *the scale; anything above forty is defined as "superlative" and the psion is tipped into special Hegemony or Putchkin secret-services training.*

Runewitch: A psion whose secondary or primary talent includes the ability to handle the runes of the Nine Canons with special ease.

Sedayeen: 1. An accredited psion whose talent is healing. 2. (*archaic*) An old Nichtvren word meaning "blue hand." *Note: Sedayeen are incapable of aggression even in self-defense, being allergic to violence and prone to feeling the pain they inflict. This makes them incredible healers, but also incredibly vulnerable.*

Sekhmet sa'es: Egyptianica term, often used as profanity; translated: "Sekhmet stamp it," a request for the Egyptos goddess of destruction to strike some object or thing, much like the antique "*God damn it.*"

Seventy Days War: The conflict that brought about the end of the Republic of Gilead and the rise of the Hegemony and Putchkin Alliance.

Sexwitch: (*archaic: tantraiiken*) An accredited psion who works with Power raised from the act of sex; pain also produces an endorphin and energy rush for sexwitches.

Shaman: 1. The most common and catch-all term for a psion who has psionic ability but does not fall into any other specialty, ranging from vaudun Shamans (who traffic with *loa* or *etrigandi*) to generic psions. 2. (*archaic*) A normal human with borderline psionic ability.

Shavarak'itzan beliak: (*demon term*) A demon obscenity, exact meaning obscure.

Sk8: Member of a slicboard tribe.

Skinlin: (*slang:* dirtwitch) An accredited psion whose talent has to do with plants and plant DNA. *Note: Skinlin use their voices, holding sustained tones, wedded to Power to alter plant DNA and structure. Their training makes them susceptible to berserker rages.*

Slagfever: Sickness caused by exposure to chemical-waste cocktails commonly occurring near hover transport depots in less urban areas.

Swanhild: Paranormal species characterized by hollow bones, feathery body hair, poisonous flesh, and passive and pacifistic behavior.

Synth-hash: Legal nonaddictive stimulant and relaxant synthesized from real hash (derivative of opium) and kennabis. *Note: Synth-hash replaced nicotiana leaves (beloved of the Evangelicals of Gilead for the profits reaped by tax on its use) as the smoke of choice in the late twenty-second century.*

Talent: 1. Psionic ability. 2. Magickal ability.

Werecain: (*slang:* 'cain, furboy) Altered human capable of changing to a furred animal form at will. *Note: There are several different subsets, including Lupercal and magewolfen. Normal humans and even psionic outsiders are generally incapable of distinguishing between different subsets of 'cain.*

extras

orbit

meet the author

LILITH SAINTCROW was born in New Mexico, bounced around the world as an Air Force brat, and fell in love with writing when she was ten years old. After taking second place in a fiction-writing contest sealed her addiction to the written word, it's often been supposed that she has ink instead of blood filling her veins. She currently lives in Vancouver, Washington, with her husband, two small children, and a houseful of cats. Find her on the Internet at http://www.lilithsaintcrow.com.

supplementary
materials

A Few Notes on Danny Valentine's World

Hopefully, after five books I have earned enough indulgence to provide a few notes. I am at least confident that those uninterested will flip past these pages. After all, who reads these things? *Besides* grammar junkies like me, that is.

I have often been asked about Danny and how she occurred to me. I've answered that question elsewhere. Another source of constant comment and query is Japhrimel and where he came from.

To be honest, he wasn't supposed to be more than a one-book character. Really, in the book I set out to write, he double-crossed Dante and left her holding the bag, infected with a demonic virus. The rest of the series he was pretty much a foil to her humanity, sort of a Mephistopheles.

Then he had to go and fall in love with her, and develop wings. Which just goes to show you can't trust a demon.

I realize now with twenty-twenty hindsight that Japhrimel was actually informed by the legends of the Nephilim, angels who fell in love with human women and fell (supposedly) from grace as a result, fathering huge progeny while also teaching humanity "forbidden" arts such as sorcery, city-building, and medicine. I had heard this legend for years, although my only clear memory of it is in Madeline L'Engle's *Many Waters*. I suppose when you study metaphysics and the occult you can hardly get away from all sorts of odd stuff. I'm only glad Japh didn't take after Cthulu or Aiwass. Or, say, old-school vampires—the type that suck your blood out through your toenails or nostrils.

And people say mythology is *boring*.

I have always been of two minds about legends and myths. One part of me looks for the psychological truth hidden inside. The other—the ravening storyteller, no doubt—likes to play the *what if* game, with lots of sauce. *How can I invert this legend? How can I play with this story? What makes it work? How can I tinker with the engine?*

So Japhrimel dug around in a vast mass of scholarship, research, half-forgotten legends, and references from books devoured since my high school days, and came up with a coat made of whole cloth—demons instead of angels falling, and the consequences of those unions. Many Gnostic and occult traditions hold that nonhuman intelligences taught humanity "forbidden" arts against the will of a God who wanted only slaves, an act of compassion and defiance both sides paid dearly for.

I remember calling Japh a Promethean figure once, and it amused him so much I had trouble getting any actual work out of him for weeks.

Then I killed him, and that might have taught him a lesson if he hadn't known I would be bringing him back. Damn demon.

So Tierce Japhrimel, like every good character, rummaged through the dustheap at the back of my mind and came up with something wonderful, something I took as a writer takes these sorts of things—a gift not to be examined too closely in the heat of creation, for fear of the magic draining away.

Danny's world was another fish entirely. She was very definite about what had happened historically and what was going on now in her world, and had very strong opinions about both. Some things I had often thought about—what would happen if individual spiritual experience was no longer co-opted by "organized" religion, what a relatively clean hover technology would mean for transport of goods and people, what might be the likely ending point of fundamentalism in the twenty-first century—were about what I'd expected. Other things, like the fear of psions and the pop culture and day-to-day government administration of a world six hundred years in the future, were a surprise.

Please note, dear Reader, than I am in no way implying Danny's world is a utopia, dystopia, prognostication, or social commentary. I am fully aware that any imagining of the future says more about the imaginer than the imagined, so to speak. I strove for logic and a historical tone where I could, and had fun where I couldn't. Like, with slicboards. I mean, come on. Flying skateboards? Even after *Back to the Future*'s many reruns, flying skateboards are still *cool*.

However, I like to think that I've read enough history, both for schooling and for fun, to say with some certainty that people throughout the ages are largely the same. The issues that resonate with a regular-Joe type of person in my own time are largely the same issues that would resonate with a regular-Flavius Roman, or a regular Han Chinese. We all worry about those damn kids today and food and shelter, and the approbation of our social set, and where the world is going. We survive, and when we have room left over from survival we create, and we raise our kids and laugh and cry and grieve.

Not too long ago I was in a pediatrician's waiting room. There was a Ukrainian family (at least, I think they were Ukrainian) and a Hispanic family, each chattering away in their respective languages, the kids either playing or sticking close to Mum or Dad or Grandma if they were feeling poorly. I remember a glance of total accord exchanged between two mothers from different continents—a glance I had no trouble deciphering—when one child ran around in a circle making an airplane noise. The slight smile, lifted eyebrows, and rueful love in the expression was universal.

It is that moment I think of when I say the word "history." Often we forget, when studying other cultures or even our own, that people are pretty much the same the world over, with the same basic needs for food, shelter, love, and art. The diversity of cultures does not detract from that one glance shared between mothers—a glance no mommy, from the earliest furry human to whatever cyberpunk age comes next, would ever have trouble translating.

But I digress. Hey, it's an appendix. I suppose I'm allowed.

Danny's world probably says more about me and my own position as a reasonably literate middle-class citizen of America at the turn of the twenty-first century than it does about whatever future will be slouching along toward infinity six hundred years from now. The influences feeding into the world of psions and the Hegemony are many and varied—from a long list of music I've listened to, like Rob Dougan, the Cure, the Eagles, and Beethoven; movies like *Blade Runner* and *Brazil*, not to mention *The Matrix* and *Life of Brian*, and *Kill Bill* where Danny got her katana; books like *From the Ashes of Angels* and *The Devil in Love*, not to mention *The Club Dumas* and LJ Smith's *The Forbidden Game* series; and the history books that are my touchstone and, to some degree, Dante's as well. Her love of the classics springs from my own unrepentant and unabashed love for the same works, books that survive because they touch something deep in the soul. Livy and Shakespeare and Milton and Dumas and Gibbon and Sophocles and . . .

You realize I couldn't begin to list all the different influences that shaped Danny's world, any more than I could list every influence that shapes my own. Still, I am conscious of them, an underground river feeding whatever well I dredge up stories from. I am neverendingly grateful that I live in an age and a cultural-social position where I have access to a truly stunning array of human knowledge and the leisure time (however harried by deadlines and children and cats) to sample this great buffet largely at my own discretion. I am even more grateful that I am in a position to do the thing I love and was made for, telling stories.

Danny and Japhrimel's story is finished now. I don't know if I'll ever go back to their world. I don't know if I told their story the best way possible, but I told it as best as I know how. I enjoyed every goddamn minute of it. (Even revisions.) I am glad I did it.

Even if Japhrimel pulled a doublecross on me, and even if Dante is a difficult and unlikeable person sometimes, and even if I imagined a world that says more about me and my time than it ever will about the future. I had a Hell of a time.

I can't wait to do it again.

When I do, dear Reader, you're invited to come along. The story is in the sharing, after all. It would be right bloody useless if it wasn't.

The only thing that remains to be said is, thank you for reading. I hope you had a good time.

And flying skateboards are *still* cool.

introducing

If you enjoyed TO HELL AND BACK
look out for

NIGHT SHIFT

Book 1 of the Jill Kismet series
by Lilith Saintcrow

*E*very city has people like us, those who go after things the cops can't catch. We handle nonstandard exorcisms, Traders, hellbreed, rogue Weres, silvers, Middle Way adepts . . . all the fun the nightside can come up with. Normally a hunter's job is just to act as a liaison between the paranormal community and the regular police, make sure everything stays within control.

But sometimes—often enough—it's our job to find people that have been taken by the things that go bump in the night. When I say "find" I mean their bodies, because humans don't live too long on the nightside unless they're hunters. More often than not, our mission is vengeance, to restore the unsteady balance between the denizens of the dark and regular oblivious people.

And also, more often than not, we lay someone's soul to rest if killing them is just the beginning.

We work pretty closely with the regular police, mostly because freelance hunters don't last long enough to have a career. Even the FBI has its Martindale Squad, hunters and Weres working on nightside fun and games at the national level. It's whispered that the CIA and NSA have their own divisions of hunters, too, but I don't know about that.

For a hunter like me, the support given by the regular cops and the DA's office is critical. It is, after all, law enforcement we're doing. Even if it is a little unconventional.

Okay. A *lot* unconventional.

The baby I unloaded at Sisters of Mercy downtown, the granite Jesus on the roof still glaring at the financial district. They would find out who it belonged to, if at all possible. Avery came down to take possession of the prisoner, who was moaning with fear and had pissed his already none-too-clean pants.

I must have been wearing my mad face.

"Jesus Christ. Don't you ever sleep?" Avery's handsome mournful beagle's face under its mop of dark curly hair was sleepy and uninterested until he peered through the porthole in the door. He brightened a little, his breath making a brief mist spring up on the reinforced glass.

"I try not to sleep. It disturbs the circles I'm growing under my eyes. This one just brushed with an *arkeus*, didn't get much." I leaned against the wall in the institutional hallway, listening to the sound of the man's hoarse weeping on the other side of the steel observation door. Sisters of Mercy is an old Catholic hospital, and like most old Catholic hospitals it has a room even the most terrifying nun won't enter.

A hunter's room. Or more precisely, a room for the holding of people needing an exorcism until a hunter or a regular exorcist can get to them.

"A standard half-rip, then. Not even worth getting out of bed for." Avery stuffed his hands in his pockets, rocking up on his toes again to peer in the thick barred window. I'd kept the Trader cuffed and dumped him in the middle of a consecrated circle scored into the crumbling concrete floor. The etheric energy running through the deep carved lines sparked, responding to the taint of hellbreed on the man's aura.

"He was about to hand a baby over to a hellbreed. Don't be too gentle." I peeled myself upright, the silver charms tinkling in my hair. "I've got to get over to the precinct house. Montaigne just buzzed me. Maybe I'll bring in another one for you tonight."

Avery made a face, still peering in at the Trader. "Jesus. A baby? And shouldn't you be going home? This is the fourth one you've brought in this week."

I snorted, my fingers checking each knifehilt. "Home? What's that? Duty calls."

"You gonna come out for a beer with me on Saturday?"

You bet. I'd rescheduled twice with him so far, each time because of a Trader. "If I'm not hanging out on a rooftop waiting for a fucking *arkeus* to show up, I'll be there."

He came back down onto his heels, twitching his corduroy jacket a little to get it to hang straight over the bulge of his police-issue sidearm. "You should really slack off a bit, Kiss. You're beginning to look a little . . ."

Yeah. Slack off. Sure. "Be careful." I turned on my heel. "See you Saturday."

"I mean it, Kismet. You should get some rest."

If I took a piña colada by the pool, God knows what would boil up on the streets. "When the hellbreed slow down, so will I. Bye, Ave."

He mumbled a goodbye, then bent to dig into the little black bag sitting by his feet. He was the official police exorcist, handling most of the Traders I brought in unless there was something really unusual about them. He only really seemed to come alive during a difficult exorcism, the rest of the time moving sleepily through the world with a slow smile that got him a great deal of female attention. Despite the smile, not a lot of women stayed.

Probably because he worked the night shift tearing the bargains out of Traders and Possessors out of morbidly-religious victims. Women don't like it when a man spends his nights somewhere else, even if it is with screaming Hell-tainted sickos.

I hit the door at the end of the hall, allowing myself a single nosewrinkle at the stinging scent of disinfectant and human pain in the air. The scar burned, my ears cringing from the slightest noise and the fluorescent lights hurt my eyes. I needed to find a better way to cover it up, and quick.

It's not every hunter who has a hellbreed mark on her wrist, after all. A hard knotted scar, in the shape of a pair of lips puckered up and pressed against the underside of my right arm, into the softest part above the pulse.

Two days until my next scheduled visit. And there was the iron rack to think about, and the way Perry screamed when I started with the razors.

My mouth suddenly went dry and I put my head down, lengthening my stride. I'm not tall, but I have good long legs and I was used to trotting to keep up with Mikhail, who didn't seem to walk as much as glide.

Stop thinking about Mikhail. I made it to the exit and plunged into the cold weary night again, hunching my shoulders, the silver tinkling in my hair.